MW01105585

GRANITE FALLS

Kathryn Malka Blake

authorHOUSE®

AuthorHouse™
1663 Liberty Drive, Suite 200
Bloomington, IN 47403
www.authorhouse.com
Phone: 1-800-839-8640

© 2009 Kathryn Malka Blake. All rights reserved.

*No part of this book may be reproduced, stored in a retrieval system, or
transmitted by any means without the written permission of the author.*

First published by AuthorHouse 8/26/2009

ISBN: 978-1-4389-9401-7 (sc)
ISBN: 978-1-4389-9402-4 (hc)

Library of Congress Control Number: 2009906211

Printed in the United States of America
Bloomington, Indiana

This book is printed on acid-free paper.

*This book is a work of fiction. All characters and events in this book
are fictitious. Any resemblance to any real persons, living or deceased,
was unintended by the author and is strictly coincidental.*

AUTHOR'S NOTE

Words are used to describe a number of things. The most difficult task is relaying through those words the intensity of one's feelings, particularly that of gratitude. It is with sincere regret that I cannot name everyone – the list is entirely too long. Suffice it to say, that this book could never have been written without the help of many, many people, and I will always be in their debt.

Inspiration and encouragement are essential to a writer. For their faith in me, my heartfelt appreciation and never-ending gratitude to Carol Alexander, Doris Boyd, Joanne Small and Lynne Watling. To my husband, Allan, whose belief in me and this book remained steadfast through his final days.

My sincere and special thanks for all their support and technical help to Linda and Jack Waddell, and Larry Lipton. Also, Eleanor Battista, Peggy Falkner, Charlie Green and Lauren Hensley. I couldn't have done it without any of you. My deep appreciation to Father Norbert Maduzia at St. Ignatius Loyola Catholic Church in Spring, Texas.

Any errors – and I'm certain there are some – are all mine.

This book is dedicated to my aunt, Flo Green, who has stood with me through all the years, offering unequivocal love and encouragement when it was nowhere else to be found. And, to my father – my inspiration, my mentor. I have missed you every minute of the last forty-two years.

CHAPTER ONE

Ariana was upstairs in her bedroom working on her presentation for her creative writing class, but had been distracted by the wintry scene outside her window. She was able to see through the now empty branches of the oak tree to the pines lining the side yard, delineating the separation of her house from that of the Kensington's. It was so very peaceful, as it can only be immediately after one of the snow storms that passed through Thompsonville in early January. As she absently stared at the pine trees, she noticed one of the boughs, heavily laden with snow, slump while shaking its burden, leaving the dark branch to bounce gently before becoming as still as the others.

Ari, as she was known to her friends and family, allowed herself to daydream. She barely heard her mother call from the bottom of the stairs. As she stepped out onto the balcony, Ari saw her mother at the bottom of the curved stairway waving a letter. In a nanosecond, the potential significance of what her mother was waving clicked in Ari's mind and she went running down the stairs to open a letter that could greatly influence the rest of her life.

Once she reached her mother, she stopped and took a deep breath. Ari looked up at the look of anticipation and confidence on her mother's face, while her mind absorbed the return address on the outside of the envelope. Penn State – one of the three colleges to which Ari had applied.

Together, they slowly walked to the breakfast room table and sat, trying to calm themselves.

Unable to wait any longer, Ari ripped it open. She scanned the letter, not really reading it, but seeking out those most important words, *You have been accepted*, the rest of the letter a blur. With a whoop and a jump or two, Ari hugged her mom, danced around the room a bit and then sat down to let it sink in.

Of course, this was only the first reply to the college applications she had sent out. But this was a really important one – one of the two colleges she was actually considering, the other a lark. But for now, a sigh of relief that her hard work these past years would allow her to continue her education. *Although*, she admitted to herself, *I'm not quite certain what kind of career I really want.*

That would have to wait because she must, *must*, call her dad and tell him the good news. Then she needed to talk to Gabby. She wondered whether Gabby had heard anything from either college. *Probably not, or she would have called.* But, then, she hadn't had time to call her yet either – *maybe!* Ari hugged her mom again, smiled, and said, "I need to call Dad."

Linda stayed at the breakfast room table as Ari went into the kitchen to phone her dad. She could both see and hear her daughter as she called her father at the plant. Linda was not amazed by her daughter's self-confidence, but there seemed to be an extra dose of it today. She was always struck by what an awesome child Ari was, and she knew Frank felt the same. Linda could only hear one side of the telephone conversation, of course, but she knew Frank was telling Ari that he wasn't surprised. It was only the beginning of good things to come.

Linda did hear Ari ask her dad, as she looked at her mom to make sure she, too, would agree, "Can we go to the country club for dinner tonight to celebrate? And, will it be all right to take Gabby, too?" With a big smile on her face, Ari said, "Thanks, Dad. Do you want to talk to Mom? Okay. We'll see you around 6:00. Here's Mom." Ari handed the phone to her mother, gave her a big kiss and gestured to let her know when she was off the phone so she could call Gabby. Ari flew up the stairs to find something wonderful to wear while she waited anxiously to make her call.

Gabby and Ari were screaming and laughing on the phone. Gabby couldn't have been happier. They had been best friends since grammar school and, while they each had a wide circle of close friends, the two of them were inseparable. Both Gabby and Ari had applied to Penn State and Ohio State, but, to date, no word, either good or bad, had been received by Gabby from either school. That didn't diminish Gabby's joy for Ari, and she was delighted to be included in the family's celebration dinner that night.

Gabby loved going to the country club. She had been there several times over the years with the Bolans, but the club was always a special treat – her parents had never chosen to join. It reminded Gabby of the elegance of The Palm Court at The Plaza Hotel in New York City; candelabra atop pillars, golds and cream on the walls and in the fabrics, crystal and silverware glinting, while harps played in the background. Gabby's parents took her and her brother there for high tea when they visited New York during a summer vacation long ago. She came away thinking, *If there was any place on earth a princess would frequent, it would have to be The Palm Court.* Admittedly, she was only seven at the time, and the country club *was not* The Palm Court, but it was as close to it as Thompsonville had to offer.

Ari managed to get a word in and asked Gabby if she had heard from Penn State? The two of them had been chattering nonstop, and Ari thought she had been incredibly thoughtless not have asked Gabby earlier in the conversation. Of course, she knew before she asked. Gabby could *never* have kept the news to herself – she'd have blurted it out at the same time Ari mentioned her acceptance.

They had long talked about going away to college together and, while both had applied to the Penn State and Ohio State, Ari also applied to Northwestern University – just to see – Chicago being one of her favorite cities. Gabby hadn't, basically because it was so much farther away from home. Gabby's older brother, Brent, was about to become a first year law student at Yale and Gabby wanted to stay closer to home, particularly her mother.

Frank Bolan stopped at Petal Pushers on the way home from the plant. Susan was in her shop and delighted when Frank told her Ari's good news. Frank chose the most beautiful arrangement of roses, hydrangea, bells of Ireland, stargazers, and snap dragons. Then tears welled in his eyes as he wrote the note from her mother and him that he would include with the bouquet. They were so fortunate to have Ariana. They tried, hoped and prayed for children over the early years of their marriage, to no avail. Only after eleven years did they give up. Then, miraculously, it happened – their beautiful baby girl was born.

Now, a poised five-foot-eight with a small frame, shoulder-length chestnut hair and her mother's hazel-colored eyes, Ari captivated everyone who met her. She was very popular at school, quite bright, and possessed a truly wonderful outlook on life. She made everyone smile, and her parents exceedingly proud.

When Ari was younger and free for the day, she would tag along with Frank and go down to the plant. She knew everyone there and had a wonderful time watching them work. Frank saw Ari absorb the workings of the plant and, with her innate understanding of people, she asked questions about how this or that was done, why it was necessary to do that exact step in making a part, or what a particular machine did. He was always amazed by her interest, but more so by her questions. They seemed to look deeply into the process, and how it could be improved. Clearly, she was going to do something important with her life. *That* was a testament to Linda's consistent encouragement.

Susan wrapped the bouquet and added a single white rose in a separate wrapping for Ari from her personally. Frank thanked her and headed out the door to make the drive home.

Susan was one of the luckier business people in Thompsonville. Petal Pushers had originally been located downtown. But, as the retail stores closed due to lack of business, Susan saw the writing on the wall, and moved out to one of the new strip malls that now dotted the entire United States. Frank didn't think business was all that good in the mall, but he certainly believed it wouldn't have lasted at all, had it remained downtown.

Frank arrived home a little after 6:00 and was greeted at the door by Linda, the smiles and hug saying everything they wanted to share. Linda thought the bouquet exquisite, but laughed at Frank. "Are you going to do the same thing for every college acceptance Ari receives?"

Frank ended up laughing at himself along with her, knowing full well she was right. "Maybe I am overreacting somewhat. But, *it is* Ari's first acceptance – even though it may not necessarily be the one she's hoping for." Actually they really didn't know which school was Ari's top choice, but they believed Ari didn't know yet either. Frank gathered up the bouquet, took Linda's hand, and said, "Let's go see our girl."

Linda and Frank had been high school sweethearts. She from the family which had originally established Thompsonville, her maiden name, Thompson. Linda had a fun sense about her, loved to read, write and act. She acted in college and had a large circle of friends, including boyfriends, even though she knew in her heart Frank was the one. Frank was a success in his business – but not exactly what her parents had hoped for her in a husband. Not that they had disliked Frank, but he came from a working-class family and they wanted more for their daughter. After Linda and Frank had been married for several years, however, Linda's parents knew their daughter had made the right choice. Frank obviously adored her, shared her sense of humor and was his own man, not allowing himself to be coerced by others' thinking.

Linda and Frank climbed the staircase, crossed the balcony to Ariana's bedroom, and knocked briefly on her door. The door flew open. Ari saw her parents standing there with a tremendous bouquet of flowers, and she just beamed. Hugs all around, then Frank stood back looking at his beautiful, loving wife, and this child, who was such a gift, standing there with so much self-assurance, enthusiasm and grace, that it just caught his breath.

Ari read the note accompanying the bouquet and thanked her parents almost sheepishly because the words her father had written meant the world to her. "Oh, Daddy, Mom, these are gorgeous. Let's go down and put them in water right away."

In the kitchen, Ari arranged the bouquet in a vase and then noticed the simple, single white rose wrapped separately and asked her father about it. Ashamed that he had forgotten, he told Ari and Linda that it was from Susan at Petal Pushers. Ari was deeply touched, and made a mental note to send Susan a card of thanks. She took the single rose, put it in a bud vase and placed it on the table next to the huge bouquet, both to be taken upstairs to her room after they returned from dinner. Now, it was getting late, and they still had to pick up Gabby.

Gabby was waiting at the door. As she saw Frank Bolan's car make its way up her driveway, her five-foot-two, petite frame began walking toward the car. Gabby was stunning. She had long, very dark brown hair, and the darkest eyes and eyelashes, set off by creamy skin. Frank got out and held the car door open for Gabby as she settled herself in the back seat next to Ari. Gabby thanked the Bolans for picking her up and including her in their celebration dinner. Then, Ari and Gabby chattered nonstop all the way to the club. Linda and Frank smiled silently to one another, having watched the two girls do the same thing many times over the past thirteen years.

As the Bolan's car pulled into the circular drive of the beautiful old tudor-style country club, Gabby, in particular, felt the anticipation of once again entering the dining room which always reminded her of the palace of a princess. The carhops opened the doors and all four of them stepped out, and together walked up the stairs to the canopy-covered, glass double-door entry. Once inside, they climbed several more steps up to the main desk, beyond which was the huge sitting area – more like a living room – the bar, and the beautiful large dining room off to the right. The windows at the back extended from the dining room all the way through the bar area, both of which overlooked the gardens and pool, the golf course in the distance. Of course, now it was blanketed by snow. But, even at that, with the outside antique-style street lamps aglow, it was like a picture postcard of some ski resort in Colorado.

Turning right, in order to enter the large double-door entry to the main dining room, they, almost as one, noticed – actually couldn't miss seeing – Thompsonville's Mayor, Steven Hill, and his family sitting at what His Honor – as he believed he was entitled to be called – considered the most prominent table in the room.

"Holy cow," Gabby blurted to Ari, "there's HRH with her parents. Wonder what brings them here?" not adding what she was thinking, *You don't think . . . No, couldn't be.*

Just then, the maire 'd greeted the Bolans and Gabby and led them toward a table overlooking the grounds on a path which couldn't avoid passing the Mayor's table without it being obvious. As Frank smiled and said hello to the Mayor, His Honor stopped them for one of those glad-handed greetings for which he was so famous. Although he generally avoided these false bonhomie encounters with the Mayor, tonight Frank was pleased to stop and unabashedly announce that they were there celebrating Ari's first college acceptance.

Undaunted, the Mayor congratulated Ari and her parents saying, "My daughter, Harriet, is also awaiting word from, ah, several of the, ah, finest colleges in the country." Harriet blushed, but managed to maintain her calm as her father did all the talking. While she did nod at Ari, it was clear to all who may have paid attention, that the girls were not the closest of friends – not enemies, just not close friends.

Mrs. Hill and Linda made small talk, asking how each other was doing and suggesting that perhaps they would have more time to talk at the next ladies' club luncheon. As they clearly had covered all the required niceties, the Bolans and Gabby turned and continued on to their table, ready to enjoy a lovely evening.

While Frank, Linda, Ari and Gabby were seated at their table and looking over their menus, there was quite a different picture at His Honor's table. The Mayor was starting again, as this had been a particular point of frustration for him. "What were you thinking, Harriet, by not applying to any college? And, why didn't you intercede, Janet? This is incredibly humiliating to me." He couldn't imagine why his wife had not forced their daughter to do what was expected of her. She was, after all, his daughter and had an image to uphold.

Although Harriet was angry that this was being brought up again and here in public, her anger couldn't override her embarrassment. Scrunching down in her chair in an attempt to become invisible from prying eyes, she could do nothing but shrivel up inside as she suffered from this public tongue-lashing. She wanted to scream, *So what did it matter if Ariana was going to go away to college? Not everyone wants to go to college*, and her mother understood that.

Actually, what Janet understood was that her daughter was only an average student and not cut out for college. However, she felt it necessary that Harriet go for at least a couple of years, so that she could meet young, available men. She'd been unsuccessful in getting Harriet to apply this year, but, perhaps, next year. Janet wanted her daughter to live the same way she had lived for the past twenty years – as a member of the higher social strata, with a husband who would provide the entré to it through his career and professional future.

Like her mother, Harriet would never need a man for his income. She would be well provided for by Janet's family's trust and Harriet's own substantial trust fund, which would be available to her when she turned twenty-five. So, Janet jumped to Harriet's defense, reassuring her husband, yet again. "Steven, there is still plenty of time for Harriet to decide what she wants to do. Many girls take a year off in between high school and college and, besides, we can spend the summer in Europe, checking out schools there."

Steven knew that this was the same dead-end conversation he and Janet had been having for the last nine months, and he wasn't going to prevail. As persuasive as he was as the Mayor, Janet was truly the one person who just wouldn't relent her position, *regardless* of whether or not she was right. And, it was *always* easier to let her have her way.

This, he realized, was the problem from the beginning of their marriage. But, they had fallen into this pattern and now he was trapped. He was certain he never could have enjoyed his current lifestyle if Janet hadn't had all her family's money, which then allowed him to become His Honor.

As the Bolans and Gabby wound up their evening, they made their way back through the main dining room, greeting other friends and acquaintances who were finishing up their dinners along the way. As they approached His Honor's table, Frank noticed that they, too, had finished their dinners and left.

Dropping Gabby off at her house, the Bolans arrived home tired, but with a genuine sense of well-being. Almost as one, they indicated their tiredness and decided to call it a night. Frank carried the large bouquet of flowers upstairs to Ari's bedroom where she directed it be placed on her grandparents' former marble-topped dresser, while Ari took the small bud vase with the white rose from Susan, setting it on her night stand. Ari again thanked her parents for the evening, kissing them both goodnight.

Closing the door, her parents walked to their own bedroom hand-in-hand, chatting about their day and, of course, the evening.

"Frank, did you notice Janet Hill's silence when it came to Harriet's college opportunities? I was really surprised by what appeared to be almost indifference."

Frank, always trying to be the diplomat, replied. "I'm not certain that Harriet has made any decisions about college."

"Why do you think that?"

"Did you notice the 'ah's' in Steven's statement about the colleges Harriet had chosen?"

Linda, standing back from the mirror reflecting Frank's image, thought about his question and said, "Ah, no pun intended, but you don't think she's applied to any, do you?"

Frank nodded. "One only has to look behind Steven's statements sometimes, particularly when there are 'ah's' in them." Frank knew they were the Mayor's tell. "It was nice, though, that when we stopped at our other friends' tables on the way out, there were congratulations and praise for Ari and her acceptance to Penn State. Ari and Gabby even picked up an indoor tennis match for Saturday." Jennifer Lee and Karen Dunwitty, two of the girls' friends, had already scheduled a game at the Logan Park Tennis Center, so they convinced Ari and Gabby to make it a doubles match, and then join them for lunch at Dominique's around the corner. The evening had been wonderful for all of them and, as they snuggled into bed after turning out the lights, both Frank and Linda smiled the smile of proud parents.

Ari, too, was lying in bed thinking of the day's events. She felt an enormous sense of relief at receiving her acceptance to Penn State, even though she had been almost certain she would be accepted. *Her grades were good enough*, she thought, *but one never knew for sure until that letter arrived in the mail.* As she started to drift off, Ari suddenly remembered that tomorrow was Friday and another day of school. She still had to finish her presentation for creative writing this weekend – it was due Monday. *So much for college dreams*, she thought, *I'd better focus on graduating from high school first.*

CHAPTER TWO

Gabby received her acceptance to Penn State the next day, so on Saturday when the girls got together for tennis and lunch, it was a real celebration. Jennifer and Karen had both applied to several different colleges. Jennifer was most interested in the University of Pennsylvania, hoping to go on to the Wharton School, Karen was leaning toward Rutgers. This being the early days of the acceptance process for the various schools, only time would tell. For some reason, Penn State made their decisions early and sent out their acceptance letters well ahead of the other colleges.

While Gabby was an above average student, she was relieved to have been accepted by Penn State. Ari always seemed to do better in school with less effort, so Gabby was a little uncertain about her acceptance. She always felt she had great street smarts, and never lacked confidence when presented with any situation, good or bad. But her self-assurance relative to her school work was not always as high as it could have been. Gabby could cut to the crux of almost any problem and, with practical thought and determination, could figure out a solution. This, she was sure, would hold her in good stead as she went through life, but not as certain that it would be apparent through the college application process. Well, now she would just have to wait and see what Ohio State had to say.

The weeks passed, the senior prom a fond memory, and it was spring. With graduation right around the corner, the excitement grew as all the seniors from the Thompsonville High School, Class of 1992, prepared for the big day, most of them also making plans for college. The Ohio State acceptances arrived for both Ari and Gabby, now raising the question, *which school should they attend?*

Ari and Gabby spent hours and hours talking with their parents, their teachers, advisors, and each other. As the days started to dwindle down until the time they had to notify the chosen college, their excitement was tempered by the significance of that decision. Not taken lightly, Ari and Gabby, supported by their parents, decided that Penn State was the better college for them. So, next week, they would notify the school of their decisions but, as advised by their parents, they agreed to take the weekend to "sleep on it."

Now that the decision was made, a weird sense of uncertainty enveloped Gabby. *What's going on with me?* For the very first time she had the feeling that she just didn't want to go to college, even though she had been planning this along with Ari for so very long. *Am I just having a case of the jitters? Why wouldn't I want to go? What's making me feel this way?* Brent was doing so well at Yale and he was always telling her that school was great and she was going to have a wonderful time. *What is this?*

Shutting herself away in her room, Gabby paced and then sat on her chaise, searching for an answer. For hours, she looked around her bedroom and thought about her home and her family. Finally, Gabby realized that she was really happy right where she was and, despite all that college had to offer, she just didn't want to leave. She loved her life in Thompsonville and, although it wouldn't be the same without Ari, something deep down inside calmed her, letting her know that this, now, was the right decision. Instinctively, she knew what she had to do.

Gabby had spent the last few summers working in the office at her father's construction company. During the last nine months, she had even helped out on the weekends when Norma, her dad's secretary, was off. Lately, although her father didn't know it, Gabby had been looking at the plans for the new development the company was building and, surprising even herself, understood them. While reviewing the individual house plans, Gabby became excited when she felt there were suggestions she could make to actually improve on the design and layout of some of the style homes. The more she thought about this, the more thrilled she became with the expectation of really *doing* something, instead of just studying something. Now, all of a sudden, Gabby understood that, as much as she thought college was what she wanted, the idea of working on the design and layout side of the construction business energized her more than college ever had.

When Sunday morning rolled around, Gabby wasn't her usual self. She and her parents went to church and out to brunch as was their routine. Mary knew this mood of her daughter's and, sensing that Gabby would talk to her when she was ready, she kept up the dialog between Nick and herself. Gabby was extremely nervous about telling her parents her change of mind regarding college.

Although Nick supported her decision to go to college, he, given his old-school upbringing, never quite understood the need for women to pursue their education past high school. *After all, Mary hadn't gone to college and she was a wonderful wife and mother.* She cooked and cleaned, volunteered at the church and school, kept busy with the book club and mah jong to keep her mind stimulated. *She was perfect. No man could ask for more.*

While Gabby thought her father would eventually accept her decision as invariably the right one, she felt fairly certain that he would jump out of his chair when she brought up the idea of working at the construction company. She could already hear *him. Women don't belong in the construction business. What are you going to do? You can barely swing a hammer, much less have any understanding of how to build a house.* And, of course, *I don't have the kind of time it would take to train you. No, this just won't work.*

On the other hand, Mary would reassure her that she could do anything she wanted to do and Mary would work on Nick until, in some small way, he might even be convinced -- Gabby just wasn't sure this would happen in her lifetime.

So, as her parents sat opposite her in their booth at the restaurant, Gabby sat there not really listening to them, but trying to get up the courage to talk to them. Should she tell them there at the restaurant, where it would be difficult for her father to get too excited about her idea to work at the company? Or, should she wait until they got home, where her father could pace to let off steam. Unfortunately, she had to do this today because tomorrow was the day they were planning to notify Penn State of her plan to attend. Even worse, she was somehow going to have to figure out a way to tell Ari. Maybe she should go see Ari first and together they would plan what Gabby could tell her parents. What a mess!

Suddenly, without thought and unable to stop herself, she told her parents she needed to talk to them. Then, launching into a totally unplanned speech, Gabby began. "I am so sorry, Mom, Dad, but I've given it a lot of thought and finally figured out that I don't want to go to college. I know, I know. We've talked about and planned for it for so long, I guess I never actually thought about what it would mean. For the last several months I've had this uneasy feeling which I couldn't identify. It wasn't until the decision to go to Penn State was made, that I fully realized what was gnawing at me. I can't begin to tell you how sorry I am."

Dumbfounded, her father sat back and just looked at her and then looked at her mother with his face frozen in a strange questioning pose.

Gabby's mother looked at Gabby and said, "Are you sure this is what you want, dear?"

Gabby's father, on the other hand, amazed by the equanimity in his wife's voice, jumped in. "What the hell is this all about? What are you going to do? Have you given this any thought? You know you can't just sit around," he sputtered.

Mary Romano put her hand on her husband's and said, calmly, "Nick, this is something Gabby obviously has been struggling with for quite some time and trying to grasp this sitting here in this restaurant within the next ten minutes or so is not going to happen. What do you say if we just table this discussion until we can get home, think about it and discuss it again later this afternoon? Is that all right with you, Gabby?"

Tremendously relieved, Gabby said, "That's fine, Mom. I appreciate how difficult this is for you to understand, and my springing it on you this way hasn't made it any easier. It'll be great if we can talk about this later this afternoon. But, I want to assure you, I *do* have a plan."

Still confused, Nick picked up the check, paid the bill, and said it was time for them to leave. Clenching his teeth during the drive home, Mary could see Nick trying to assimilate what Gabby had just said, understanding that before sitting down again with Gabby, the two of them would have a long conversation. Mary only wished she knew now what Gabby had in mind. Then, perhaps, she could soften the blow and better prepare him for what was coming. This had really come out of the blue, but Mary knew her daughter was rock solid and would have a plan, a good plan in fact. It was her job now to convince Nick to listen with an open mind.

When they got home, Gabby pulled her mother aside as her father put his car in the garage. "Mom, I need to run over to Ari's house and tell her what's going on before the Bolans call Penn State in the morning." Mary looked at her quizzically, her eyes asking with surprise, *You mean Ari doesn't know about this?* Gabby answered the unspoken question, "Mom, I just figured it out myself overnight, and I wanted you and Dad to be the first to know."

"Go ahead, but be back by four this afternoon so we can continue our talk." Mary looked squarely into her daughter's deep brown eyes. "I know you have something in mind. I trust that whatever it is, you have thought about it long and hard, and that you know in your heart of hearts it's what you truly want." Mary then gave Gabby a kiss. "Now, go and talk to Ari. I'll talk to your father."

Nick came in the kitchen door, catching only a glimpse of Gabby as she went running out the front. "Now where's she off to?"

Mary sighed and took Nick by the hand. "Let's go in the sunroom and sit down for a while."

Finding their seats, Nick leaned forward in his chair, his arms resting on his legs with his hands crossed, and looked up from under his furrowed brow. "Did you know about this?"

Mary gazed at this, she thought, still very handsome man to whom she was married -- the dark eyes, curly hair, tan and taut body – and wondered how best to try to explain to him what she herself didn't yet know. What Mary did know was that Gabby had been uncharacteristically self-contained lately. Even though she had written that off as natural while trying to decide which college she would attend, she now understood it was something else entirely. And so she thought she would start with that.

"Honey, to answer your question, no, I didn't know about this. However, I did sense that something was out of kilter over the last month or so. Gabby almost always talks with me when she has important decisions to make. But this time, I wondered what was going on. She was keeping her thoughts to herself – really out of character for her. I didn't say anything to you because I thought it was just last minute jitters about whether or not she would make the right decision about which college to attend. I also thought there was that extra burden of not knowing whether her choice would be the same as Ari's."

"You never mentioned any of this to me."

"It was only a feeling I had. The one thing I do know is that Gabby never would have come to this decision unless she was very sure of it. One, because she and Ari have planned on going to college together for so long and, two, she must have something in mind she thinks would be better for her in the long run. This has to be very difficult for her, and I can't even imagine what she's saying to Ari right now. So, let's be patient and hear her out this afternoon, not making any snap decisions. Whatever her plans, we *must* listen and not reject them out of hand. We'll ask the questions we need to ask, take the time to think it over, and discuss it between ourselves. Then we'll sit down again with Gabby. Can we agree to that?"

Nick nodded slowly. Mary always seemed to handle the family situations best, and he thought himself fortunate to have known that the girl he saw walking to and from high school would turn out to be such a wonderful wife and mother.

"I know you're right, honey, and we'll handle it that way. I am disappointed, though. To me, it was always essential that Brent go on to college. And, while I never felt it was as necessary for Gabby, once she told us she wanted to apply, I thought, *why not?* Life now is different than when we were young, and I've always wanted the best for her. I just always thought that, from the day she was born, she'd be just like her mother. You know I've always felt somewhat inadequate because, unlike some of our other friends, I never finished college. So, on the one hand, I was living back in the days when we were young, believing she would find the same happiness by having a life being just like you. But, then, on the other hand, my own sense of not being as good as others because I don't have that college degree, well, I just wanted her to have that advantage. After all, it's the 90's now and we've had a woman run as a vice-presidential candidate. Gabby should have an education so she can become whatever she wants, not what I want. It's just such a shock." With that, he patted Mary on the shoulder and said, "I'm going to my study for a while and look over some papers. Call me when Gabby gets home."

In the meantime, Gabby had been sitting on the easy chair upstairs in Ari's bedroom, having arrived unannounced at the Bolan's door. While Ari's mother was surprised to see her, she welcomed her and sent her directly up to Ari's room.

When Gabby knocked and opened the door a crack, Ari smiled at her best friend asking, "What're you doing here?"

"I need to talk to you," and sat down somberly in the chair by the window. Ari suddenly became concerned.

"Are you okay?" Ari asked.

Taking a long moment to steel herself, Gabby tried to begin what she thought was going to be harder for her than telling her parents earlier today. Seeing the worried look on Gabby's face, Ari closed the book she had been reading and waited patiently for what was to come.

"Ari, this is so hard for me, I don't even know where to begin. In the last month or so, I just haven't felt like myself. You must've sensed it. I tried very hard to push this feeling out of my mind, not even knowing what was going on myself. It wasn't until Friday night that I, well I . . . I realized that college isn't for me. I've been going over and over it in my head, slept on it and still feel the same way. I'm so sorry. All of our plans . . . but, it's just not right for me. I think part of the reason it took me so long to figure it out was that subconsciously I didn't want to let you down. And, I worried. What was going to happen to our friendship? I love you so much, but I know that once you and I go our separate ways, we'll never be the same again and it's tearing my insides out"

Sobbing now, Gabby fumbled to unfold the tissues she had wadded up in her hand, trying to stem the tears as they poured down her cheeks. Ari went over to Gabby and put her arms around her, holding her for several minutes. Sitting on the arm of the easy chair, Ari began to understand how different things would be from now on, not having Gabby at her side. She also realized how incredibly difficult this must have been for Gabby, and began to weep quietly for both of them. Slowly, Ari straightened up, went over to her night stand, grabbed the box of tissues, and returned to the easy chair. Holding the tissue box out to Gabby, Ari said, "Whew, I thought some guy had broken a date with you."

Gabby looked up at Ari through her tears and gave her a half laugh, knowing this was Ari's way to try to make her feel better.

Ari patted Gabby's back and tried to reassure her that this was not the end of their friendship. "Nothing can ever come between us. Tell me you know that,"

As Gabby nodded, her eyes began to tear up again. But knowing this would be even harder on Ari, she blew her nose and began to laugh. "Now, maybe, you can get a real boyfriend, since I won't be around all the time." Before she could cry anymore, Gabby stood up and hugged her friend. "I need to get home and talk to my parents some more. I just dropped all this on them at brunch this morning and leaving them to come to grips with it, came flying over here to tell you. We'll talk more tomorrow. I'm so sorry, just know that I love you." Ari and Gabby hugged for a minute, Gabby squeezing her tightly. Then, pulling away, Gabby turned toward the door, leaving quickly before her sobbing started again. Ari, in a daze, wondered whether all that had really just happened.

In what seemed to be less than a moment later, Ari's mother knocked on her bedroom door. Hearing Ari tell her to come in, Linda opened the door with a questioning look on her face. "Is everything all right, honey? I caught Gabby leaving out of the corner of my eye. She usually says goodbye, but not a word today."

Ari sat down on her bed and looked up at her mother. "Mom, Gabby's not going to Penn State, in fact, she said college wasn't for her."

Linda Bolan gently asked her daughter, "Do you think it's the money? Because if it is, maybe Gabby could get a scholarship."

Ari looked at her mom and thought about what she had just said. "I don't think so. I'm not really quite sure what it is, but I'll find out more tomorrow. She's going home to talk to her parents again -- she only told them this morning. So, no, it doesn't really sound like a money issue." Ari was thankful this was happening now and not later when they wouldn't have time to figure it all out. Maybe Gabby would change her mind or, perhaps, whatever it is that's bothering her can be resolved. In any event, they still had three weeks before the Penn State deadline.

Gabby walked into her house with bloodshot eyes. Mary took one look at her and sent her up to her room telling her to wash her face, take a little nap and then come downstairs. Her father and she could wait.

Mary found Nick in his study, told him how Gabby looked, and that she sent her up to her room to take some time for herself before coming down. After Mary left his study, Nick thought he should go up and check on Gabby himself. Knocking gently on her door, Gabby opened it with such a forlorn look, that Nick could only take her in his arms and hold her for several minutes before whispering, "We love you sweetheart. Everything will be fine, I promise you. Come down when you're ready, and we'll all figure it out together."

Gabby kissed her dad on the cheek, murmured, "Thank you, Daddy," and closed the door in order to regroup.

About an hour later, Gabby heard the telephone ring and, realizing it was Sunday afternoon, knew it was Brent calling from Yale. Gabby loved her brother dearly, but right now she really didn't want to talk to him. Gabby was sure her parents would tell him what was going on. Knowing how much he loved college, she just couldn't bear to hear him chastise her for her decision, or endure his attempts to change her mind. No, it was better to wait and talk to him later, after she had talked with her parents more and they knew where she was coming from. After all, she felt certain there would be a lot more to discuss after her plans were revealed. *This has already been a tough day*, she thought.

Combing her hair and brushing her teeth, Gabby straightened herself up to finally go down and talk with her parents. It was 5:05 now. She was a little more than an hour late, but she had done as her parents told her. Feeling somewhat rested, and even better than she thought she would, she was now on her way down the stairs in a more assured state than she had been two hours earlier.

Stepping into the kitchen, her mother turned from the chopping board and asked Gabby if she felt better and was ready to talk. Indicating she was, Mary smiled, suggesting that they would all be more comfortable in the sunroom.

Peeking into her dad's study, she prayed he was going to understand and accept what she was about to propose. Her mom would support almost anything Gabby would choose to do; it was her dad who was the question mark. Nick heard the door, saw Gabby and smiled. He could see that she was feeling better. She told him they were going to go out to the sunroom now, and could he join them. Proud of the way she was handling herself now, Nick said he was right behind them.

The sunroom was an addition Nick had put on several years before, and it truly was a wonderful room. Enclosed in glass during the winter months, which was replaced by screens in the summer, it was the room the family used most often. Surrounded by the backyard view of the early spring flowers and budding trees, Mary, Nick, and Gabby sat on the comfortable chairs and sofa that seemed to meld the indoors with the outside during the summer and made a cozy spot to keep warm during the winter. The sun was close to setting as they walked into the room, so Mary turned on the lamps casting a warm glow over the room, as they all prepared for what they were going to hear and say.

Nick, leaning forward in his chair, slowly began. "Gabby, I apologize for jumping off the deep end in the restaurant earlier today. Both your mother and I were surprised by what you said, although, admittedly, your mother less so. While we're disappointed by your decision, we both love you very much and we'll try to understand what it is you're going to tell us in the next hour or so. So, unless your mother wants to say something, you have the floor." With that, Nick sat back in his seat to listen to Gabby outline her plans.

Mary, sitting next to Gabby on the sofa facing Nick, gently patted her daughter's hand. "Go ahead, honey."

Gabby started, somewhat hesitantly at first. "As I told you earlier today, this is not something that just came over me. It's been building up for quite some time, without my being able to identify the problem. It was never my intention to hurt or disappoint you, please believe me. But as time went on, and then we committed in our minds to Penn State, this sense of foreboding came over me and wouldn't go away. Once I realized that I didn't want to leave you and Thompsonville, even though Ari wouldn't be here, I felt this great sense of relief. I'm not sure how to explain this to you. Please understand, it's not fear that keeps me from going to college. It's that I don't believe that it's the right path for my future. Would it keep me from it? No. But it's four years I'll have wasted not going for what it is I do want to do. You both know that I'm ambitious and have very strong opinions – thank you both very much for that. I also love creating things. When I realized that part of my sadness in leaving Thompsonville would mean leaving the construction company, I just *knew* it would break my heart."

As Nick started to lean forward again, Gabby stopped him. "Wait Daddy, let me finish." Gabby saw Mary give Nick a glance and knew she could continue without interruption. "Over the past year or so as I've worked for you, I've been sneaking looks at your plans for this house or that development. I've learned from going to the library and studying blueprints, how to read and understand them, and what the symbol's mean. I have ideas I think would work well, and even make some of your homes work a little better, without any appreciable increase in costs."

Breathing deeply and forcing herself to sit up as tall as she could, Gabby continued, "This is my proposal. I would like to come and work for you at Regency. My plan is to go to the different job sites, sit in on meetings – I promise not to say a word unless asked – learn all I can from anyone and everyone, and do all this without pay for the first six months. We can reevaluate any salary after that, if you think I can make a contribution. However, I *will* stay and do this job for one full year, learning all I can, with an eye to becoming a part of the company after that year is up. I expect no special favors, other than the one I'm now asking." A small smile quickly appeared and disappeared from her lips.

"Dad, Mom, this is something I really have to try. I love working with the people. I love the idea that I can help build something and can perhaps even use my head *now*, rather than waiting, to have an input into homes that are the most personal and important investments our customers make in their lifetimes. So, I guess that's it."

Gabby sat, still erect, waiting for the objections from her father. Her mother just held her hand and Gabby was so grateful to have her.

Nick took his time before he spoke. "Maybe I'm wrong in what I'm hearing Gabby, but it sounds like you have an interest in architecture. If that's the case, you'll need to go to college. Perhaps Penn State isn't the right college for that, but we can look into others for the spring term, if that's what you want to do. Otherwise, I can't imagine what you'd do in a construction firm. But, I'm willing to listen. You said you had some ideas after looking at some of our plans for the new development. Before we discuss this any further, I'd like you to come down to the office and show me what you have in mind. I'd also like you to tell me at that time more about what it is you actually plan to do, other than 'learn the business.' And then, what's your goal? What do you plan to do once you *have* learned the business? After we've discussed your possible role in the company, your mother and I will talk it over and then sit down with you again. So, can you come down tomorrow before lunch, say 11ish so we can discuss this?"

"I'll be there with bells on."

"Mary, okay with you?"

Mary nodded, and gave Gabby's hand another squeeze, "Good. Then is everyone ready for dinner?"

And off they went, Gabby first, feeling somewhat lighter having had this conversation and not facing a tirade from her father. She knew it wasn't over, but she had a chance. Tomorrow morning before going to the office, she would head over to the library and put together some of the materials she might need to help prove her point, and perhaps potential value of her working there, to her father. Yes, this had indeed ended up a better day than she originally anticipated.

At dinner over at the Bolan's, Ariana's father noticed how uncharacteristically quiet it was at the table. Normally, this was the time when everyone caught up with each other's day and was usually quite lively. Looking back and forth between Linda and Ari, Frank asked, "Why the silence?"

Linda waited for Ari to answer and looked in her direction giving her the lead. Ari then told her father about Gabby's visit and surprising announcement. While Frank thought this was a very unhappy development for Gabby, and he knew how disappointed Ari would be, he really didn't quite understand the impact it was having on her. Waiting for her to say more, Frank kept looking alternately between Linda and Ari.

Ari simply said, "Dad, I'll know more after I talk with Gabby again. But for right now, I'd like to wait before we notify Penn State. We still have some time."

"You're not thinking about giving up college are you Ari?"

"No Dad, just give me a few days, please." Frank looked at Linda who was also looking at Ari, so he couldn't catch her eye. Ari then asked to be excused and hurried upstairs.

"Don't worry Frank. Ari has worked too long and too hard not to go to college. I think this is just a shock for her because they'd been planning it for so long. I can't even imagine what Gabby's parents are going through right now. Ari will digest what Gabby has to say in the next day or two, and then she'll be able to accept it better when she knows the why of it.

We both know Ari wants to go to college, so let's just give her the time she needs to understand it."

Waiting until it was past the dinner hour, Ari called Gabby hoping to make plans to get together the next day. Not wanting to tell Ari about her plan until she knew it was going to be okay with her dad, Gabby just said she was meeting her father tomorrow, and could they make it Tuesday instead? In her heart, Gabby knew she had to do this and would figure out a way so her dad had to agree, but she still wanted to wait until he said yes before telling anyone else, even Ari. Agreeing to lunch on Tuesday, they made plans to meet at Augustino's, a more upscale downtown restaurant, which wasn't very busy during the lunch hour.

"Are you okay, Gabby?"

"I'm fine, really. See you Tuesday." Hanging up, they again wondered what was going to happen to their friendship now that they were going to be so far apart.

Monday morning, after looking over the calls, mail, and work status sheets from the weekend, Nick sat behind his desk thinking about Gabby. She was due in about twenty minutes and he was concerned that he would have to end up disappointing her. When he started Regency, he had already been in construction for several years. He had started right out of high school, working side-by-side with his uncles and cousins. The work was grueling – not the kind of thing a woman did. Where did Gabby think she would fit in, if not an architect? Surely she didn't want to go out on the sites with the men. He had built his reputation on the quality work he had done and then began to train his employees to do the same. If any of his employees were seen doing shoddy work, he was immediately fired.

Nick's company, Regency Development Corporation, named by Mary, became highly successful, he believed, because of his strict adherence to quality. Regency was one of the top, if not the top, construction company in the tri-state area -- almost always the builder of choice. Nick thought, *Maybe she just wants to start out as president. Am I ready to retire?'* Shaking it off, Nick decided to get a cup of coffee before Gabby showed up. Just as he opened his office door, Gabby came down the hall, a book bag of sorts in her hand, toward his office. He poured himself a cup of coffee asking Gabby if she would like some. Gabby declined, thinking, *I'm just ready to do this.*

Gabby walked into her dad's office, sitting down in one of the chairs facing his desk. Nick took his seat behind his desk and set down his coffee. Not sure who was to begin, Nick started. "I'm looking forward to hearing what you have to say, Gabby – particularly your suggestions regarding some of the plans for the new Huntington Forest development out at Clark's Corner."

"Dad, would you ask Norma to bring in the design plans for the Tuscany and the Belvedere homes that are a part of the mix of styles to be built at Huntington Forest." As Norma was about to hand the plans to Nick, he motioned his head toward Gabby, and Norma handed them to her. Taking the blueprints, Gabby laid out the plans on Nick's conference table just as Norma was closing the door. Nick stepped around his desk and began to walk over to the table, Gabby thinking, *Well, here goes. Don't mess up.*

Gabby put the blueprints for the Tuscany on top, and searched through the stack to locate the one detailing the kitchen. Shifting it to the top of the stack, she began. "Dad, if you look at this layout for the kitchen cabinets and appliances, I want you to look specifically at the way the cabinets go around in a 'U' shape. Because the kitchen is long and narrow, the 'U' allows only two small center cabinets and two corner cabinets. Then the shorter part of the 'U' becomes a peninsula separating the eat-in part of the kitchen from the working part. This makes it difficult for more than one person to work in the kitchen at any given time. Part of this design was probably determined because of the location of the door to the garage. What I would like to suggest is that we cut the peninsula off from the 'U,' thereby eliminating one of the corner cabinets, giving us room for three regular cabinets and one corner one. Most women don't like those corner cabinets. They just end up being a catch-all for things that are not used all that often, and end up stuffed, as a junk drawer might. Then, let's build an island, which we can move closer to the eat-in part of the kitchen. This is the thing women now want most in their kitchens. And, it gives the appearance of the kitchen being larger. A kitchen is probably one of the things that is most important when choosing a house. Regency's are out of date.

Okay, let's move onto the Belvedere, unless you have some questions about the Tuscany?"

Switching out the plans of the Tuscany for those of the kitchen of the Belvedere, Gabby went on. "Here the change is not as dramatic. But if you notice, you have the refrigerator between a row of cabinets, leaving only a one-width cabinet on the end. This is not only a waste of counter space because it's not continuous working space, but ends up being cluttered with odds and ends on it, having been rendered useless due to it's size and location. Furthermore, the counters and cabinets surrounding the refrigerator dictate the size the refrigerator must be to fill the gap or it looks silly. Move it to the end of the counter, again giving the kitchen a more sleek appearance and the bonus of more working space. I'd like to recommend a change in the lighting for all the kitchens and even the bathrooms. Those that are indicated by these drawings, the boxes for the florescent lights in the kitchens for instance, are outdated."

Sitting back away from the blueprints, Gabby took a deep breath as she prepared to wrap up. "Dad, at the moment this is all I can specifically point to, but I really haven't had a lot of time to study them. Perhaps, I won't even have any other suggestions, but I think that if I'm allowed to do as I propose, I can come up with other ideas which will make our homes a little more up-to-date and even show better. So, that's it. What do you think? Any questions? I'm a little nervous, so *please* say *something.*"

Nick, not wanting to show her how impressed he was by her observations and suggestions, said she'd made a very nice presentation. He was, however, somewhat skeptical about whether this island idea was all that popular. So, he asked her, "Why do you think this island idea has so much appeal?"

Thankful she had taken the time to stop at the library that morning, Gabby went over to her bag and pulled out some photocopies of pages from decorating magazines. Spreading them out on the conference table, she showed Nick how each of the magazines' pictures was featuring kitchens with islands in them.

Nick was now truly blown away, not only by Gabby's suggestions, but that she had the foresight to bring backup documentation to support her suggestions. She clearly had thought this through and offered a professional presentation. "This is very interesting and I'm impressed with what you've shown me here. But, I'm still a little unclear as to how you plan to make this a full-time job. Let's sit down and talk about this a little more."

"Dad, I know this is a little off the wall, but here's what I'm thinking. Right now you don't have anyone working directly with the vendors or covering all the jobs you have going. While at this point I don't know enough, well hardly anything, about the actual construction process, I know enough when there isn't a crew on site or whether they're doing a shoddy-looking job. I can deal with the vendors and can even work to see that the lighting, faucets, knobs, appliances, etcetera, are the current styles, and that what we order, is what we need and what we get. From time to time, if I find there are other things I think could be improved upon, I'd like to be free to make suggestions, as I did here today. I'd like to sit in on meetings, as I told you, to learn the rest of the business, all in an effort to end up as your right-hand man. I know you have Uncle Tony, and he's wonderful on the construction side. But you're the one who runs the company, and I think I can help in that area where you really don't have anyone else. The company is busy enough with all its projects. You can't possibly do it all, and that's where I think I can make a contribution. Again, no salary for the first six months. Of course, I'll have to live and eat at home. After that, we can negotiate if you think I'm making a difference. But, with or without salary, I get a year's trial."

Nick sat back and said, "I'd like to take some time to think this over. There are both business and personal considerations here. Your mother and I will talk this over and, as we told you last night, we'll sit down with you again after that. Regardless of what we decide, I am proud of what you've done today. Now, how about some lunch, just father and daughter, no business talk."

Gabby realized she wasn't going to be able to eat a bite until she calmed down. She also knew it would be extremely difficult to have a conversation with her dad at this point without wondering what her parents would decide. So, with that, Gabby thanked her dad, told him she was too nervous to have lunch, and gave him a kiss.

She began to gather her things and then went to straighten out the blueprints. Nick told her, "Just leave them. I'll get them later." He actually wanted to consider her suggestions a bit longer while having the blueprints at hand. *They sounded good, but are they feasible?*

Opening the office door, Gabby turned to her dad and said, "See you later, Daddy. Thanks for listening to me," and she walked out of the room, closing the door behind her.

Nick was glad to hear he was "Daddy" again because, during Gabby's presentation, she had called him Dad. He wondered whether that was a conscious choice on her part.

Gabby was full of nervous energy and really didn't quite know what to do with herself for the rest of the afternoon. She thought about going home and talking to her mother, but that might be difficult at this point, even though her mother was her best friend. Well, her mom and Ari. Gabby still wanted to wait to talk to Ari until she knew what her parents were going to say -- so that was out. Maybe some window shopping at the mall.

Eventually, she ended up at Logan Park, not too far from the tennis center. As she sat on a park bench watching the birds as they flitted around searching for worms for their babies, Gabby ran over and over in her mind the meeting she had just had with her father. It was so hard to know where she'd come out on that. He had said he was proud of her and impressed by her presentation. But was that the father talking or the businessman? Could he see what it was she was trying to do for him and for Regency? Maybe she should have spent more time looking at the blueprints -- perhaps there was something else she could have offered as a suggestion. Gabby wanted this so badly. She knew he had reservations and didn't know whether she had been successful in overcoming any objections he or her mother might have. Lord, this could end up being one of the longest days of her life. Gabby couldn't sit any longer. She started walking to work off her nervousness and, eventually, the afternoon started to pass. Finally, it was time to go home.

Walking into the kitchen, Gabby could smell her mom's meat sauce cooking on the stove. One of her favorite smells, she asked, "Spaghetti?" but then saw the lasagne pan on the counter and was really excited. She loved her mom's lasagne probably better than any other dish in the world. She went over to her and gave her a big kiss. "Mom, you're terrific. Thanks. Is there anything I can do to help?"

"How about setting the table. Then, we'll boil the noodles and cut some veggies for the salad. That'll give you some time to change before your father gets home. We'll eat in about an hour." Gabby washed her hands, and pitched right in. When they finished, Gabby thought it the perfect time for her to go and clean up, thereby giving her parents some time to talk alone. While she didn't expect any answers tonight, she didn't want to be in the way when her father got home.

So, taking her mother's cue, Gabby said if there wasn't anything else she could do, she'd go upstairs then and change. Off she went, running up the stairs and into her bedroom. Thinking she needed to be doing something, Gabby decided to take a shower and wash her hair, knowing that would take about as much time as the lasagne, and she wouldn't be sitting around wondering what she could have done differently.

Nick walked in the house while Gabby was still in the shower. He kissed Mary and asked if Gabby knew that they had met today. While Nick almost never came home for lunch or even made time for it, today, after Gabby left, Nick called Mary asking if she could meet him for lunch. Mary thought that was a good sign for Gabby. Apparently Nick was not going to dismiss Gabby's plan out of hand, so there must be something he wanted to discuss with her when Gabby wasn't around.

Mary had started their lunch by saying, "Gabby must have done something this morning which impressed you."

"She did and I still am blown away by her. I didn't know she had any interest in Regency, much less the determination to research and learn what she did. This, though, is part of my concern. If she could do this on her own without being taught what to do, doesn't that show that she should go to college?"

Mary nodded, understanding his reluctance. "Most kids go to college to figure out what they want to do with their life. Gabby apparently has already figured out what she wants, and now is asking to take the appropriate masters' course in order to excel in her chosen field."

Nick, almost confirming what Mary had just said, asked her if she knew that Gabby had run to the library this morning so that she could be prepared for some of his questions regarding her suggestions. "And," Nick said, "she was so professional, particularly for her age. On the other hand, I'm not sure she can do what she wants. She doesn't know anything about building a house, or how to run a business for that matter." At this point Nick went on to explain to Mary the idea of Gabby being his "right-hand man" (or was it "woman?"). Nick asked, "How do I explain this to my employees? How do I explain it to Tony? She has no experience in construction and, all of a sudden, she's my 'right-hand man?'"

"She'd just be training, Nick. Gabby's only trying to make a career choice by doing this. After all, Tony brought TJ in, and it shouldn't be any different just because Gabby's a girl." Mary also reminded Nick that when he decided to go off and start Regency, he really only knew the construction side of the business. "You learned as you went and I think you could benefit greatly by having someone help you out on the business end. Gabby's right, you have Tony, but he's not a businessman.

Aside from the business aspect of this decision, this is also your decision as a parent. You know, Nick, it's not only a parent's responsibility to educate their children by sending them off to school, but to help them make the right choices for their lifetime by giving them every possible opportunity a parent can provide. We, and you more specifically, are in a position to make this happen for her. I think we should support her decision, even though it's not what we had originally planned."

"My last big concern is what if she's wrong? What if after a year or even less, she realizes she should have gone to college, Mary? What then?"

"Then she'll reapply to Penn State or perhaps another college where she can study architecture if that's what she wants. I don't think we can play the second-guessing game at this point. But let's ask her what she thinks. In the meantime, why don't you take the rest of the afternoon to think about this and we'll discuss it more tonight." Mary and Nick then enjoyed their lunch, after which each went their own way until work was over and Nick would go home for dinner.

Feeling refreshed after her shower, Gabby made her way downstairs for dinner. As everything was served, Mary and Gabby joined Nick at the kitchen table. It was very quiet. Both Mary and Nick were enjoying their dinner when they noticed that Gabby was really only pushing her food around on her plate.

Mary knew that until this matter was resolved, Gabby's stomach would remain in knots so she said to Nick, "Honey, I don't think Gabby will eat a thing while this decision is hanging over her head."

Nick finished chewing some lasagne and pushed his chair back from the table. "Gabby, both your mother and I want to support you in this, but I'm concerned about how you will be received and perceived not only by the other employees of Regency, but also by the vendors and other business people. Another big concern is what if you decide you've made a mistake and then want to go to college? You could end up losing a year, maybe more. I don't know how colleges view this type of situation."

Gabby thought about it and then said, "Daddy, Mom, I can't do anything about what other people think. I can only do the best job I can, learning all I can, and making myself valuable to both Regency and you. As to college, I don't believe in my heart that I'm making a wrong decision. But, what if I call Penn State and see if it's possible for me to defer my enrollment. That way, if I'm wrong, I have a cushion and it'd be almost like I just took a year off between high school and college. I think lots of kids do it – I even think that's what Harriet Hill is going to do."

Nick and Mary looked at each other, Nick already knowing that Mary was willing to let Gabby "go for it"as she had said earlier that day. Then, knowing his wife was right, said, "Gabby, if Penn State can give you a year, certainly your mother and I are willing to do the same." With that, Nick stood, and said, "I think we all would like to have a glass of red wine with our dinner, don't you, Mary?"

As she turned the corner onto Columbia, Ari was thinking about what Gabby was going to tell her this afternoon at lunch. Augustino's was on the next corner and Gabby pulled into the parking lot adjacent to the restaurant. Ari thought she was early, but as she parked her car, she noticed Gabby's mom's Chrysler LeBaron convertible already tucked away in the back of the lot, away from the trees. Turning off the car, Ari rushed inside to see Gabby and get the scoop from her. She knew Gabby had been very conflicted, and felt guilty about not going to college with her. Ari was incredibly anxious to hear what Gabby had in mind and then figure out what she could say to ease her friend's guilt.

Meanwhile, inside Augustino's, Gabby was thinking she was very fortunate Penn State was going to allow her to defer her admission, although she knew she wouldn't need it. Gabby was sure she could learn enough about the construction business in one year that her parents would have no doubts. But she was glad to be able to reassure them that college would be there, just in case.

Ari saw Gabby seated at a square table for four over by the mural on the back wall of Augustino's. The restaurant was a lovely Italian favorite for many in Thompsonville, but there had been a slowdown during the luncheon hours, due to many of the downtown businesses moving out to the suburbs.

As the maitre d' led Ari back to the table, she was glad to see the huge smile on Gabby's face. Taking her seat, she could barely wait for the maitre d' to leave before turning to Gabby. "Well?" Obviously there was no need for small talk leading up to the big issue between the two girls; they were simply too close to stand on ceremony.

Gabby could barely sit still. "I don't even know where to start because I'm so excited. So much has happened in the last couple of days . . . Okay. First of all, I want to apologize again for backing out on our plan for college. I really did struggle with the decision. Not because I was unsure about what I wanted, or in this case didn't want, to do, but because I didn't know if I could pull it off."

Gabby took a deep breath and continued. "You know I've been working at Regency for the past few summers and helping out on Saturdays when my father needed me. Well, over the past year in particular, I've been really paying attention to what was going on and how it worked, especially the new developments. I'd been looking at the blueprints and sometimes I would see something I didn't think made sense. I've been going to the library and looking at the architectural magazines; *Architectural Digest*, *Metropolitan Home*, and the like, and the do-it-yourself magazines. Suddenly last weekend, I realized that what I really want to do is work for my dad and get involved in the construction business.

Right before I went over to your house on Sunday afternoon, I told my parents I didn't want to go to Penn State – but I hadn't yet told them what I did want to do. So, when I saw you, I didn't want to say anything because I didn't know if they would agree to my plan or not. After leaving you I went home, recharged myself and then sat down with my parents in the sunroom. I laid out my idea of learning the business and then being his right-hand man. They listened, but understandably they were reluctant – my Dad more than my Mom, of course. It eventually came down to my meeting my dad at his office Monday to present how I thought I could make a contribution to the company. I outlined some changes based upon my ideas as we looked over the blueprints, and he listened. I must've done something right. I'd gone back to the library that morning and made some copies of pages from the architectural magazines backing up some of my suggestions – because he then said he'd talk to Mom."

"Wait a minute. You want to work at Regency rather than go to college? Am I getting this right?"

"I know, I know. But let me finish. When my Dad came home for dinner last night, it seemed as if he'd already made up his mind – he must have talked to Mom sometime earlier in the day – anyway, that's what I'm going to do and I am sooooo excited. Of course, one of their big concerns was my giving up Penn State, well college altogether. So I promised them I'd call Penn State and see if they'd defer my admission in case things don't work out. They will, but things will work out, I just know it. So there, in the short time before the waiter comes back, you have it all. Except, of course, how much I'll miss not being with you. But I'll be here when you come home for holidays and I can even go and visit you too."

"I had no idea . . . I am really excited for you. Really. This comes from out of nowhere, but then again I knew you liked helping your dad out – but permanently? I do have to tell you though, I never saw you this excited about college. I'm going to miss you terribly, but now that we've talked, I think you've made the right choice for you and that's what's important."

Gabby could see that Ari meant what she was saying, so she sat back and smiled saying, "It *is* the right choice for me. Thanks, pal."

"Now, *I* have a confession to make," Ari said sheepishly.

"What? What kind of confession?" Gabby was shocked, and sat there staring at her best friend. After all, she felt as if she was the one letting Ari down -- *What is this all about?* They then both noticed that the waiter was back and they hadn't even looked at their menus. Picking them up quickly, Gabby ordered the Mediterranean Pasta and Ari asked about any specials, choosing the veal in white wine sauce topped with asparagus. The waiter topped off their iced teas, thanked them and disappeared to place their orders.

When Ari looked up after the waiter left, she laughed because Gabby was again staring at her wide-eyed, her expression saying, "So?"

"Well, I'm kind of thinking that I might change my mind and go to Northwestern."

"You're *what?*"

"Rethinking Penn State. I haven't even mentioned this to my parents yet because I'm still thinking about it. Northwestern was kind of a fluke – I never thought I'd get in. But it's such an awesome university, well, so is Penn State, but Northwestern is in the Chicago suburbs and I think it would be terrific to live there."

"Holy cow!" Gabby said. "Maybe it was meant to be! I mean my deciding not to go to Penn State and your applying to Northwestern 'as a fluke' as you call it, just maybe . . . "

"Well, as I said, I haven't made up my mind, but I'm seriously considering it. Now that I've talked to you and I see how happy you are about your own decision, I'm more comfortable now thinking about what it is that I'm going to do. I don't want you to think I would have been unhappy going to Penn State, but this is an opportunity perhaps just too good to pass up. And, as you say, it may have been meant to be."

"When are you going to talk to your parents?"

"Probably tonight. I don't want to jump the gun, but I'd love their input and, of course, they are the ones paying the bill. I think this is so exciting for both of us and, if I do go to Northwestern, you can still come visit me there. When are you starting to work for your dad?"

As Gabby was about to answer, lunch was served. Both Gabby and Ari toasted each other with their iced teas and began to dig into their meals.

Gabby then told Ari a start date really hadn't been discussed yet and, that even though she wasn't going to college, she really wanted to go on all the shopping trips with Ari and the other girls. "Just because I'm not going to college," Gabby said, "I'll still need work clothes for my new career, and my school wardrobe just isn't what I have in mind."

They both said, "deal" at the same time and again dug into their lunches. After lunch, as they walked to the parking lot together, they made a date to go shopping on Saturday, and Ari promised to call Gabby after she had talked to her parents about Northwestern.

Ari did talk with her parents that night. Both Frank and Linda were surprised but, of course, they both had known about Ari's application to Northwestern. They talked about the differences between Penn State and Northwestern, both in terms of the education each would offer and also the differences in living experiences of the big city versus a small town. Ultimately, Frank and Linda told Ari it was her decision to make and that either choice would be a good one; it was a matter of preference only she could determine.

Having called Gabby to keep her in the loop, Ari then began to consider in depth the idea of Northwestern vs. Penn State.

CHAPTER THREE

Graduation day was glorious in all respects; the weather perfect, the speeches not too long, and the families expectedly proud of their graduates. Jennifer Lee was heading to the University of Pennsylvania as she had hoped, Karen Dunwitty was accepted at Bryn Mawr, but was still waiting to hear from Rutgers, with most of the other girls going off to their chosen schools.

The notable exception to this was Harriet Rose Hill. Harriet had told everyone she was taking some time off this summer to decide what she was going to do, but that she was very interested in the Sorbonne, and she and her mother would be spending most of the summer in Paris to check it out.

Ari decided Northwestern would be the school for her and was eager to get started. She and her parents had taken another trip to Chicago to check out Evanston and the school again. Coming away more impressed than she had been the first time, it clinched her choice and there was no looking back after that.

Following the ceremonies, the graduates gathered with one another knowing their paths would not cross again for some time to come. Ari, Gabby, and Jennifer were off talking about their plans when Doug, who had been Ari's prom date, and Sean, Gabby's, came up to talk with the girls. Both Doug and Sean were off to volunteer in South America before heading to college in the fall.

Looking sheepishly at the girls, Doug asked if they could all get together for dinner before they left for Peru. Jennifer wanted to back off thinking they were asking Ari and Gabby for dates, but they said no, they wanted her to join them too. In fact, they thought they could make a night of it with Josh and Larry and maybe Karen could make it. Everyone thought this was a fine idea. They had all been friends for a long time and there was no real romance between any of them, either past or present, which might make the dinner awkward. They made plans to meet Thursday night at The Inn at the Park because the boys were leaving the following Saturday.

"Dinner with the boys" as Ari, Gabby, Jennifer and Karen called it, was a huge success. They were typical graduates, glowing from their accomplishments and with all the hope and optimism for their futures.

Doug and Sean's trip to South America was an experience they had been looking forward to for several months. After arriving, they would trek to a small village in Peru near the Amazon River to help the villagers with their planting, housing repairs and, they hoped, the chance to work and play with the children of the village. It was a summer-long commitment, allowing them only a week back home before heading off to college. The dinner group decided they would try to get together again before going their separate ways.

While Ari and the other girls were getting ready for school, Gabby had already started work at Regency, Nick giving her only a week off after graduation. "Now that you're in the construction business, you have to be prepared to work hard, particularly during the summer months when we're the busiest. But," he reminded her, "you'll have the benefit of not working the week between Christmas and New Years, when we're closed so all our employees can spend time with their families."

Gabby did spend most of her Saturdays with Ari, and often with Karen and Jennifer as they prepared to go away. Even though Gabby knew she was going to miss being with her friends, she was so into learning everything she could about her new job, she spent almost all her free time going to the library and researching new designs shown in the magazines. After spending almost every night there, Gabby finally decided that she should subscribe to the magazines she thought were the best for what she was trying to learn.

On the Saturdays when Gabby wasn't with Ari or the other girls, she would take a ride to the various developments of other construction companies, just to get a look at what they were doing. She also made it a point to check out some of the houses that were up for resale, particularly when she knew there had been some renovation work done. All of this was done not as a secret from Nick, but just something that she wanted to do on her own. She took it all in and started to look at houses in a whole different way, and unbeknownst to her, it was safely filed away in her head for later use.

Brent stayed in New Haven for the summer having found a job at the law library. He thought it would hold him in good stead to become as familiar with the library as possible. He had heard he was going to be spending a great deal of time there once fall came and he was officially a first year law student at the University. Brent called Gabby frequently after she first announced that she didn't want to go on to college. But he, too, became comfortable with her decision, particularly after their parents had reassured him that college would still be there if she changed her mind.

Brent couldn't understand it. He was the consummate student; he loved college and was the bookworm of the two. Brent had dreamed of being a lawyer for what seemed like forever. Remembering back to when he had the measles and was stuck in the house for a week, there had been this very old movie on TV called To Kill A Mockingbird. Thinking that Atticus Fitch was a very smart, gentle and compassionate man, both as a lawyer and the sole parent for his young children, Brent never considered anything else. It was the law or nothing. He thought of himself as blessed for being able to pursue the law, particularly at Yale.

Brent knew Gabby could do just about anything she wanted to, so he was pulling for her, and their phone conversations had eased back into the close brother/sister friendship they had always shared.

Somehow the days just flew by. Doug and Sean were back with wonderful stories and pictures from their two months in South America. The reunion of the dinner group was as good as the graduation dinner itself. But it, too, had come and gone.

Ari was leaving in two days and by the end of the week, the entire group would be spread out among their chosen colleges. Thompsonville would be a different place from that she knew and Gabby was starting to feel lonely already.

As the crisp scent of fall fell over Thompsonville and the leaves were turning their flaming colors of red, yellow and orange, Gabby was well into her fourth month at Regency and beginning to think she might not make her one-year deadline. There was just so much to learn. And, while she was making headway with parts of what it took to build a house, she felt she was a long way from understanding what it took to build a whole development, much less run a company that did. Frankly, she was somewhat amazed at just how difficult it was to get into the swing of things having her father as a boss. But, because of the Jeep Nick had given her, she was able to get to the job sites easily and function on her own. She was learning about the vendors and their inventories and the scale of the needs Regency had when they undertook a new development.

Gabby again started running back and forth to the library trying to do more research about all the different fixtures offered, and the best way to do that was on-line. She had taken a couple of computer classes in school and had learned enough to know it was becoming imperative to have a computer if one was running a company. Gabby knew one of her most difficult jobs was going to be convincing her father that Regency needed several. In order to do that, Gabby knew she would have to take a more intensive computer class than she had taken in high school. If her father was to even consider this, she had to know enough about how to work it to answer his questions, and then someone had to use it at Regency in order to train others. Gabby decided she would ask the librarian where she had learned how to use the computer. Mrs. McLaughlin was only too pleased to tell Gabby she had learned at the community college in an evening class taught by a Mr. Jerry O'Neil, who was very knowledgeable. He even had a local company that sold and maintained computers.

On a mission now, Gabby called the community college to find out about their evening computer class. As classes had already begun, Gabby decided it might be best if she could meet with Mr. O'Neil and talk with him privately about what she was trying to do for Regency and the best way to go about it. As Tuesday was the night the class was scheduled to meet, Gabby went over to the college on the chance that Mr. O'Neil would have some time to talk with her. Gabby stood at the door to the classroom before class was to begin. When Mr. O'Neil arrived, Gabby asked if she could have a few minutes of his time. Glancing at his watch, Mr. O'Neil asked if she could arrange to either meet him after the end of the class or perhaps next week before class.

Making plans to meet in the classroom after class was over that night, Gabby wandered off to find a place to get a cup of coffee. While Gabby roamed the halls of the community college, she spied a schedule for the evening classes that were offered. Stopping to read it over, Gabby happened to glance at a class called An Introduction to Architecture, and was intrigued. The instructor was an architect by the name of John Traymore. *This could be very interesting*, Gabby thought. Although she wasn't interested in becoming an architect, it might be a very good idea if she had some understanding of what it was all about. Glancing through the brochures and other giveaway materials at the information desk, Gabby found one for the class and put it in her purse to call about tomorrow.

Now, she wandered out of the building, spotted a coffee shop across the street and walked over to wait out the time until she was to meet with Mr. O'Neil. Sipping her coffee, Gabby decided to read the brochure about the architecture class. She thought that it really might be right on for her needs – not too technical. Just, as advertised, an introduction. Still thinking about the class, Gabby almost didn't notice it was time for her to meet Mr. O'Neil. Grabbing her bag, Gabby went running back across the street and up the stairs to the door of the classroom as the students began piling out.

After the exodus settled down, Mr. O'Neil motioned for her to come in and sit. Gabby shook hands with the instructor and sat down at a desk, thanking him for making the time to chat with her. She outlined Regency's business and her part at the company, also telling him about her father being a hard sell for this idea.

Mr. O'Neil listened intently and agreed that it was wise for Regency to make use of computers. According to him, computers were the wave of the future and were now being used regularly by attorneys and businesspeople with a terminal in almost every office – they were no longer the big old systems available to only a few computer-savvy people in each organization. Gabby explained that because Regency was a construction company, the need for a computer for each employee was not the same as corporate businessmen or lawyers, but she did think that perhaps four or five of the inside people could make very good use of them. Also, she thought the best way to approach this was for her to learn more about what the computer could do for the business and she wondered if she could take some private lessons from him.

Mr. O'Neil was taken by the intensity and determination of this young woman. He offered to give her the hour after each of his Tuesday evening classes, if that would work out for her, at a price that a recent high school graduate could afford.

Delighted by his willingness to work with her, Gabby accepted his offer and promised to be back next Tuesday night to start her class. Humming as she left, Gabby felt she had had a very productive evening, and was looking forward to seeing Mr. O'Neil again next week. She realized he was a very attractive man; his dark hair, creamy skin and those dark green eyes were striking, even if he was too old for her. *Oh, well. Back to earth*, she thought. *I need to get home and get something to eat.*

The next morning, as she had promised herself, Gabby called the college and inquired about the architecture class. Learning there had been only one class she had missed, Gabby enrolled over the phone and went running down to the college at lunch to pay the required fee.

That afternoon, Gabby spent some time out at Phase One of Huntington Forest, the name of the new Regency Development at Clark's Corner. Gabby had become a more accepted sight there, at first having been heavily scrutinized by the construction workers. But Uncle Tony, her father's brother and the construction chief for Regency, and his son, TJ, short for Tony, Jr., had worked with her, teaching her and, by their example, the others fell into line.

Gabby liked to go out and check on the progress of the homes. Still relatively early in her training, she wanted to see how things went together, step-by-step, thinking that was the way she would understand the whole process better.

TJ, Gabby's cousin, walked her over to the Belvedere model where the studs for the walls were being put up. Of course, Gabby had been to many homes that were in the process of being built with her father, but not at such an early stage of construction and certainly not with an eye toward understanding each process and it's importance in timing and order in the scheme of it all.

Touring the site, TJ explained the rooms and their positioning, the width of the walls and the layout for the electric and plumbing. Gabby noticed one of the workers out of the corner of her eye watching her. As soon as she looked directly at him, he quickly turned his head back to nailing one of the studs. "Who's that?" Gabby asked, as he was someone she didn't recognize. Most of the guys were old-time employees of Regency, but she hadn't seen him before.

"He's a new employee, hired on to help with all the work being generated by this new Huntington Forest Development. Remember, this is only Phase One of the project, with three more to go. His name is Mike Franconi, Joe Franconi's nephew from Detroit. He came down here because there wasn't a lot of work up there. He's a very good worker and we're glad to have him. Why?"

"Nothing, really. It's just that his face isn't familiar to me and I like to know everyone's name in case I need to ask any questions." With that they finished up with their tour of the site and Gabby made her way back to the office for the rest of the day.

Evanston was very different from Thompsonville. So many people and so many places to go, and this was only a suburb. Ari was enthralled by all the goings on at Northwestern. After registration, class selection, and moving into the dorm, unpacking and just getting settled was a big deal.

Her roommate, Emily Gorman, actually was from the Chicago area, but choose to live on campus away from all the doings at her house. Emily had one older sister, three younger sisters and one younger brother. She called it, *sheer pandemonium, and not a fit place to live or study*. Emily was a brunette with long wavy hair, soft brown eyes and a fabulous figure. She loved sports, and in many ways reminded Ari of Gabby. Emily was much more into school though and spent a lot of time studying, even early on.

When they did go out, Emily would take Ari downtown. They went to Uno's and sometimes to some of the clubs on the near north side and around Rush Street. Sometimes they just went down to Michigan Avenue on Saturdays. Ari loved it. The sights, the people, the shops, restaurants – all candy to her eyes. She thanked her lucky stars she ended up in Chicago; she just couldn't imagine herself anywhere else.

Ari called Gabby often and was so glad to hear Gabby's excitement when she talked about her work. When Gabby told her about the classes she was taking and why she was taking them, Ari thought this really was what Gabby wanted to do with her life and while they were not together now, they were each doing what worked best for them.

As the days passed at Northwestern, Ari was really in the swing of things. The dorm was always abuzz with people and she had made friends quickly. Several young men asked her out, but there was no one she thought of as special at this point. The classes were challenging and Ari worked hard to do well in all of them.

And then, almost without warning, it was Thanksgiving and Ari was headed home to Thompsonville for the first time since her parents had dropped her off at school three months earlier.

On Tuesday, Ari took Amtrak to Pittsburgh where her parents were waiting at the station. During the drive home, Ari talked nonstop about school, Chicago, Emily, and life in general. As Ari stepped into the kitchen, the scent of the house was immediately familiar, warm and comforting; she knew she was home. She took her bag from her father and asked if she could call Gabby, saying she couldn't wait to see her.

Linda laughed and said, "Sure." As Ari ran up the stairs to her bedroom, Linda turned to Frank saying, "This is what it's going to be like now. Too few days home and too many things Ari wants to do during the short time available."

Frank nodded. "It's a good thing Thanksgiving dinner is ours. It is, isn't it?"

"You know it is. Don't forget your father is expecting to be picked up at 12:45 p.m. sharp on Thanksgiving Day. He doesn't want to be late for dinner or miss the football game."

Ari didn't even unpack before she got Gabby on the phone. The two of them were chatting away like crazy when Gabby said, "Wait a second, we're talking on the phone as if you're still in Chicago; I'm on my way over."

Ari saw Gabby's Jeep come up the driveway and ran down to the front door, throwing it open even before Gabby could ring the bell. They fell into each other's arms and didn't let go for a long moment. Feeling the chill in the air, Ari dragged Gabby into the house and they went into the living room where Frank had started a fire in the fireplace.

Plopping down on the sofa, Ari started asking tons of questions about what Gabby had been doing and whether she had seen any of their other friends or when they were arriving home for the Thanksgiving holiday. Gabby and Ari were still talking two hours later when Linda appeared in the living room to ask Gabby if she would like to stay for dinner.

Not realizing they had talked that long, Gabby was embarrassed that she hadn't even said hello to Ari's parents or noticed the time. While Ari was begging Gabby to stay, Gabby explained, "I wish I could, but there are a couple of things I need to do at work. After all, it's Tuesday and a work day for me."

Thanking Linda for the invitation, Gabby picked up her purse and started toward the front door. As she was leaving, Gabby said, "I told my dad I'm taking Wednesday and Friday off this week to spend some time with you and some of our other friends in for the holiday weekend."

"That's great. I didn't even ask, is Brent coming home for the weekend? It would be fun for all three of us to get together again."

"No. He's staying in New Haven for Thanksgiving, but planning a nice long Christmas break here at home."

Since Ari didn't have any siblings, Brent had always treated her like a little sister along with Gabby when they were young and they had all been very close. The three hadn't had a lot of time to spend together over the past few years, particularly with Brent away at school. But whenever they could, they would try to get together, catch up and just generally have a good time.

The girls made plans to meet the next day and, in the meantime, Ari would call Jennifer and Karen and see if they could join them for lunch down at The Blue Frog, one of their all-time favorite hangouts.

The Blue Frog Diner was downtown, and a favorite of many. The legend went that it was named after the frogs that swam and jumped in the rock-filled streams running down the hills surrounding Thompsonville. Apparently Claudia Ruchenzi's father spent a lot of time up in the hills as a young man and noticed the frogs looked blue to him in the cool morning light as they made their way from rock to plant. When he opened the diner, he thought the name would serve as a wonderful memory for him and others who had spent time lazing by the rocky beds of the cool mountain-like streams.

The diner sat in the middle of a block of retail shops, some of which had closed, but the diner stayed busy. It seemed that the diner was the place people went when looking for comfort food, familiar faces, and local news before it hit the papers. Breakfast was a specialty and the locals met there almost daily. It was also the place with the best burgers and fries in town and the diner had been adopted as the "place to go" by most kids from their high school years and after. In the summertime, one could smell the burgers and fries from a block away; it had the old-time screen doors and large overhead fans spinning from high ceilings. A throwback to earlier days, the floor was black and white linoleum squares, the tables black Formica, and the fountain stools red naugahyde encased inside stainless round forms with the pedestals bolted to the floor, as they had always been. The menu had remained basically the same, although the prices changed over the years.

Gabby and Ari walked in to meet Karen and Jennifer who had come in from Philadelphia. Karen ended up at Bryn Mawr and loved it. And, it was close to Jennifer down at the University of Pennsylvania. The girls were excited to see them already chatting with Debbie, Chris and Christine and noticed several tables filled with other young people, some from their class. Stopping to say hello at a few tables, the girls made their way back to hug their former classmates.

Debbie, Chris and Christine were just finishing up so, after chatting with them for a few minutes, Ari, Gabby, Karen and Jennifer made their way to a clean table so they could order lunch and find out everything that was going on with their two other friends.

Jennifer loved Philadelphia. The city was quaint, old-city style with row houses, cobblestone streets, tons of parks and museums on the one hand, but also vibrant with it's new office buildings and corporate businesses on the other. Jennifer said she had been to the Free Library and the Rodin Museum, among others, and that she was captivated by the lights outlining the boathouses along the Schuylkill River.

Karen had spent some weekends down in Philadelphia with Jennifer and they had seen the sights together. And, Jennifer had gone up to Bryn Mawr, only a thirty minute train ride away. They had cheered the Villanova Wildcats football team at a home game and window shopped in Wayne and Spread Eagle Village. Both said they had made friends with several girls in their dorms and were settling into the college lifestyle.

Gabby brought everyone up-to-date on her work, telling them how much she loved it. She admitted she hadn't had much time for anything else and, besides, everyone was gone. Then she thought a second and said "Wait, *almost* everyone is gone."

With all eyes on her sensing something was coming, Gabby eyes sparkled. "I guess you haven't heard that HRH is back from Paris? Evidently, she decided that the Sorbonne was not for her either. She took an art class or a fashion design class, maybe both. Anyway, she didn't like it. Word is, she and her mother spent the summer shopping, with a few side trips to the South of France and Italy. I'm not sure what she's going to do, but I'll bet it has nothing to do with work or school." Gabby had been the one to name Harriet Rose Hill "Her Royal Highness," better known as HRH.

Harriet was pretty much spoiled by her parents, especially her mom. Her mother reared her to be just like her and she did a really good job of it, which left Harriet a very lonely child. As far as anyone knew, HRH's major accomplishment, and one she never let anyone forget, was when she developed a new strain of roses, which she quickly and unashamedly named the "Rose Hill Rose" after herself.

Apparently Harriet had started tagging along with her mother when she went to the garden club and became interested in gardening, and roses in particular, at that time. No one knew for certain if Harriet had really developed this new strain herself or not, but she had taken credit for it nonetheless. It was just her way.

Harriet was not beautiful. She was about five-foot-six, maintained her posture after years of repeated commands to do so, kept her figure, dressed impeccably, although that had not always been the case, and had become quite attractive over the years. Her auburn, almost red, hair was wildly out of control when she was young. Now, it was part of her fashion statement. She kept it long and well-styled, often making heads turn.

As a child, little did Harriet's classmates know that inside, during all those years, she had shied away from them because of her lack of self-confidence and was, in fact, quite lonely. Then, as she grew older, she became more distant which, on its face, appeared haughty and snobbish. At least that was how they perceived her. Ari sensed that Harriet's shyness may have been a defense mechanism, but HRH had seldom given any of the girls the time of day. Consequently, they ended up making plans that didn't include her, which further reinforced her lack of self-esteem.

Having caught up with one another, the girls began making their way to their cars. The air had turned crisp and there was a hint of snow in the air. The girls all hugged, promised to get back together again soon, and headed back to their own homes in anticipation of the next day's Thanksgiving Day celebrations.

Linda was up early setting the table and working in the kitchen when Ari came downstairs. Ari looked at her mom sheepishly with an apology for not being up earlier to help her. Linda knew Ari kept a tight schedule at school and was certain that sleeping in was a treat for her rather than her normal routine. Linda nodded toward the hot pot of coffee and Ari quickly grabbed a cup and then routed through the pantry until she found the cereal.

Sitting down at the table, Ari began to eat her cereal when her mother asked, "What's new with the girls?" Ari generally kept her mom up-to-date on what was happening with her friends, but she hadn't really had a chance to discuss yesterday's get-together with her in depth. So, Linda and Ari sat at the kitchen table talking and laughing as they always had.

Linda was surprised to hear about Harriet. "Do you have any idea what's going on with her?"

"Oh, Mom. It's been a long time since I've had a conversation with Harriet. She's kept pretty much to herself over the last few years and she didn't even go to the senior prom. I thought she was going to go on to college because that's what Mayor Hill told us that night at the club. But then I heard that Harriet was going to spend the summer in Paris with her mom checking out the Sorbonne – now she's home. None of us really knows what her plans are."

"I'm very sorry to hear that, Ari."

As they continued their conversation, Frank came in from his study to get another cup of coffee. "I see you girls haven't missed a step even though Ari's been away at school," Frank said.

At that, Linda looked at the clock on the microwave. "My word, where did the time go? I need to finish up in here, Ari and I need to dress, and you'll need to leave soon to pick up Grandpa Bolan."

Grandpa Bolan, Yuri, was Frank's father and the founder of the machine parts repair shop which later became Bolan's Machine Works, Inc., which Frank now ran.

Ari adored her grandpa and always made it a special point to spend time with him whenever she could. He was alone now, Ari's grandmother, Marta, had passed away several years ago and Ari thought her grandfather was lonely. Of course, Yuri denied this, claiming he had many young ladies he spent time with, but Ari just wasn't so sure.

Ari was captivated by her grandfather's life, and had actually based one of her writing class papers on it. She learned that Yuri had immigrated to the United States in 1928. His name was changed at Ellis Island when he arrived by intake attendants who found it too difficult to pronounce. So, like many others, his name was shortened. He was so overjoyed to be in the United States that he thought Americanizing his last name was a sign that life would be all he had dreamed before he left Czechoslovakia.

Yuri was strong-willed, but at seventeen lacked the education and working background to fit in easily, and his broken English made it even more difficult. He was determined, energetic and eager to start his life in America and took odd jobs in various small stores in New York City as a stepping stone, knowing he wanted more.

New York was teeming with immigrants and the city was hot and overcrowded, not to his liking. He made his way down to Philadelphia, then a large city but still much smaller than New York, and he felt more comfortable there. While attending church, Yuri met and was befriended by another Czech who had come to America several years earlier. Boris took Yuri under his wing and started him as an apprentice in his small machine part's repair shop. There Yuri thrived. He loved the work and learned quickly. When 1929 and the crash came, business became almost nonexistent, except that people found it less expensive to repair machines than to buy new ones. Boris kept Yuri on as he was such a good worker and moved him into his apartment. Together they kept the business going and themselves above water financially.

Yuri even managed to save money and, as business improved, ended up saving quite enough to go out on his own – a long time dream of his. He just didn't know where. He liked Philadelphia and certainly had done well there, but the city was too big and not the beautiful countryside that other parts of America offered. He wanted the hills and streams, the beauty that was so close to that of his beloved Czechoslovakia. Again, Yuri began dreaming of the place that would feel more like home to him and yet offer all that America did.

During that time in Philadelphia, while still working and living with Boris, Yuri met and fell in love with a beautiful young woman named Marta. Marta had moved to Philadelphia in search of work during the Depression, but longed to return to her family in Thompsonville in the lush hills of West Virginia, atop the deep slopes over the Ohio River.

When Marta first brought Yuri home to Thompsonville to meet her parents, he was welcomed with open arms. Checking out Thompsonville, Yuri and Marta's father thought there was a need for a machine part's repair shop. Yuri felt he had, at last, found the place to build his home and his life in America. In Yuri's mind, the deal was done.

Yuri and Marta went back to Philadelphia to make their plans to move back to Thompsonville, and for Yuri to thank Boris for everything he had done for him over the years. Within three months, Yuri and Marta had moved to Thompsonville, arranged their wedding, found a home, and Yuri had set up shop in a small garage-style building on 3rd Street downtown. That was 1934 and Yuri never regretted any of it.

Today, Ari knew she would hear some of the story again. Once in a while, she would learn something new that her grandfather would remember from out of the blue. She never tired of hearing his stories and missed not having known Yuri's sister who had stayed in Czechoslovakia. There were distant cousins somewhere that her dad kept in touch with from time to time, but there really wasn't anyone else.

Linda's sister, Ellen, and her husband Bruce, were going to be with their oldest daughter and her family for Thanksgiving, along with Linda and Ellen's brother, Bob and his family. But, the whole brood would be at the Bolan's for Christmas Eve as usual. It was always one of Ari's favorite times with the entire family together.

Grandpa Bolan didn't disappoint during Thanksgiving dinner. As always, he was very interested in and supportive of Ari's activities. They talked about life in the big city and life, in particular, in Chicago. Grandpa Bolan had been there many times as a young man meeting with some of the manufacturers whose parts he repaired, some trips at the request of customers, other times to promote business by showing manufacturers how to upgrade their equipment.

There was lively chatter among all four of the Bolans. As dinner was coming to an end and Linda brought out the pumpkin and pecan pies, Grandpa Bolan became quiet. He accepted another cup of coffee and sat back in his chair. "I've made reservations for a Mediterranean cruise for next May."

Ari was excited for her grandfather and asked all about the ports of call, how long he'd be gone, and who he was going with?

Shocked, Linda and Frank just looked on. Frank knew he would have to address this with his father in private, his concern clearly being an eighty-one-year-old man going off halfway around the world and without a companion, at that.

At Gabby's house, it was elbow-to-elbow family. Mary never tired of having the family in, and at Thanksgiving they were all there. Uncle Tony and Aunt Carmen, cousin TJ and his sister, Jessica and her husband, Aunt Rose and Uncle Ed, their two sons, Eli and Joseph, Aunt Angela and her husband Carl with their son Dominic and two daughters, Amy and Stephanie, Nick's parents, Joe and Mary Romano and Grandmother and Grandfather Campagna. The only one missing this year was Brent, and, while he wasn't there, the family was so proud of him and his accomplishments at college and now law school, they would toast him and his future, celebrating the family as if he was sitting in his ususal chair.

On Friday, after the lavish dinners, football games and family fun, the dishes were done and put away. Everyone had delighted in another holiday shared with those they loved. Ari and Gabby spent some time together and then again on Saturday. Frank and Linda took Ari to the country club and spent as much of Saturday as they could with her. Soon, it was time for her to go back to Chicago, and it seemed as if there just hadn't been enough time.

Ari rode the train back to Chicago, feeling more alone than she had when she first started Northwestern. Obviously Gabby was loving her life, which was so separate and apart from hers, that Ari felt an emptiness she couldn't quite explain. Shaking off the feeling, she started thinking about what she had to get done before the Christmas break.

Arriving back at the dorm, Ari found Emily there anxiously awaiting her return. The two hugged and sat, each of them telling the other about their holiday. Emily had, of course, just been across town at her parents. She said they had a wonderful dinner and she enjoyed being with her family, but had chosen to come back to the dorm on Friday. Surprised by this, Ari gave Emily a look of astonishment. She couldn't imagine leaving her parents early. But then again, she didn't have young siblings, and didn't live just forty-five minutes away.

"I met a guy last week before Thanksgiving. He didn't go home over the weekend as his family lives in California, so he asked me out. He's very nice and terrific looking. I couldn't say no. So, back I came in time to go out Saturday. We went into the city, walked the Miracle Mile, had dinner at a pubby-type restaurant and just had a wonderful time. He's asked me out for next Saturday too. Ar, I really like him."

"Amazing. I'm gone for five days and you fall in love."

Emily laughed. "Don't pick out any maid-of-honor dresses yet -- we've only gone out once."

Later that night, Ari thought about how easy it was to slip back into her other life here at college. While she had only known Emily for a few months, the two had grown very close. She hadn't even realized herself what a big part of her life Emily had become.

So, school was back in full swing, Emily was seeing more and more of Matt, her new friend, and Ari buried herself in her classes. As Christmas neared, the dorm was abuzz with the students making their plans for the holiday vacation. Ari asked Emily if she would like to go home with her over the holidays, but Emily said, "Thanks, Ari. Maybe another time. Christmas is a big deal at my house and I have to be there. It'll be lonely without you around, and Matt's going to California to be with his family – that'll make it even worse." Still, they were excited, and before they knew it they were hugging each other goodbye and wishing the other happy holidays.

CHAPTER FOUR

Christmastime in Thompsonville was glorious. The town was blanketed in fresh white snow and the Christmas lights on the shops and restaurants twinkled in the brisk winter air, giving the town a Norman Rockwell feel.

Ari and Gabby were together again, and spent their first few days running around town buying Christmas gifts and seeing old friends. Brent was home, and took the girls to lunch the day before Christmas. He was full of his usual good humor and admittedly was enjoying running around New Haven, his classes, and the law library as the proverbial first-year law student. In other words, like a crazy person. He confirmed there was little time for sleep or other worldly pastimes, but he wouldn't trade it for anything else in the world and couldn't imagine his life if he couldn't practice law.

Ari talked about Northwestern and how much she enjoyed school and Chicago, about Emily and, of course, how much she missed not having Gabby with her.

Gabby couldn't stop talking about Regency, her evening classes and how positive she was that she had made the right decision. Timidly, she announced that she'd met a young man in her architecture class and that they had gone out a couple of times.

Ari nearly jumped out of her seat. "You didn't tell me that." Needless to say, the inquisition began. Ari wanted to know everything, and Brent, being the protective older brother, wanted to know even more.

Gabby just smiled and said, "His name is Jason Marsh, he was in the Army and was over in Kuwait and Iran in Operation Desert Shield and the early part of Desert Storm. He's just starting to get his life back together and he's enrolled in night school – just to get a feel for it before next fall. He lives in Shelton, which is really pretty far away, but he likes the commute. He's very nice, very shy, cute, blond, fairly tall – at least for my five foot-two inches – and I think you two will like him."

Ari was thrilled for her friend. "I can't wait to meet him."

Brent, also very interested in meeting this young man his sister was so interested in said, "You should invite him over during the holidays."

Knowing exactly what he meant, Gabby laughed, responding "Maybe I'll do just that."

They then made plans to go to the Junior League Christmas Party together, which was being held at the country club on Saturday night. This was *the* big holiday party, and this year Harriet Rose Hill was part of the committee which was putting it together. Both Gabby and Ari were looking forward to it and they especially wanted to find out what was going on with Harriet. It seemed as if no one really knew what she was doing with herself these days except, of course, helping host this holiday party.

Frank and Linda had been spending a great deal of time discussing Grandpa Bolan's planned cruise. Frank was vehemently against it. "I don't think he should be carousing all over the globe at eighty-one years of age. And, to top it off, he's planning on doing it alone."

Linda said, "Frank, he's certainly not 'carousing' and hardly 'doing it alone.' After all, he won't be alone on the airplanes and there definitely will be lots of people on the cruise," even though she knew what he meant. "Are you suggesting that it would be better for him to wait a little while, perhaps a year or so, before going?" Frank caught her sarcasm, of course, and gave her a look to let her know he got it. But he was less than happy.

Linda knew that he was afraid for his father, so she eased back a little. "Frank, I know you're concerned that something might happen to him while he's away. So am I. But we can't be his jailers. He's not ill. He's old, yes, but he has his medicines, knows when to take them, is generally able to keep up with others, and enjoys being around people. I don't see why he would be any less able to do those things, whether he's on a cruise or here at home. And if, God forbid, his life were to end on this trip, at least he was doing something he really wanted to do.

We shouldn't be able to dictate what he can or cannot do, no matter how concerned we may be. We certainly wouldn't want anyone telling us we can't do what we want. And, I think I can safely say that neither one of us would want anyone dictating to us how we should live if we make it to eighty-one. Remember, he's been alone and truly hasn't done anything one could call fun since your mom died. He deserves it, and the fact that he wants it, well, I think it shows he has a great attitude toward life and we shouldn't diminish his confidence or enthusiasm in any way."

Frank wasn't altogether convinced, which was why he and Linda had been having that same discussion since Grandpa Bolan announced the trip at Thanksgiving. Linda knew that Frank would eventually come around, but in the meantime they would parry back and forth. She was somewhat concerned that he might bring it up the next day when Grandpa was there for their Christmas Eve celebration, although it might be somewhat difficult with all of Linda's family there as well.

On Christmas Eve Day, the Bolan household was busy putting the finishing touches on the dinner their families would share before the real party began. Frank picked up Grandpa Bolan early so that he could be on hand when the rest of the family arrived.

Arriving at the house, Grandpa was stunned by the magnificent tree set in the entry hall in the curve of the bannister at the bottom of the stairway. It was at least fifteen feet tall and one could walk around it and watch the lights twinkle as they climbed the stairs. It was done entirely in gold and white. When Gabby had seen it yesterday while visiting Ari, she thought it, like the country club, was reminiscent of The Palm Court. Linda had gone all out this year, buying new ornaments to replace the old store-bought ones from ages ago, but had kept all the families' personal keepsakes, some of them handmade by relatives long passed. Grandpa had brought gifts for everyone and Linda was always amazed by his ability to go out and do all that shopping on his own.

As they stood in the entry admiring the tree, Ari came running down the stairs to greet her grandfather. He was always delighted to see her. She was his only grandchild and the light of his life. She wasn't exactly the spitting image of her grandmother, but there was the hint of her and her beauty which he couldn't define, but felt every time he saw her face.

Moving to the living room to await the others, they barely sat down when the doorbell rang. In came Linda's brother, Bob, along with his son and two daughters. Bob was divorced and holidays were hard for him, but he put on a brave face for the benefit of all, especially his children. As they were closing the door, Ellen, Linda's sister, and her husband and two daughters pulled into the driveway. Within minutes everyone was together again, smiling, hugging, and settling in for their celebration.

The dining room table had been pulled out to accommodate the two leaves necessary to seat twelve comfortably. The "kids," most of whom were on the verge of adulthood, with only one of them, Bob's daughter, still a young teenager, chose to sit together at one end of the table. This had been the norm for family celebrations. They were really good friends, in addition to being cousins. As they were about to begin their meal, Frank proposed a toast welcoming all as was his tradition, and giving thanks for all of them. It was a great evening and the dinner was delicious as usual. After dessert, everyone headed back into the living room to visit some more. Ethel, a lovely lady Linda often hired to come in and help her, brought the coffee, cognac, sodas and chocolates in and set them on the coffee table for everyone to enjoy. As the evening went on, gifts were exchanged and a wonderful sense of contentment was felt by all.

Soon, all too soon it seemed, the grandfather clock announced it was 11:30 p.m. and Ellen and her family knew they had to go if they were going to make the midnight service on time.

With that, Bob and his family also gathered their things to leave, although they weren't heading to church, but home. Bob lived only about a mile from Grandpa Bolan's so he offered to take him home, which Grandpa accepted gratefully. All in all, the evening was exceptional and the three Bolans turned off the lights and headed off to bed.

Christmas Day at the Romano's was a bit more hectic; grandparents, parents, children, all totaling nineteen very animated Italians. Life was always good, even if it wasn't, at the Romano's. They were a family in the tradition of old-time Italian families, laughing and singing and eating. No one ever had a bad time at the Romano's. Nick's toast was always "Insieme per ritrovarsi," meaning "together again as we were before," which was his way of saying, "may we always be as this," and the entire family cheered as one.

To Nick and Mary there was no greater joy than having the family together, all well and happy. They wanted it to go on forever, realizing it couldn't, but knowing that the family would persevere because of the roots they had helped establish.

Earlier that afternoon, Nick had asked Gabby if she had a few minutes to talk. Making their way into Nick's study, Gabby was wondering, *What's this all about?*

Nick started by clearing his throat. "I know I promised you this week off, but I was hoping you wouldn't mind it if I asked for ten minutes of your holiday to discuss Huntington Forest with me.

"Sure, Dad."

I'm somewhat concerned about what's happening with the economy, particularly in the short term, and I think we'll have to be smart in order to do well over the next six months to a year. I've told you the feedback from your suggestions about the kitchens of the Tuscany and the Belvedere was very good. It's my sense that people will have many different new homes to choose from due to larger than normal inventories, and we'll have to offer more style for the same price -- if we're to compete successfully.

I've heard you've been spending time visiting the other new developments as well as studying the architectural and remodeling magazines, all in addition to your class at night school. I think you're ready to put that knowledge to good use, if you're willing.

As you know, we're planning on breaking ground for Phase Two in early March. I was wondering if you'd take some time to see if there are any other suggestions you might make to enhance our designs before we begin? We'll need time to evaluate them, draw up the new plans for the crews and make sure we have the correct materials, cabinets; doors, appliances, lighting, etcetera, for which we'd make you responsible. We know this is a lot, but what do you think?"

Gabby took a moment to control her excitement. Here she had been thinking she wasn't catching on fast enough, and now her dad was asking her advice on the planning of the next year's activity for Regency.

"Dad, I'd love to do that. Would I be restricted to making only kitchen suggestions?"

"No, we'd like you to review all the plans and make suggestions wherever you think they make sense. Understand, however, not all of your suggestions will necessarily be adopted."

"I've seen so many things which I think would really make us stand notches above the other builders. Of course, besides any new ideas, I'll have to do tons of research re cost analysis and availability, including minimum buying requirements, and so on. Which brings up something I've been meaning to discuss with you."

"Uh Oh."

"You know that in addition to taking my architecture class, I've also been taking a private computer course. What you probably don't know is that the instructor not only teaches but owns a company which designs systems for small businesses. I think Regency needs to have that capability and I would like to invite Jerry O'Neil to meet with us at Regency so that we can talk about what it could do for us."

"Gabby, whoa. I'm not sure we need a computer system and, even if we do, I'm not sure that now is the time to invest in one."

"Could we just talk to him? You might be surprised."

"Well . . . I guess we could. You've made sound suggestions so far, so I'm inclined to at least listen to what he has to say. But, no promises."

"Dad, I don't know that we need a whole system at this point, but I know what a tremendous asset even a personal computer hooked up to the internet would be to us now. And, if the economy is getting worse, a computer can save man hours and find lower pricing on some of our materials. We could end up saving money."

"Since we seem to have made this into a meeting, there's one more thing I would like to discuss with you."

"Okay," said Gabby.

Nick handed Gabby an envelope. "Here's your year-end bonus. You've worked hard for it and we clearly believe you deserve it. In addition, inside the envelope is a sheet setting out your new salary, the requisite withholding, insurance, and information on the company's retirement plan. This is not meant as a carrot to deter you from college, should you decide that is what you want to do in the fall. It is a measure of our appreciation for your work, your attitude and your determination to go that extra mile. We want you to know we see your efforts and are rewarding you for them and, on a personal level, how very proud I am of you."

"Oh, Daddy, the bonus and the raise are wonderful, I'm sure. But, I'm more excited about the fact that you trust me to review the plans, make suggestions and then be a part of the team to implement them – I couldn't have asked for more. Thank you."

Gabby hugged her father as Mary cracked the door a little bit, about to ask if she was interrupting. Seeing the smiles, she opened the door all the way and congratulated her daughter on her accomplishments, adding "Now that your meeting is over, it's time to get the house ready before the family arrives for Christmas dinner."

Christmas came and went and then it was Friday. Gabby had a date with Jason Marsh, and Brent was right at the door when Jason rang the bell. Gabby was embarrassed by Brent's obvious desire to pump Jason about who he was and what he was doing with Gabby. Quickly, she grabbed her coat and told Brent that they had to get going or the movie was going to start without them.

Jason showed a flash of surprise, but covered it well as Gabby took his hand and headed toward the door. Jason pointedly stopped and turned, offered Brent his hand and said, "It was nice to meet you, Brent. We'll talk again another time. Goodnight."

Brent was impressed because, although Jason had recovered quickly, Brent knew that Gabby was just getting Jason away from the interrogation ASAP. Brent shook Jason's hand saying, he, too, was pleased to meet Jason. With that, Gabby closed the front door behind them.

Jason and Gabby were going out to dinner, but not to the movies. As they headed down the snow-covered road, Jason asked about the movie routine.

"My brother thinks of himself as my protector -- it's been that way ever since I can remember. Now that I'm older and he's not around much, well, I'm a little more self-sufficient than I was at six, which is basically the same age as he thinks of me now."

Actually, Jason was surprised to learn that Gabby was only eighteen; she seemed so much more responsible and level-headed than most eighteen year olds. Still, he had to remind himself that he was twenty-three, which was quite a bit older than she and, because of his Army experience, he had seen more than other twenty-three-year-old men who had not gone to war. He thought he had to be careful. He had a lot riding on this relationship and he wanted to take it slow and get it right.

They went to Augustino's for dinner, which Jason had learned was one of Gabby's favorite restaurants. He held her hand and they talked for hours not realizing it had gotten so late. On the way home, Gabby asked Jason if he'd like to go with her to the Junior League Christmas Party the next night, apologizing for the lateness of the invitation. She was disappointed when he said he couldn't make it. Gabby soothed her feelings by reminding herself that it really was awfully late to expect someone to be free the next night. And, after all, they did have plans for New Year's Eve.

After Gabby and Jason left, Brent closed the door behind them, and turned back into the hall. *Now what do I do?* He wondered. He went into the kitchen where Mary and Nick were talking and sharing some wine. Mary was cutting up some fresh parsley for her Frutta di Mare dish of shrimp, scallops, and clams in cracked black pepper pasta tossed with olive oil. Mary smiled at Brent, inviting him to have some wine with them before dinner. As Brent poured himself a glass, Mary asked how it had gone with Jason.

Nick watched as the two fell into a pattern of conversation that seemed so easy, he never ceased to be amazed. Both Brent and Gabby had this wonderful friendship with their mother not many parents enjoyed. Mary knew Brent would be at the door when Gabby's date arrived, and so as not to appear to be too overbearing, and because she and Nick had already met Jason, she had engaged Nick in a conversation about his meeting with Gabby that afternoon, which drew him into the kitchen.

Brent admitted that Jason seemed nice enough, but he hadn't really had a chance to talk to him.

Mary noticed that Brent was lacking his usual good humor, but wrote it off to his concern about Gabby. He hadn't been around for the last few years when Gabby had started to date, so this was new to him. Also, he had always taken his role of big brother very seriously, so this, coupled with her decision not to go to college, had caused him a great deal of worry.

What Mary didn't know was that Brent had become restless, so when she tried to ease Brent's mind about Gabby, he surprised her by saying, "Mom, I am concerned about Gabby, but I think this is more a function of the fact that I just don't know what to do with myself here. I love being home and being with the family, but now I'm anxious to get back to my real life of school, study groups and especially the law library. Besides, from what you and Dad have told me about Gabby and her contribution to and amazing transition into Regency, I'm elated that she seemed to know what was right for her and had the self-assurance to stand up for it. I'm just thinking about going back to New Haven early. There's plenty of work for me to do there."

Mary looked at Nick and back at Brent. "We'd be so sorry to have you go back early – it seems we don't get to see you nearly enough. Why don't you wait and go back after the holiday party tomorrow night? I know Gabby wants you here and so do we. If, after the party, you decide to go back early, I think we'll all understand."

Brent nodded his assent, poured his parents and himself another glass of wine and asked if he could help with dinner.

It seemed as if everyone who was anyone was at the country club on Saturday night. The main sitting area/living room had been turned into part of the dining room because the dining room had wood floors for dancing and the sitting room was carpeted. Even Hiz Honor, which Brent had dubbed him, much to his chagrin, had to give up his table to sit at a makeshift table in the sitting area which was not nearly as prominent as his usual position in the dining room. Not being so concerned about being seen, the Bolans and Gabby and Brent sat with the Lees at a lovely table in the back half of the main dining room, but abutting the area left open for a dance floor. Stanford Lee was President of The First National Bank of Thompsonville and Jennifer's father. Her mother, Stephanie, was a longtime member of the Junior League and was very active in Thompsonville society and its charities.

The evening was magical for Gabby even though Jason wasn't there. Several of Ari and Gabby's friends, both male and female, were there and they were never at a loss for a dance partner. While sitting out one of the dances, Gabby was approached by John Traymore who apologized for interrupting. "May I have the next dance, Miss Romano?"

Stunned, Gabby gathered her wits, turned to her parents and introduced John Traymore to them, saying he was an architect and her instructor in one of her night school classes.

Watching the couple make their way to the dance floor, Nick asked Mary about this. Mary said she was sure that Gabby was as surprised as they were and that she had never mentioned this man, other than in the context of her course. Mary made a mental note to ask Gabby about this later -- *this could be trouble*, she thought.

Ari was on the dance floor with Doug, her senior prom date, and hadn't noticed what was going on until the two couples almost bumped into one another. Doug was guiding Ari away from the potential collision, so Ari didn't have a chance for an introduction, much less an explanation.

Harriet Rose Hill never looked better. She was more at ease with herself it seemed and, probably because of her responsibilities with the party, was less under her mother's and even her father's thumbs. Harriet stood tall and looked lovely in what seemed to be a Paris original. That, of course, was entirely possible. Ari made a point of congratulating Harriet on the party and complimented her on her dress and the way she looked in general. Harriet thanked Ari and said it was very good to see her, asking whether she was enjoying herself.

As they chatted, Ari was surprised to learn that Harriet's newly acquired self-assured appearance was really only a false impression. Where Harriet had been quiet and aloof and quite shy before, Ari now felt Harriet was just going through the motions and really didn't care to hear answers to any of her well-mannered, if badly disguised, questions.

Harriet, now clearly in her HRH persona, made it a point to tell Ari about the article in tomorrow's paper about tonight's party and her part in it. Also, she was certain there would be photos of the evening, as well as coverage of her trip next week back to New York and the south of France for the season. "I just have to get out of here. I'm sure you agree with me, now that you've seen life in the big city. I simply don't understand people who live in small towns like this for an entire lifetime. I certainly have no intention of doing so."

Taken aback by Harriet's railing, Ari wished Harriet a good trip and excused herself to go back to her table. *Incredible*, she thought. *Where did all that come from? Certainly she had never been that vituperative before. She must be very unhappy with herself.* She then felt very sorry for Harriet.

Brent saw three of his former high school classmates, all three girls, two of whom had married and were there with their husbands. He danced with Melanie and was glad to talk with her; she had finished college and was now working in California for a major aerospace company.

None of his former male high school classmates were there, he believed, because they were either in other cities pursuing their careers or they just weren't the Junior League type. Brent also danced with Gabby, Ari and Jennifer and then spent some time talking with Gordon Reed, one of Thompsonville's local attorneys. Brent enjoyed learning about Gordon's practice and then answered some of Gordon's questions about Yale and his experience there, reminding Gordon that it was very early on in his law school days to really have a handle on it, other than to say he already missed being away from it.

Just then, Mary and Nick interrupted to say hello to Gordon. After a moment or two, Mary mentioned that she and Nick were getting ready to leave and asked Brent whether he wanted to ride with them?

Inside, Brent jumped at the chance to leave; he had never been very comfortable in large social settings. Shaking hands with Gordon, Brent said goodnight, as did the Bolans, and they began to make their way toward the front door. Brent wondered about Ari and Gabby, just as Nick said that the girls were going to ride home with Doug; they were having entirely too much fun.

Indeed, the social section in the Sunday edition of The *Sentinel* did have coverage of the gala at the country club the evening before. And, yes, there was a photo of HRH, noting below her photo that she had been a part of the Donations' Committee and was, of course, the daughter of Hiz Honor. Ari studied the picture and, pointing it out to her mother, asked "Do you think Harriet looks happy?" Linda thought it an odd question, but answered saying, "Seldom do people appear anything other than posed in these newspaper photographs. It seems that The *Sentinel* doesn't have a candid photographer like they do at *Town & Country* magazine, unless someone volunteers. Why do you ask?"

Ari said little. "Oh, I don't know. I had this conversation with her last night. She told me she was heading off to Europe again, with a stop in New York City, but really didn't seem to have any plans for the future past the next couple of months. I just thought it was sad, that's all."

CHAPTER FIVE

Gabby spent as much time as possible with Ari while she was still home, as well as getting together with Karen and Jennifer. When she wasn't with the girls, she poured over the blueprints for Phase Two. She ran back and forth to the library, reading magazines and copying articles and pictures she thought would help in her attempt to design the interiors which would be more closely attuned to current trends, and all this in a cost-effective manner.

On New Year's Eve, Gabby went out to dinner with Jason. They spent the evening talking, Gabby thought too much, about her new task at Regency, and then dancing to the band that Lion d'Or had hired for the midnight celebration. Gabby had never been to the restaurant before and was caught up in it's elegance and absolutely fabulous French food. Even dessert, *Wow* she thought. Lion d'Or was just over in Washington, though Gabby had never heard of if before. She was smitten with the restaurant and she was definitely becoming more and more smitten with Jason Marsh.

When Mary had asked Gabby about John Traymore, Gabby said she was as surprised as anyone that he was there and just thought he was being nice by asking her for a dance.

What Gabby had noticed was that a cute young worker at Regency, Mike Franconi, made it a point to be visible when Gabby was on site.

She had a feeling that he was trying to get her attention, perhaps get up the nerve to ask her out, and she kind of liked his interest in her. She thought it was very good for her ego, even though she really didn't want to see anyone other than Jason.

Brent went back to Yale on Monday morning after having spent Sunday with the family at church, their regular brunch out, and watching the football games with his dad. Brent was amazed that he wasn't the only one back at school early. Actually, he learned some of his fellow students had stayed over, so he easily slipped back into the routine, albeit without classes.

One of his study group partners, Stacy Cohen, was there and they made plans to spend New Year's Eve together. Brent and Stacy had an easy-going working relationship and they joked about their date for Wednesday night. They spent the evening at Mory's Temple Bar, a long-time law school hangout and private club, along with several other students, where they all had a terrific time ringing in the new year.

On Tuesday, Hiz Honor drove Harriet to the airport in Pittsburgh. She was on her way to spend three days at The Carlyle in New York City and then on to Europe.

He admitted to himself as the plane took off on its journey that he didn't really know Harriet all that well and, frankly, what he saw, he didn't much like either. Harriet was becoming more and more like her mother, but to a large extent he knew he was also at fault.

Steven Hill married Janet Dorrance with something close to love for her, but definitely out of the love of her family's money and position. Interesting how they both had very similar traits, but, at best, have an arms-length marriage. This, he believed, allowed him his numerous relationships, although he considered them to be mere peccadillos. After all, he rationalized, it's an entitlement for those in the political arena, as history has shown. His only interest, outside of being important and his romantic interludes, was golf at the country club where he wielded a big stick with the boys, whether it was a political stick or a golf club.

He had spent most of his married life making his rounds with the voting public, playing the game as it were, playing golf and having his little secret flings. He had tried to get Harriet to go on to college and couldn't imagine what she had planned for herself. Perhaps exactly what it looked like – a mirror image of her mother, and for that he felt very sorry.

He was glad his mother didn't live near Thompsonville to see Harriet. She would have been so disappointed. As it was, his mother barely spoke to him, and Janet never tried to keep in touch with her. This all stemmed from the fact that she knew he had sold himself out for a cushy life, for which he was paying dearly.

Ari spent New Year's week in Thompsonville. When Saturday came around and it was time for her to go back to Chicago, she could hardly believe how fast the holiday vacation had come and gone. She had been surprised when Gabby told her Brent had become restless and headed back to school early. Ari couldn't understand how what seemed so fast for her, must have seemed so slow to Brent.

But, back she was. She and Emily spent most of Sunday doing their favorite thing – shopping on the Miracle Mile. After all, the after-Christmas sales were in full swing and they had some Christmas money to use for just that purpose.

Sunday evening Emily had plans to go to a pub with Matt Lansing who had also just returned to school from his holiday vacation. Emily asked Ari to join them and when Matt arrived, he simply insisted – he wasn't the kind of guy you said no to. They had a great time. *Pizza and good friends*, Ari thought, *nothing better!*

When Emily and Matt decided to go to a movie though, Ari begged off, saying she still had some unpacking to do and wanted to get some rest after the long train ride in order to be ready for classes when they resumed the next day. Waving, Ari headed back to the dorm ready for life to fall back into its regular routine.

And so went January. Gabby and Ari would talk every so often, each trying to keep up with the other's life. It was strange, Ari thought. They were still close, but their lives had taken such different tracks and in such a short period of time. Ari was comforted by the fact that even though they weren't together daily, their friendship had never been in jeopardy.

During one of their conversations, Gabby told Ari about an article that had appeared in The *Sentinel*. Apparently, HRH was flitting around Europe, specifically, the article mentioned, skiing in Switzerland, and that she had been seen with some very important people. Gabby said she had no doubt that this had been reported to The *Sentinel* via mommy, Janet Dorrance Hill. She further reported that there really wasn't anything important in the article, but she was sure that if mommy had anything to do with it, there would be more later.

Gabby had finally been successful in setting up an appointment for Jerry O'Neil to meet with her father and her at Regency. After the two had met, shaken hands and all three were settled, Jerry eased into the conversation by saying that he would like to spend most of the meeting just listening to Nick and, of course, Gabby as they described their business. That way, he explained, he could better tell them what benefits a computer system might have for them.

Nick briefly outlined the business, and Jerry asked some questions.

After an uncomfortable pause in the conversation, Gabby jumped in. "You know, Dad, the accounting department could make use of the computer for keeping it's payables, receivables, receipts, balance sheet, P & L's, and various banking transactions on line. Also, can you imagine how much easier it would be to know what's in inventory, what isn't in inventory, and what we need by merely clicking a mouse? It could help tremendously. Just think, it could keep Regency from overbuying and thereby losing money on unusable materials.

Then there's the benefit of being able to view on-line what new products manufacturers are showing in appliances, lighting, bathroom fixtures, kitchen and bathroom cabinets, flooring, tiling, etcetera. Not only do on-line websites show these products, but they give information on measurements, pricing, bulk pricing, shipping, again, all at the click of a mouse. I'm sure there are other uses, but those are the primary needs as I see them."

"Gabby is quite accurate in delineating Regency's business needs from a user's point of view." Jerry said. "What she may not have thought about is the potential sales asset Regency would have by maintaining its own website and presenting your homes and developments on-line. Imagine buyers and real estate agents being able to click to your site and see your product and how it compares to the competition. By showing pictures of your model homes, you could potentially increase your foot traffic and therefore your bottom line significantly.

I would like to work up a proposal for you which would address those needs we've discussed, as well as any I think might be useful. Then we can sit down again, maybe next week if you have time, and discuss the plan."

Nick interrupted, "I never thought about the sales aspect of a computer and Regency's use of a website, so if you would include that as part of the presentation as well, I would appreciate it."

Making an appointment to meet again the next Tuesday, Gabby and Nick both thanked Jerry as they walked him to the door. Walking back to their individual offices Nick said, "I was prepared to think this was a waste of time but, Gabby, it looks like you've had another good idea here. I'm looking forward to next week's presentation."

For the next meeting with Jerry, Nick asked Tony to sit in with them. Nick had told Tony about what had taken place at the first meeting and about how he thought Gabby may be right again.

Tony wasn't so sure. He was a hammer and pliers kind of guy, but he recognized the fact that as construction chief he was focused almost solely on that aspect of Regency. Now, he needed to listen from Nick's point of view.

As the meeting transpired, Tony began to think that this guy Jerry was a really smart fellow. He addressed, step-by-step the accounting benefits, how to track sales and estimate future sales based upon Regency's assumptions, Gabby's points about materials and their availability through on-line sites, inventory, forecasting for timing of crews to coincide with delivery of materials, and hiring needs.

He then went on to talk about Regency's own website which would be used as a sales tool for their developments as they had discussed. It would be designed to tell the story of the company and allow contact for information directly from the site via e-mail.

This was so much more than Nick had ever believed possible that he began to think the cost of it was going to be way beyond their means. Tony was overwhelmed by the entire scope of what this computer could do. He couldn't even imagine who would be able to do all this, particularly on the construction side. *Certainly not him*, he thought. Gabby was thrilled and hoped her father saw the potential for Regency by doing this.

Nick sat back and started to ask *the* question. "I'm extremely interested in going ahead with the system, assuming it's something within

Regency's financial ballpark. Frankly, though, it sounds as if it'll cost a great deal of money. If the entire system is too expensive, perhaps we can do it incrementally."

"I have prepared this written proposal for you. You'll see that in addition to the installation of the system, we will train the employees you designate, as well as perform any maintenance required on the system without charge for one year after installation. I've also included a list of several companies in the area whose systems we've installed. Please feel free to call them. I'm going to leave this with you and let you talk among yourselves. If you have any questions now, I'll be happy to answer them. If not, or if you have questions after reviewing this material, please call me. I think you'll be pleased with what we can do and what a system can do for Regency. I look forward to your call and working with all of you."

Nick said, "Let me walk you out. Jerry, thank you again for your time. I learned far more than I anticipated and I promise to study the written presentation in detail and in a timely fashion." Jerry walked to his car for the drive back to his office, hoping he had covered all of Nick's concerns.

That night Gabby and Nick could talk of nothing else. Mary, listening to the exchange, clearly saw the potential of having such a system and she became as excited as both Nick and Gabby were. Mary asked "Nick, have you had a chance to look at the written presentation yet?"

"I have, but I haven't had a chance to really study it."

"What about the cost?" Mary prodded. "Surely that's something you looked at. Is it anywhere close to what you originally anticipated?

"Actually, it's less, but not significantly. However, it's going to do so much more than I ever dreamed, even after last week's first meeting. It could be worth every penny."

"Then you've decided to go ahead with it?" Mary asked.

"I haven't made a decision yet. I wanted to get your take on it and also want to talk with Tony." Nick laughed. "I don't need to ask Gabby what she thinks, do I sweetheart?" Gabby blushed, but agreed she was squarely behind the entire system.

Nick continued. "It's clear having Gabby on board has brought great innovation to Regency and, that, with her help and insight, I see great potential for the future."

Even though the economic outlook for real estate was not terrific, Nick went ahead and ordered the computer system for Regency thinking that in the long run it would end up saving the company money and time. As the computers were delivered and installed, Gabby was excited with the prospect of their use, and Nick was right behind her. Nick had even started to read all he could about computers and their use, as well as the power of the internet. Jerry was giving daily hour-long lessons to the staff. Nick also took a class with Jerry every day but they were more intensive and lasted one-and-a-half to two hours in length. For this reason, Nick's lessons began at the close of the business day, which meant that he was free to concentrate on the lesson and not the demands of business.

On Thursday, February 25th, after a long day at Regency and his almost two-hour lesson with Jerry, Nick drove the icy winter roads home. Tired, but pleased that he was finally picking up on how the computer system and the internet worked, Nick was reviewing in his mind the material he was putting together for Regency's home page.

Lost in thought, Nick almost didn't see the headlights of the truck coming down the road from his left. Slamming on the brakes, Nick was able to slow his car down. At that same moment the truck driver tried to slam on his brakes, hit a patch of ice and the truck went out of control, swerving to the right. There just wasn't enough time to stop the collision. Because of the weight of his vehicle, the truck driver wasn't able to stop it from hitting Nick's car full force, directly into the driver's door. Nick didn't have a chance.

The truck driver ran and pulled Nick out before Nick's car burst into flames, but there was nothing he could do for him. Through his tears, he said he was so sorry to Nick and Nick only managed to say, "Mary, tell Mary . . ." and then nothing.

The flames must have attracted someone's attention because as the truck driver continued to cradle Nick's head in his arms, he became aware of sirens cutting through the dark winter night. When the emergency vehicles arrived, the policemen first on the scene began to pry the truck driver's locked arms from Nick. They saw there was clearly nothing that could be done for him.

The driver was in a state of shock and was immediately attended to by the paramedics upon their arrival. Slowly, slowly, the truck driver began to calm down with the help of a Valium and the soft words of the paramedics. As he became more responsive, the police on the scene came over to the ambulance to ask him some questions regarding the accident. It soon became clear to them that it truly was an accident and asked the truck driver to get in touch with them after he was released from the hospital.

Mary had become somewhat accustomed to Nick's later than usual arrival home from work since he began working with Jerry and the new computer system. Snuggled on the sofa in the sunroom, Mary was watching a movie as she waited for Nick to come home.

Outside, it was dark and cold as the two police officers pulled into the driveway in front of the Romano's house. This was one of the worst jobs for a policeman. They both hesitated before going up to this lovely home to break the bad news to the deceased's loved ones.

Mary almost didn't recognize the bell; some of the TV commercials these days used doorbells which were difficult to distinguish from one's own, which she found unnerving. Realizing it was her bell that was ringing, Mary made her way to the front door, wondering, *Who could be calling this late?*

Opening the front door, Mary gazed at the two police officers and immediately knew something had happened to Nick. "Where is he . . . What hospital? Is he okay?" Mary cried.

The officers asked if they could come in a moment, while taking her by the arm to support her as they stepped inside. "Ma'am, we're sorry to have to tell you that your husband was in a car accident this evening. Unfortunately, he didn't make it. We're so sorry, please let us walk you inside, get you settled and answer any questions we can."

Mary was unbelieving. In a fog, she allowed the officers to guide her into the kitchen and sat her down at the table. One of the officers brought Mary a glass of water. She didn't see the glass being offered to her, so the officer just set it down on the table in front of her. "Where is he?" she asked quietly.

One of the officers sat down so as to be at Mary's eye level and started to answer her questions. "Your husband is at the medical examiner's office. You may go there as soon as you feel able. What we know right now is that your husband was driving down the street and didn't see an approaching truck. There wasn't a light or stop sign, so there was no one at fault. The truck driver couldn't stop the truck due to a patch of ice on the road. He feels terrible. He was able to get to your husband and pull him out of his car before the gas tank exploded, hoping he could save him. Unfortunately, it wasn't to be.

According to the officers on the scene, the truck driver cradled your husband's head; his last words were for you." As the officer repeated Nick's last words, Mary finally felt the full impact of what was being said to her, and she began to weep uncontrollably. Giving Mary a few minutes to regain some degree of control, the officer sitting at the table asked, "Is there anyone we can call for you, your doctor, a priest?"

Mary, still sobbing in between her words, said she needed to talk to her daughter and then call her son. "Perhaps you could get a hold of my daughter. She's at Mario's with a young man by the name of Jason Marsh. Also, Father Frank over at St. Thomas'. If you could do that, I'll call my son in Connecticut and my husband's family here in Thompsonville. Please, my daughter," with that Mary broke down again.

Mary wept quietly now. The officers brought her some tissues, and began to make the calls to Father Frank and to headquarters requesting that an officer go down to Mario's in an effort to locate Gabby and bring her home.

Finding Gabby at Mario's, the officer who had been sent out to find her, drove her home. Gabby kept asking what this was all about, but the officer said that her mother would talk to her when they got there. Gabby knew that what she didn't hear was that her parents would talk to her, and she was afraid that something had happened to her dad. She hoped it was only something at Regency that meant her father had to be there to handle it. But then, why would they send the police? As she was driven up the driveway, Gabby saw the other police car and knew in the pit of her stomach it was her father.

Running into the house, she called frantically for her mother. A policeman came out of the kitchen and directed Gabby to her mother, still sitting at the kitchen table. Kneeling beside her mother, Gabby put her arms around her and quietly, almost in a whisper, asked, "What happened?" Mary turned to look at her daughter through her shockingly red eyes and told her what Gabby feared most, that her father had been killed in a car accident on his way home from the office. The pit in Gabby's stomach now became a horrendous blow to her solar plexis and she could barely catch her breath. "Oh my God, no. Are you sure?" she asked looking at the police. Their expression confirmed it. "It just can't be."

Mary stroked Gabby's hair and told her to sit down. "Gabby, will you call Aunt Rose for me, please. Father Frank is on his way." It seemed to the police that now that Gabby was there, the mother in Mary took over and she was beginning to gain control of her emotions — at least those she exhibited in public.

Gabby did as she was told and called Aunt Rose. Her Aunt and also Uncle Ed said they were on the way over. Somehow, while Gabby was on the phone with her Aunt, Father Frank had made his way into the house and was now sitting at the kitchen table talking with Mary. The officers saw that things were now well under control at the house and told Gabby they would be leaving.

Mary saw them as they started to walk out the door and thanked them for being so kind to her. They again offered their condolences and walked out the door. Father Frank then suggested that Mary and Gabby come sit with him in the living room. Gabby said she would be right there, that she would make a pot of coffee, but he should take her mother to a more comfortable chair as soon her Aunt and Uncle would be here too.

Gabby decided she should call Uncle Tony. He would call the rest of the family and it would be one less thing for Mary to worry about. Gabby's heart was broken, but because she thought she should take some degree of control on behalf of her mother, she found the strength to make the call.

Of course, Uncle Tony was already in bed asleep — morning comes early for those on construction crews — and Gabby was so sad she had to wake him. As he seemed to come out of his sleep-filled stupor, Gabby eased into telling him what had happened. Fully awake now, Tony had apparently turned around to tell Aunt Carmen, as she could hear some conversation in the background. Tony said back into the phone that he and Carmen would be there soon; they were going to make some phone calls to the family first. Grateful, Gabby said that Father Frank was at the house with her mom and she was sure her mom would appreciate seeing both Uncle Tony and Aunt Carmen.

Gabby wanted to talk to her brother, though she wasn't certain her mom wanted her to tell him or whether she would rather do it herself. She thought the only way to know the answer to that question was to ask her mother, and she thought she had better do it before everyone showed up. Slowly walking into the living room, Gabby went over to her mother and sat down right next to her. "Mom, we need to call Brent. I can do that if you want me to, or perhaps you want to do it yourself."

Waiting for her mother to answer her, Gabby looked into her mother's eyes in some way assuring her that she could do it. Mary nodded, understanding her daughter, and said "Why don't you get him on the phone and talk to him. When you're finished, let me talk to him."

Gabby said she would. She softly told her mother she had called Uncle Tony, and he and Aunt Carmen were on the way; they were calling the rest of the family.

Mary gratefully smiled at her daughter, and simply said, "Thank you, honey."

After everyone had been notified, the family and Father Frank had come and gone, and Brent was trying to find the first flight out of New Haven, Mary and Gabby were finally left alone. Mary was still sitting in the living room trying to assimilate everything that had happened. She asked Gabby to come sit by her and then just held her for a long time. Quietly sobbing on and off for over an hour, Mary murmured so softly that Gabby barely heard her say, "I can't believe this, we thought we had years . . ."

Gabby held her mother closer. "Let me take you upstairs to bed, you're exhausted and you need to get some rest." Unaware she was doing so, Mary stood and let Gabby lead her up to Nick's and her bedroom. Gabby helped her as best she could and then put her into bed, staying until her mother had drifted off into a restless sleep.

When she was sure her mother was in a deep sleep, Gabby went off to her own room, washed up and climbed into bed. Gabby was exhausted, but her mind wouldn't let her sleep right away – so many things to think about, but those things would have to wait for another day. Her father had to be laid to rest.

Brent arrived home the next day. Uncle Tony picked him up in Pittsburgh after having gone down to the medical examiner's office to make the legal identification of his brother's body. Mary wanted to make the funeral arrangements herself so, with Gabby's help, they went down to the funeral parlor and then met with Father Frank about the service. By the time

Brent got home with Uncle Tony, most of the major arrangements had been made and Brent did the best he could to console his mother and sister.

Brent was at a loss. All the books he had read and studied over the years hadn't prepared him for this. While he would have given anything to bring his father back, he had never suffered a personally devastating situation and couldn't even begin to think of what to say to his mother. Even his relationship with Stacy — she was his first real girlfriend, and they were still together. So, no lessons there.

Fortunately for all three of them, the Romano/Campagna family was quite large, very close, and there almost nonstop, helping them try to come to terms with what had happened.

Mary went through the weeks before and after the funeral in somewhat of a daze. Suddenly it was over, Nick was really gone and most of the family had gone back to their everyday lives. Mary, Brent and Gabby were left alone in their own grief, knowing they too had to get on with their lives, yet not quite ready for life without Nick. Regency had closed for a period of mourning but that, too, was now back in full swing.

Mary knew it was up to her to actually get them back on track. Asking Gabby and Brent to join her in the sunroom almost a full two weeks after the funeral, Mary started, "I want to thank you both for being such rocks during this painful time. But, now, we have to address the future. Brent, you need to return to Yale — I would think by the end of the week. It's something your father would have insisted upon."

"Mom, I appreciate that, but I'm concerned about leaving you. Are you going to be all right? I know having Gabby here will be a big help and you're a strong woman, so you'll do fine in time. I guess what else I'm asking is, are you going to be all right financially?"

"I'll . . . we'll be just fine. Your father and I saved over the years and, while we weren't wealthy, I'll be able to maintain the house and our lifestyle, including your law school tuition, Brent. The larger issue is Regency."

Gabby's head snapped up as she heard this. "What's the problem with Regency?"

"It's not really a problem yet, but some decisions will have to be made as to how we will continue, or it could become one later. I've asked your

Uncle Tony to come over so that we can all talk about this. What you probably don't know is that your father and I owned eighty percent of Regency, the other twenty percent belongs to Uncle Tony. Any decision we make, we must all make together."

Almost on cue, Uncle Tony rang the front doorbell and Brent opened the door leading him into the sunroom. As he settled into an easy chair with his back to the glass wall, Tony could tell by the silence and the fact that all eyes were on him, Mary had already told Brent and Gabby the reason for the get-together.

Waiting for him to speak, all three were surprised when Mary began. "The last few weeks have been extremely difficult for all of us. During that time, somehow I've been able to hear Nick's words as he laid out his plans for Regency. I would like to see that we follow his dream, and I will do everything in my power to make it come true.

First of all, and perhaps most important, Regency has a tremendous amount of money tied up in the Huntington Forest development and, frankly, we can't afford to just stop, we would lose everything. So, given that, and also the investment we have made with our employees, our equipment, our office building, as well as the new computer system, there is no question we must continue on until we have at least completed and sold Huntington Forest. Tony?"

"I agree, although I'm not sure we should *plan anything* past Huntington Forest. And, as far as this computer thing with a website for us, well, I don't think that makes any sense either."

Gabby was about to jump out of her chair when she saw her mother almost imperceptibly shake her head at her as she caught Gabby's eye. "Tony, in order to accomplish the task of selling out Huntington Forest in this market and at this point in time, the internet might be our greatest sales tool. Nick had been working on the company website and the cost of putting this all together was and is a part of the contract we already have with Jerry O'Neil."

Raising his hand to his chin and unconsciously rubbing it, Tony thought about what Mary had just said. "I guess you're right about that," he said. "But, who's going to run Regency? I can do it, I guess, with Gabby's help, but then we'll need someone to run the crews. Maybe TJ?"

Mary said, "Gabby's going to run Regency's day-to-day operations, with my help, your help, and whatever other help she thinks she needs."

Gabby, for the first time ever, her mother thought, *was absolutely speechless.* Tony's eyes almost jumped out of his head and his mouth was wide open.

Finally, finding her voice, Gabby said, "Mom, there's so much I don't know . . ."

"And what you don't know, you'll learn. Your father and I always discussed everything about Regency; every move, every idea, everything. Your father was so proud of you, what you'd accomplished in such a short time. Anyway, I'll be right here. Your Uncle Tony is the most capable construction chief your father ever knew. Frankly, it is almost easier to replace your father's job with you, then to try to replace Uncle Tony with anyone else."

"But Mary, Gabby's only nineteen. What does she know about running a business?"

"As I said, Tony, I'll be here and so will you. Gabby has been learning from her father and, as you know, has been responsible for some of the most important updates that have ever been made by Regency. We're in it until at least the end of Huntington Forest. After that, we'll revisit this. But for now, we must continue. The stock market took a hit last fall, real estate is in a slump, but we have fared better than most, in large part due to Gabby. If we don't present a strong commitment to continuing Regency in the same manner as under Nick, the banks will pull our financing, we won't be able to pay off our loans and we'll lose everything. So, are we all agreed?"

Brent looked questioningly at his mother wondering whether she had been under such extreme emotional stress, she didn't know what she was doing. But she looked confident and he had to say, "You're all in a better position to make this judgment than I am, but if Mother backs it, I'm right behind her."

Uncle Tony nodded and then all eyes were on Gabby. Very slowly, as if trying to come to terms with all that had been said, Gabby said, "Thank you all. I recognize what a tremendous responsibility you are handing me and I promise I'll do everything I can to make this work. Thank you."

Gabby got up and hugged her mother, Uncle Tony and Brent. Her brother said, "Wow, Sis, who knew? If you need anything, and I mean anything at all, please call me, but as far as I can tell, I'm the odd man out here. It appears that Regency is once again in very capable hands and, as long as you're sure about my leaving, Mom, I do need to get back to law school." Even as he said it, Brent was very concerned about the pressure that had just been placed on his sister's shoulders and pondered how she would survive the enormous responsibilities just handed this very young and relatively inexperienced woman.

CHAPTER SIX

Eventually, life fell into a routine. Gabby was so busy now; she had meetings with the bankers to assure them Regency was still on track and that there were no major changes in the plans as they knew them. Receiving their support, but still understanding that Regency was under a microscope, Gabby then went on to talk with all the suppliers, the entire office staff and then, jointly with Uncle Tony, the construction crews. Norma did everything she could to help Gabby get comfortable in her father's old office and make sure Gabby was up-to-date and familiar with business issues which had upcoming due dates. Gabby didn't know how she would have even begun without Norma.

Gabby missed her father terribly. There was a hole so deep within her that, had she not been consumed by Regency and the need to keep it above water for the family, she wasn't sure she could have continued. But work was her comfort and her salvation. And there was his presence. Even though Norma had made his office Gabby's, she sensed his being, as if willing her on.

Mary was available at home every night to help Gabby with whatever came up during the day where Gabby felt she needed a sounding board. They worked hand-in-hand, and it became a routine they both found comfortable.

Mary was still amazed by how she had handled the meeting with the family. She knew that if she had not made herself appear very strong and in total control of what she was saying, Tony would have stepped in and taken over, leaving Gabby in the wake. Mary had been, and continued to be, very determined not to let that happen, not just for Gabby's sake, but also for the entire family's future. Mary and Nick had talked about Nick and Tony's frequent disagreements, caused mostly because Tony just couldn't see the big picture. Tony was a terrific chief of construction, but he didn't understand running a business, and that just building a nice house didn't make a construction business successful. He never could have negotiated with the banks, for example, and that was going to be one of the most important aspects of keeping Regency on its feet over the next year or two.

Ari had been desperate to get back to Thompsonville and help Gabby through the loss and funeral of her father. While grateful for her friend's concern, Gabby insisted that things were far too hectic for them to spend any time together. Gabby spent many hours on the phone with Ari in that first month after her father's death. Just as Mary needed Aunt Rose and Aunt Carmen, Gabby needed Ari. When she told Ari about what was going to happen at Regency and her part in it, Ari was beside herself. After all the congratulations, Gabby quietly admitted to Ari she was somewhat overwhelmed with the whole task. During their frequent talks, Ari encouraged Gabby and often restated the fact that her mother would not have put her in charge unless she had confidence in her ability.

Gabby also admitted to Ari, "There's something else, Ar. Just before my dad was killed, Jason had been talking about taking the next step in their relationship."

Ari was almost speechless. She managed to ask, "How do you feel about that?"

"I really haven't had the time to think about it seriously with all that's happened. I do know that I love him."

"Gabby, I'm not about to tell you what to do. But, please don't act too quickly, particularly with everything else you have going on." Ari feared it had to be fairly serious, though, if Gabby was telling her about it. She hoped her words of caution carried some weight. She didn't think that

Gabby should be making any important decisions about her personal life this soon after her father's death.

Jason *had* been hinting around about marriage. He wanted to ask Gabby on Valentine's Day, but sensed that she wasn't ready yet – perhaps she thought it was still too early in their relationship. After Gabby's father died, Jason feared his efforts had been wasted. He saw less of Gabby and he was certain her feelings for him had diminished. In the meantime, Jason tried to keep busy with his studies, although he told Gabby he was always available if she could get away for dinner or a movie. Whatever, he'd be there. He was enrolled in classes at Carlton Junior College and took a small studio apartment in Thompsonville to be closer to both school and, of course, Gabby.

While Gabby was very busy at work, she eventually fell into a routine and was able to free up her weekend evenings to be with Jason. With the relationship back on track, Jason felt a sense of satisfaction. Mostly they went to dinner. Jason found out quickly that if they went to a movie, Gabby soon fell asleep, so they spent their time together talking and laughing. He had become a very important person in Gabby's life. Not only did they talk about their past experiences and hopes for the future, but Gabby found herself confiding more and more in him. He always seemed to listen carefully and give her good advice. As this bond became stronger, Gabby felt it less necessary to rely on Ari or even her mother as often, and it felt wonderful, empowering.

During the late fall and early spring, The *Sentinel* had been reprinting articles from other newspapers and magazines about Harriet Rose Hill's escapades in New York, around Europe and the Mediterranean. One article reported her attendance at a charity ball, another an interview where she showed off her new puppy, a wire-haired terrier named Winston. The reporter had asked if he had been named after Winston Churchill and Harriet had dismissed that notion, immediately saying, "Don't be silly. He was named after Harry Winston, of course, my favorite jewelry store."

Several articles included pictures showing her at different soirées, each with a new escort and other notables, one being an Italian prince. She apparently had become a popular member of the jet setting group and was highly sought after for charity events and other glamorous galas given by the rich and famous.

The latest article reported she would be spending most of her time over the summer in New York City where she was chairing a charity ball to be held in early fall.

In April, Jason asked Gabby to go away with him for the weekend. He had booked a room at The Inn at Little Washington as a surprise. Having heard so much about the Inn, she was totally delighted and couldn't wait to go. It was on this weekend that Jason finally asked Gabby to marry him. She could not have envisioned a more perfect place to spend this most romantic weekend.

Jason found the most beautiful peach-colored roses, tied them with a black velvet ribbon at the end of which was a sparkling, round diamond set up high, he said, because he wanted everyone to know she was already taken.

Gabby never thought about saying no. She had been Jason's from the beginning and she had known it. Only the last couple of months had proven her even more right. He was there for her, his shoulder and his advice were solid, and she loved being able to banter ideas back and forth with him. She knew this was right and couldn't wait to get back to tell her mom and call Ari and Brent.

Arriving home late Sunday evening, Gabby found that her mother had already gone to bed, so she and Jason would have to wait to tell Mary about their engagement. Gabby kissed Jason goodnight and happily went upstairs to her room. She was too excited to sleep, however, and, since it was an hour earlier in Chicago, Gabby decided to call Ari with the news.

Ari was awake, having just arrived home from a date. Gabby tried to ease into the news, but Ari could hear the excitement in Gabby's voice and finally said, "Give it up, Gabby, I know there's something going on."

Gabby just laughed and told her best friend about the proposal and then the entire weekend's events leading up to it. While Ari was still concerned that this was happening too fast, it was clear from Gabby's excitement, that this was exactly what she wanted. And, so far, Gabby had been pretty good at figuring our what was good for her. So, the two of them couldn't stop talking and laughing, and even started to plan the wedding.

Finally after an hour's conversation, they both knew they had to get some sleep and regretfully hung up the phone. Gabby, still excited, turned out the light and crawled under the covers knowing she had to be at work in just a few hours and that always required her full attention. Smiling, she eventually slid into sleep.

When Gabby entered the kitchen the next morning, Mary was reading the paper while enjoying her coffee. Asking Gabby how the weekend had been, Gabby couldn't wait to flash her left hand, watch the look of surprise on her mother's face, and then ran to hug her. Mary was truly surprised. She knew, of course, that Gabby was smitten with this young man, but she really didn't think they had known one another long enough to have made such a commitment. Gabby said, "Oh, Mom, he's so wonderful and I know this is right, I've known since the very beginning, well almost the very beginning."

All Mary could say was "Sit down, honey, tell me everything."

Gabby looked at her watch. "I'd love to, Mom, but can we do this tonight? I'm really running late and I have a meeting scheduled in a half hour." Giving her mom a squeeze, Gabby started toward the door.

Mary could hardly say anything except, "Okay honey, drive carefully," and then she was gone.

On the phone that afternoon, Gabby and Jason decided they should take Mary out to dinner that night. The plan was that Gabby would go home and have some private time with her mother and then Jason would pick them up around 7:30 for dinner. This way, Gabby and Jason felt that Mary could ask the motherly-type questions that always came with this kind of announcement, and Jason would have plenty of time to clean up after his classes and a necessary stop at the library.

Dinner was easy. Both Gabby and Jason seemed very much in love, and Mary enjoyed watching them interact. Mary did have questions, however. " Have you set a date yet, or have you thought about where you're going to live?"

Before Jason had a chance, Gabby answered. "I think a holiday wedding would be nice. In fact, I think it'd be terrific. Besides being the holidays, Brent and all my girlfriends will be home for Christmas break. We really haven't talked about where we're going to live."

Jason seemed somewhat disappointed with the date, but said, "I was hoping it would be sooner, but I understand your thinking, honey."

"Jason, what about your family?" Mary continued.

"My parents were killed in a fire and I was raised by various foster parents after that. When I became too old to be in the foster care system, I didn't know what to do with myself, so I joined the Army. I spent two tours of duty in the Service and was discharged sixteen months ago. Then I enrolled in junior college last fall under the GI Bill. Now I'm finding my way around being back in school."

"I'm so sorry about your parents, Jason. It must have been very difficult for you. Now that you're back in school, do you have any particular interests career-wise?"

"I think architecture will end up being my final choice – that's where I met Gabby, in our architecture class. But I also find computer science very interesting as well."

While Mary had many more questions, she sensed that what she really wanted to know about him would be found out over time. Questions and answers are good as far as they go, but generally one finds out considerably more about a person by watching their behavior. Besides, she hadn't heard anything that sent out a warning signal.

"Well," she said, "I think that's enough of an interrogation for one evening. However, I would like to give you a party. Nothing large, just family mostly, so that everyone has a chance to meet you. Our family is quite large, and it'll be easier to have everyone meet you all at once, rather than drag it out over a series of dinner parties. You can probably expect lots of questions from them, as well." They all agreed and Mary toasted Gabby and Jason, wishing them luck.

At the family party, Gabby was aglow. Mary made the announcement and Jason was immediately whisked off by various members of the family as they questioned and congratulated him. It was a wonderful party and it seemed that the family had welcomed him as if he had been around forever.

The one exception to this was Uncle Tony. He felt, somewhere in his gut, that this guy was just *too* smooth. Maybe it was because Gabby was only nineteen. Maybe it was because they had just lost Gabby's father a little more than two months ago. *Whatever it is*, he thought, *I'll just have to do a little snooping.*

Without telling Mary and certainly not Gabby, Uncle Tony enlisted his son TJ as well as some of his police buddies to check Jason out. With their help, Uncle Tony did confirm that Jason had been a foster child; he had spent two tours of duty in the Army; he was enrolled in college and had a small apartment in Thompsonville, where he paid his rent and utilities on time. He had no police record, and Uncle Tony was beginning to think he was all wrong about him.

After TJ had spent fourteen nights and all day on Saturdays and Sundays over those two weeks following Jason, he reported back to his father that Jason hadn't done anything out of the ordinary. He went to classes, studied at the library, saw Gabby almost every night and went out to a couple of diners when he wasn't with Gabby. So, finally, Uncle Tony began to believe his concerns were unwarranted and kicked himself for being so suspicious and apparently way overprotective of his niece.

Jason was anxious. He wanted the wedding to be sooner than Christmastime. He told Gabby that he had been alone for so long that now he just wanted to be with her, to belong to her. He had suggested eloping to Las Vegas the night he proposed. But, Gabby had told him, she just couldn't do that to her family, particularly since it had been only two months since her father had been killed. It just wouldn't be right.

Jason also raised the question of where they would live. Gabby was so inundated at work that frankly she had not given that a great deal of thought. Certainly they couldn't live in Jason's studio apartment. She thought that living at home with her mom probably wasn't the best idea either.

Jason mentioned that perhaps they could live in one of the new houses at Huntington Forest. Gabby didn't think they could afford them. Clearly this was something that would require some further discussion and investigation. Finances were not something they had discussed in depth before. Gabby knew Jason had some money saved from his time in the Army and that his college was being paid for largely by the GI Bill. But Jason wasn't working now, how would they be able to pay for a house at Huntington Forest?

They were well into the spring selling season. Gabby had been meeting with Jerry O'Neil about Regency's website; it had been up and running as of the beginning of May. There were still things that needed to be tweaked, but it was there and it looked great. Gabby was working on a mailing to all the local real estate agents about the site, and she planned several print ads in The *Sentinel*, as well as the local county magazines, which were directed mainly at new home buyers. There was a traffic counter on the website, so she was hoping that she would soon have some feedback on the site's success. She had her fingers crossed.

The real estate market was not good and the outlook not much better. She needed to sell a third of the homes in Phase Two by June 30th, when their next quarterly loan payment was due. If not, the family would have to decide whether or not to put up their personal money in order to keep Regency afloat, and then only until the end of September. And, of course, by then, they would have to have sold nearly seventy percent in order to keep the loan going for Phase Two and to have any chance for Phase Three.

By mid-June, Gabby was under pressure from Jason about setting a date for their wedding, and from the business. Regency was still short of its sales goal that needed to be met in the next two weeks. She tried to assure Jason that their marriage was her long-term priority, but that for right now all her efforts needed to be channeled toward meeting Regency's sales requirements and financing obligations.

Mary, too, was after Gabby to set a date for the wedding. As it was, it was going to be difficult to find a date and a caterer that would be free during the holiday season. Gabby tried to explain to her mom, as she had Jason, that she just couldn't focus on that right now. She did promise to sit down with Jason the beginning of July to concentrate on wedding plans and they would tell Mary as soon as a decision had been made.

True to her word, Gabby and Jason spent the Fourth of July weekend choosing the date of Thursday, December 23rd for their wedding. Regency had not met its projected sales, but they were only short two sales, and Gabby was meeting with the bankers on Friday to see what arrangements could be made. She and Jason told Mary the date, but said any planning would have to wait until after that meeting.

Knowing the pressure Gabby was under, Mary carefully suggested that, perhaps, since Gabby was so busy at work, she could call Father Frank, and Judy over at Sweet Nothings, to make certain that date worked for both of them.

"Mom," Gabby said, "we have a little problem. Jason isn't Catholic. I'm not certain, but I don't think we can be married in the church, at least not the Catholic Church."

Mary sat, stunned. That was not one of the questions she had even thought about asking. She just took it for granted that Gabby would want to marry a Catholic and remain in the church. Finding her voice, Mary said, "Well, perhaps that is something I can ask Father Frank and, if he can't marry you in the church, can he marry you at all? If not, what are your options?"

Gabby looked at Jason and he just nodded. The truth was that Jason really didn't care about a church wedding, but he went along with it to keep Gabby happy. As far as he was concerned, Vegas was the only way to go. Looking back at her mom, Gabby said "Thanks, Mom, that would be a big help." And that was how it was left.

Later that week, Mary found out that Father Frank could marry them but that, before he could do so, Gabby and Jason would have to go through a marriage preparation process which included classes and interviews with a priest. At the conclusion of that process, Gabby and Jason could then receive a special dispensation from the bishop – the entire process taking approximately six months. So, December 23rd was out of the question.

Gabby and Jason were alone at dinner after Mary told Gabby what she had learned. Jason, secretly delighted, said, "I think it's going to be impossible with your business responsibilities and time pressures, given the chosen date of December 23rd, to find someone who will marry us other than a Justice of the Peace or a Judge. I think we should reconsider going to Las Vegas. I'm concerned about the pressures on you with Regency and now with the complications about a church ceremony, maybe eloping is the best solution. If we go through the special dispensation process, we won't be able to marry for another six months at the earliest. I don't want to be without you that long. We can be married in the next few weeks my way."

Still unwilling to give in to the idea of elopement, Gabby said "I really will take some time to think about it now." She hadn't thought that this was going to be such a big issue, and she was starting to feel uncomfortable about being married outside of the Catholic Church. She knew she hadn't really focused on it and basically had, unfairly, left it up to her mother. Promising herself a long night of introspection, she told Jason she would see him Friday night and that she was sure she would have an answer by then. And again that was how it was left.

Gabby kept her promise, but knew she needed to talk to Ari and then maybe even Brent. Her conversation with Ari was unexpected.

"Maybe you should step back, Gabby, and take some more time to plan the wedding. What's wrong with a summer wedding – as in next summer?"

"It might be easier then," Gabby allowed, "because business could be better. But, I really can't count on that. Besides, we want to be together now."

"Then you need to think about getting married in some sort of a civil ceremony. Maybe even HRH's father could marry you."

"Wouldn't that be a hoot? Except, then I'd probably have to invite Harriet and I'd worry that the wedding wasn't up to her standards as 'Thompsonville Jetsetter of the Year' or something." They both giggled. "Thanks Ari. I'll think about it. Talk to you later," and then hung up. She knew Brent would have a similar reaction to Ari's and almost decided not to call him, just to save having to hear it again.

Brent didn't disappoint. "Gabby, have you even thought about what it would mean to the family if you don't get married in the church? Even more, how *you* would feel?"

"I have, honestly. Brent, I love Jason so much and we're going to get married. It's just a question of how and when. The church part is becoming less important to me."

Brent didn't like what was happening to Gabby. She was still Gabby, but even as a little girl when she would get herself in a box, she would fight until she found a way out and it wasn't always the best way either. Brent thought she should wait until next year. "Gabby, what's the rush? I know you love Jason and can only imagine how you feel. But, after all, Dad just died. Don't you think you should wait?"

"By Christmas, Dad will have been gone for ten months, that's not an unreasonable amount of time. I think I'm just making too much of all this. Thanks Brent, I appreciate your advice."

"Gabby, no matter what you decide, well, you know I'll be there."

Gabby started thinking alone now. She thought about what Ari said and about what Brent said. She also knew what her mother was thinking, even though she hadn't said anything to her. It all boiled down to the fact that she loved Jason, he loved her, and they wanted, *needed*, to be together now. She also knew that with Regency's business on the edge as it was, she wasn't going to have a lot of spare time to plan a wedding. As the evening wore on, Gabby became more convinced that Jason had been right all along. They needed to elope!

That decision made, Gabby turned her thoughts toward where they would live. She decided that because Regency's future was so much up in the air, she just couldn't rely on her salary to buy a house at Huntington Forest, or anywhere else for that matter. Since Jason needed his money for school, the only logical thing to do right now was to live with her mom until they had a better handle on their financial future.

When Gabby told Jason about the decision to elope, he was ecstatic. It was Friday evening and he said "Let's go. We can go to Vegas tomorrow morning, spend the day, get married tomorrow evening, have a wonderful night there, and return home as Mr. and Mrs. Jason Marsh early Sunday evening. What a perfectly wonderful weekend."

"Wait a second. Sit down. That's what you wanted to hear. What may not be to your liking is that I think we have to live with my mother for the time being." Gabby explained the reasoning behind her thinking and, while he wasn't excited about spending the first year or so under the same roof as his mother-in-law, he knew she was being practical. Besides, that would allow him to spend less of his savings, and that was a good thing.

So, agreed they were, and they were very excited. The question for Gabby now was whether they should tell her mother they were going to get married in Las Vegas over the weekend, or should they just go?

"Gabby, part of the excitement of an elopement is the secrecy. Let's just keep it between us. It'll be more fun, don't you think?"

"There *is* a thrill about it I just can't explain. Okay, tomorrow, Las Vegas it is. Oh, Jason, I'm so happy." They spent the rest of the evening making their plans for the weekend and, without wanting to leave one another, finally said goodnight, knowing they wouldn't have to leave each other again after this weekend.

Gabby was up early Saturday morning. As she packed an overnight bag, she sang along with her CD. She was incredibly happy and couldn't wait until 8:30 when Jason was going to pick her up for their drive to the airport in Pittsburgh and then off to their wedding in Las Vegas and the rest of their lives.

When Gabby went down to the kitchen to get some coffee and wait for Jason, she found a note from her mom saying that her regular hair appointment had been moved up, and she'd be back from the hairdresser around 10:00. Gabby was disappointed she wasn't going to be able to share her news with her mom before she left, but then thought again about how delicious it was to have such a wonderful secret. She wrote her mom a note saying that she and Jason were going off for the weekend, and they'd see her Sunday evening when they returned.

Jason and Gabby arrived in Las Vegas a little after 1:00 on Saturday afternoon. Jason had phoned ahead and made reservations at Caesars Palace. After checking in, Gabby told Jason she wanted to go down to the shops and find something special to wear that evening for their ceremony. Gabby took her time and found a spectacular dress and some shoes for her wedding. *Something about new shoes*, she thought, *always make a woman feel more special.* Arriving back in the room, Gabby actually trembled with excitement when Jason told her he had booked their ceremony at the Chapel of the White Bells for 7:30 that evening and dinner at *Spago*.

The ceremony was beautiful. Jason surprised Gabby with a bouquet of white roses and lilies of the valley, they had a photographer take several pictures, and then enjoyed a beautiful dinner. It seemed that the day had flown by as they toasted each other with champagne and barely made it to the bedroom before all their clothes had been stripped off. All of a sudden it was Sunday, and they were headed back to Thompsonville. While Gabby was very happy, she just couldn't believe it was all over. *All, that is, except telling her mom, Ari, Brent, and the rest of the family.*

Mary was in the sunroom watching television when Gabby and Jason came in. Mary turned down the volume on the TV and turned to greet them. "How was your weekend?"

Gabby sat down by her mother on the sofa and Jason stood on the other side of the coffee table. "Mom, Jason and I got married this weekend. We were in Las Vegas, well we weren't just in Las Vegas, we went there to get married. We thought it over and it seemed to be getting too difficult with the church thing and the Christmas holidays and then, of course, all that's happening at Regency. Well, we just thought this was the right thing for us." Gabby reached across the table for Jason's hand. As he took it, Gabby looked back at her mother. "I hope you're as happy as we are."

Mary hugged Gabby, stood and went around the table to hug Jason too, welcoming him to the family. "Well, we're going to have a big reception with all your friends and the entire family, then we can all share in your happiness. We can do this now, over the summer, when everyone is home from school without having to wait for the holidays."

"Mom, that's a great idea. What we wanted to discuss with you, though, was that we think it would probably be best if we took you up on your offer and lived here with you for a while. Money is tight and we don't want to get ourselves in a financial bind. Right now I have to concentrate on Regency, and Jason needs to concentrate on school. So, is it still okay with you?"

"Of course it is. It's wonderful, and I'm delighted you'll *both* be here. I would've been upset if you hadn't asked."

"Thank you 'Mom,'" said Jason, and Gabby laughed as she saw the look on her mother's face.

"Mom, I'm going to grab some clothes for tomorrow and take them over to Jason's. He hasn't given notice at his apartment, so he'll have to do that. Then I'll help him pack up and move what he wants over to the house. During the next month or two, we'll be back and forth. We just wanted to tell you our good news tonight so you wouldn't worry. Mom, I'm so happy. I'll talk to you more tomorrow. I love you."

After Gabby and Jason left, Mary sat alone in the sunroom with the volume on the TV still turned down. *Am I just being a typical mother who is concerned with the elopement, or is there really something that isn't quite right about this whole picture?* Unfortunately, she knew, there was nothing she could do about it now. Gabby was a married woman and there wasn't anything about Jason she didn't really like; *I'm just being silly*, she thought. As Mary attempted to dismiss those thoughts from her mind, she found she couldn't get back into the movie she'd been watching, so she turned off the TV and headed up the stairs to her bedroom. As she lay awake, Mary started to plan the reception she would give Gabby and Jason, while hugging Nick's pillow, hoping that Gabby did indeed know her own heart.

The good news was that foot traffic had picked up at Huntington Forest. Regency had thrown an open house for real estate agents in early June where the apparent attraction began. They were shown the website and Jerry O'Neil had given them a brief tutorial on how to use it as a sales tool. Gabby had handled herself beautifully. The changes she had made to the plans seemed to take everyone aback. When Gabby told them the sales prices had not changed dramatically, and they saw the incredible upscale touches made to the houses, they knew they would be showing Huntington Forest to many clients in the near future. Gabby told the real estate agents, I'm sweetening the pot by offering vacation packages for two to Hawaii for any agent selling more than five houses, no matter how many of you do it." There was a loud buzz, and a huge round of applause erupted.

Mary stood back and smiled. Even Uncle Tony nodded approvingly, telling Mary that she'd made a great decision when she put Gabby in charge.

Not only had Gabby earned the respect of the Regency employees, but also many real estate agents and even a few bankers who had been skeptical of a nineteen-year-old taking over the helm of a corporation as large as Regency. The real estate agents rose to the occasion and, soon, Regency was outselling its competition with their plain vanilla homes, versus the streamlined, architecturally interesting, and no-nonsense styling of the homes at Huntington Forest. But that was May and June. If anything, the real estate market had slowed even more and, while Regency was outselling its competition, they were still behind in their target sales.

Gabby and Jason were almost finished packing up Jason's apartment and had moved his essentials over to Mary's house. The rest of his stuff was going into storage. Mary was seeing less of Gabby and Jason than she originally thought she would. Gabby was working as hard as she could, talking to real estate agencies in order to promote Huntington Forest, as well as offering weekend seminars and open houses to home buyers about the current market and it's long term potential.

Jason was gone every day. If he wasn't in class, he was at the library studying. They tried to have dinner with Mary three nights a week, so she wouldn't be lonely. But, they were newlyweds, and wanted some private time to themselves. They often went out to dinner, when they had the time and no outside diversions, and discussed what was going on in each of their lives.

Jason would talk about his classes, and how much he enjoyed his architecture classes in particular. Gabby often told Jason about the plans she had for the next section at Huntington Forest and Regency in general. She found that Jason listened intently and consistently had sound advice for her. She was very happy and also thankful that she and Jason seemed to be on the same page in their ideas for Regency.

The reception was elegant. Mary held it on the terrace of a beautiful old estate overlooking magnificently manicured grounds. Mary had asked Judy, a longtime friend who owned Sweet Nothings, to cater the party, and Judy had outdone herself. It couldn't have been more perfect. Brent was there making the toasts along with Uncle Tony, TJ, Aunt Carmen and the entire Romano family, the Campagna's, their extended families and almost all of Gabby's friends from school.

Ari came home for the weekend. She had taken a summer job along with Emily back in Chicago and needed to be back at work on Monday. Josh and Larry were off somewhere in Burma or Thailand, doing work for yet another relief organization. Harriet was in Paris. Otherwise, everyone seemed to be there.

Mary was standing back near the double French doors leading from the house to the terrace feeling very happy for Gabby and watching her enjoy Jason and their day with their friends.

Uncle Tony wandered up beside her, and for a few moments stood next to her in silence. "You know," he said, "I was skeptical of this young man back around the time we first met him."

Mary turned to him with a questioning frown around her eyes. Looking up at him, she asked, "Why didn't you ever say anything to me?"

"Mary, we had just lost Nick. You were, we all were, under a tremendous strain. Losing him, the company's uncertainty, I just thought it was best if I handled it on my own. I did check him out though. He pays his bills on time, he is in school as he said, has no police record, and, at that time, went home or to the library every night he wasn't with Gabby." Tony turned back to look at Gabby and Jason.

"I guess that's all one can ask, but I wish you had told me. I had my own concerns early on and would have felt much better knowing then what you're telling me now. I'm glad Gabby knew better than both of us. But, thank you for telling me now." With that, they both made their way back to the guests and enjoyed the rest of the celebration.

CHAPTER SEVEN

It was slow going. Nearing the end of September, the weather already cooling, and Regency still needed to sell eight more houses in order to meet their financing needs. While Gabby had been thinking ahead about the next phase, in the hopes that there would even be one, she was feeling the weight of those eight houses. Too nervous to eat, she lost weight. Then the stress really got to her, and she wasn't feeling well at all. She was concerned that she just wasn't cut out to run a company the size of Regency, with all it's ups and downs. Mary had jumped in as much as she could, but, frankly, Gabby had been handling so much of it by herself for the last several months, Mary was not up to speed at a time when it was absolutely necessary.

Jason also helped. Gabby had started to count on him more than even she knew. He began to spend more time at Regency to help her out and had even taken over some of her weekend seminars in an effort to give Gabby a break.

It was on one of those Saturdays when Jason was heading up one of Gabby's seminars that Gabby suddenly realized that maybe she wasn't just sick; she couldn't remember the last time she had her period. *Holy cow*, she thought, *could I be pregnant?* Running down the stairs, Gabby grabbed her mom and sat her down in the kitchen. "Mom, maybe I'm pregnant."

Mary immediately ran down to the drug store for one of those early pregnancy detecting tests. Mary was hardly able to contain herself; *a grandchild*, maybe. She hardly thought of herself as old enough to be a grandparent – *I'm only forty-six! Well, that's not unheard of; many grandparents are younger than forty-six.* She just felt she was way too young. Rushing into the house, Mary handed Gabby the box, gave her a hug and said "Let's find out."

Staring at the box in the privacy of Jason's and her bedroom, she began to consider taking the test before Jason knew what was happening. Gabby knew she needed to know right away. *But what if I am? Shouldn't Jason be the first to know, not my mother? But, then, I'm putting the cart before the horse,* she thought. Taking the test was a snap. Too easy. Standing over the sink, she stared at the stick for what seemed forever, but then, there it was. All the problems of Regency seemed to dissipate, and she let out a shout of happiness.

Mary rushed in and looked at Gabby who just nodded at her. They were both laughing and crying at the same time. Gabby laughing because she was so happy, and Mary, laughing in between her tears, because Nick wouldn't be around to see his first grandchild.

But the happiness was there and Gabby asked, "What time is it? I need to tell Jason." Discovering it was only 2:30 and the seminar was still going on, Gabby decided to drive over and surprise him.

Standing in the back of the room, Gabby heard Jason talking to the potential home buyers and thought, *he's really good at this.* Then as she tuned in a little more, she heard him make some promises on behalf of the company he had not discussed with her. He was also assuring buyers he would be here at Regency with an open-door policy, should they ever need to discuss anything. *What is this all about?* She wondered. But then, the seminar was over, the attendees applauded and went up to talk with Jason personally.

As the room thinned out, Jason noticed Gabby for the first time and ran up to her. "Why are you here? Are you all right?"

She laughed. "More than all right, I'd say." Looking at her quizzically, she took him by the arm and walked him out to her car which was parked right up front. "Jump in. I could use a milk shake."

After they were seated and had placed their orders, Jason leaned forward. "What's this all about, honey?"

Gabby, smiling and playing with the straw the waitress had left, looked up. "It's about needing more room at home." Letting that sink in a minute, Gabby then said, "We're pregnant, Sweetheart."

Jason was stunned. "I, ah, I thought we were waiting until we could afford it better. Did you forget to take your pills? What happened?"

"Oh, Jason. I thought you'd be happier about this. We *did* talk about getting pregnant."

"Well, yes, we did. Only, I thought we were going to wait until we were more settled. You know, in our own place or something – just more settled. But, I'm thrilled, Gabby, really. It's just that it's so much sooner than I expected. Is it a boy or a girl . . . when is it due? Wow. This is really something."

Gabby's milk shake and Jason's malt arrived and they clanked glasses as if they were drinking champagne. "Jason, I probably shouldn't have sprung it on you this way. It only occurred to me this afternoon that the reason I haven't been feeling well was, well, what it is. I took one of those at-home pregnancy tests and immediately came flying over here to tell you. We still have to confirm everything at the doctor's office and he'll give us a better idea of when. I'm thinking June, though."

"June, that's really something."

While Gabby wasn't really feeling any better, now that she knew what the problem was, she was back at work, dealing with business as usual. The doctor confirmed that the due date was early June -- probably the 4th. She was told she was healthy, even though she had morning sickness, and not to worry about anything; these things had a way of taking care of themselves as long as the mother took care of herself.

Jason insisted he continue to help her at work. He expressed concerns about her working such long hours, and how she was going to take care of a baby with all the responsibilities she had at Regency.

Jason and Gabby talked at length about their living arrangements too. "Gabby, I really think we need to find our own place and not stay here with your mother after the baby is born. It's been a long time since there's been a baby in the house, and I'm concerned that it'll be too much for her. This might be the time for us to find our own place."

"Oh, Jason. I don't know . . ."

"There are some really nice houses in Huntington Forest, Gabby. I know we agreed to wait until we had more money in the bank, but I think this changes everything."

"Jason, I'm still concerned about the money. We have some money in the bank, but I don't think it's nearly enough."

"I can give up some of my classes, maybe just go to night school. Then I can work during the day to help pay for everything. I'm not sure what I can do, but . . ."

"Jason, I'm really against your giving up your college work. I know we need more than what Regency pays me for what's coming, but giving up school?"

"What if -- now this is just an idea Gabby -- but, what if I can work with you at Regency on a, let's say, 30ish hour work week? I'm already doing some of the seminars and working with the real estate agents. Most of that work is on the weekends, which would leave me some time for a couple of day classes and transfer some of my other classes to the evening. We could just make it a real job, instead of my only helping out. Then, I can be there when you have the baby, and we can work out some sort of split shift after that."

"I don't know, Jason. But it's a possibility. I'll think about it and talk to my mother and Uncle Tony." Gabby thought that the idea had some merit. Jason had been her sounding board for several months now, well, actually, since they'd started dating last fall. They agreed on just about everything, and she certainly was going to need someone there until she could get back on a full time basis. *This might be the solution*, she thought. *Then, when I'm back at Regency, Jason can go back to school, maybe do some consulting work to help supplement our income. Yes, this could work.*

They still hadn't figured out where they were going to live. Mary wanted them to stay at the house, but understood their desire to finally be on their own. Gabby and Jason started looking at apartments, but the ones they thought would be big enough for their needs were very expensive, *almost as much as a house*, Gabby thought. Jason also saw that the costs to rent were very high, which again made him think that they might be better off in a house. So, Gabby and Jason started looking at some small starter-homes that were up for resale. They really didn't like what they were seeing.

This confirmed to Gabby that, even though it would be expensive, renting was the way to go. That way they would have the flexibility to upgrade or downgrade as their financial situation dictated.

But, Jason wanted a house and he wanted it *now*. This was their first real argument and Gabby couldn't believe how angry he became. Never having seen Jason behave that way, Gabby immediately stepped back and asked herself, *What's really going on here?* She concluded that it was the fact that he wasn't the breadwinner, that they'd needed to live in her old room at her mother's house, that he may have to give up school, and that he was letting her down because he couldn't take care of his own family. She thought, *It must be emasculating for Jason*, and her heart went out to him.

Gabby's solution wasn't really a solution at all. Gabby sat Jason down one night and laid out the frustration she felt about not being in a position to buy a house now. "I understand how you feel. I wish it could be otherwise." These words, and many others along the same lines, helped diffuse his anger and break down the wall he had built to protect his emotions. Gabby was able to get Jason talking and, while it took more than one conversation, they finally agreed that they would stay with Mary through the holidays and then, perhaps, they would have a better feel for what they could handle financially.

Fortunately, Regency's September sales were better than expected. Instead of selling eight houses, they sold thirteen and they still had a few interested buyers, according to the real estate agents. Gabby was elated and hoped this might be the end of the down real estate market. But, alas, only one of the interested buyers actually bought a home, and sales slowed again until after Thanksgiving.

Gabby started planning Phase Four and was beginning to rethink the mix of houses that would be built in that final section. Remembering her own search back a few months earlier, Gabby thought, *Why can't we build just a few smaller houses with a little more contemporary flair than our normal traditional-style homes?* Gabby played around with reducing the total number of square feet by cutting out the living room and family room duplication, and opening up the common rooms, thereby almost totally eliminating the traditional hallway design so that the house had a less formal feel. *We could cut our construction costs, and still offer a high quality product at a lower price point.* Gabby ran the numbers with the help of her office accounting staff, but she determined that the costs they had in the land would preclude them from making the necessary profit for the banks and Regency's own needs. *If we can just get through this crunch,* she continued thinking, *I'll look into making something like this work. If we can buy the land at the right price and then apportion it for smaller houses than those at Huntington Forest, this could be a winning concept for Regency.*

Gabby ran the idea by her mother but asked her not to tell anyone, including Uncle Tony and especially not Jason for the time being.

Mary asked, "Why not?"

"Because it's too early to even think about a whole new development, and I don't want Jason to get his hopes up that this could be the answer to our housing problem."

Regency, Gabby, Jason, Uncle Tony and everyone seemed to be in a holding pattern for the rest of 1993 and even into the spring of 1994.

Gabby met with Regency's board, and while the company had not met its year-end projections, they again had come very close. Mary and Uncle Tony decided they would cash in one of Regency's CDs to finance this modest shortfall as well as the ongoing day-to-day business operations. Both Mary and Uncle Tony were very grateful that Nick had purchased key man insurance on himself for the benefit of the company. This allowed them to purchase CDs for just such a purpose. If it was going to be necessary to cash in another one during the spring, they would do so, because not to, would end up costing them far more. While the bank had some concerns, they had been doing business with Nick and Tony for many years and while Gabby was young, they believed in the family work ethic and the formula used as the base of their business. So, again they dug in.

Jason was still in school. With Gabby spending more and more time at Regency trying to improve the spring sales, they had less time together. Jason was spending a great deal of his time at the library because, he said, he didn't like being home alone, even though Mary was there.

The pressure was really beginning to show on Gabby. It wasn't just the pregnancy or even Regency and its problems, there was something else she just felt uneasy about, but couldn't put her finger on it. Maybe she was only imagining it, but Jason seemed more distant. And, he was seldom there in the early evening when she could make it home on time. When they did spend time together, Jason's interest in her seemed to turn to mere tolerance.

His interest in Regency never waned, however. He talked to her about the company and never failed to be at Regency on the weekends working with the real estate agents and any potential buyers who attended the open houses and seminars. Additionally, he had made himself an office in one of the small conference rooms, and kept himself busy reading reports and catching up on the company's day-to-day business.

Gabby and Jason took all the classes offered to first-time parents. When Gabby found out that the baby was to be a girl, she was thrilled, although, admittedly, she also would have been thrilled had it been a boy. Nicole was on top of their short list of names, along with Elizabeth and Stephanie, although in Gabby's mind, Nicole was the only choice. Jason didn't participate much in choosing the baby's name, but said he was thrilled about the prospect of being a daddy.

Gabby and Mary did all the shopping for the baby's arrival. Mary was anxiously awaiting the arrival of her first grandchild and, as with almost every about-to-be first-time grandparent, bought virtually everything in sight. With Gabby and Jason still at Mary's house, Mary set up the guest room for the new arrival.

With the late spring came new potential home buyers, and Gabby and Jason's baby daughter, Nicole. Gabby spent more time at home -- Jason at Regency. Little time was left for Jason's school work, and even less for the two of them to spend together. Jason started using Gabby's office for meetings, Norma told her, but Gabby dismissed it as his needing more space for visitors to sit, and perhaps view whatever they were discussing. Mary became increasingly concerned, but Gabby assured her that he was just trying to do his best.

After several weeks of being an at-home new mom, Gabby knew she needed to get back to work. Mary was delighted for two reasons: one, she would have lots of time with her new granddaughter and, two, she really was concerned about what was happening at Regency with Jason there. Both Norma and Uncle Tony told Mary about all the meetings he was having with their architects, accountants and suppliers, not to mention his continuing relationships with the real estate agents and potential buyers.

On the first Monday back at the office, Gabby was surprised Jason wasn't there. She knew he wasn't at home. Maybe he was at school. Sitting down with Norma and Uncle Tony, Gabby started to get a picture of what had taken place over the past six weeks during her absence. She found that everything seemed to be in order and she was pleased with the spring sales to date. She thought Jason had done a really fine job and she was proud of him.

Brent came in from New Haven to see Nicole, but wasn't able to stay long. He had accepted a summer associate's position at one of Washington, D.C.'s most prominent law firms and needed to get back there and settled in. This was a huge opportunity for him and he wanted to make certain he did the best job possible.

Last summer he'd taken a summer associate's position at a venerable old Boston firm, thinking it was exactly where he wanted to practice law after graduation. He loved Boston with its neighborhoods, academia and history and had focused last year's search for a summer position on Boston. He spent almost the entire summer working on cases involving some of the large Boston-based corporations which the firm represented.

This year he had wanted to get a taste for something different and was excited to find a place at the D.C. firm. Stacy spent her previous summer's internship at a firm in D.C., and had piqued his interest in the possibilities that city had to offer.

Ari arrived home from Northwestern and spent a couple of days with Gabby and Nicole before Gabby went back to work. Other friends also stopped by to see Nicole and, of course, there was a revolving door of Romano family members, dropping by to help.

Jason was becoming more and more scarce. When he was home, it was almost as if he was disinterested in both her and the baby. Struggling to find out what was happening, Gabby finally asked "What's wrong Jason? You aren't home much and when you are, well, you're indifferent."

Jason had prepared for this confrontation, although he'd hoped he could have hidden his feelings better in order to delay it. His patience was beginning to fray, and he knew he needed to get it under control. "Nothing, except I'm finding it increasingly difficult to have to live here with your mother, particularly now that Nicole is here. It's your mother's house and not ours and sometimes I'm just plain uncomfortable being here. It's not like we can really relax, she's always around."

"But, Jason, there's no way we could handle all this without her help."

Then, it came. "Also, I know I need to get a real job now and frankly I don't know what I'm trained to do. I could re-enlist or maybe apply to the police academy, but I've seen enough of fighting and guns, and I would rather not do that. Without a degree under my belt, I feel as if the only thing left for me is a job at Home Depot or WalMart. I'm sorry, Gabby, I don't know what else to tell you. The pressure is getting to me."

Mary sensed the tension between Gabby and Jason and grew concerned. She chose not to say anything thinking Gabby would talk to her when she was ready. And she did. The day after Gabby's talk with Jason, Gabby sat down with her mother, repeating Jason's and her conversation of the previous night.

Mary listened carefully to what Gabby was saying and tried to comfort her. Gabby broke down in tears. Her mother held her, gently rocking her while rubbing her back. Finally Mary said, "Gabby, I don't know what to say. I've known for some time there was something not quite right between you and Jason, but this is far more serious than I thought. Every new marriage needs a period of adjustment, and living here with me was another adjustment which may have been too much for Jason. I want you to dry your eyes now and get ready to go to the office. Then, tonight when you come home, we'll talk about this some more."

When Gabby arrived home that evening, Mary and Nicole were waiting for her. Mary took one look at her daughter, thinking she looked very tired. "Gabby, why don't you change into something comfortable and then come down so we can talk. I have an idea."

Even though she was tired, she was also intrigued. After washing her face and hands, Gabby changed into jeans and a tee shirt as she wondered what was on her mother's mind. Walking back to the kitchen, Gabby picked up Nicole and started talking and cooing, with her little daughter smiling that toothless smile that just melts a mother's heart. Mary suggested they take Nicole into the sunroom where they could be more comfortable while they talked.

"Gabby, I've been thinking about what we talked about this morning and your situation with Jason. What if we were to find a small parcel of land and build some of those smaller houses you talked to me about several months ago? I know it wasn't practical then for Huntington Forest because of the costs involved and the fact that the individual parcels had already been surveyed and approved by the county. But, if we, and by 'we' I mean Regency, were to build a small cluster of smaller homes using the new ideas you envisioned, not only would that be a good test for those plans, but you could design your own home and buy it from Regency at cost."

"Wow, Mom. Do you think we could? With business so iffy right now, I'm not sure this is a good time to go *experimenting*."

"I've given it a good deal of thought today and here's the way I see it. Because real estate is down right now, we can probably get a good buy on a piece of land. And, because we're not buying as large a parcel as we have in the past like those for Huntington Forest and The Estates at Coldwater Creek before that, we can build just a few homes, keep our construction crews busy for a little while, get you and Jason a house, and test the waters all at the same time."

"Mom, this could be a really great idea, and you are the majority shareholder of Regency, so what you say goes. But, have you thought about this objectively? Would you be considering this if I weren't your daughter and in this situation? I'm going to have to try to step back and think about it objectively, too. And, then, of course, talk to Jason. I know this is a spectacular offer on your part, but I'm not sure how Jason will feel about it and then whether we can afford it, even at 'cost.'

I've had an idea of my own I'd like to run by you though. You know Jason has been covering for me at Regency on the weekends and also during the week, when necessary, for the last few months. I was wondering what you think about hiring Jason part-time to continue doing what he's been doing for free at Regency till now. Besides giving him a small income, I think it would do wonders for his self-worth and still give him time to continue all or some of his classes at Carlton J.C. Additionally, it will allow my weekends to remain free so I'll have some time with Nicole that I wouldn't otherwise have."

Mary was quiet for a few minutes as she thought this over. "I think that could work out on a temporary part-time basis. We don't know where Regency will end up and with our plans on hold for a large new development we won't have as much work for him to do. But it could be a good thing for everyone concerned. You'll need to run it by Uncle Tony, although you ultimately have the authority to hire and fire as you see fit. I think it's important though that this be on a *temporary part-time basis.*"

When Nicole started to get fidgety, Mary and Gabby made their way to the kitchen to feed the baby and get themselves something to eat. It seemed clear that Jason was not going to be home for dinner again that night. Gabby and Mary ended up throwing together some salad and pasta and treated themselves to a glass of wine. Jason walked in as Gabby was getting ready to put Nicole down for the night, not allowing Gabby and Mary a chance to finish their conversation.

As Gabby was putting Nicole in her crib, Jason asked in a somewhat snippy tone of voice "What was it that you and your mother had your heads together about tonight? Probably, some *new* reason as to why we need to live here *forever.*"

Having had just about all she could handle of Jason's recent moods and, without thinking, Gabby whipped her head around and said, "No. It was about our building a house and giving you a part-time job at Regency. I'm a little tired of your attitude and suspicions, and maybe the house and the job are not such great ideas at this time. If you're hungry, why don't you go downstairs and find yourself something to eat. Furthermore, if you're tied up at the library and aren't going to make it home for dinner, call – it's the way grownups behave. I'm tired and I need to get some sleep before Nicole's two o'clock feeding. Goodnight." With that, Gabby climbed into bed and turned off her bedside lamp.

As she scooted down under the covers, turning her back toward Jason's side of the bed, Jason came over to give her a kiss and try to make amends. He could see that this was not the time to try to talk with her, so he just kissed her on the side of her head and walked back to the door to go downstairs and raid the icebox. Making his way down the stairs, all he could think was, *Damn, I hope I didn't screw things up.* A job at Regency and their own house was just what he'd been aiming for.

Gabby calmed down over the weekend as she had some time away from Regency and time to think about what had happened between her and Jason. Jason had tried to talk to her since that night, but she'd put it off insisting that they talk about it over the weekend when neither of them had other commitments. So, here it was, Saturday afternoon. Mary offered to take Nicole to the park, giving them time to talk without interruption. Gabby had talked to Uncle Tony Friday afternoon about her plans for Jason. Uncle Tony actually thought it was a good idea -- he knew Gabby hadn't had much time to herself lately. He, too, stressed the point though that hiring Jason should only be on a temporary part-time basis. Gabby pondered why both he and her mother had made such an issue of it but, since that was what she intended, she just brushed the question to the back of her mind.

Jason quietly walked into the kitchen. "Gabby, would now be a good time for us to talk?" They walked into the sunroom and took seats opposite one another with the coffee table separating them.

"Gabby, I am so sorry for the other night. You know how pressured I've been about a job and not being able to provide for you and Nicole. It's not meant to be an excuse, but I hope you'll forgive me. I love you so very much and, now that we have this beautiful daughter, I just can't imagine life without you two. Problem is, I still don't know how to take care of you and Nicole properly. Maybe our rushing into getting married wasn't the right thing to do, but I just couldn't wait for you to be my wife so that we could be together forever. I am so, so sorry."

Gabby melted. She wasn't the woman who had snapped at Jason the other night and, trying to be tough wasn't working either. She went over to the couch and sat down beside him. Without saying anything, Gabby leaned forward and tentatively gave Jason a kiss, then another one, and then another. Soon they were in each other's arms kissing as if they were still on their honeymoon and clearly forgiving each other. As they held each other, Gabby slowly said, "Why don't we talk about what my mother and I were discussing the other night?"

"Only if you want to, sweetheart."

"First of all, the idea about a house for us. Several months ago when we were looking for a house but hadn't been able to find one, I had this idea. I wanted to do a series of houses that weren't in the 'traditional' style we've always done in the past. I thought we could do a new open-design concept, but we determined back then that it wasn't possible with the financial burdens of Huntington Forest. Now, though, my mother thinks we can do a small sampling of the new concept house, one to be ours, on a new yet-to-be-purchased piece of property."

Jason was overjoyed. He couldn't believe that they were finally getting a house – *It was about damn time!* Even though they would have to wait until it could be built, he was ecstatic and hugged Gabby tightly.

Encouraged by his reaction, Gabby pressed on. "Now, about a job at Regency. We'd like to offer you a part-time position to do the same things you've already been doing, but now you'll get paid for it. It would only be on a temporary basis, until I can get back to work full-time, but it'll bring in some extra income we'll need for a house. And, because it'll be part-time and a good part of that is over the weekend, you'll be able to continue on with your classes."

Jason tried to be tactful. "Honey, that's a wonderful offer. It's just that I don't think I can continue on with my classes for the time being."

"Why not?"

"Well, working at Regency and trying to go to class and study is extremely demanding. As it is, I'm falling behind at school. I haven't been able to keep up since Nicole was born. But I've been glad to do it. As a long-tem commitment, even a temporary one, I don't think it's something I can do and still go to school. But, I've been thinking too, and I've come up with something that might work. I was thinking about getting into real estate -- as an agent. I wasn't sure how that would work because, while I was studying for the exam, I wouldn't be earning any money. Plus, it takes time to really get started in the business. But, if I can work at Regency for a while as I'm breaking into real estate, this could work for us. What do you think?"

"What about school?"

"Well, I'd have to put it on the back burner for a while. But, once I start making money in real estate and Regency is over the hump and no longer needs me, I can go back to school. Sweetheart, let's think about this some more and talk tomorrow. Tonight, I'd just like to take you out to dinner and spend a lovely evening with my beautiful wife."

Gabby and Jason did have a wonderful evening. They talked about the idea of their new house and what it would be like; what they would like to see it have. All the plans a young couple envisions when starting out were alive again for both of them.

"Gabby, this is my dream; a plan for our future, in our own home, with me working and providing for my family. As long as we're working toward something together, there's nothing that can stop us."

Gabby was back on the same cloud she had been on when she and Jason had fallen in love and married. She thought to herself, *well, we've weathered our first storm. Thank God it's over.*

CHAPTER EIGHT

Mary was so glad to see Gabby happy again. Jason finished up his class commitments and then told them at Carlton Junior College that he would need to take some time off between semesters while he straightened out some family issues. Now that he was enrolled in real estate school and employed by Regency, he was clearly a much happier man. He was home almost every night for dinner and spent lots of time with Gabby, Nicole and Mary.

The search for the perfect piece of property was on. Jason needed to be sponsored by a licensed real estate broker in order to take his real estate courses and become licensed by the state. Gabby asked Jason to talk with the manager of his soon-to-be real estate company to keep an eye out for that small parcel of land for Regency. The manager was very happy to accommodate Jason as he knew that Regency could become a very large account for his company. Jason was assured that he would receive a finder's fee if he found the right property before he was licensed.

The summer months passed quickly, and Regency's sales started to rebound. Gabby was beginning to see a light at the end of the tunnel and was definitely feeling better about building a house -- when and if they ever found that perfect piece of property. Gabby looked at quite a few parcels of land and questioned whether the right piece would ever come along.

Jason was doing a great job at Regency and working hard on his real estate career. He had finished his classes in real estate school, passed the state exam and was now in training at the real estate firm. He'd even managed to list a property, along with another agent, during his training period. Quite pleased with himself, he was always talking about ideas he had to get more listings or how to meet more people who could end up being clients. Things were good.

Then, one day when Gabby left work early to take Nicole to the pediatrician, she was rounding the corner of one of the back roads she sometimes used in order to avoid rush hour traffic, when she noticed a sign tacked to a tree in a heavily wooded section in the hills of Thompsonville. The sign was old and tattered but it still clearly read, "For Sale by Owner," and listed a telephone number. Gabby immediately pulled over and scribbled down the number, wondering how she'd missed it before. Hopeful, she was determined to call the number at her first opportunity.

Everything was terrific at the doctor's office. Nicole had gained several pounds, but still on the slim side. She'd grown and generally appeared to be healthy. Nicole had a booster shot, which made her somewhat cranky. But by the time they arrived back home, Nicole was smiling again. Gabby gave Mary the good report and then, all of a sudden, remembered the old sign she had seen on the tree.

In her enthusiasm, Gabby searched in her purse, found the number and picked up the phone. An elderly woman answered and Gabby was certain she had a wrong number; that the sign was indeed an old one. "Hello. I'm sorry to bother you, but I'm calling about a piece of property in Thompsonville that has an old 'For Sale' sign on it. I'm wondering if it's your property or if you know anything about it?"

"Oh my. I haven't thought about that in a long time. My husband put up a sign on that land several years back. It's part of the property we built our own home on thirty-two years ago."

Surprised and excited to hear that it was the old woman's property, Gabby asked, "Is the property still for sale? If so, perhaps you would prefer that I speak directly with your husband."

The woman, who now introduced herself as Priscilla McCutcheon, said, "I really don't know about selling it now. My husband passed away several years ago and frankly I forgot about selling the land."

"Mrs. McCutcheon, I might be interested in that property. Do you know how many acres are for sale?"

"Well, dear, I think there are about seven or eight and there's a creek, but I really can't remember all the particulars. I'd have to look through my husband's old files."

"Is there a chance I could meet with you and look at the property?"

"Oh yes, I think I would like to sell it. I could use the money, but not if you're going to put in some big store or anything."

Gabby laughed. "Actually, I'm thinking about building a few houses there, one would be my own home – we'd be neighbors. I'm also with Regency Development Corporation. You may have heard of us. We've built many homes in and around Thompsonville and I'd be happy to take you over to see some of them if you'd like."

Mrs. McCutcheon seemed to really like what Gabby was saying. "I would be glad to meet you. I'll look through my husband's papers and then call you. Thank you so much for calling, dear."

Hanging up the phone, Gabby couldn't hide her excitement. "Mom, this could be it." She jumped up and hugged her mother and her daughter, whispering to her that "Mommy may have just found your new home."

Jason came in about an hour later. He was tired but Gabby couldn't wait to tell him about her potential find. She certainly didn't expect the reaction she got from him. He was almost livid. "What do you mean you called the number without letting me do it? If you'd let me call, I could've gotten a commission on the sale. This way I don't get anything."

Gabby was shocked. "Honey, assuming she would have listed it, it only would have meant the property would probably end up costing more. I'm sorry, I should have thought about that but I was just too excited thinking that I may have found our new home. Besides, we don't even know at this point whether the property will be right for Regency or us."

Jason calmed down immediately. "Gabby, I'm sorry I yelled at you. But, in the future, I certainly hope that you'll think about me a little more. Remember, we're a couple and need to act in each other's best interest. I'm going to go wash up now. I'll be down in a little bit."

Jason climbed the stairs still fuming. Sometimes he just didn't understand Gabby. *Why had she done that?* He was certain he could have twisted that old woman around his little finger, probably getting the property for less than Regency was going to have to pay. That is, *if* they buy it. He knew he was tired, but this was getting way more difficult than he had bargained for. Knowing it was essential to keep Gabby happy, he managed to calm himself before he went back

downstairs. Then, he realized, he was actually getting what he wanted all along, he just wasn't going to get paid for finding it. Worse things could happen.

Gabby went out to meet Mrs. McCutcheon and look at the property. Mrs. McCutcheon's home was down a long drive around the corner from where Gabby had seen the sign. As Gabby drove back under the canopy of trees into the clearing, she was taken aback by the beautiful craftsman-style house that could have been built by Frank Lloyd Wright or the team of Greene and Greene back in their heyday. This house was clearly not that old, but it was a beautiful piece of architecture, and there was no question that it had been custom-built.

Mrs. McCutcheon met Gabby as she came up the steps to the house. Welcoming her, she led Gabby to the great room with its wall of windows exposing a panoramic view of the dense growth of trees in the backyard. Gabby couldn't help but ask lots of questions about the house and Mrs. McCutcheon clearly liked this young woman who seemed to understand the design, as well as know about the architects of the time.

After a tour of the house, they sat on the screened-in porch and enjoyed some iced tea. They started to talk about the property itself. "Mrs. McCutcheon, our plan is to build only eight or so houses on the property. The actual number will depend on the land itself and the location of the creek you mentioned. As I told you over the phone, my husband and I, along with our baby daughter will be building our personal home on the property, which will be one of the eight or so built. Were you able to find out how many acres are involved and whether or not you have a survey of the property?"

Looking embarrassed, Mrs. McCutcheon handed the file to Gabby. "I'm sorry, dear. Here, why don't you look this over for yourself, my eyes aren't so good anymore."

Reviewing the file, Gabby found that the entire property was ten acres, but that included the property upon which Mrs. McCutcheon's house sat. The survey showed the house but didn't define its acreage as a separate number. "Mrs. McCutcheon, I would like to know how much you are asking for the property, and if it would be possible for me to see it."

"Oh, of course, my dear. I can have my grandson come out and drive you around if you like. It's totally fenced in, at least it used to be. Tom always took care of making sure that sort of thing was done. I'm not sure about the price. In the file you'll see what Tom thought we should sell it for, but that was quite awhile ago. It probably needs to be appraised or something. I'm sure my grandson can have that done too, if you think you're interested. It would be very nice to have you so close by. I don't really know any of my neighbors anymore, and I'm not as young as I used to be."

"Would it be all right if I took a peek around the property now?"

"You just go ahead, dear. If you'll please drop back by after you're finished so I know you're safe. Then we can decide if you want any more information."

Gabby promised she would, and set out to explore the property on her own. The parcel was so overgrown from years of neglect, it was difficult for Gabby to determine where the creek was, or even where she was at any given moment. She loved the hills and the trees. It was going to be a challenge to save the setting, *but it couldn't be more perfect,* she thought.

Excited, she went back to Mrs. McCutcheon's. "I like the property very much, but there are some things which need to be considered. I'm going to go down to the land office to research the regulations related to subdividing it. There are other questions, of course, but I'm getting ahead of myself. Could your grandson make a photocopy of the survey for me, as well as any other pertinent information he might have?"

"Of course, my dear. I'll have him take care of that."

"Thank you for the tea and the lovely afternoon, Mrs. McCutcheon. I look forward to seeing you again."

Driving down the long driveway away from Mrs. McCutcheon's house, Gabby thought she had found the setting and hoped things would fall into place for her and Regency.

It wasn't easy. The property almost entirely surrounded Mrs. McCutcheon's house. It was going to be tricky to leave the trees around her house untouched, create a new street, and place the houses so they didn't encroach on their neighbors' privacy. While the parcel by law could have been divided up into ten lots, because of the positioning of Mrs. McCutcheon's house and land and because of the topography, it seemed that seven new houses were the most they could build there. Some of the lots would be larger than others and that made Gabby think she could successfully mix the smaller house idea with a couple larger than originally intended. It might make the entire development more of a hamlet than one of those new cookie-cutter type subdivisions.

Gabby met with the architects, outlining her ideas for the new subdivision. They named it "Pheasant Run," and Gabby loved the fact that this was the first group of houses she was going to totally oversee. The houses were different, and each one, while different in its layout, was designed to take maximum advantage of the large trees, offering each owner a very private setting.

The duplication of the living room and family room was eliminated as were the hallways found in a more traditional style house, allowing room for extra closets. The rooms were larger, including the bathrooms. The kitchens all had large center islands and none had four walls as found in your typical traditional house. Gabby made a point of putting in only top-of-the-line appliances as well as special custom touches, such as pasta sinks, chandeliers over the islands, and magnificent exhaust fans over the commercial stoves. The kitchens were truly a gourmet's delight.

After the first house was finished and decorated, Regency threw an open house for real estate agents which was extremely well received. Within ten days, all six of the houses had contracts on them. Gabby was amazed. They had sold out in *ten days!* Realtors were trying to convince Gabby and Jason to sell their personal home, the seventh of all the houses in the development. Mary and Uncle Tony were elated and wanted to use the same open-concept designs in their next subdivision. Gabby said she wasn't sure that was such a good idea but she would take the next week and think about it.

Because of the success at Pheasant Run and the continued strengthening of their real estate sales, Gabby knew Regency needed to decide what their next step would be. They just couldn't have their construction workers sitting around without anything to do.

Jason was delighted with Pheasant Run too. As it was now fall, real estate had fallen off somewhat, which made his life a little less hectic. He spent just as much time working though, explaining to Gabby it was important to keep his name out there so he would have a great spring and summer next year. To Gabby, it seemed as if Jason was finally happy. And, soon, they would be moving into their new home.

Gabby called another meeting of the Board. After everyone was settled, Gabby took the lead talking about how Regency was doing in general. "I've given a lot of thought about what Regency's next step should be. We have two options here. One, Regency could build another huge subdivision like Huntington Forest or, two, it could build smaller developments like Pheasant Run."

Uncle Tony was the first to jump in. "Why can't we build houses like Pheasant Run's in our next large subdivision?"

"The reason Pheasant Run was such a success is that it's not a typical subdivision, which is fundamentally what Huntington Forest is. Think about it, at Pheasant Run the lots were larger, the houses were not placed on the lots in rows facing the street -- the entire feel of the development was one of a small village, not a large community. People will pay a premium to have a custom home that's not like their neighbors, even if it's smaller.

Unfortunately, Thompsonville just doesn't have a large enough market for that price-point home. We can incorporate some of the ideas, combining rooms, for instance, but we can't do top-of-the-line things like we did in Pheasant Run in fifteen hundred houses or so. If we were to try to duplicate Pheasant Run on a large scale, I'm afraid that the higher costs necessary to make the houses custom would end up eating away any profits, assuming we can sell them. Oh, people would love them, but not enough would be able to afford them."

Mary asked, "Gabby, where do you come out on this?"

"Mom, Uncle Tony, I think the most practical choice for Regency now is to continue with larger developments, updating the interior layouts as we did in Phase Four of Huntington Forest. Should smaller pieces of property become available from time to time, we can build a more exclusive enclave á la Pheasant Run, but larger subdivisions should continue to be our main focus."

Reluctantly, Uncle Tony agreed, as did Mary, and the decision was made. Once again, the search was on for the right property; their next project scheduled to break ground in the spring of 1995. Gabby would talk to Jason as soon as she got home and ask him to begin looking through all the property listings.

Jason was glad to be involved in Regency's search for properties. He hadn't really thought about being on the commercial side of real estate, but this could be a big bonus for him if he could find properties for them from time to time. He was also anxious to move into their new home. Jason had staked out a room which would be his office as had Gabby, and he was looking forward to being able to have his own space. The move was scheduled for the following Tuesday and, even though they had missed the Thanksgiving deadline, both he and Gabby were looking forward to spending Christmas in their new home with Nicole.

Gabby and Mary went furniture shopping, selected paint colors and wallpaper and watched as Gabby's new house came close to being completed. The furniture and drapes would be delivered the following week, and then it was just a matter of settling in. Fortunately, Gabby had that week off during the holidays, closing Regency as was her father's tradition. Jason was planning on spending a good portion of that time at home as well, although he now wanted to concentrate on finding that property for Regency.

Mary was still going to have Christmas dinner at her house and, even though Brent would be home and Gabby would help when she could, she realized she needed help. Linda Bolan always raved about Ethel and how helpful she was to Linda when she had guests. So, this year, she finally broke down and asked Ethel if she was available to help her out. Ethel was delighted that she was able to do so, and Mary couldn't have been happier.

Ari was also home for the holidays. She spent a good portion of Gabby's week off helping her set up her new house. She was so excited for Gabby. The house was fantastic, the development had obviously done very well and Nicole was growing into such a beautiful baby girl. Ari was convinced that Gabby had the whole world on a string. While Jason was in and out, he spent most of the time Ari was around working in his office or out scouting properties. Gabby took Ari and Nicole over to Mrs. McCutcheon's house as she delivered a Christmas gift to her new neighbor. Mrs.

McCutcheon invited them all in and they spent a lovely hour chatting with one another while enjoying Christmas cookies and tea.

Mary wanted to continue watching Nicole even after they had moved. Gabby was certain that her mother wanted to be with Nicole every day but she was concerned that now that they weren't at Mary's house any longer, it would be too much of an imposition. She talked to her mother about this and eventually Mary came up with the solution. Apparently Ethel had told Mary she would be interested in doing some additional work for her if Mary needed the help. Since Ethel had helped Linda Bolan with Ari when she was young, perhaps she could stay with Nicole two or three days a week, and that would help everyone. Gabby would feel better if her mom had more free time for her friends during the week, and Ethel could use the additional income to help supplement her retirement income. It was a terrific solution. Ethel was enthusiastic and grateful that they had thought of her.

CHAPTER NINE

The holidays were over. Ari and Brent returned to their respective cities and schools and Gabby returned to Regency.

Only Jason hadn't seemed to change his routine after the holidays. He had found a large tract well beyond Clark's Corner which was a bit farther away than Regency usually liked to build, but it was becoming increasingly more difficult to find properties closer in. They continued to look for something closer to Thompsonville, but time was growing short and there didn't seem to be any other options if they were going to keep their crews busy.

Another agent in Jason's office found that the old Sturgis Estate, which was located in a very exclusive section of town, was being offered for sale. He did some research and determined that the property could be split into three additional lots, two if they situated the houses similar to those at Pheasant Run. Gabby ran the small piece of property by her mom and Uncle Tony. Both were excited that they could build two exceptional houses on that property, in addition to reselling the original estate house. Regency committed to that property, as well as the one past Clark's Corner and Regency was back in full swing for 1995.

Brent could hardly believe he was in his third and final year of law school. The three years had flown by. It had been both exhilarating and exhausting, and he had loved every minute of it. He had learned, well maybe not learned, but recognized, that he loved the research, the minutiae of the law. He was not the type to become a trial lawyer; the staging, the crowds, the theatrics, they were not for him. He also found that to be true in his personal life. Large parties were not to his taste, and he avoided social situations which led to small talk by generally small-minded people.

Stacy Cohen and Brent had been seeing each other since that New Year's Eve get-together in 1992 and enjoyed an easy-going relationship based upon mutual respect, a lively exchange of ideas, and a shared goal of improving everyday situations through the practice of law.

Both Stacy and Brent had received offers from some of the better law firms in New York, Washington, D.C., and several smaller cities. Brent was thinking long and hard about his choices. He had received an offer from the Boston firm where he had clerked after his first year of law school and also one from the D.C. firm where he spent his second summer.

Brent thought he would never want to live anywhere other than Boston, but he was having second thoughts. He loved Boston, no question, but the work at the law firm was fairly repetitive and probably would continue to be so. He couldn't envision himself doing the same thing for the next forty years of his life.

On the other hand, the firm in Washington was an international law firm with both business and clients from all over the world. The opportunity to practice in many different areas of international law was of great interest to him. He loved the learning process and believed that the D.C. firm, with its diversity, might offer more in that respect.

And, too, Stacy and he had spent a great deal of time touring D.C. during their second year clerkships. They had visited the monuments, the many buildings of the Smithsonian and the art galleries. Then there were the bistros on 19th Street, Connecticut Avenue and, of course, Georgetown and Old Town Alexandria, and they hadn't had nearly enough time to see everything. While Washington wasn't Boston, it was a great town with a strong international flavor.

Graduation wasn't far away and it was time to make their decisions. Ultimately, it came down to the fact that the offers made by the D.C. firms to each of them were far more interesting career-wise than those made by other firms. Brent accepted the offer made by the international law firm where he had clerked and Stacy was headed for a boutique law firm specializing in mergers and acquisitions.

They would be packing up and moving in just a few months' time and were headed down to Washington in April in order to find themselves apartments. While their new positions started in June, they knew that their summer months would be spent primarily studying for the bar.

As the routine of everyday life began again, everyone's schedule took shape, that is, everyone's except Jason's. Gabby was spending lots of time with the architects. Gabby named the two lots on the Sturgis Estate, "Sturgis Place" and "Sturgis Ridge." The larger development out past Clark's Corner, to be developed in four phases, was named "Ashton Park Estates."

Gabby planned that the two new Sturgis houses would be top-of-the-line, larger than Pheasant Run's houses and would, accordingly, be in the upper price range for Thompsonville. This meant she had to hit the nail on the head for these two designs. She also discovered that the original Sturgis Estate manor house was not in the best of shape – it, too, would require renovating and updating if they were to get top dollar for it.

Gabby wanted to rework some of the older plans used in Huntington Forest as they were the basic concept for the new Ashton Park development. Without going super high-end, Gabby wanted to upgrade what was economically sound, while using some of the more contemporary open floor plans used in Pheasant Run. Redesigning the layouts while still maintaining the approximate sale price, would require a great deal of work.

When Gabby was finally able to finish her work and get home at night, Jason was seldom there. Ethel had started making dinner for Gabby, like Mary did when she was there with Nicole. When Jason did get home, Gabby would ask if he wanted any dinner and what he was working on, knowing there was very little real estate activity in the deep throes of winter. Jason would have something to eat on occasion, but rarely had an answer to Gabby's questions. She was certain she smelled liquor on his breath and even thought there was a hint of perfume once or twice. Jason hardly paid any attention to Nicole. Once again, Gabby began to see his darker side.

After several weeks of this continued behavior, Gabby knew she needed to get to the bottom of it. "What's going on with you Jason?"

He stood back with a look of hatred in his eyes. "Don't you ever question me. What I do is none of your damn business."

Gabby was so shocked by his retort that, without thinking, she stood up to him, demanding, "What do you mean by that? I'm your wife and the mother of your child. I'm really tired of your never being home, your complete avoidance of Nicole and your apparently newly acquired habit of having too much to drink – wherever it is you do that."

Jason's eyes turned from contempt to loathing as he yelled at her. "Shut up, bitch," smashing her across the face. He picked up his coat and stomped out of the house leaving Gabby in tears, devastated.

Calming down after the tears, Gabby became angry. The more she thought about what he had just done, the more furious -- livid, actually, she became. She knew that she couldn't live like this and, while she normally deferred to him in order to keep the peace, that acts of violence would not be tolerated. Gabby seldom backed down from anyone or anything, but she now admitted to herself that he frightened her. And, she didn't know how to face him. *They had,* she thought, *bridged the gap of his lack of career, his inability of being able to contribute to the family as well as their living with her mother. What was wrong now?* These were warning signs that, in retrospect, she should have recognized. He clearly needed professional help. *How could she get him to see that? And, what should she do in the meantime?*

Jason didn't come home until the middle of the night. He slept on the sofa in his office and didn't get up to say anything to Gabby before she left for work.

Gabby likewise didn't say anything to anyone about Jason, his new habits or their fight. He started coming home earlier in the day, but went directly to his office. Gabby tried to talk to him about seeing a psychologist, but he merely dismissed her suggestions. He didn't seem to care much what Gabby was doing and continued to ignore Nicole. He no longer fought with her, and a truce, bordering on indifference, enveloped their relationship. After a couple of months of this, he fell back into the same pattern of coming in late, drunk and belligerent. She had stopped caring.

Ethel knew there was something terribly wrong. It seemed that the days Mary was there, Jason made more of an effort to show up somewhat sober. Ethel had seen enough. She convinced herself that she needed to intercede, and made a point of going over to Mary's house one night and telling her everything she had seen.

Mary also sensed there was some tension, but had no idea things were as bad as Ethel painted them. Now that Mary knew about things at Gabby's house, it explained to her why Gabby had been so tired and out-of-sorts lately. She knew she was going to have to talk to Gabby.

Gabby hadn't talked to Ari in almost a month. She'd withdrawn into herself not knowing what to say to her best friend and, not wanting to be a burden, thought it best if she just tried to work it out by herself. The problem with this tactic, she was beginning to understand, was that it just wasn't working. The longer it went on, the more depressed she became, and the less able she was to handle anything except work.

Coming home late one night in April, Gabby found Jason waiting for her in the family room. Gabby thought, *Good. Maybe we can clear the air.*

Jason poured a glass of wine for Gabby and, as she sat down, said, "Gabby, I want a divorce. I've hired an attorney and we'll be filing next week. I think it would be best if you moved back home with your mother so that she can take care of Nicole and you won't have to worry about the house."

Gabby laughed. It was a nervous laugh of utter disbelief. As she gained control, Gabby started to get angry. "Jason, there is no way I'm leaving this house. As for you, it's almost a relief to hear you say you're planning a divorce. That's all I have to say right now. Anything more, you'll hear from my attorney. Goodnight and Goodbye."

"Well, I have no intention of leaving the house either." Stomping off to his office, Jason slammed the door loudly as Gabby quietly sat and sipped her glass of wine.

After a few minutes, Gabby checked on Nicole and then went back out to the family room to call her mother. Reaching for the phone, Gabby thought, *How am I going to tell her this?* but dialed knowing somehow the words would come.

They came slowly at first. As Gabby told her mother the events of the past hour, Mary sat quietly with her mouth open listening to her daughter.

"Gabby, I think you and Nicole need to come home immediately."

"Mom, I can't. It's not really practical with the baby and all her things and, besides, you'll be here first thing in the morning anyway."

"Absolutely not. I'm on my way over now. I'll just pack an overnight case and be right there."

Gabby didn't even try to talk her mother out of it. Right now she needed her mother and needed to be held.

Mary called Ethel, told her what was happening, and asked her if she too could be at the house first thing the next morning. Mary's thinking was that, *Two people besides Gabby would be better than just one.*

Mary and Gabby sat on the couch in the family room for quite some time. Mary told Gabby, "Honey, you're going to need to get a lawyer if Jason is planning on filing papers next week."

"Well, we have the lawyers who represent Regency. They're quite good."

"They're good for what they do for Regency, Gabby, but you need a lawyer who specializes in divorce. I'll ask around. Also, you should ask Regency's law firm if they have anyone they can refer you to."

Gabby started to cry and told her mother she needed to go to bed. Mary wanted to stay with her daughter, but Gabby wanted to be alone. She cried herself to sleep and was surprised to find it was 9:20 when she awoke the next morning. She went to check on Nicole and was gratified to see both her mother and Ethel playing with Nicole as if nothing had happened. Mary told Gabby that Jason had left, but said he would be home later.

Gabby knew she was in no shape to go to work. She called Regency's attorneys and was given the name of a local divorce lawyer. Gabby called him and they set an appointment for later that afternoon. Gabby returned home after meeting with the lawyer and told her mother. "There has to be another divorce lawyer in this town." Mary went to look for the yellow pages, while Gabby sat and played with Nicole, trying to gather herself.

Thinking it was a relatively warm spring day, perhaps what she needed was a walk. Bundling up Nicole, she began to push her around the neighborhood in her stroller. Gabby soon realized she had ended up in front of Mrs. McCutcheon's house and that the lovely old lady was standing at her open front door waving at Gabby and Nicole. Waving back, Gabby started to push Nicole back toward their house, but Mrs. McCutcheon waved them in.

Gabby really didn't want to talk to anyone right then, but she knew Mrs. McCutcheon seldom saw anyone, and it would make her happy to see Nicole. Gabby picked Nicole up from the stroller and went up the stairs to Mrs. McCutcheon's front door. Nicole was happy with the cookie the old lady gave her and Gabby could see that she was being eyed carefully by this wonderfully astute woman.

"Gabby, I might be old and can't do some things, but I can tell there's something off about you today. Are you all right?"

Gabby couldn't hold it together. Her nerves were too raw, and the memory of Jason's words too cutting. She started to cry almost uncontrollably. Mrs. McCutcheon found a box of tissue and handed it to Gabby, sitting down on the sofa next to her. She leaned Gabby into her small body and held her as she cried. Nicole crawled over to her mother and grabbed onto her leg, not really knowing what was wrong with her mommy, but holding on for dear life. Gabby gathered herself and reached down for Nicole, held her for a while and then set her back down on the floor to play with the blocks Mrs. McCutcheon kept for her. Gabby then told this wonderful old lady about her situation, saying it had just happened, and apologizing for not being more in control of her emotions.

Mrs. McCutcheon listened to her new young friend and her heart went out to her. As if it were meant to be, Mrs. McCutcheon asked, "Have you found a lawyer yet? Because if you haven't, perhaps you should talk to my granddaughter in Pittsburgh. She's a very good lawyer and I know she can practice here, too. She actually lives about half way between here and Pittsburgh, and I think you two would get along very well together." Mrs. McCutcheon went over to her desk and looked up her granddaughter's numbers, wrote them all down along with her name on a piece of paper, which she gave to Gabby.

Thanking her profusely, Gabby realized they needed to get back to the house before her mother started to worry about them. Waving goodbye, she and Nicole headed off in the direction of their house.

Mary was glad to see her daughter and granddaughter head up the drive a few minutes later. Both Ethel and Mary had been concerned about Gabby and Nicole's long absence. When Gabby and Nicole were inside, Gabby told her mother about her visit with Mrs. McCutcheon and that her granddaughter was a lawyer.

"Good. A woman lawyer might be very good in this type of situation and, truthfully, Thompsonville doesn't have much to offer by way of a good divorce attorney. At least not as far as I can tell."

"Mom, I'd like to go call her now. If you'll excuse me, I'll make the call from the study where I can talk without you-know-who hearing any of the conversation." Nicole was only ten months old, so it wasn't as if she could understand the conversation. But Gabby was certain she would be able to interpret her sadness and anger, and she didn't want her daughter upset.

Carolyn Maxwell took Gabby's call immediately after her secretary told her she had been referred by her grandmother in Thompsonville. Gabby gave the attorney a brief synopsis of her problem and liked Carolyn's immediate understanding of the situation and it's urgency. While Gabby told Carolyn she would be able to meet her in her office in Pittsburgh, Carolyn said that she was planning on being at home in the morning and, if Gabby would like to meet her half way, they could sit down and get to know each other over a cup of coffee and see if there was some way in which Carolyn might be of help.

Gabby immediately felt better. Later that night after Ethel had left and well before Jason came in, Mary and Gabby called Brent in New Haven. Brent said he had been trying to reach Mary since last night, but there had been no answer at home. Relaying the new developments to Brent, there seemed to be recognizable anxiety in his voice. From everything they were telling him, he had no doubt that this guy just wasn't any good for his sister. Being so far away, Brent felt helpless and wondered whether his mother would be strong enough to shoulder his sister's devastation. As they spoke, Brent became increasingly convinced that this divorce was the best thing that could happen.

Gabby told Brent about Carolyn Maxwell, Mrs. McCutcheon's granddaughter, and that they were going to meet in the morning. She also told him that she had met with the attorney Regency's counsel had suggested, but she wasn't very comfortable with him.

Brent wrote down Carolyn Maxwell's name, planning to check her out. Even though he wasn't there, perhaps this was something he could do to help. Brent was furious. He knew he had to calm himself down if he was going to be of any help to his sister. *How did he miss seeing this coming? The guy was just too slick.* Brent asked them what they really knew about Jason?

Mary answered, "I never told Gabby this. I'm sorry honey. But, at one point, Uncle Tony had his doubts about Jason and checked him out with his friends on the police force. He even had TJ follow him for a couple of weeks."

"So," he finished for her, "they didn't find anything that led Uncle Tony to believe he wasn't the good guy he portrayed himself to be."

Mary confirmed that and asked Brent, "Is there anything you can do?"

Gabby apologized over and over again that this was happening so close to his graduation, but she just didn't know how to deal with it.

"I need to think about this for a day or so and you should keep things to yourselves. In the meantime, please write down everything you know about Jason and send it to me." He was angry with himself he hadn't done this earlier, but was somewhat mollified by the fact that Uncle Tony had.

Brent thought about Gabby's situation that night and the following day. As a matter of fact, he thought of little else. He asked Stacy to meet him and laid out what his sister and mother told him, wondering out loud if she had any ideas.

Stacy immediately said, "Check him out. There's something wrong here with someone who has no past. You're telling me this guy has no family, no friends, no anything? It smell's bad and I just don't believe it." Stacy wouldn't let up until Brent agreed he would look into Jason again, once he received the information from his mother and sister.

Gabby tossed and turned the entire night and awoke early the next morning as the ugly reality of the day's task filled her mind. Having had enough, she got out of bed and wandered into the kitchen, brewed coffee and sat, looking out the window as the beautiful trees enveloping their lot became better defined as night turned to dawn. It was quiet now, the birds just beginning to awaken. Even Nicole was still asleep.

Gabby tried to figure out how it had all come to this? She and Jason had been so in love. Was it just too much for him too fast? Believing this was a very strong possibility, Gabby felt a weight of responsibility for the destruction of her marriage she didn't want to accept. Of course, there was her job. It took so much of her time away from him, and then Nicole coming along so fast. She wouldn't trade Nicole for anything. But had Gabby contributed to this as much as she was beginning to believe?

She then heard the cooing and other telltale sounds coming from Nicole's room letting everyone know she was awake and ready to get out of her crib. She heard her mother's voice as she started a good morning dialogue with Nicole and realized she now only had a few minutes to say her own good mornings before hurrying to dress in order to meet Carolyn Maxwell.

Gabby was a few minutes early and thought she may as well be seated. Carolyn Maxwell had told her she would be in the last booth on the left of the restaurant by the windows. Gabby was surprised there was a young woman already sitting in the booth and considered taking another one when the young woman arose and walked up to Gabby with her hand out, introducing herself simply as Carolyn.

Gabby thought, *This can't be right. I'm only twenty-one, but this girl/ woman looks like she's only nineteen.* Gabby shook Carolyn's hand and found herself being steered toward the specified booth with a gentle hand on her back.

Gabby and Carolyn sat across from one another and Carolyn started making small talk, recommending the French toast rather than the pancakes, and generally easing Gabby into a more relaxed state of mind. They chatted about Carolyn's grandmother and how Gabby had come to know her, about Nicole and about Regency. It wasn't until after they had finished their breakfasts that Carolyn said, "You mentioned that you have a problem. What can I do to help?"

Gabby began by telling Carolyn everything she could remember, including the smash across the mouth, Jason's total indifference to Nicole, his career problems, everything. She also told Carolyn that Jason wanted her to move back with her mother where they had been living up until about five months ago.

Carolyn asked many questions, including whether or not Gabby wanted this divorce, what their financial situation was, including their incomes, in whose name the house was deeded, and the like. She also said "It doesn't sound to me that he's interested in getting custody of Nicole, but what do you think?"

Gabby was shaken. Up until that moment, there wasn't even a small inkling in her mind that Jason would want custody of Nicole. *But, oh my God . . . .*

Carolyn told her she was sorry she had to bring it up, but it was necessary for her to know everything he might want in order for her to better know how to handle this case, if Gabby wanted her to handle it. Gabby was clearly at a loss for words.

Carolyn started to talk about what normally happens in divorce situations and assured her that children were usually awarded to the mother. She further stated that because Gabby was the major breadwinner in the family, this too would help. She talked for quite a while and finally Gabby began to relax, recognizing that Carolyn was bringing the custody issue up because it was a possibility, but generally not the norm.

Gabby and Carolyn talked for nearly three hours. When Gabby was ready to leave she told Carolyn she wouldn't want anyone else handling her divorce except her, and how very grateful she would be if Carolyn accepted the case.

"I wouldn't have it any other way."

Carolyn thought Gabby was now okay to drive the distance back home so, with that, they got up and started for the door. Outside in the parking lot, Gabby again thanked Carolyn and then gave her a quick hug and walked away to her car for the drive home.

When Gabby arrived back at the house, Jason had left for the day, and her mother and daughter were playing on the floor. Gabby told her mother about her meeting. "I really liked her, Mom. I asked her to represent me and now, I guess, I'm in the process of getting a divorce. I never thought that, as a nice Catholic girl, I would ever be in this position."

Mary blinked, thinking, *How did I miss this? I need to talk to Father Frank.* Focusing back on the conversation, she said, "Brent called. He told me to tell you he'd looked into Carolyn Maxwell's reputation, law school and general legal skills and that, 'This gal's a shark.' Apparently this is a good thing, so I'm very glad you like her."

Gabby was thinking, *Brent must have the wrong person. This young attorney is probably just out of law school, so she can't be much of a shark. But, that's okay. I like her anyway.*

"Oh, Mom, Carolyn told me that 'under no circumstances am I to move out of this house.' So, for the time being, I'm afraid you'll need to come here when you can to help with Nicole. I need to think about going back to Regency too, but not today. I'm just worn out from this morning. Would you mind if I went in and took a nap?"

Gabby slept fitfully. She really didn't think that Jason wanted custody of Nicole, but the fear of it permeated her very being. She knew there would be many more meetings with Carolyn and there would probably be other things she hadn't thought about which might come into play. It dawned on her that afternoon that she really had no idea about Jason's financial situation. She knew he had saved some money from his time in the Army and that the GI Bill was paying for his classes, but how much did he really have? Was he financially capable of taking care of Nicole if he wanted to? And, then again, the guilt. *What have I done?*

When Jason arrived home that night, Gabby handed him one of Carolyn's business cards as she had told her to do. "This is my attorney. In the future, any communications regarding our divorce should be directed to her. Please inform your attorney. And, oh yes, just so there's no misunderstanding, Nicole and I will be staying in this house all through the divorce as well as long after it's over, so you need to find another place to live."

CHAPTER TEN

Divorce is debilitating. Gabby's proceeded at, what seemed to her, a snail's pace. She went back to work a couple of days a week, but still wasn't up to her old self. Clearly the divorce was taking its toll. Gabby, Mary and Ethel, along with some of Gabby's relatives and Mrs. McCutcheon, kept Nicole happy and generally away from all the negativity it involved. Nicole was a very happy child and was working on her first steps. When she stood up at the coffee table on her own and took even just one step alone and then fell, she would clap her hands as if to say, "good girl!"

Jason refused to move out of the house. He apparently had been told not to do so, just as Gabby had been. Jason's lawyer, a local man from Thompsonville, filed the papers and, of course, once they were a matter of public record, as is usually the case in a small town, everyone knew. Jason had filed on the basis of "irreconcilable differences," which was the standard. It kind of left everything on the table if one wished to pursue contributing factors, but if both parties ended up getting what they wanted, they could both walk away without airing their dirty laundry. However, Jason didn't just want to walk away, he wanted to walk away *rich*. In fact, *very rich*. He was asking for alimony, lost wages, partial ownership of Regency, the house, and sole custody of Nicole.

Carolyn called Gabby to arrange a meeting in Thompsonville? "Gabby, he's asking for the moon. But stay calm -- I'll be there in a couple of hours. In the meantime, let's keep this to ourselves until we have our talk."

Gabby knew it was bad. If Carolyn was on her way down to Thompsonville, it must be awful. Immediately her heart began pounding at an abnormal rate, knowing he was asking for custody of Nicole. Beside herself, Gabby barely held together until Carolyn arrived.

After meeting Mary, Carolyn suggested that it would be a good time to take Nicole out for a walk. Maybe they could stop by her grandmother's for cookies? As Mary pushed Nicole down the drive in her stroller, Gabby turned from the window. "He wants Nicole, doesn't he?"

Carolyn took Gabby by the hand and, without responding, led her to the sofa in the family room. "Gabby, he's asked for everything." As Carolyn laid out the entire list of wants, Carolyn had to repeatedly reassure Gabby that this was just the beginning of the negotiations and, from everything Gabby had told her, she believed he was using Nicole as a tool to get the things he really wanted. In other words, everything else.

They talked for over an hour and finally Gabby began to see that this was Jason's wish list and Carolyn was right, he probably wasn't going to get everything he wanted. Further, Carolyn said they were going to fight this aggressively, and then repeated what she said earlier about the court seldom giving custody, particularly that of a baby, to the father unless there was some reason such as drugs or physical abuse. Carolyn stayed as long as she could, but finally told Gabby she needed to get back to Pittsburgh.

When Mary saw Carolyn's car drive away through the trees, she thanked Mrs. McCutcheon for letting them stop by, bundled up Nicole and headed home as quickly as she could. Whatever it was Carolyn had come to say, Mary knew Gabby was going to need her.

All Gabby could say when her mother and Nicole came in the door was that she needed to lie down for a while. Gabby leaned over to whisper in her mother's ear, "Jason has asked for sole custody of Nicole, along with everything else he thinks he can get, including part of Regency." Mary tried not to look shocked, but it was clear on her face that this was way beyond anything either of them imagined could happen.

Gabby went directly to bed. It didn't matter that it was only late afternoon. She was incapable of managing anything more today. Tomorrow she would try to think rationally about what Carolyn said and what Jason demanded. She knew, for instance, that Regency was totally out of the question. *Where the hell did he get the idea that he could get any portion of Regency?* Certainly he knew that even she didn't have an ownership interest in the company. Maybe he thought her mother would just roll over if he's holding out for custody of Nicole. *Lord, what a mess!*

Gabby thought about everything Jason had asked for. Other than Regency, she and Jason held all their other assets jointly, including the house, the furniture, and bank accounts. That is, all their bank accounts except Jason's cash stash from his time in the Army. She knew there was a possibility he could get some sort of alimony. She was going to have to leave that, along with the house and their other assets, up to Carolyn. Gabby wished she had something to fight him with but, the truth was, she really didn't care about anything other than Nicole.

Carolyn was in the middle of preparing the Reply to the Petition for Divorce that had been filed ten days earlier, when her secretary buzzed, announcing a call from someone named Brent Romano. Carolyn thought, *What is this?* wondering whether she should even take the call. Picking up the receiver, she answered "Carolyn Maxwell."

Brent started right in. "Ms. Maxwell, I'm Gabby's brother. I've talked to Gabby. I told her I had some information about Jason and the divorce, and she asked me to call you directly."

Carolyn was intrigued. "You know, of course, that I can't say anything to you. But if you have something you wish to tell me, I'll be glad to listen."

And, glad she was. Brent had decided to have Mr. Jason Marsh checked out again – Stacy's advice had been right on. "I made some inquiries about private investigators used by my law firm and, while most of them don't involve themselves with this kind of investigation, I was given the names of several others who came highly recommended." Apparently in the mid-1990's, private investigators no longer needed to be local. While a local presence was sometimes necessary, most of the work could be done through data bases available to almost anyone who knew how to use the internet.

"I hired a firm by the name of I Spy Investigations and, just today, received a call from one of the investigators, passing along the firm's findings. They're sending me a hard copy, which I'll copy and pass along to you.

To start with, Jason Marsh isn't this guy's real name. Somewhere along the way he found a death notice or worked in a mortuary or something, but came up with a deceased boy whose name was Jason Marsh and obtained his death certificate. Then, our Jason applied for and received the real Jason's birth certificate, a social security number, and various other pieces of identification, assuming the deceased's identity. The investigators think this happened around our Jason's age of seventeen or so, but clearly sometime before he became an adult. Even private investigators can't get into juvenile records, they're sealed. So, their thinking is that he did something very wrong to want to change his name. His real name, by the way, is John Marshall, and that's the name under which he got married."

"He did what? Did he get a divorce?"

"No, but let me go on. Believe it or not, there's more. Jason or rather, John, did serve in the U.S. Army using the Jason Marsh name, which is how he had all that back pay available to him as well as GI benefits.

John, on the other hand, is still married to the girl he married using his real name when he was nineteen back in Virginia. They have two kids and she lives in a trailer park not too far from John's family. The whole string of them, including the wife, has police records, mostly involving theft, but John and his wife specialize in fraud and extortion. The investigators somehow got their hands on telephone records showing communication between John/Jason and his wife all the while he's been living in Thompsonville. So, clearly, she had to know what was going on and this seems to fit in well with the extortion charges for which they were under suspicion.

I'm not certain how you would like to handle this, and I'm not going to begin to make any recommendations. Please use this as you will. From what Gabby and my mother tell me about you, I'm certain that whatever you chose to do, will be the correct course."

Carolyn didn't find herself dumbstruck often, but this was certainly an exception. "This will teach me. Gabby told me your uncle had already checked out Jason through the police and had him followed, to no avail. Normally I do have someone investigated by a firm I use locally, but I trusted that the police would find anything there was to find. Perhaps my firm wouldn't have found anything either, I'll never know, but I can't thank you enough for all your help. I'll be glad to see the hard copy of your investigator's report and they'll probably end up with a new client, me, after this is all said and done. Would it be possible for you to call your firm back and ask them to overnight a copy of the report directly to me, I would really appreciate it? Thank you again so very much Brent. I'm sure you just saved your sister a whole boatload of heartache."

Carolyn received the investigator's report the following morning and it said precisely what Brent said it would. She thought, *This is going to be like taking a howitzer to a duel.* There was no way Jason/John could get out of this one and, with the attorney he had representing him, well, it was all but over. Carolyn called Jason's attorney that afternoon asking for a meeting between he and his client and she and Gabby. He wanted to know what it was all about and she simply said she wanted to iron out some of the details, letting him think this was going to be a negotiation. Carolyn spent several hours after reading the report dictating documents which she planned to use in the meeting.

Gabby understood the reason for the meeting, but wasn't so certain she wanted to be in the same room with Jason for this little tet-a-tet. Knowing it was something she had to do, she told Carolyn she would make herself available whenever it was scheduled.

Jason received the call from his attorney telling him that Gabby's attorney wanted to have a meeting with all four of them. He also told Jason that he believed this was going to be a settlement meeting and it could be the big ending he was looking for.

Jason was ebullient. He thought about all the times he had to make nice for that little bitch and suck up to her mother and uncle. He was so proud of the way he had done it. The elaborate weekend he had planned for their engagement, the nudging on the elopement, knowing that she was so tired from trying to run Regency she couldn't stand up to the pressure, the "Oh, I can't go to school and pay the bills and take care of my family," everything he felt compelled to do to get to this point.

He was certain Gabby would give him anything so that he wouldn't take that awful kid away from her. That meant the house; she'd walk away, he knew. He'd get some cash, probably alimony, too -- Gabby earned more than he did. And there was a chance that Mary might give him some small percentage of Regency, but he really didn't care much about that. He really wanted that house. He'd sell it and buy *his* wife a new house, getting her and those two snotty kids of theirs out of the trailer park. That was the payday he'd been working for. He'd bank the money so he could pull this scheme again. It had worked beautifully, although next time he had to figure out a way to make it work faster. This had been entirely too much work. That bitch was going to find out what a fool he'd played her for, and he couldn't wait.

The meeting was scheduled for Friday morning at 10:00 in the main conference room of Regency's headquarters. No one was late. Jason looked squeaky clean and all done up in his best suit. His attorney looked like a tired one-horse-town lawyer. Carolyn and Gabby watched them enter the building from their vantage point in Gabby's office.

Gabby sensed that something big was about to happen. Carolyn had told her that she had discovered some information about Jason which would make him back down in his demands, all of them. So, while Gabby was unaware of the specifics -- she told Carolyn she really didn't want to know them, as long as she walked away with Nicole -- she trusted Carolyn was going to make him back down, she would get her divorce, and she and Nicole would be free from him, even though he was still Nicole's father.

Carolyn's strategy was to let Jason and his attorney wait in the conference room until 10:15 or so, wondering what was about to happen. They were fidgeting in their seats as Gabby and Carolyn walked in and took their seats across from the two men.

Jason's attorney waited in the deafening silence and, finally unable to control himself, "blinked first," as they say, asking, "Well, what do you have to offer?"

Carolyn didn't like this man much, so she was going to take a great deal of pleasure in watching him squirm while she hammered Jason/John. Carolyn said to Jason's attorney as she pulled some small stacks of papers from her briefcase, "I'm not certain you know what a bad boy your client has been."

The attorney looked at his client and Jason just looked back at him, shrugging, as if to say, *I don't know what she's talking about.*

Carolyn placed a stack of papers in front of Gabby and slid one over to Jason and one to his attorney. Jason, in his smug and supercilious manner, thought this was the written offer Gabby was making so, assuredly, he turned them squarely in front of him and began to read. He was barely down the first page of the private investigator's report when he began to sink lower into his chair. The attorney had been reading too and was now looking at his client as if he were some unknown monster.

Jason said, "Where'd you get this rubbish? None of this stuff is true. What're you trying to pull here?"

Carolyn thought, *Ah, the true colors coming out.* She waited as Jason and the attorney both finished reading all the papers in front of them.

Quietly, but firmly, Carolyn said, "We can send you to jail for this. It is called 'extortion,' among other things and, trust me, I have checked with the District Attorney and it is criminal and prosecutable. You, young man, have a choice here. You can walk away from this marriage with nothing, and I *mean nothing, zero,* or we can press charges against you in criminal court."

"Well, you can't do that" said Jason. "Tell her, I was married to her and I'm entitled to alimony and at least half of everything. And, don't forget that kid."

Gabby cringed and grabbed Carolyn's knee under the table. Carolyn patted Gabby's hand assuringly and continued to wait for Jason's attorney to respond.

Jason's attorney turned to his client as if seeing him for the very first time. "If this is true, there is no way you are ever going to get anything from this woman. You'll be lucky if she doesn't throw you in jail even if you decide to walk away. I suggest you do whatever it is Ms. Maxwell tells you to do."

Carolyn pulled out several other stacks of paper and Jason said, "What's this now?"

Carolyn again slid one over to Jason and one to his attorney as well as one over to Gabby. "This is the Agreement you are going to sign giving up all rights to any property, cash or otherwise, held jointly in Gabby's and your name. This is not negotiable. It also states that you recognize you have no claim on any of Regency's stock or assets, because they were never part of any property held by you and your wife jointly, or even by her, severally."

"I'm not signing that. As a matter of fact, I'm not signing anything. If she doesn't give me the house and alimony, I'll take Nicole and she'll never see her again." With a nod and a humph, Jason crossed his arms and sat resolutely in his chair.

"Jason," Carolyn said calmly, "that's just not going to happen. In addition to the Agreement in front of you, I have prepared a document here which states that you relinquish any and all rights to the child known as Nicole Marsh and further that you impregnated her mother solely in order to use the child as leverage in any divorce proceedings."

"But, I'm her father."

"Oh, you are. No question about that. However, what good will that do you while you're in jail. You see, not only can we prosecute you for extortion, you have also committed bigamy and, let's not forget, that your wife, and I mean your first wife, aided and abetted in this whole fiasco. Not only will you be going to jail, she's going too.

Then there's the matter of lying to the government. You see, you enlisted in the armed services of the United States using a fake name and with a prior record, which you lied about on your application for service. Are you getting the picture here? Your past has caught up with you big time? I don't think you want the Federal government in on this, do you?

If you're not in jail when Nicole comes of age, perhaps she'll agree to see you then. In the meantime, you sign these papers, you sick son of a bitch, before I no longer offer you a choice."

When Jason heard the Federal government mentioned, he knew he was licked. He sighed and signed both papers. Jason's attorney signed as Witness and couldn't wait to get out of the conference room and out of Carolyn's reach.

Carolyn added that all his belongings had been packed up from the house and that he could pick up the boxes on the way out. "You are never to set foot in or near that house again, the locks have been changed and we have a restraining order against you as well. An officer is outside the conference room in order to serve it as you leave. If you attempt to contact Gabby, Nicole, Mary or any other member of Gabby's family or her friends, if she even sees you or hears that you are in the area, we *will* prosecute you."

Jason just glanced at Gabby and almost spitting, said, "I should've gotten something for all the miserable time I had to spend with you." He then turned and stormed out, banging the door against the wall.

Gabby was amazed. "Is it over, is it truly over?" she asked Carolyn.

"It is and we couldn't have done it without your brother's help." Carolyn explained how Brent had gone out and hired a professional investigator who was able to find out far more than the usual skip-tracer, even more it seemed than the police had been able to find out when Uncle Tony had asked for their help. "You see, sometimes people, if they knew how to look, could find out who was deceased and steal their identity. This was far easier years ago. Now, many of the loopholes that allowed that to happen, have been closed, but Jason found one before then and you see what he was capable of doing."

"Brent told me some of it before I asked him to call you. I knew there was a first wife, but I certainly didn't know they were still married. I didn't know a lot of it. Frankly at this point, I don't care. I don't care about it or him anymore. He's out of my life and I'm only moving forward from now on. I have my daughter; my mother and I will regain our sanity, and we'll have peace once again."

Gabby embraced Carolyn and couldn't let go for the longest time as she tried to stifle her tears of relief. "I'm certainly going to owe my brother a big one for this, but thank God for family and friends, including their lawyers. May I take you to lunch and celebrate, maybe call your grandmother to join us?"

"You know, I'd like that," and off they went.

CHAPTER ELEVEN

It was June and everything was green again. Gabby was settling into life without Jason, which meant without strife. Nicole turned one and was into everything. She was bright and inquisitive, just as Gabby had been, and she brought a smile to everyone as she seemed to enjoy every day and what happened in it.

It seemed that everything was easier. Regency, and its attendant work schedule, was still extremely busy, but the stress wasn't there. They had started building Phase One of Ashton Park Estates and had held their first open house two weeks earlier. The new open floor plans were well received, but it was still too early to tell how that would translate into sales. Gabby hired a young woman to take over for her at the seminars and deal directly with the real estate agents in their marketing efforts. It was Gabby's original marketing concept which had worked so well for Regency, and the one Jason had continued while Gabby was pregnant with Nicole.

The big news seemed to be that HRH was coming back to Thompsonville with a handsome, very wealthy young man with whom she had been seen on the Continent. All this by way of articles in The *Sentinel*, which were, for the most part, reprints of other papers' stories. The whole town was atwitter. Apparently Hiz Honor and Mrs. Hill were throwing a huge party at the country club so all their friends could meet this young man and reportedly many of Harriet's jet setting friends were also to be in attendance.

As Gabby read this in the paper, all she could think was, *My, my, all this right here in River City,* paraphrasing a line from one of those old movies her mother watched, The Music Man. Gabby had no illusions about being invited, but wished she could be a fly on the wall for this one.

Ari had arrived home in late May in time to help celebrate Nicole's first birthday. She'd decided not to stay in Chicago that summer and work as she had the previous two years. She was going to take the summer off, maybe take a trip to Italy or France before her graduation next spring and then, hopefully, start her career, whatever that turned out to be. Ari couldn't believe the change she saw in Gabby now that the divorce had gone through.

Mary in the meantime had been talking to Father Frank. Mary's concern was Gabby's and Nicole's status in the eyes of the Church. Since Gabby hadn't been married by a Priest or in the Church, was she a married woman or had she lived in sin? Was Nicole Catholic? Mary didn't think so; she hadn't been baptized. And, now that Gabby was divorced, was that recognized? Furthermore, would Nicole be considered illegitimate?

Father Frank assured Mary that Gabby would unquestionably be welcomed back to the Church and further that Nicole was able to be baptized there. Father Frank even told Mary he was looking forward to performing the ceremony.

Gabby quickly set the date and asked Ari to be Nicole's Godmother and Brent to be her Godfather. It was a glorious day and now that that was settled, Gabby's life was truly her own again.

Gabby was surprised to see a hand-addressed -- calligraphy no less -- cream-colored envelope on the kitchen island when she arrived home one night from work. That evening she had become involved with Nicole, talking to her and watching her dance around the room, then sitting down to dinner with her and Ethel, the envelope slipped her mind. What a blessing Ethel had been and Nicole seemed to be thriving in both Ethel's and her mother's care during the day while Gabby was at Regency.

As Gabby was putting Nicole down for the night and Ethel was about to leave for the day, the telephone rang. Gabby kissed Nicole goodnight and waved goodbye to Ethel as she took the receiver from Ethel's hand.

"Gabby," Ari asked, "did you get any invitations in the mail today?"

"I don't think so. Oh, wait, there *is* a fancy envelope here, I just haven't had time to open it yet. Why?"

"Just open it."

As Gabby did so, Ari waited silently on the other end of the phone. "No way. There's just no way I would be included in this . . ."

"I know. I can't believe it either. I've only seen her the one time since I left for Chicago, you know, that holiday party at the club."

"Do you think HRH even knows we were invited? It has to be some sort of mistake, wrong list or something. Maybe she's just trying to show off, you know, celebrity stuff or royal stuff. I'll tell you one thing, mistake or not, now that I have the invitation, I wouldn't miss this for the world."

Ari said, "I know, I'm looking forward to it too." With that they started making plans about what to wear and where to buy it.

Harriet had arrived home with her friend, Paolo Bertalucci, ostensibly an Italian prince and, according to the paper and those who had seen the duo around town, an extremely handsome man. The gala being given by HRH's parents at the country club was the following Saturday evening, and it was arguably the most eagerly anticipated event in Thompsonville. Ari and Gabby decided not to take escorts. This particular evening might be a great deal more fun just meeting HRH's friends and watching all that would take place. They were not disappointed.

As they climbed the stairs from the entry of the country club up to the main sitting area, Ari and Gabby had to stop themselves from gasping at the incredible decorations and the beautiful gowns and people before their eyes. Gabby had chosen a simple but very sleek long black evening gown that showed off her petite figure. Ari found a cream and gold St. John knit at Saks Fifth Avenue in Chicago that fit her beautifully. Neither was overdressed. They were certain they were looking at some of the most fabulous evening gowns available in New York and abroad.

The club had hung cream-colored moire in a drape-like fashion narrowing the doorway into the main dining room and the bar in the back.

More candelabra had been brought in. Massive flower arrangements of calla lilies, white hydrangeas, roses with gold spray-painted curly willows and ivy trailing from the elaborate urns were everywhere. The waiters were wearing white wait jackets, rather than their normal black attire.

Moving into the room with the other arriving guests, they were greeted warmly by both Hiz Honor and Mrs. Hill. Mrs. Hill looked as if she had walked out of a magazine in her silver evening gown, accessorized with an outstanding diamond and emerald necklace and diamond earrings. The evening was living up to its expectations.

As Gabby and Ari mingled during the cocktail hour and as the hosts continued to welcome their guests, they noticed there were very few people there from Thompsonville. They were happily watching the beautiful people, when to their surprise, HRH approached them with a young man who just *had to be* the one referred to in the papers. Harriet was very gracious and introduced Paolo and invited the two girls to join them so that she could introduce them to some of their other friends.

Harriet announced to her friends that Ari and Gabby were her two best friends from Thompsonville and while Ari was finishing up at Northwestern University, Gabby was President and CEO of the largest residential construction company in the area.

Ari leaned over and whispered, "Gabby, what makes Harriet think you're the President and CEO of Regency?"

"Actually, I'm about to be. It just happened. I don't know how Harriet found out – maybe through Stanford Lee at the bank. Anyway, I was waiting to tell you until after all the papers were signed. My mother and Uncle Tony must think that I've done a pretty good job over the past three years. I'm really excited."

"You deserve it, Gabby. Congratulations."

As the group chatted, Ari and Gabby began to realize that this group of HRH's new friends seemingly did little other than attend parties and sporting events, buy whatever they wanted, and make sure they were seen and reported on doing it all.

They were seated at one of several tables comprised exclusively of Harriet's friends. There didn't seem to be many couples. Most of them just seemed to be good friends. HRH and Paolo were seated at Hiz Honor's table along with Jennifer Lee's parents, Stephanie and Stanford, The First

National Bank of Thompsonville's President, Gordon Reed, the attorney and his date, and another couple the girls didn't recognize.

Inside the dining room, the tables were magnificently adorned with more fabulous flower arrangements, candles and beautiful china. There was a stage with a small group of musicians playing softly during the dinner hour who, they were told, would play dance music after the main course had been cleared.

And then the dining experience began. The waiters moved elegantly and quietly through the crowd serving course after course of some of the most delicious food offerings Ari or Gabby had ever tasted. After each course they were certain they couldn't eat another thing, until it was placed in front of them. During the meal, Ari and Gabby spent some time talking with the other guests at their table. One of the women, approximately their age they thought, seemed quite nice and more down to earth than some of the others with whom they had spoken.

As they chatted, the waiters served champagne and the band struck up a musical introduction of someone about to speak. Hiz Honor rose to welcome their guests en masse and again introduce Prince Paolo Bertalucci. "My wife and I are pleased to announce Harriet's engagement to Paolo. The wedding will take place in New York during the holidays. We hope you all can be with us on that happy occasion. To Harriet and Paolo."

No one, it seemed, was surprised. And while neither Gabby nor Ari was taken aback by the engagement, they ended up after the evening was over being surprised they had been invited to be a part of it. Ari and Gabby decided they were there as "Harriet's best friends from Thompsonville," only because they thought HRH would have felt foolish not having any friends from home at the party. They were there solely for her to save face in front of all her rich jet setting friends.

The party and the announcement of Harriet's engagement to the Prince were, of course, reported in The *Sentinel*, and this time it wasn't a reprint. There were tons of pictures. Gabby and Ari were in one of them. They didn't remember seeing the photographer, but realized they should have known, given that it was thrown by the Hills, the event would have to have one. Harriet's friends were, for the most part, heading immediately back to Europe to attend the next event, the exception being a small group of her apparently closest friends and Paolo. They had been seen about town and, while they only stayed on a few days after the party, they were photographed and noticed by all the locals.

As the summer wore on, Thompsonville returned to normal. The Hills were apparently busy planning Harriet's wedding; Mrs. Hill in Paris and New York, and Hiz Honor busy doing whatever it was he was doing, including acting on his official duties as Mayor.

Ari went to Europe as she had wanted, visiting Italy and France and then ended up meeting Emily in London for a week. She was excited she had the opportunity before really becoming a grown up and having to go to work for a living. Ari returned home to unpack and get herself organized for her final year at Northwestern.

Ari and Emily's senior year at Northwestern went quickly. Emily decided she wanted to pursue a career in public relations. She had studied public speaking, advertising, and creative writing, and found it satisfying to be involved with people who created rather than conformed to specific sets of facts and figures. Emily met hundreds of people through her father's business and, because she was from Chicago, she felt certain she could quickly put her contacts and creativity to good use. Fortunately, she was able to find a job as an intern at a prominent public relations firm almost immediately. Her job search was over.

Emily went with Ari to several job fairs in the Chicago area, Ari still unsure what she wanted to do job-wise. Several job fairs and many job interviews later, Ari was getting discouraged that nothing seemed to strike her as just what she wanted to do. After a good deal of frustration and, knowing that she had to make a decision, she ultimately decided she would take one of the many offers which had been made to her by securities firms and accept one from the Chicago branch of a major New York City stock brokerage firm.

In the meantime, Brent and Stacy had both passed their bar exams on the first try. They celebrated with each other and with members of both law firms and then settled into their specific work assignments at their respective firms.

Stacy loved Washington and so did Brent. Now that they both lived in the District on a permanent basis, they found many places to go that weren't tourist spots and began to see, live and feel the pulse of the ethnically and culturally diverse dynamics of this center of international power. They were meeting many young people from anywhere and everywhere and their circle of friends expanded exponentially. It was a heady experience, and both were very glad they had made the decision to accept jobs in Washington.

Their work, it seemed, continued to require more and more of their personal time. During the first few months in their new jobs the concentration had been on their bar exams, but now they were really a part of their individual firms, albeit only as first-year associates.

Stacy thrived on the work. To her, mergers and acquisitions was the most exciting specialty in the law.

Brent was assigned to one of the senior partners of his firm specializing in taxes. But, because the firm itself didn't limit its practice strictly to taxation, he had been brought in on a variety of issues as required by other lawyers. He, too, was extremely busy with an abundance of work involving very different types of issues, and it was a great learning experience for him. As much as he thought he had learned in law school, it amazed him how much he didn't know about the actual practice of law. He often wondered if it would get easier for him and require less of his time the longer he practiced. He was very glad he was one among several first-year associates at his firm and they all seemed to be in it together, making it easier for each.

CHAPTER TWELVE

It was almost impossible to believe, but in what seemed like the speed of a bullet train, Brent and Stacy's first year as working attorneys was about to end. Neither one of them could put a finger on where the time had gone, but there was a sense of satisfaction that it would soon be behind them. New associates would be joining their firms, and they would no longer be the new kids whose names were not always remembered by the partners.

Ari and Emily graduated. Linda and Frank Bolan as well as Grandpa Bolan made the trip from Thompsonville to watch their little girl receive her diploma. After the ceremonies, Ari and Emily announced to their families that they'd found an apartment in Lincoln Park they'd be sharing and invited everyone to go see it, even though they wouldn't be moving until the following week. After the viewing by both sets of parents and Grandpa Bolan, the entire group took the graduates out to dinner to celebrate their accomplishments and toast their future careers.

Harriet married in New York at Christmastime, as announced. The New York papers' society pages as well as *Town & Country* had large spreads of the spectacular wedding. The reception was held at Tavern on the Green and the photos showed off the magnificent restaurant as well as the extravagant decorations set off by the floor to ceiling windows and crystal chandeliers. Ari and Gabby were sorry to have missed it, but Gabby was involved with Nicole and her first big Christmas, and Ari was busy at the time putting together her resume and investigating possible career options. Actually Ari didn't want to go alone and, since Gabby wasn't going, well, she didn't think Harriet would miss her all that much.

Harriet and her Prince husband went off to an undisclosed location for their honeymoon. Gabby and Ari wondered if Harriet was now a Princess. But, whatever her title may or may not be, she looked happy in the photographs and both girls were genuinely delighted that she had at last found love after having been brought up in a home that was so skewed in its family values.

Harriet and Paolo were seen and photographed along with their friends all over the world. All of Thompsonville kept up with them through The *Sentinel*, which continued to reprint articles from other publications, as well as tidbits supplied by Harriet's mother, Janet Dorrance Hill.

Seldom, but once in a while, Harriet would go to Thompsonville to visit her parents. She would fly in and out without really spending any time in town. Once she called Gabby. They chatted, bringing each other up-to-date on their activities. But, truthfully, they had such different lives now, they simply said how great it must be for the other and made promises to keep in touch in the future.

Nothing much changed for any of them over the next several years.

Ari went through what she thought was the most boring and tedious training program she could imagine. She often wondered during the training process why she had chosen a career at an investment firm. She wasn't particularly fond of, or good with, numbers, but she found that she had an insatiable appetite for business. She loved learning about the different companies, their management, financial structures, almost everything that didn't involve the math. She learned that math wasn't what made an investment advisor at a brokerage firm. Oh, one had to understand it well enough, but the firm had specialists who made recommendations based on the math and that wasn't really her job.

As the first few years passed, Ari was becoming more successful and she settled into what she thought life was all about. Work, cover her financial responsibilities, and date once in a while when she found someone she thought could be interesting. Unfortunately, she found she was mostly disappointed in that regard. Most of the men she came in contact with through business were married, although that didn't stop them from making advances. She and Emily were still roommates and enjoyed a busy social life with lots of friends. Lincoln Park with its sidewalk cafes, small storefronts and small community feel, was a perfect location. They loved living there.

Emily, on the other hand, loved what she was doing. She had shown herself to be a huge asset to her firm and, because of her creative writing ability, was more than just another one of their public relations executives. She had, in her own right, established relationships with most of the new movers and shakers in Chicago, while still maintaining the relationships with the power brokers of old she knew through her father. It was becoming known on the street that, if you wanted something done in Chicago, you went directly to Emily. Ari was certain that a partnership was not too far away for her.

Stacy was on a fast track, too. She spent almost every day and many evenings at her office working on this or that merger or acquisition. She couldn't get enough of it. She pushed herself to the limit. So much so that, when one of their transactions was completed, she literally had to take time off to reinvigorate herself. Her efforts were not unnoticed by the partners in her firm and, as new projects came in, the partner in charge would invariably ask for Stacy. Her relationship with Brent took the brunt of her success. But, when she could make time for a social commitment, it was with Brent and they continued to enjoy a relationship they both found comfortable.

Brent's legal career was every bit as demanding. He had been spending a great deal of time lately dealing with government officials as he acted on behalf of some of the firm's clients, both foreign and domestic. His contacts with members of Congress and their staff members, along with State Department and Justice Department officials encompassed the most interesting work that he had been involved with since joining the firm. His friendships blossomed with many of these new contacts and Brent found the bantering among this very bright group of people exhilarating.

After four years of the same thing, Ari was growing restless. She did a good job and enjoyed working with her clients very much, but there was something lacking. One Saturday, while strolling around Bughouse Square, Ari happened to overhear a young man talking with several others about a relatively young State Senator hoping to get elected to the U.S. Congress. Ari sat on a bench close enough so that she could continue to listen without appearing to be eavesdropping. Something about this young man's earnestness and clear belief in his candidate seemed to hit a chord in her.

Ari had not been particularly interested in politics. Frankly, there wasn't much going on politically in Thompsonville. Of course, they knew about the presidential races and even some of the major congressional races, but Thompsonville wasn't a regular spot on the campaign trail, so she rarely paid attention. There was the mayoral race in Thompsonville, but Ari couldn't even remember the name of any opponent of Hiz Honor. Somehow, he always seemed to end up being the Mayor.

Ari thought she might take a look into local politics. After all, she figured, since she was now a taxpaying resident of the state, she probably should be more involved in affairs that might end up being an issue which could be of concern to her.

She was captivated. She had no idea what went on under the generic term "politics." Along with her classmates in Thompsonville, she had taken civics classes, but never remembered it being as fascinating as she now thought. She began to watch CNN and read parts of the newspaper which she had seldom glanced at before. She didn't get involved to the extent she ever attended any rallies or volunteered, but she felt that knowledge of one's local politics was an important responsibility for every adult, and she determined that she would always try to be up on the issues.

Gabby, Nicole and Regency were blossoming. Gabby had firmly established her place as CEO and President of Regency, no doubt about her abilities any longer. She had recently determined that while the rest of the country was enjoying a healthy U.S. economy, Thompsonville was not as strong perhaps as other small towns. This she attributed to the fact that they were in the Rust Belt, where the shuttering of manufacturing facilities and the closing of steel mills was prevalent. Therefore, Gabby decided, Regency needed to stop investing in large residential developments in the Thompsonville area which ultimately may end up not having enough buyers.

So, while Gabby continued with the small high-end homes which had been so successful at Pheasant Run and Sturgis Ridge, she was also thinking about trying something new. When she purchased the property known as the Sturgis Estate, which she subsequently subdivided, the main estate house was found to be in a state of ill-repair. Gabby loved renovating it, and was now beginning to believe that with some of the lovely older homes in Thompsonville, Regency should form a division which would be involved strictly in renovating homes, both for their own account and on behalf of homeowners.

She began testing the idea and found that while there were some home remodelers in the area, and they did have a couple of big box home improvement stores, the Regency name stood for quality and unique design, making the new division a hit from the very beginning.

Jerry O'Neil continued to work with Gabby on Regency's website and Gabby enjoyed bouncing ideas off him regarding business in general, in addition to the company's computer needs.

Nicole was growing like a weed too. Kindergarten was only a wink away, and Nicole was already reading and speaking above her age level. Ethel was slowing down and Gabby was glad that she wouldn't have to spend so much time at the house once Nicole's school started. Gabby started a fund, unbeknownst to Ethel, which would help supplement her Social Security benefits when she would finally have to give up working. Gabby hoped Ethel would be around to dance at Nicole's wedding, but wanted to make certain Ethel would be taken care of, should her health become an issue.

Uncle Tony started talking about retiring. Gabby couldn't imagine running Regency without Uncle Tony. He assured her that, just because he wasn't on the site every day, he would only be a phone call away, should she need him. TJ had pretty much taken over most of Uncle Tony's responsibilities and was stepping into his father's shoes quite smoothly. Ultimately though, Uncle Tony announced that he would continue working through

1999, but, after that, it was the new millennium and time for the next generation to fully take control.

Gabby really hadn't thought about it that way, but indeed, she had stepped into her father's shoes as the next generation, and now it was time for TJ to fully assume his father's place at Regency as well. She had not really focused on her mother's aging or Uncle Tony's, but now it was a reality starting to creep into the back of her mind. She wondered, *Why had she recognized that Ethel was getting older but not her mother or her uncle?* Maybe it was because Ethel was so much older than her mother or maybe she just thought her mother would always be there. It was hard for her to believe that she was twenty-four years old and had been running Regency for six years now.

Mary became very busy on her own. She made quite a few new friends who were either divorced or widowed and still kept up with most of her longtime friends, many of whom were still married. It had been difficult at first. Married friends invited her to many dinners and other social functions after Nick died, but as time passed, it became awkward to be the odd-man or, in this case, odd-woman out. Mary took some photography classes at the local community college and formed a gourmet club for singles which took off like a wildfire.

The "Orphans' Gourmet Club," as it became known, grew as many of the older, but not yet senior, residents of Thompsonville became single for whatever reason. It was at one of these dinners that Mary met Brian Armstrong. Brian was a widower and a recent retiree from the refrigerator manufacturing plant on the outskirts of Thompsonville. He had been alone for several years now, but he had been busy at work as the plant manager until his recent retirement.   Brian and Mary seemed to enjoy being together and had become fast friends. Cooking was their favorite thing to do. While Mary had always been a very good cook specializing in her own creative pasta dishes, Tony's taste ran more to the basics. That was, until he savored her creations. Now, she and Brian spent a lot of time together creating new dishes and then enjoying them by themselves and with other friends. They went to the movies, bowled and even spent a couple of weekends away exploring the countryside while antiquing.

Ari had been involved in the local political scene now for a couple of years, but it was now well into the presidential race and Ari was entirely caught up in it. Politically, it was the end of an era. President Clinton was about to leave office, and who the new president would end up being was up in the air. The economy tightened, it seemed, partly due to the uncertainty of the American public in their choice for their next President, as well as the dot com bust. Whatever the reason, it wasn't getting any better as the end of the year approached.

The "experts" on the Street predicted a weak economy for the foreseeable future and only time would tell how long and how bad it would end up being. She saw a loss of confidence in the stock market and a serious drop in her business. She was afraid of what was to come.

As Jerry O'Neil watched the millennium approach, he decided he had waited long enough. From his first glance at Gabby when she was interested in learning the computer from him for her new job at Regency years earlier, Jerry was smitten. The more he worked with her, both in those early classes and then later as they began working together at Regency, Jerry thought he had never known such a captivating woman. She was strong, smart, dedicated and incredibly beautiful.

He watched as Jason came into her life, seen her anguish through her father's death and could do nothing but stand by helplessly as her husband betrayed her and her beautiful daughter. Through it all he loved her.

He decided at the time they met that Gabby was too young for his then age of twenty-nine and thought he could wait patiently for two or three years. He had never considered that another man might come along. Other boys she would date, yes, of course. But marry, no.

Now Jason was well out of her life, Nicole was a little person and Gabby had again become that self-confident, determined and strikingly beautiful woman he had fallen in love with so many years earlier. They had worked together for so long, shared a business lunch or dinner here and there enjoying each other's company, or so he wanted to believe.

And so, a week before Christmas in 1999, Jerry O'Neil made his first move. He went over to Petal Pushers and ordered a dozen white roses to be delivered to Gabby's house that evening. He stood and carefully wrote the card that was to be included with the flowers.

Susan Cranston waited patiently as Jerry finished the card and paid for the flowers. Susan smiled to herself thinking, *Now, this is a man for Gabby.*

It was nearly 7:15 when Susan was finally able to get away from the store and deliver the flowers to Gabby's house. She rang the doorbell. Peeking through the window, Gabby immediately recognized Susan. Opening the door, she said, "Susan, Hi. What's all this?"

"Hi Gabby. This is for you." Susan handed the box of roses to Gabby. She started to walk back to her car when Gabby asked if she wouldn't like to come in? Susan smiled and said, "Thanks, Gabby, but I need to get home. Enjoy the flowers. Goodnight."

Gabby walked slowly into her kitchen and set the box on the island, opened it and found the card sitting on top of the beautiful roses. Gabby wondered, *Who's sending me flowers?* as she pulled the tiny card from the envelope. The card read, *Please have dinner with me on New Year's Eve. I'd like to get to know you better outside of the office. I'll call you tomorrow. Please say yes.* The card was just signed, *Jerry.*

Gabby didn't believe her eyes. *Jerry? Jerry O'Neil? Must be,* she thought. She had always liked him and had even found herself relying on him and his opinions, but she had never thought he was interested in her as anyone other than a fellow business associate/client.

The more she thought about it though, the more she liked the idea of spending some time with him in a social setting and knew she would say yes when asked the next day. She was smiling now and surprised to realize that this was an invitation she liked a great deal.

CHAPTER THIRTEEN

Business was slowing everywhere. There were announcements of employee cutbacks from major manufacturers around the country, service companies were hurting and there was a general feeling of unrest.

One of Thompsonville's major employers, the refrigerator manufacturing plant where Brian Armstrong had worked for so many years, was closed by its parent company. The refrigerators were to be manufactured in Mexico, along with many other products whose companies had moved their manufacturing facilities to Mexico in order to capitalize on the substantially lower workers' salaries versus those of the U.S.

Thompsonville was in a squeeze. Real estate values were down and the local population was declining. As other smaller plants, companies and retail shops closed, there was a significant impact on the local economy.

Gabby felt fortunate that Regency had stopped developing major residential communities when it had. There had been some downsizing, but for the most part many of the original construction employees of Regency had joined the company at or very soon after her father and Uncle Tony had started it, so they too were nearing retirement.

Regency was still working on home renovations and, on occasion, reconstruction of houses for its own account. Regency managed to maintain a high degree of the renovation business due to their outstanding reputation and exceptional design detail. What they couldn't resell immediately, they rented and then invested in several apartment complexes. After renovating them, they sold them as condominiums, giving the company a steady cash flow. While they weren't making the kind of money they did when building major residential developments, Regency managed to stay in the black and that was an accomplishment in the current business environment.

Jerry O'Neil wanted to be with Gabby more than anyone he had ever known, but felt that pressing her would be a wrong move. He wanted her to really get to know him outside of business; his sense of humor, and his family, such as it was. Jerry's mother was still alive and full of mischief. She played bridge with the girls, played golf with whomever was available and was seldom found without something to do. Jerry's sister, Julie, was also fun. Gabby enjoyed getting together with them, seeing them interact and watching carefully how they treated one another. During all this, Gabby wouldn't allow herself to grow close to Jerry. *I'm probably being way too overprotective*, Gabby thought. But she remembered how terribly hurt and horrifically used she had been by a man whose name wasn't even his own, much less had any of the moral character he portrayed to her.

Gabby thoroughly enjoyed their New Year's Eve dinner. They dined at Dominique's and danced to the band that was performing there for the occasion. They shared stories of their youth and laughed at each other's antics. They talked about Nicole, and Jerry seemed to really listen and care. They made a concerted effort not to talk about business but inevitably they did, although not Regency.

Jerry talked about his business, how he had started it on a shoestring right out of college. He said that many of the things he now knew had been self-taught, including the "how to run a business" part, adding that much of what one learns after leaving school is at least as important as, or more important than, one's formal education. The proof of his success was the current size of his company and the fact that it had clients across the United States.

They talked about the economy nationally and, then, of course, locally.

Then the dance music began and they spent the next two hours dancing. It was, Gabby thought, a lovely way to welcome the new year and the new millennium.

Gabby was getting to know Jerry and liked what she saw a great deal. She invariably thought about how different Jerry was from Jason, or, rather, John. She noticed Jerry often spoke about his family and his youth, where Jason hadn't. Jason steered clear of any of that kind of conversation she now knew because he hadn't lived the life he was trying to convince her he had. Jason always was about what he would do if and when he had the chance; that his loss of family while he was young, or his service in the Army afterward, had denied him the kind of life that he was aiming for. Little did she know that *she* was his meal ticket to that life.

Jerry was different and she was glad for the chance to spend time with him. He almost always included Nicole, planning outings to the zoo, the park, picnics, and meals out. She saw him interact with Nicole and thought, *This is the kind of man every daughter wants for a father.* She tried hard not to fall for him for that reason alone, but knew it was more than that and let herself, once again, trust a man.

Brent was working all the time and yet he didn't spend as many hours at his office as Stacy did at hers. Slowly they started to pull away from each other, not consciously, but away nevertheless. Stacy still loved what she was doing and lived it, breathed it, and, truthfully, it consumed so much of her thinking, there was room for little else.

Brent started to question the value of their efforts. Stacy spent almost every waking hour working on a merger or acquisition that probably wouldn't benefit anyone other than the powers behind the deal and, of course, Stacy's law firm with its exorbitant fees. Brent logged more than 2,600 billable hours a year at his firm and knew several other associates who billed even more. There was now that competition for partnership.

Brent just didn't understand what he was accomplishing even after five years at the firm. *Was this the way it was to be?* In two years he would be up for partnership. *But, then what? Will I make it?* He knew that even to make partner he would need to become more effective in bringing new clients to the firm. As he analyzed it, he knew from past experience he wasn't the party type, the social guru who could go out there and bring in the new business which was so important to the health and wealth of a firm. Stacy could, but that wasn't his strength. Brent always loved the law, but he always thought that through his practice of it, others would benefit.

And, if I should make partner, then what will my life be like? Will I be able to have a family and also spend time with them, watching my children at sporting events, recitals, growing up? What about my wife? Will she want to spend so much time raising our children alone, seeing me maybe only on weekends and holidays with just that "special trip" once a year? Will she be happy?

As he considered all these things over almost a year's time, Brent realized that "his wife" wasn't Stacy. In all the thoughts about his future, the wife he considered never was Stacy.

Almost immediately with that realization, Brent knew that the happiest he had been in Washington, other than enjoying the city and all it had to offer, was when he spent time with his "Hill friends" debating new legislation and how it could help or, in some cases, hurt mainstream Americans. His friends were energized by their work and their part in it. Brent knew he wanted to work with people in a way which would improve their lives. What he was doing now, well, just wasn't it.

Brent took Stacy to dinner the first night she was available. They went to L'Auberge Chez Francois in Great Falls because he believed they would have less of a chance of being interrupted and/or recognized there, and because it had such a lovely relaxed setting out on the deck under the trees with the Potomac running behind them.

Stacy knew something was up and was afraid Brent was going to ask her to marry him. As they sat and ordered cocktails, Stacy got to the point. Asking nicely, Stacy said, "This is lovely Brent, what's the special occasion?"

Brent had wanted to work into this, it was just his way. But Stacy always got right to the point. "It's not really a special occasion Stace, but I've been doing a lot of thinking lately about my career at the firm. It's basically that I don't think Washington is the place for me. I can't see myself spending the rest of my life essentially doing the same things I'm doing now and missing so many of the things I experienced growing up that, as a parent, I would miss passing on to my own children. I wanted you to know this now before I made it public at the firm."

Stacy was astonished. Perhaps because she and Brent hadn't spent as much time together as they had in the past, but she couldn't imagine how she had missed seeing this coming. "What will you do if you leave the firm?"

"I'm not sure." He then let all his thoughts spill out, talking about his envy of those of his friends who were doing work they loved and then followed it with the questions he had in his own mind. "Stace, we've been together a long time and have a wonderful friendship, I hope you know this isn't about you."

"Do you want to work on The Hill, is that the type of work you're thinking about? If so, I'm sure you could find something with your wonderful background. I'll help, of course."

"I've thought about looking up there, but I'm just not sure that's the answer either. Like I said, I just wanted you to be the first to know."

"So, what's your plan?"

"I'm going to talk with Ben, my supervising partner, next week. I think he'll understand. I'm not sure our managing partner will, but I'll just have to deal with that later. I'm working on an antitrust case which is just about settled. There are a few other cases where I'm involved, but they're essentially team efforts at this stage and they can cover for me if the firm wants me to leave right away."

Brent spent the rest of the weekend walking. On Saturday, he walked down on the Mall, spent time sitting on one of the many benches scattered around the grounds of the Viet Nam Memorial and, later, leaning against a pillar at the Lincoln Memorial, staring up at the statue of a man whose intensity, strength and confidence were depicted so convincingly in deeply chiseled white marble. One could not help but stand in awe of this man whose presence was captured so magnificently in this statue, this homage to one of America's greatest presidents.

On Sunday, Brent walked up into Rock Creek Park. There were many people out enjoying the park on this almost cool Sunday afternoon -- joggers, couples walking hand-in-hand and families out with their children. Brent found it easy to get lost in the crowd and in his own thoughts as he meandered along the paths that wound their way through the park.

Uncertain about where his future should be directed, Brent thought that if he could only tackle the question as he believed Lincoln would, it might become more clear to him. *Now*, he thought, *that's an idea! First, let's take the givens.*

Brent knew he didn't want to stay with the law firm and while he envied his Hill friends' jobs, he also saw their frustration when the bills they had worked so hard to pass ended up not passing or even not making it to the floor of their respective house. Brent also knew he wanted a family.

Then, using what he thought would be Lincoln's thinking, he realized he already had a family. Families don't start with each young man as he marries and has his own children. One's family is what was there before you, guided and loved you through the years and continued a thread of belonging which could never be replaced. If one of Brent's priorities in life was to have a family like the one in which he grew up, why was he trying to do it away from that family?

And, as he continued that path of logic, couldn't he practice the type of law he had always wanted in Thompsonville? There, unlike Washington, perhaps he could actually help his neighbors and friends. The people of Thompsonville were a part of his family too and he decided that his practice had to include the effort of giving his friends and neighbors of Thompsonville the best representation that could be had. While the practice of law may be less challenging at home, the personal satisfaction of being able to help others, take the moral high ground if you will, would far outweigh any potential, if farfetched, aspirations of creating new law for the benefit of all.

Brent was energized. He looked toward the sky and announced, "Thank you, President Lincoln" and walked back through the park enjoying the sights and sounds which he had blocked so successfully just a few hours earlier.

That night, Brent told Stacy his decision. Stacy thought about their conversation over dinner Friday night and knew Brent was making the right decision for himself. While Stacy could not understand how one could be drawn away from Washington, she somehow believed that Brent was one of those people who would end up unhappy and unfulfilled here, but thrive in a smaller arena like that of Thompsonville.

"Brent, I want to wish you the best of luck. Lately -- I'm sure you've realized it too -- our lives have taken different paths. I'll always love you, but I want to stay where I am, become a partner and, yes, do this for the rest of my life. I'll never regret us, our years together in New Haven and then here in Washington. You've been a very special part of my life, but I can see that your life will have more meaning for you in Thompsonville. I'll miss not having you around, but I'll always be here if you need a friend."

The weakening of the economy was affecting Ari too. Layoffs were announced at most of the major brokerage houses in New York, and one of them was hers. The numbers were staggering, but so far Ari was still employed. And then it happened, a second round of layoffs was announced. Within the week Ari and several of her co-workers were told they were out of a job.

Ari never actually thought that she could lose her job. She had done well, had many satisfied clients, and always met her quota. That was until this past spring. She hadn't lost her clients, it was just that so many of them weren't in a position to continue investing in a marketplace that was so shaky. Some of her clients had also been laid off; senior executives with large corporations and many of those clients were considerably older than she. Ari knew they were concerned about their futures. She understood them and their concerns, now thinking she was one of them.

Ari started networking. Through Emily and Ari's own contacts, she began making calls, updating her resume and answering many blind ads, most of which never responded. Ari finally decided a headhunter was the way to go. She found one she liked a great deal and together they again rewrote her resume and then targeted specific companies which might still be hiring.

Almost everything came to a stop during the Christmas holidays, which convinced Ari it would be a good time to visit her parents. Ari hadn't been home in several years and she needed to be around friends and family. Something about being laid off, not fired, just laid off, made one question one's own ability and self-worth. Of course, it didn't help that no one had even invited her in for an interview either. She felt that a break might be a very good thing right now.

Linda and Frank were waiting for her in Pittsburgh. Ari couldn't believe she hadn't seen them in almost two years, since their last visit to Chicago. Falling into her parents' arms, Ari knew this was exactly what she needed right now. On the way home they chatted about everything and then talked about what plans they wanted to make for the holidays. Grandpa Bolan was getting up there in age and they all wanted to be with him for Christmas as always. This year, though, it would have to be at Grandview Manor, an assisted living facility and his new residence.

Ari told her parents about Brent's move back to Thompsonville. Gabby was so excited when she called Ari to tell her the news. While she hadn't gone into a great deal of detail, Gabby said Brent felt he would be happier practicing law in Thompsonville than he was in Washington. Ari was anxious to see Gabby, her goddaughter Nicole, who looked so beautiful and grown up in her recent photos, and then to find out what was going on with Brent and see him again. She couldn't believe the last time they had seen one another was Nicole's baptism. That was more than five years ago. *Whew, how did that happen?*

Brent met with his supervising partner in Washington the very first thing on Monday morning, having gone in early specifically to catch him before the day's responsibilities took over his schedule. It was more difficult than Brent expected, but there was no hesitation about his decision. Ben was surprised and disappointed. He had developed a real respect for Brent and thought he was a fine lawyer, even though he knew Brent would never be a rainmaker for the firm.

Ben conceded that he had some of the same thoughts as a young lawyer and, although he was sure he had made the right decision for himself, he often lamented the fact that his family saw much less of him than he would have liked. He told Brent that unfortunately that was the price one paid to be a successful attorney in the political capital of the world. He added, remorsefully, that it shouldn't have to be that way, but it was.

Once Brent had made his decision known, it became easier. It seemed to take a very long time for the month to pass. Brent packed up his apartment, actually taking very little. His furniture was still the odd assortment of furnishings acquired by a first-year associate who becomes so wrapped up in work, that little attention is ever paid to upgrading his home environment. Most of that went to the Salvation Army. Brent shipped most of his books and personal belongings home to Thompsonville and, as the day came for him to leave, he picked up his suitcase and one small carry-on bag and stepped onto the plane with no regrets.

Brent settled in temporarily at his mother's house. Mary was thrilled to have him home. Since Gabby and Nicole had moved into their new home, Mary had thought that the house was, well, just a house. With Brent there, it was a home again. Brent was appreciative of his mother's willingness to let him stay there for the time-being, but he knew she had a friend and needed her privacy, just as he wanted his own.

He spent his first days home with his family. He was so happy to have the time with no outside pressures to get to know his niece and to actually get to know his sister again. When he had last lived in Thompsonville, Gabby was still in her early teens. Although they had talked on the phone a great deal over the years, he hadn't really spent any length of time with her since she became an adult, a mother and the head of the family business. They talked about his decision to leave Washington and return home, his plans both short- and long-term, and they talked about family.

After those first few days, Brent was anxious to get to it. He had looked at the real estate ads for office space in Sunday's paper, but there weren't many ads. Maybe it was the economy.

Brent decided he wanted to be downtown near the courthouse and county offices that serviced the needs of the community. While many of the other lawyers, though admittedly there weren't really many in Thompsonville, but a large percentage of them, had their offices in some of the newer office buildings on the outskirts of town. Brent wanted to be close to the action. Perhaps it was merely the familiarity of being downtown as he had been in Washington, but somehow it just felt right to him. Brent rode around downtown and, after looking at all the buildings available, he thought the task amorphous without the assistance of a real estate agent.

He was surprised to see how depressed a large part of the downtown area appeared. He was well aware of the economic downturn in the country and even knew of its impact on Thompsonville. But, because he hadn't spent much time back home in many years, he really hadn't seen the toll it had taken on this once lovely town. The office space abutting the county offices and courthouse were in better shape than those nearer the river, and appeared to be occupied. There were service companies, which supported the various activities of the government that occupied much of that space, and of course some retail space, and several restaurants.

Brent along with his new realtor, Jack Caldwell, spent several days checking out the downtown spaces that were available to lease. The very few that were in close proximity to the courthouse were largely overpriced to Brent's thinking. On the other hand, while he was willing to go somewhat against the grain of where the clients were, Brent didn't want to be the lone pioneer in the now almost deserted retail section of downtown Thompsonville.

In its heyday, downtown had been a thriving county seat with a truss bridge crossing the Ohio River, the eastern side of which was Thompsonville. Following Main Street into town, directly in front of one was the county courthouse, standing tall in the distance. Main Street, which only became Main as it crossed the bridge, ran straight into the center of the courthouse allowing traffic to turn only left or right onto Capitol. The streets that crossed Main were the numbered streets, beginning with 1st Street, which ran along the river. As the numbered streets got higher, fewer rental properties were available and the higher the rental prices became.

Jack asked Brent, "Have you thought about buying an entire building downtown? While rents are very high in the area, sales prices for many of the buildings are uncorrespondingly low." Brent, frankly, hadn't considered anything remotely like investing in real estate at this point in his life. But, as Jack continued, Brent started to listen. "You can buy a building, have your practice on one floor, perhaps the ground floor, use one as your residence and the other one or two floors as rental properties."

Brent was intrigued, if, perhaps, not quite convinced. He asked Jack to show him some of the properties that were for sale. Jack and Brent decided to meet again the next day which would allow Jack time to put together the offering statements on the various listings and make appointments with the listing agents to show the properties.

Brent wanted the time to think more carefully about this idea and also run it by his mother and, even more importantly, Gabby. While Gabby was on the residential side of real estate, she kept herself apprised of the real estate market generally and would be able to offer sound advice about this new possibility.

Brent called Gabby. "Gabby, would it be all right if I dropped by tonight? I have something that I need your opinion on." Gabby was excited that Brent wanted her opinion on anything and was delighted that she might be able to do something to help him get started back in Thompsonville.

Brent arrived at Gabby's, played with his niece before her bedtime, told her a story and then kissed her goodnight. Nicole was enjoying the attention from her long-lost uncle and godfather, now back in her life on a regular basis. After Nicole dropped off to sleep, Gabby poured herself and Brent a glass of wine and, with bottle in hand, they moved into the family room.

Brent relayed to Gabby everything he had seen for the last few days; the properties available for rent and their specifics, as well as his general impression of all the downtown real estate and its condition. He then told her what Jack had suggested about the possibility of buying a building, the rental potential and the bonus of having his residence there as well.

"Did you see anything you liked?"

"I'm only in the very early stages of considering this, Jack only mentioning it for the first time today. It's what I wanted to get your opinion on before I get too invested in the idea. Jack and I are going to look at the first 'for sale' properties tomorrow. So, no, I haven't seen anything yet."

"Brent, I'm not sure I can be of much help to you. I'm not that familiar with real estate in the downtown area, particularly commercial real estate, although I know it's quite despressed. Are you certain that your want your practice located downtown? Do you think you really need to be that close to the courthouse?"

"I'm sure that's where I want to be. Sis, I've thought about this long and hard and, whether I rent or buy, I want my office to be downtown."

"Well, then, let me tell you what you probably already know. The economy in Thompsonville has been deteriorating over the years." She stressed the loss of businesses, the loss of jobs and therefore the loss of discretionary income of Thompsonville residents. In her element now, Gabby continued. "While there is some economic strengthening predicted in the near future by 'those who know,' I'm not so certain that smaller towns such as Thompsonville will benefit versus larger cities where there's a highly diversified business base and a large population of well educated and/or highly-skilled workers.

So, not to rain on your parade, I think it basically boils down to the numbers – frankly, it almost always does. If you can buy a building which would incorporate both your office needs as well as your living needs, and you can do that at or near what it would cost you to rent an office and pay rent on an apartment, this could be a very good option for you."

"Should I be watching out for anything specific?"

"Obviously, you don't want to end up with a building which would require a great deal of renovation – that could be extremely expensive. And, you can't count on any rental revenue from outside sources. If you are lucky enough to rent a floor or even just some office space on an extra floor, that should just be considered cream and should never enter into your equation in terms of whether or not you can afford it.

I'm not sure this is what you wanted to hear and I don't want to crush your idea, it could work out very well for you. Let's look at the numbers. I think you should go into this with an open mind."

"I will. Thanks, Sis."

"You and Jack look at buildings. When you have an idea of what's available downtown that you like and you have all the information on them, including prices, taxes, insurance, square footage, as well as comps, let's sit down and talk again. You know I'll be happy to look at any building you find interesting and, when you get serious, we'll get TJ out there too so that we can get a general idea of how structurally sound it may be.

My last piece of advice is to *take your time*. I know you've saved over the years. I don't know how much and I don't need to know. However, be sure you keep at least one year's worth of living expenses available to you in the bank until your practice catches on and you can cover your expenses through your fees. Remember, you can always live at home rent free. So, if the dollars aren't there now, maybe renting a small office for a year and then revisiting the idea of buying, might be your best answer."

Brent thanked Gabby and left. He wasn't discouraged. In fact, Gabby had confirmed his thinking and knew, based upon what she said, he could do this. The condition of any building he might choose and its location were critical factors. Money probably wasn't going to be the issue if the building was structurally sound. He had saved a good deal of his salary while in Washington and his bonuses were substantial, those too being banked for his future. He was just going to have to wait and see what Jack came up with the next day.

CHAPTER FOURTEEN

Ari was starting to unwind. She hadn't realized how uptight she had become over the past several months, if not the entire last year. She luxuriated in the comfort of her old bedroom, allowed her mother to make her breakfast, and enjoyed those early hours with her mother as they chatted over their morning coffee. Ari went down to the plant with her dad as she had done when she was much younger. Some of the faces she remembered were no longer there, but her heart soared when she could walk right in and almost pick up conversations she had years ago with so many others she had known for so long.

Frank Bolan had built up the machine parts company which was started by his father in 1934 after he first moved to Thompsonville. When Yuri started the business, he was the only employee. By the time Frank joined his father, the company had nine employees. Frank spent his first several years traveling to many of the cities where his father had opened up client contacts. Through Frank's continued efforts, their client base increased significantly. At its height, Bolan's Machine Works employed 55 people.

That was the thriving business Ari remembered. The one where her father had taught her the rudimentary principles of business, to which she held fast in everything she now undertook.

Business had slowed over the past couple of years and Ari was concerned not only for her father and his business, but also the impact it might have on her parents' financial well-being. She worried about her Grandpa's situation and the huge financial drain it, too, had to be. What no one knew was that Frank had stashed away enough money for his family to live quite comfortably for the rest of their lives. Frank was a saver and a pillar of the community, having donated to the poor both personally and through his company for many years. He had invested wisely and neither Linda nor Ari would ever have to worry, although they didn't know that.

Having spent most of the day with her dad, Ari went back to the house, took a little nap, and decided she needed a "Gabby fix." She called her best friend and invited herself over to Gabby's house for some play time with her goddaughter and the requisite glass or two of red wine with her goddaughter's mother. *Well,* Gabby thought, *a glass or two of wine just wasn't going to be enough to cover everything they needed to catch up on.* Gabby suggested that Ari spend the night and Ari immediately took her up on her offer.

The friends played with Nicole while Ethel prepared dinner. As Ari's companion when she was a little girl, Ethel admired what a lovely young woman Ari had become and was proud she had been able to play a small part in the process.

After dinner, Nicole having been read a bedtime story by "Aunt Ari" and then falling off to sleep, the girls settled down in the family room. Gabby started a fire, grabbed the bottle of wine and their two glasses and she and Ari curled up on the comfortable sofa. Gabby told Ari that Nicole was going to get spoiled. "Last night a story from Uncle Brent and then tonight one from 'Aunt Ari.'"

"We'll have to get more storybooks, I guess. Believe me, I love it. Not to change the subject though, tell me what's going on with Brent and his move back to Thompsonville?"

Gabby told Ari the story, the reasons behind it and his plans. Ari was ecstatic it was a positive move on his part, not something he had to do.

Gabby was about to ask Ari what was happening with her and her job search when the phone rang. Answering, Gabby said, "hello," and a smile came across her face. Ari knew this had to be Jerry on the other end of the line. Gabby and he chatted for a couple of minutes when Gabby said into the phone, "Jerry, if you're finished with work, why don't you stop by for a little while? Ari is here and I'd really like you to meet her. Great. Oh, have you had dinner yet? Okay, good, so have we. We'll see you in a little bit. Bye." Gabby turned to Ari, "I hope that's all right with you. I really do want you two to meet."

"I'm anxious to meet him, Gabby. You've told me so much about him over the last several months, I need to see him for myself – make sure he's real." Gabby blushed, then they chatted on, enjoying each other's company and the warmth of the fire as they sipped their wine.

About thirty minutes later, the doorbell rang and Gabby jumped up to answer it. Jerry was standing at the front door with a pink pastry box and a warm smile on his face. Gabby welcomed him in, taking his coat and the box. Jerry said, "I just happened to be passing that little French bistro/pastry shop and thought that you and Ari would like to join me in dessert."

Gabby set the box down in the kitchen and then took Jerry's hand and led him into the family room to meet Ari. They liked each other immediately.

Ari thought there was something very calm and reassuring about Jerry that had been lacking in Jason. While she didn't want to make comparisons, it was inevitable that anyone who had known Jason and then met Jerry, would do just that.

They enjoyed their treat and Jerry stayed about an hour. With a wink to Ari, he excused himself. "I know you two have a lot of catching up to do." As Gabby walked Jerry to the door, Ari could see that there was something special between them.

When Gabby returned to the family room, Ari simply said, "I like him a lot."

"I do too." And then Gabby got quiet.

After a fairly long silence, Gabby finally got to ask Ari about her job situation. Ari told her everything. She told her about the hurt, rejection if you will, of being laid off, the frustration of not being able to find a new job, and the lack of self-confidence that comes with all of it.

"Gabby, I have to admit that it never was my dream job. But I was successful at it and there was a sense of purpose. I was only one of thousands who are hired directly out of college by the large brokerage houses in New

York. Even though you eventually end up with your own clients, you're still just a number in the whole scheme of the business. And to top it all off, I still really don't know what I want to do with my life. I'm hoping to get my head back on straight so I can go back to Chicago with a positive attitude and find a new job I can really relish."

"You'll do it, Ari. I know you will."

"You're right, and tomorrow's another day."

As Ari climbed into bed, there was a knock on the door. Gabby peeked in to see if Ari was still awake. Ari looked up at Gabby. "What's up? Is Nicole all right?"

Gabby nodded, came in slowly and sat on Ari's bed. "Ari, I haven't told this to anyone, not even my mother, but Jerry has been asking me to marry him."

"Oh, Gabby, that's terrific. From what I saw, I think he's wonderful. Why aren't you shouting this from the rooftops?"

"I think I should be, but I'm so concerned that what you saw, what I've been seeing, well, maybe that's just not who he *really* is. I wasn't so smart before, I can't afford to make another mistake. Now I have Nicole's interests to think about. It's not just me anymore."

Ari put her arm around Gabby and gave her a hug. "Gabby, this is so different. Before, with Jason -- no one knew him. He came from nowhere and claimed he had no family. He met you, targeted you if you will, made it his job to have you fall in love with him, and all that in about nine months. You've known Jerry for what, eight years now? You've worked with him and met his family. He grew up here, he's been in business in Thompsonville since he got out of school and he's a respected member of the community. I know you're scared, but this man is *not* Jason. If you have other hesitations, if there's something else you're not telling me well, then, okay, maybe he's not right for you. Only you can decide that. Just don't let your fear keep you from happiness. If that were to happen, Jason will have won after all and Nicole could end up being the biggest loser."

Gabby hugged Ari back and murmured, "Thanks, pal."

The next morning when Ari went downstairs, everyone else was already up and Ethel had arrived, making breakfast for those who wanted it. Ari poured herself a cup of coffee and sat down at the kitchen table with Gabby and Nicole. Gabby was running late so she only had a minute to thank Ari for spending the night. "Is there any chance you can stay again tonight?"

Ari thought about it a minute. "I'd really like to, but I think I need to spend some time with my parents first. Maybe we can do it again next week."

On Saturday, Jerry had a date with Gabby and Nicole to visit the pumpkin farm so that Nicole could pick out her own pumpkins for Halloween. They decided they wanted to pick one up and carve it for Mrs. McCutcheon too. So, the plan was to design, cut and decorate all the pumpkins that afternoon and Jerry would then stay for dinner after their hard day's work.

Gabby had her video camera so she could get some movies of Nicole wandering through and sitting in the middle of the pumpkin patch, á la the Country Baby, who sat surrounded by bushels of apples in the movie Baby Boom.

Nicole carefully examined all the pumpkins, as Jerry held her hand, answering her questions. He pointed out all the choices which might be good for outside their front door, for Mrs. McCutcheon's porch and which one might be her special pumpkin. As they chatted back and forth, Gabby kept the camera going just to capture what a fun day it was.

Jerry stooped down to Nicole as she was studying yet another one. "Nicole, would *you* like to be *my* special pumpkin?"

Nicole looked up at Jerry. "How can I be a pumpkin, silly?"

"Well, if I were to be your daddy, you could then be my special pumpkin."

"For always? Not just Hall'ween?"

"Yes, sweetheart, for always. What do you think?"

Nicole threw her arms around Jerry and held onto him tightly. He looked over at Gabby, who was still unconsciously filming through her tears. He tilted his head questioningly and mouthed, "Will you," then saw her nodding, as she dropped the camera, and ran into their arms.

There were tears and laughter, Nicole said, "Mommy, Jerry's gonna be my daddy and I'm gonna be his special pumpkin, that's okay isn't it?"

Gabby hugged them harder. "It's better than okay, it's better than just about everything."

Gabby retrieved her camera and they headed back to Gabby's house with an assortment of pumpkins. While they were designing the jack-o-lanterns, Brent called to ask if he could drop by to discuss his real estate finds.

"Come on over. You don't know it, but you just volunteered to help cut pumpkins. I'm going to call Ari too, she has all kinds of questions about you, she may as well ask them directly. Plan on staying for dinner. Jerry's here. We'll make it a little party."

After talking to Ari, Gabby called her mother and invited her too. "Mom, do you have the makings for your Frutti de Mare? I've sort of invited everyone for dinner and don't have anything in the fridge, except salad fixings."

Mary laughed. "Not a problem, I'll bring everything for the dish and even make it, if I can be excused from the pumpkin cutting ceremonies."

When Mary arrived, she really had brought everything: the ingredients for her pasta dish, fresh bread, salad already made with her special dressing on the side, and, best of all, Ethel. Gabby was glad her mother had thought to include her and told Ethel that she was only allowed to stay if she sat down to dinner with everyone else.

Everyone had a great time working on the pumpkins and joking around with each other. Brent hadn't met Jerry before but, of course, Mary knew him and soon Brent was getting along with Jerry as if they had known each other for years. When Jerry realized they had everything for dinner except dessert and maybe an extra bottle of wine or two, he drove off to pick them up, making a quick stop at his house. He returned an hour later and helped put the dinner together as best he could without getting in the way of all the ladies of the house.

The men were shooed out of the kitchen so the ladies could get some real work done. Jerry and Brent ended up out on the back deck chatting as old friends. Jerry knew about Brent's search for an office and they ended up talking about downtown real estate for a half hour or so before they were called in for dinner. They all had a wonderful time together at dinner. There were jokes, stories and a true sense of people really enjoying one another.

"Nicole, how did you enjoy going to the pumpkin farm and choosing your own pumpkins?"

"I liked it a lot, Aunt Ari. But the best part is that now I'm going to be Jerry's special pumpkin, because he's going to be my new daddy."

Everyone stopped talking, looked at Nicole as if they questioned what they had just heard and then all heads turned to Gabby and Jerry. Gabby smiled. Jerry's smile was even larger. Then everyone started talking at once.

Gabby tried to answer all the questions as they were being asked, but then Nicole said, "Mommy, you know you have the movie in the camera." Gabby was startled by the realization that Nicole was right. She had videotaped the whole thing.

Jerry said, "Gabby, if you don't mind, why don't we all just watch the movie? If everyone can wait a few minutes until we finish dinner, we'll all go see how Nicole got a new daddy. Gabby?"

Gabby was anxious to share the story, but thought she could hold out until after dessert. "I'd love it."

Jerry brought in the pink box from the bistro and set it in front of Gabby. Ethel brought in the dessert dishes as Gabby arranged the various pastries on a cake stand.

Mary eyed the pastries. "What's that?" she asked, pointing to a decadent looking piece of chocolate cake. Perched on top sat a sparkling diamond ring. Gabby gasped as she saw it.

All of a sudden Brent said, "Wait a minute, there's another one!"

Gabby looked at Jerry now, her expression saying, "What's going on here?"

"Maybe I can help you serve, Gabby." Jerry walked over to Gabby's side and placed the slice of chocolate cake in front of her, slipping the ring on her finger. He leaned down and kissed Gabby, whispering something in her ear. Turning, he calmly took the other piece of cake with the small ring on it and served it to Nicole, who quickly put her new ring on her own finger. Brent rose and proposed a toast to the new family, saying how genuinely pleased they all were that he was now a part of all of them.

When everyone but Jerry had finally left, and Nicole was asleep in her bed, he and Gabby went down to the family room. Jerry cradled her in his arms as they sat on the sofa in front of the fire. Gabby's subconscious had finally freed her from any remaining reluctance, and she lost herself in Jerry's warmth and embrace. Now, she eagerly returned his kisses, his touch, and allowed her senses and body to respond as never before.

Jerry noticed the difference. He held her tenderly and kissed the top of her head. "Why now? What changed? It's not just the fact that you finally said yes, but you seem to be more relaxed, perhaps more sure of your love. Is that it?"

"Oh Jerry, I've been in love with you for such a long time now, but I was so afraid, for me, for Nicole. I didn't trust myself that I would make the right decision this time. It wasn't you. I kept my fears to myself and guarded my emotions for you and my reactions to you.

Then, the other night when Ari stayed over, I finally broke down and let it all out. I probably should have talked to my mother earlier, but somehow, this time, I wanted someone who could be more objective. Ari made me realize a lot of things I couldn't see because I was so close to my own fears. Once I understood, there was never a question in my mind that I wanted to be with you for the rest of my life and have you be a part of Nicole's life. You know, she adores you almost as much as I do."

With that, Gabby shared with Jerry the most unguarded and totally trusting moments she had ever spent with anyone. Until that night they had never made love. Jerry didn't want to push Gabby and, ultimately, he was right. He sensed that she would have repelled his advances and undoubtedly run for the hills -- all that mistrust of men running through her head. Now, Gabby gave herself willingly and unabashedly and she and Jerry slowly and softly melted into one another's beings.

They never discussed Brent's real estate issue. On Sunday, Gabby called Brent and apologized, asking if he would like to spend a couple of hours that afternoon going over his stuff. They agreed to meet at 2:00, which gave Gabby and Nicole enough time to run over to Mrs. McCutcheon's to deliver her gift. Mrs. McCutcheon was delighted with her jack-o-lantern and promptly put in on the front porch in anticipation of Halloween.

Nicole was so pleased that Mrs. McCutcheon made a big deal over the gift and told her all about how she picked it 'specially for her. She was becoming quite the young lady and she oozed exuberance in all she tackled. She promptly announced to Mrs. McCutcheon that Jerry was going to be her new daddy. The lovely older lady, who had grown to love this family, was thrilled with the news. She wanted to know all the details, but Gabby told her they had just decided yesterday and hadn't really discussed the particulars yet.

When they arrived home, Brent's car was in the driveway. They sat at the kitchen table and spread out the listing information on the various properties, while Nicole sat at the island drawing pictures of pumpkins.

Brent was excited. He could barely contain himself as he began to tell Gabby about what he had found. Gabby couldn't remember seeing Brent this excited about anything. Normally he was one to sit back and quietly think about what was being said before putting in his two cents -- and then, only if he was asked.

"Jack and I spent the first part of the day driving around the entire commercial area of downtown, street by street. It was clear the buildings by the river are in the worst condition and slowly, as we went from 1st Street up through 7th and then Capitol toward the courthouse, the buildings were better maintained and occupancy increased. The number of buildings available for sale also follows a similar pattern as do the asking prices. So, given that, it was easy for me to eliminate the two buildings that are currently for sale within a stone's throw from the courthouse.

Based on what you told me regarding the costs of renovation and that there's really not much else going on near the river, I have also pretty much eliminated those buildings as well. That is, unless you know of one that I should look into. That left these," as he pointed to a stack of listings in front of him. Next, he pointed to the stack in the upper right-hand corner of the table. "These are the ones from around 1st to 3rd Streets, which I brought just in case you wanted to look them over. Here's a map of downtown." He unfolded a large detailed map of the city streets, laying it flat in front of them so that they could both look at it.

"Okay, Brent. Let me get my bearings here. You've eliminated these by the river and two by the courthouse. Am I correct?"

"You are. Now, from what I've eliminated, we're left with the area from about 4th Street up to 7th and then from Main Street over to Columbia. You know Augustino's Restaurant, that's on the corner of Columbia at 7th, that's pretty much the outside perimeter of my search area. Then, on the other side of Main, we have about three blocks before we hit the beginning of the industrial area.

Interestingly enough, Jack is totally correct. I can afford to buy in most cases less expensively than I can rent office space. I've looked at quite a few buildings, but there are three I really like.

One is the old cannery on the south side of town on Preston between 4th and 5th, really the beginning of the industrial area. It's huge, but the cost per square foot is considerably less than the others. It has a commercial elevator and the property takes up the entire block, some of which is a parking lot, it's not all building. It's wide open inside. Almost entire floors without walls, just large pillars, I'm assuming structurally necessary. The ceilings are very high and the windows are wide and tall. It's the least expensive per square foot of the three buildings."

"I'm not sure you want to go there, Brent. It might be okay during the day, but if you're planning on living there too, well, you probably have better choices."

"Actually, I do, or at least I think I do. Next we have a smallish building at 4th and Columbia. It's a three-story brick building that was renovated at one time into a luncheonette on the ground floor with all the restaurant equipment still in place, the top two stories divided into office space. Not particularly well done, but it has been updated. This is a good deal also. The cost per square foot is more than the cannery, but there are fewer square feet. It wouldn't require as much work to make it useable, but I'd end up with a building where I could use one floor for my office, one for my living quarters and then I'd have to rely on finding a tenant to rent the ground floor."

"That could be difficult for you with so much other retail space available in the area."

"Lastly, we have a four-story brick building which was at one time Spenser's Boutique and Salon. You may not remember it. At one time Spenser's was *the* place to shop in Thompsonville. It's been rented out over the years since Mrs. Spenser died and they closed the doors. Some of the original beauty can be seen and some of it was either 'modernized' or replaced as it wore out. But the building has a sense of elegance I can only recall seeing in major cities. It's more expensive, but it has four floors, each one approximately 2,000 square feet, an elevator, and the top floor, which was never finished to be open to the public, has lovely large windows both on the front and back sides of the building, fairly high ceilings, and beautiful brick walls that run down both sides.

Gabby, I love this place. I can afford it and I don't think it would cost that much to renovate, hopefully, mostly cosmetic work. Will you come and look at it with me on Monday? Can we take TJ too?"

"Whoa, slow down, Brent. First of all, where is this edifice?"

"I'm sorry, Sis, I'm so excited, I forgot to tell you. It's on 5th and Ashland, which makes it only three blocks to the courthouse and a block off Main. There's plenty of street parking and there's a public parking lot just up the street toward the courthouse."

"That sounds like a good location. It's close to the Blue Frog then."

"The Blue Frog is on 6th and Main, but on the south side of Main. Still it *is* close and almost everything is in walking distance. Even the few retail shops which are still in the area are close by, although mostly more toward the bridge and the river."

"Brent, where are the papers on this Spenser building?" Brent handed them to Gabby and she began to read. "This building isn't cheap Brent. Can you afford it?"

"It is expensive, probably more than I wanted to spend. But in the long run, I think this is the best investment I can make. And, I'm not only talking about the real estate investment, I mean in my own personal career and future. I don't normally get carried away or make any decisions by gut, but I have to tell you Sis, this just feels right."

"Okay, let's go take that look at it on Monday. I always start the week with a meeting of my department heads. That's 8:30 a.m. We'll finish by 9ish and that would probably be a good time for me to steal TJ away, too. I think you might want to ask Uncle Tony to look at the building as well. Let's face it, his experience is far more extensive than TJ's. Remember, both Dad and Uncle Tony worked on some commercial properties before they started Regency. So, if you can get an appointment for around 10:00 with Jack to show us that property, I think it'll work well for all of us. Did you want us to look at any of the other buildings too?"

"Well, I guess we could."

"It would probably be a good idea, just for the sake of comparison. While you've seen several properties downtown, we haven't, and that's not the market we're generally familiar with. It would help me, for my own peace of mind, that I'm giving you good advice."

"It's a date, Sis. Thanks so much."

"You're very welcome, but you know you'll owe me one," Gabby said laughing.

When Jerry arrived to pick Gabby and Nicole up to take them to dinner, Nicole was waiting at the door with a hug. "I thought daddies lived in the same house with everybody else. Aren't you going to live with us?"

Jerry laughed inside but knew that this was a very serious question to Nicole and it deserved a serious answer. "Well, Nicole, daddies do live in the same house with their families, but you know that legally I'm not your daddy yet. What that means is that your mommy and I have to go to the city and get a piece of paper saying we can get married and then find someone who can do it. Not everyone can marry people. But, once we do that, then we can all live together and I'll be your daddy for real. Okay?"

Nicole glumly said, "Okay," as tears welled up in her eyes. "But I thought you were already my daddy."

"Nicole, I am, only it's not written down yet. Your mommy and I will take care of it. I promise you."

Gabby overheard most of the conversation as she was on her way to answer the door. She smiled at Jerry and looked down at Nicole, who was tugging on her jacket. "Mommy, Jerry says we need to get a paper from the city, can we stop and get it today? Then he can live with us and be my daddy."

Gabby bent down toward Nicole. "This is very important to you, isn't it sweetheart?"

"Oh, yes, mommy. Everybody has a daddy 'cept me."

"Well, then we'll see what we can do to get that paper as soon as possible."

Nicole hugged her mom and wiped her eyes knowing that her mommy could do anything. And, besides, Jerry promised too.

That night, after they enjoyed their pepperoni pizza from Mario's, Gabby and Jerry sat down in Gabby's family room and decided that they wanted their wedding to be held as soon as possible because they wanted to start the rest of their lives together and because it would remove any confusion Nicole was now experiencing.

"We have so much to be thankful for; my best friend is in from Chicago, my brother has returned home and it's almost Thanksgiving. Do you think we could pull this off in the next six weeks? I think it would make a wonderful Christmas gift to each other and also for Nicole."

Jerry looked at Gabby, kissed her tenderly, acknowledging his agreement and held her with the promise of a happiness that was yet to come.

CHAPTER FIFTEEN

Gabby found herself on cloud nine Monday morning. She didn't say anything to Nicole at breakfast about Jerry's and her plan to hold their wedding over the holidays until she was sure they could get everything in place. If they couldn't make it happen, she didn't want to let Nicole down.

On top of wedding plans swirling in her head, Gabby had her regular staff meeting at Regency and then her promised meeting with Brent downtown. It was only 8:00 on Monday morning, and she was already running hard.

After the staff meeting, Gabby asked TJ to join her, telling him what they were up to. TJ was excited about his cousin returning to Thompsonville and was happy he had been asked to help look at buildings for his new office space.

When Gabby and TJ arrived at Jack Caldwell's office downtown, Brent and Uncle Tony were there waiting for them. They decided to take two cars to see the three buildings Brent was interested in, as well as a couple of others Jack thought would make good comparisons per Gabby's request.

They toured the cannery which was as huge as Brent had told her. She saw why he was interested in the building. It was a clean palette, with tons of light and space. But, she thought it was too large and wasn't really in a good part of town for leasing office space to other tenants. Uncle Tony and TJ cautioned that the upgrading of the mechanicals, plumbing and electric would be expensive, and that it undoubtedly would cost a fortune in maintenance. Gabby also feared that building it out into smaller offices would have a high price tag.

The smaller building over on 4th and Columbia was a better option and would work well for Brent's purposes. The price was right even though there would be a large cost in removing the ground floor kitchen from what had been a restaurant, and reworking all the added walls. It would be less expensive to leave the kitchen on-site, but finding a tenant with those specific needs was probably close to impossible given the area's decline in occupancy. Uncle Tony and TJ told them that the renovation work Brent thought had been done to this building was almost exclusively cosmetic. It would be costly – almost an entire gutting of the building – and it didn't offer any real room for growth, not to mention that it was farther away from the courthouse and the area was a little more iffy in Gabby's mind.

Jack saved the best for last, as had Brent when he described Spenser's to Gabby initially. Nothing, as they walked through an intricately cut glass door into a foyer of white with small black diamond-shaped accents marble floor, white pillars and a magnificent winding black wrought iron staircase, could begin to describe her sense of being blown away by what was one of the most elegant buildings she had ever been in. Gabby really didn't remember this place, and she knew she would have, had she ever been there before.

Brent watched her as her eyes roamed around the main floor. He whispered to her, "Didn't I tell you?" Even though some of the marble was chipped or broken, the mirrors were blackening, there were holes in the walls, some with wires protruding, and the entire place needed paint badly, the underlying beauty was evident.

They dutifully went from floor to floor, but Gabby knew from that first moment, this was the building. The entry itself spoke of success, and what lawyer ever wanted to portray anything other than success. And what a place to call home.

Uncle Tony and TJ were off doing their thing and Gabby knew that Brent was anxious about what they would find. They finally emerged from their inspection and told Brent that the building had been built with what was then top-of-the-line materials and mechanicals. They said there would be some upgrading necessary, but it was minimal based upon what they could see.

Structurally, it was as solid as they came. All of the buildings they had seen would require new air conditioning and electrical. The plumbing materials used here though were in far better shape than the other buildings and, interestingly enough, the bathrooms, other than what would become the master bath on the fourth floor, were so magnificent that updating them with today's bland styling used in commercial properties would be a sin.

Gabby then went to see the other buildings Jack had thought she needed to see. There was nothing in those other buildings that made Gabby think Brent would be making a mistake with the Spenser's building.

Gabby told Brent, "You know I love the Spenser's building. But, you need to take a long look at what the costs are going to be. You'll need to get companies in to check out the air conditioning, plumbing and electrical, as well as the elevator. Based upon what their quotes are, you'll have a better understanding of what you could afford." Gabby gave Brent the names of some companies specializing in those areas, but cautioned him, "Some may not handle commercial buildings, but I'm sure they can refer someone reputable."

Feeling that she had done everything that she could do for him, she wished him good luck. She was about to leave, when she turned, "Oh, by the way, Jerry and I are thinking about a December wedding. Don't make any travel plans until you've checked with me."

Brent gave her a hug and said, "I won't," and thanked her again.

After handling all the things that had piled up while she had been gone that morning, Gabby called her mother and then Ari. She told them Jerry's and her plan and that she needed to reach Father Frank right away to find a date that would work.

Father Frank was very happy for Gabby. He, of course, knew about all the horrors she had experienced with Jason and was certain that, this time, she had found a wonderful man in Jerry. He had known Jerry and his family for many years and Jerry's parents had been regular worshipers at his church until his father died. They discussed dates and honed in on two. Gabby asked Father Frank to save them both . . . she'd let him know.

Gabby's next call was to City Hall to find out about getting a license in Thompsonville. It was actually almost as easy as Vegas, even though Thompsonville wasn't in the business of tourist weddings. Gabby then called her mother back to enlist her help in arranging the reception. "Honey, I'll talk to a few caterers I know. The difficult part though will be finding a place during the holidays that's not already booked. I'd love to have you get married here at the house. Think about it."

Gabby and Jerry set December 22nd at 4:00 p.m. for their wedding. They each set about making a list of those they wanted to invite. It was clear when they put the lists together that if they invited everyone, Mary's house couldn't accommodate the group. Mary did succeed in convincing her longtime friend and retired caterer, Judy, to come out of retirement to do the catering.

So, all that was left, was the place. Gabby thought about the country club. It was still one of her favorite places. As a child, she had dreamed of being married there. Even though they weren't members, maybe, with Frank and Linda Bolan's help they could use it. Gabby and Ari spoke to them, and they were going to see what they could do. There were a couple of restaurants which might be available, but then they couldn't have anything, except what was on the restaurant's menu, with no outside catering.

Nothing was working. The country club was completely booked for the season and even though there was nothing scheduled at 4:00 p.m. on the 22nd, there was a private party at 7:00 that evening, and they needed the space clean and the chef working on that party earlier in the day.

It seemed that their only option was to cut back on the number of guests and hold the wedding at Mary's house. While cutting back on the number of guests was not what she wanted, Gabby was determined that the wedding was going to take place on the 22nd.

Ari was standing by with the invitation proofs provided by the printer waiting to insert the address of the reception, when Gabby got a call from Brent. "This time, you owe me, Sis."

"Okay. Why?"

"Because I am now the proud owner of Spenser's and I can have everything downstairs fixed up in time for you to be married on the main floor. How would you like to walk down the staircase on your way to becoming Mrs. Jerry O'Neil?"

"Holy cow. Wow! Are you serious? You bought the place?"

"I did indeed, and it's only fitting that it be the site of your wedding. It will hold everyone on your original lists and it will be grand, don't you think?"

"Brent, this is terrific, but are you sure? The place looked like it needed a lot of work before anything could be held there."

"I've been promised that it'll be ready in time. And, even if I have to do some of the work myself, you will get married there."

"Oh, Brent, I'm so excited. Thank you, thank you, thank you! You didn't tell me that you'd made a decision, much less an offer. Can you come over this weekend and tell us all about it? Jerry will be so pleased for you too."

Gabby was ecstatic. Jerry also thought that holding the wedding in Brent's new building was a splendid idea. He hadn't seen it of course, but he had heard all about it from Gabby and, if Gabby was happy, it was all that was important to him. Mary was thrilled that Gabby was going to have the wedding she wanted, and even more gratified that her children had come together to work on each other's problems.

Then Gabby called Ari, telling her the news. Ari promised she would get the draft invitations to the printer immediately now that she had an address. "Gabby, I'll do whatever it takes in order to make this happen – that includes setting marble flooring or painting the entire building myself."

Gabby laughed. "Be careful what you wish for kiddo. In this case, you may actually be called upon to do just those sorts of things."

With the wedding set and Brent's building under contract, Gabby gave a sigh of relief, sat back, and smiled.

Jerry and Gabby told Nicole about the wedding, when it was going to be, and her part in it. Nicole, with noticeable relief written all over her face, almost cried, now believing that Jerry was truly about to become her "Daddy."

On Saturday morning when Brent went over to Gabby's to tell her all about his purchase of the Spenser's building, Mary took Nicole to the movies, so that Brent and Gabby could talk without interruption.

Brent laid out all the numbers for Gabby. He had done a thorough job checking everything out. But then, that's just what Brent always did.

He talked with Jack before making any offers, and found out that the building had been on the market for quite some time. Apparently there had been some earlier offers, but the potential buyers wanted to tear the building down and put up a new, nondescript building. That had been several years earlier when Mrs. Spenser's husband was still alive, but he wanted the beautiful old building to live on. Now that he too was gone, the Spenser children really didn't care. They had reduced the price, but there hadn't been much interest because of the local economy or lack thereof.

Brent went in offering 25 percent less than the asking price. The owners countered, and Brent ended up paying 15 percent less, but with several incentives, including the sellers paying his closing costs and up to 5 percent of the purchase price in putting the elevator in good working order and passing current safety inspections.

Brent put down a hefty deposit on the building and had no trouble getting a mortgage on the balance. He told Gabby he had enough to fix up the building, including adding a full kitchen and master bath on the top floor for his apartment, a small kitchen and several bathrooms on the law firm's floor, as well as building out whatever walls might be needed for both his living quarters and the rest of what he presumed would be office space.

In truth, Brent still had enough in the bank to weather the next couple of years. He was clearly happy with his decision and couldn't wait to have the building finished. Gabby was thrilled to have her brother living back in Thompsonville again. They enjoyed the rest of the afternoon chatting and laughing about old times and then their hopes for the future.

Responses to the wedding invitations began coming in. The most astonishing one of all was from HRH. Not only was she coming, she was coming alone.

Apparently, Harriet decided to spend the holidays with her family and her husband had chosen not to. Some of the recent reprints in The Sentinel had shown Harriet at several soirees, but not Paulo. Ari and Gabby wondered what that was all about, but then these tabloids didn't always photograph every married attendee with their spouse.

When Gabby told Ari that HRH was coming to the wedding and that she would be there for the holidays, Ari decided to invite Harriet to lunch. Even though they hadn't been close in school, Ari felt that Harriet had been reaching out to her and Gabby, and she wanted to give their formerly reclusive classmate a welcoming gesture other than the formal invitations they had been exchanging. Harriet happily accepted Ari's invitation to lunch.

They met at Raison d'Etre and Ari was surprised by how much easier it was to talk to Harriet. When they were classmates, Harriet was always aloof. Ari was pleased to see that she was much more outgoing. She believed that it was due to the fact that Harriet now had a large circle of friends, traveled internationally, and mingled with so many people at the social functions she attended.

They started out chatting about some of their former classmates and then went on to discuss what Ari was doing. Harriet seemed sincerely sorry that Ari had been laid off, assuring her she would find something else soon.

Then, the Harriet with whom she had just been talking, became a different person. *It seemed as if Harriet was talking to a reporter,* Ari thought, as she began to talk about her life since graduating from Thompsonville High. Harriet talked about her apartments in New York and Paris. She talked about the French Riviera, the Cannes Film Festival, skiing in the Alps, her husband's family estate in Italy, and all the social events, both in the U.S. and abroad.

Ari left the lunch uncertain as to why Harriet had even decided to join her. While Harriet certainly was more outgoing than she had ever been, she seemed to be just as self-centered. *What was she trying to accomplish?* she wondered. *Is that her way of trying to reach out or is Harriet just as vacuous as she seems?*

Brent was working day and night on getting the building ready for the big day. He had enlisted Uncle Tony's help along with a host of other relatives and friends, and swore everyone to secrecy that the building was behind schedule, knowing Gabby had a full plate. Gabby became suspicious. It was *way* too quiet. She stopped by the building in order to check it out for herself, and ran smack-dab into Ari, Uncle Tony and almost everyone else she knew, working furiously to finish up in time. Staring at the mess, her throat had a stranglehold on her words.

Ari was the first to catch sight of her. "Gabby," she screamed, "what are you doing here?" Everyone stopped. Brent went running up to her as Ari, Uncle Tony, TJ and even her mother looked on, aghast.

"Now, Gabby, it's not as bad as it looks. I promise you, Sis, it'll all be cleaned up in time."

"Brent, there's no way you'll have it finished . . . "

"Yes, we will. You know how, that in order to organize things, one has to make a mess first. Well, this is the mess. Truly, most of the work is done – we're in the clean up stage. We'll be ready."

"Why didn't anyone tell me?"

"Obviously, because we didn't want to worry you, Sis. You have enough on your hands."

By then, everyone had gathered around her. "Gabby, we have more than a week before the wedding," said Uncle Tony. "Think about the houses we build; we can do a lot in ten days. You know that. Have I ever missed a deadline?"

"Well . . . no. Not that I can remember. But, this is . . . well, it's just . . . you know, a shock. I had no idea."

"Don't worry about it, please. I know it doesn't look like it, but we will absolutely be finished, maybe not with time to spare, but finished. The building will be sparkling, at least the part of it the guests'll see, and you'll have the most beautiful wedding ever. Look at me. You believe me, don't you?" Gabby nodded. "*Tell me* you believe me, Gabby."

"I believe you, Uncle Tony. Thank you for doing this – Thank you all for doing this."

Gabby walked away almost in tears, even though she knew her uncle always met his deadlines. But the uncertainty lingered, and it was unsettling.

Gabby and Jerry's wedding day seemed to arrive overnight. The building was spectacular. Uncle Tony was true to his word and, even though many of the guests had callouses and sore backs, the *crew* was very proud of the work they had done.

The bottom floor of the building was stunning with its marble flooring looking as if it were new, the black wrought iron bannister decorated with sprays of star lilies and ribbon and the chairs covered in cream satin placed in semicircular rows facing the altar. Not an exposed wire or unpainted wall to be seen.

Brent guided Gabby down the staircase and up to the altar. She felt her father's presence and knew that he, too, was escorting her. There, at the end of the aisle, before the altar, stood this exceptional man, whose love for her was unequivocal. Standing beside Jerry was Nicole. It was unorthodox as wedding etiquette went, but to Jerry and her, it was perfect. They were her reason for being and, soon, they would be as one.

The wedding was everything she ever dreamed of – not even The Palm Court would have been as beautiful. Surrounded by their families and friends, Jerry and Gabby exchanged vows and then picked Nicole up as they walked back down the aisle, now a family.

Right on the heels of the wedding came Christmas and then New Year's. It was a blur. Gabby and Jerry enjoyed a long weekend in San Francisco and then returned home in order to incorporate their two households into one, before heading back to work after New Year's Day.

Harriet returned to New York without another word to anyone.

Ari began to feel anxious and unsettled. She had spent as much time in Thompsonville as she thought she could afford.

Ari visited Grandpa Bolan at Grandview Manor several times. He hadn't missed a step. The ladies swarmed around him, and he seemed to enjoy every bit of their attention. It was now more difficult to find time to visit with him, due to all his social commitments. With a twinkle in his eye, he whispered to Ari, "You're still my number one girl, and don't you ever forget it."

Now that the holidays and Gabby's wedding were over, with the start of the new year, it was time to begin the job search again in earnest. That could best be done in Chicago.

Arriving home, Ari and her headhunter decided that they needed to expand her search, as the economic situation had not improved over the last quarter. They spent the next several months responding to every possible lead, sending out resumes to every company they thought might be in a position to hire, regardless of where they were located. There were some nibbles, but nothing solid. As the months passed, Ari became more and more disheartened, and again her self-confidence began to break down. She struggled getting dressed every day, forced herself to call people, and began to question her self-worth.

One day in May when Ari didn't think she could be much more depressed, she answered the phone to hear her mother on the other end of the line with a voice that didn't sound normal. Ari immediately knew that there was something wrong. Asking just that, her mother replied, "Ari, your father has been having some problems which we didn't want to bother you with, but, yesterday, well, the doctor confirmed to us our worst fears. It seems that your father has cancer of the liver and the outlook isn't good. We're now reviewing our options, but unless something dramatic happens, or we can get him into some new-drug testing program, we're looking at, at best, nine months. Hold on, honey. Your father wants to talk to you."

"Dad . . . oh, Dad . . . "

"I know, sweetheart. We're so sorry to have to tell you this over the phone or to burden you with this at all. You have enough on your plate right now."

"I don't care about me. What can I do?"

"Nothing, sweetheart. We're going to follow the plan that the doctors set out for chemotherapy and/or radiation and, as your mother said, do whatever else may be necessary. This is serious, but we *are* going to fight it. We don't want you to worry. We felt we had to tell you what was going on, but we'll have to get back to you in a couple of days to tell you what the final plan will be."

Ari couldn't speak. She mumbled something about "what ifs," but basically was rattled. She could only think about getting off the phone, and then maybe waking up from whatever awful nightmare she was having. After hanging up, Ari just sat on the couch in her apartment unable to move, staring at the phone. *This is just not happening*, she thought. She sat there for hours in a state of horror.

When Emily arrived home, she found Ari sitting in the dark, hugging herself. Emily quickly threw a blanket around Ari's shoulders as she sat there shaking, while continuing to hug herself. Emily fixed a pot of tea and sat down with Ari, trying to figure out exactly what was going on.

After some tea and soothing talk from Emily, Ari began to tell her roommate about the call from her parents. Ari told her that she had been sitting there all afternoon since getting the call, trying to figure out what she should do. "I have to go home, Em."

"Of course you do," Emily replied, as she put her arm around Ari's shoulder.

"But I don't know when I'll be back. It may be a couple of months or it could be a year. I don't know what to do. I don't have a job and my bank account is dwindling. I think you need to find another roommate, because my half of our rent is something I can't afford to continue while I'm gone."

"Stop that kind of thinking. This is still your home whether or not you pay rent. When you come back, everything will be in its place. I really don't want another roommate, so if it's not you, it's no one. I think you need to concentrate on packing up your suitcase and forget about everything else."

Ari began sobbing again. After a few minutes she calmed down. "Whatever happens with my father's cancer, it won't be good or easy on my mother. I need to be there for my father and then, afterwards, I'll need to be there for my mother. This is not just something that I have to do, but I *truly* want to do. Whoever or whatever I am today is due to their unconditional love and support, and we need to be together and deal with this as the family we are and have always been."

Emily continued patting Ari on the back. "Take some time, go home, be with your family and don't worry about anything here. Now, come on, dry those eyes and I'll help you pack."

CHAPTER SIXTEEN

Gabby and Jerry set about doing the paperwork necessary for Jerry to legally adopt Nicole. Gabby contacted Carolyn and asked her if she had the time to prepare the papers but that if not, her brother Brent had moved back to Thompsonville and was in the process of setting up his own practice. She told Carolyn about the building downtown, his plans to have his office there, rent out some of the extra office space and live on the top floor.

Carolyn was shocked. As she had talked to Brent during Gabby's divorce, she found him to be very bright, his thoughts cogent and well articulated. She knew that he had practiced at a major international law firm in Washington, D.C., and couldn't imagine what would make a successful attorney practicing in such a high-powered environment choose to leave and set up shop in a small town. Granted, Thompsonville was a county seat, but it had relatively rudimentary legal matters – she was certain he would become bored.

Carolyn told Gabby that if Brent wasn't too busy setting up his practice, she would be happy to let him handle Nicole's adoption. "At some point, I'd like to meet him in person – I'm down there often."

It wasn't long after that conversation that Carolyn called Gabby asking for Brent's office telephone number. Carolyn mentioned that she was planning to be in Thompsonville on a new matter and thought it might be a good time to meet Brent. Carolyn had ulterior motives. She had checked Brent out thoroughly with the ABA, his former law firm in Washington, and even two of Brent's former D.C. clients. Everyone had nothing but glowing words about his work and him personally.

For some time, Carolyn and her partners had been looking to open an office in Thompsonville due to the amount of work they did there. The problem was that while there was a good deal of work, it wasn't enough to require a full-time lawyer's presence, or justify the cost of operating an office there. Truth be told, there really wasn't an attorney in their office who even wanted to work in Thompsonville full-time. With Brent now establishing an office there, maybe Carolyn's firm could rent some space from him. Carolyn's firm could just use the office when necessary. She thought that this was a very good plan indeed.

Brent was surprised to hear from her. Work on the mechanicals, electric and plumbing had all been completed. The commercial floors of the building were still shells, waiting to be built out depending upon the needs of the tenants, although his office space was almost finished. Brent's penthouse, however, was far from complete. Fortunately, there was no urgency in moving out of his mother's house. Besides, he still hadn't focused on buying the furniture which would make his new living quarters a home. Carolyn and Brent set a date to meet for lunch at Augustino's, and then tour the available office space in Brent's building.

Carolyn was immediately taken with Brent, which again made her ask herself, *Why would a young man with such promise leave a coveted position and influential career in Washington, D.C.?* And so, she asked him exactly that.

Brent hesitated before he spoke. "Washington is a very heady place. I have friends on The Hill who bought into the process with nothing but the best intentions, then became disillusioned. It entraps one into believing you are doing good for the people when, in fact, little gets done on their behalf due to the legislative process. Let's just say I found private practice there to be empty and unsatisfying. I found the lawyers intelligent and stimulating, but at the end of the day, it just wasn't enough for me to want to continue doing the same thing for the rest of my life."

Brent was everything she believed him to be and more. Not only was he bright, articulate and comfortable in his own skin, he was handsome. She immediately saw the resemblance to his sister, the dark hair and eyes, even though his skin was on the olive side and he stood quite a bit taller than Gabby, probably, she guessed, around six feet. *Soon*, she thought, *some lovely young woman would snatch him up.* Carolyn wondered how he had stayed single for so long, particularly in D.C. *Now, who did she know . . . ?*

Carolyn's initial reaction to Brent's building was exactly what he hoped for when anyone new walked into its foyer. She stared at the tall ceilings, the marble floor, the winding staircase and was overwhelmed by the sheer magnificence of the building.

Brent explained that the ground floor had been completed first, as Gabby and Jerry needed a space for their recent wedding.

"I am so sorry I wasn't able to be here for that. I'm certain it was lovely, particularly now that I see the setting."

"It was beautiful, and I know Gabby was very sorry you couldn't be here." Brent continued to show Carolyn the building. She saw the open space available for tenants, and the yet to be completed kitchens and bathrooms which were to be a part of the common areas for the leased offices. They discussed which part of the space she was most interested in and how much square footage she anticipated needing, the rent and other issues which would impact their plans. She asked Brent whether he was providing common facilities to be shared by the tenants such as conference rooms or even a receptionist. Brent admitted he hadn't considered providing those facilities since he anticipated leasing to firms rather than individuals. He conceded that this was something he might consider. "I think that will depend on the needs of my tenants. Since I won't be building out the walls until I have a signed lease agreement, I can make adjustments as necessary. Is that the type of space your firm is looking for – shared facilities?"

"We would like to have access to a conference room, certainly. You're already providing kitchen and bathroom facilities, so that's not a problem. As to a receptionist, I'm sure we could get around that with call-forwarding. Most of us now have cell phones, too. Let me talk to the partners back in Pittsburgh and then we'll be in touch with you. Thanks, Brent. You have a beautiful building."

Ari's homecoming was less than joyous. Gabby and Jerry met her at the airport. With her parents at one of the many doctors who would now be treating her father, Ari couldn't have felt more alone walking into her empty childhood home. It even felt different. It was almost as if she were a stranger there – not quite comfortable in this seemingly familiar place.

Jerry carried Ari's suitcase up to her room, allowing Gabby and Ari just a few minutes alone. Ari offered coffee, but Gabby knew, instinctively, this was not the time to chat. She hugged her friend and told her, "Anytime you need me, no matter what . . ."

Ari cried as she locked the door behind them. Knowing she couldn't let her father see her this way, she immediately went up to her room and splashed cold water on her face. Her mother had told her that they would be home around 4:00, so Ari needed to fix her face before they arrived. Ari knew this was not going to be easy for her mother either, but she was determined to do her best and not make it any more difficult for them than it already was.

Ari was not prepared for how different her father looked from when she had last seen him only a few months earlier. She had put on a pot of coffee and was sitting in the kitchen when they came in. She rushed to hug and kiss them both, holding back the tears that were already forming in the corner of each eye. Fortunately, her mother took over the conversation, allowing Ari to get herself back under control. They sat in the kitchen, drinking coffee and started to feel their way around the conversation.

Frank had a good attitude and assured Ari, as he had Linda, that he was going to fight the cancer by doing everything the doctors recommended and then some. They discussed the treatment options and their potential side-effects.

Ari immediately asked, "What can I do?"

"Sweetheart, there isn't anything. Just your being here is enough." Frank replied.

Linda, on the other hand, had a very specific idea of what Ari could do. "Ari, your father wants to go down to the office as if nothing were happening and as if he still had the stamina to work. I'd like you to help him do what he needs to do there. Somehow, between the two of us, we'll try to keep up with him."

It wasn't easy. The treatments were intense and Frank often found himself unable to do anything but sleep. Even eating had become difficult.

When he could go down to the office, he seldom could stay for long. It soon became apparent that Ari was going to have to learn everything her father could teach her about the business in a crash course, if they were going to be able to keep it afloat.

Ari was frustrated. But, she admitted, it was better than the deep depression that had set in because of her being unemployed. She now knew how crippling it was to lose one's self-confidence and fall into the utter desperation that came with it. She used to believe, as most people do, that depression was an indication of mental disease. Boy, had she found out differently. Now, even though she never wanted to work at her father's company, she found herself feeling that she wasn't worthless. She even started to believe there was nothing that she could have done to avoid being laid off; it was merely a function of the economy and, sooner or later, she would find the right job for her.

Her father's health and strength with it were failing at a rate which scared her. She and her mother would sit and talk when Frank was resting. Ari watched the stress of her father's illness take its toll on her mother too. As much as Ari, Hospice, and outside aides helped, Linda was suffering from lack of sleep as she listened to every move Frank made just in case he needed her for something. He was becoming less mobile and she struggled to help him get up, sit down, and walk; every possible move he tried to make, hampered by this insidious disease. His appetite was gone and his ability to swallow anything was significantly impeded, so much so that he stopped trying to eat.

Ari was glad she could be there for her mother, and thought that no one should have to go through this. Not the patient, their loved ones, or the caregivers.

Then, one Tuesday morning in September, their already stressed lives were rattled to the bone. At first, when Linda called Ari at the office, Ari assumed that something had happened with her father. Linda could hardly speak. "Ari, turn on the TV. I can't believe it. An airplane just flew into one of the Twin Towers in Manhattan."

Before Ari could sit back down in her chair, another airplane flew into the other tower. Of course, not having seen the first airplane, Ari thought she was looking at a taped replay of the accident. Ari and Linda watched in silence as they began to comprehend that there had been another airplane which flew into the second tower, and that *this was no accident.*

Ari called George and the others into Frank's office. They stood silently as they watched in horror. The replays of the crashes, the pandemonium of people running in the streets with clouds of ash rising behind them, and the endless camera shots of the buildings as they burned and crashed to the ground. In about the length of an employee's commute to work, the world had changed. There were continuing reports of other targets, then a plane flew into The Pentagon and another which, due to the bravery and unselfishness of its passengers, crashed in a field in Pennsylvania, killing all on board, but saving the lives of countless others. No one could work any longer that day. They all left for home, each in a state of shock.

While their world had not felt safe since the beginning of Frank's illness, this attack seemed so senseless that both Linda and Ari were overwhelmed. They knew they were losing their battle against Frank's cancer, but they were doing everything they could to fight it. This was something different, so alien, it lacked comprehension. And, they couldn't stem the tears.

The 9/11 attacks left everyone in the country with a sense of apprehension. In the days and weeks that followed, everyone called everybody they knew to make certain they were okay. There were unending pictures of missing people on the news, and everyone's hearts were ripped apart by all the casualties suffered at the hands of mad men.

Through it all, Linda and Ari continued on with Frank's care. His condition continued to deteriorate. Psychologically he, too, had been hit by the utter senselessness of these terrorists' attacks. As Linda and Ari tried to deal with it all, Linda finally admitted to Ari, that there wasn't much hope for her father. Linda thought that if he could just make it through another Christmas, now only six weeks away, and see the family together again in a happy setting, it would give her husband great pleasure. It was something she desperately wanted for him. She also told Ari that Frank often told her how glad he was that she was there and how very proud he was to be her father.

While Frank couldn't make it down to the plant anymore, he did ask Ari if she felt everything was going all right. He often asked about the men, and asked to be remembered to them when she next saw them. Actually, the company was in fairly good shape, in the sense that it didn't have large creditors and their assets exceeded their liabilities. Ari had dug into everything she could get her hands on and studied it carefully.

Fortunately, there was one employee who had been there for many years. *Well*, Ari thought, *they all had*, but George Swerling was one of the company's longest serving employees. Ari had known him since she was a young girl. George was there when she first started going down to the plant with her father, and always made time to talk with her and answer all of her many questions. She liked and trusted him then, and she did so now. These days, she often sat down with George to discuss matters regarding the business, now that her father was too ill to do so.

The manufacturing business had been declining over the past twenty years or so, mostly due to the lack of machinery still used for manufacturing purposes in the U.S. The upside was that there were very few places where one could find the parts, or which had the capability of rebuilding the machines that some companies required for their operations.

Ari's spare time was almost nonexistent. When she was free, Ari would spend as much time as possible with Gabby and her family. Jerry wasn't always available, as his business was in high demand, but the girls often found themselves together and enjoyed their times immensely. On occasion, they would make it a foursome – the girls, Jerry, and Brent. While Ari had many friends in Chicago whom she really liked being with, there were few in her mind who could compare with Gabby and Brent, and now Jerry. They were truly special, and Gabby and Brent had been so for a very long time.

Brent's law practice grew steadily as his reputation spread. The Regency account, along with his other clients, kept him busy enough, *but he could use more work*, he thought. Brent and Carolyn worked out an arrangement for her firm to rent a small space in his building. Another firm, which had been officed in an outlying area, decided to move closer to the courthouse, and ended up leasing a large portion of the third floor. So, while he still had space available to rent in his building, he had more than covered his "nut," and he was grateful. Brent enjoyed the comradery among the small group of lawyers, and seemed to be settling into small town life.

There was little being reported in The *Sentinel* lately about Harriet. It was Gabby who had noticed it first. Ari couldn't understand how she had missed it, but Gabby insisted it was considerably more difficult to notice the absence of something, unless one was expecting to find it.

Ari decided to call Harriet's mother. After reintroducing herself to Mrs. Hill, Ari told her that she was concerned because she hadn't heard from Harriet lately and there was little being reported in The *Sentinel*. Mrs. Hill sounded somewhat nervous in her reply. "Harriet is at her apartment in New York, if you wish to speak with her. I assume you have the number."

"I do. Thank you, Mrs. Hill."

"I'm sorry to be so short, Ari, I was just in the middle of something. Please, call Harriet. I'm sure she would like to hear from you."

Harriet was very glad to hear from Ari and, frankly, surprised. After exchanging niceties, there was a long silence in the conversation.

"Harriet, I was wondering how you're doing. I haven't heard from you in a while and there haven't been many articles reprinted in The *Sentinel* lately."

Harriet seemed sad when she replied. There was a tiredness in her voice Ari couldn't remember ever hearing before. "Oh, Ari, I don't know . . . Paolo and I have separated, but it isn't common knowledge yet. Paolo's in Italy at his family's home and plans to be there for some time to come."

"Harriet, I'm so sorry. I didn't know."

"No. Of course you didn't. I was in Paris for the first couple of weeks after the separation, but the paparazzi was unrelenting, and I found my-self unable to go out in public without them trying to photograph me or get a story. It's only marginally better in New York. But here, one can get lost as nowhere else in the world. Though, sooner or later, when you try to attend functions for charities with which you're affiliated, they catch up with you. I'm thinking about coming home for a while; I'm less vis-ible there. Except, at home, I'd lose whatever privacy I have here. I'm not sure what to do. Obviously, I'm not thinking clearly right now. Please don't tell anyone about this. I'll call you if I come home. I'm sorry. I have to go." With that, Harriet hung up and Ari found herself staring at the receiver in disbelief.

While Ari was fairly certain Harriet didn't know about her father, she wasn't sure she had ever been involved in a conversation with someone who was quite as self-absorbed as Harriet had been here. As always, however, Ari found herself making excuses for Harriet's behavior, and allowing that she was suffering badly. Never having been married herself, Ari couldn't imagine the devastation that must come with the unraveling of such a deep relationship.

True to her word, Ari didn't mention anything about Harriet and Paolo's separation, but did tell Gabby that she had spoken to Harriet and she was doing okay. Not two days later an article appeared in The *Sentinel* announcing the separation, with photos of Paolo at the fall showing of a promising new Paris designer with a very lovely, very young model, who was just becoming known.

According to Gabby, some of the others in the photographs were some of the friends they had met that night at the country club when Paolo had first been introduced to Thompsonville, and Harriet's engagement to him had been announced. Ari thought how incredibly difficult it must be for Harriet to even think about facing those friends now.

Gabby was the first to hear that Harriet was in Thompsonville. It was several weeks after the article had appeared in The *Sentinel*. Apparently, Harriet had been back at her parents' house for some time. Gabby learned of her return when Harriet began looking at a couple of the new houses Regency had built in one of their small, exclusive upscale communities, á la Pheasant Run. The rumors spread rapidly.

Eventually, Harriet called Ari. "Ari, I'm sorry for not calling you sooner. I was at a very low point when you called me in New York. Please excuse my behavior – I wasn't myself. Your call was very much appreciated."

"Don't worry about it, Harriet. Are you doing better now?"

"Yes, somewhat. I bought a house here in Thompsonville and want to get together with you and Gabby to catch up. I'll bring you both up-to-date then. See you soon."

CHAPTER SEVENTEEN

The holidays were not a happy time in 2001. There was still a pall over the entire country from the terrorists' attacks and, while most people went through the motions of trying to make it "Christmas as usual," their hearts were burdened. There was fear for the children and how they reacted psychologically to the horror of it, as well as concern that we as a country were not prepared to protect our citizens. In short, nerves were raw. Retail merchants, the travel industry, and certainly the stock market had taken a hit. Most people were praying that 2002 would prove to be a better year.

Harriet left before she and the girls had the chance to get together. Apparently Paolo called Harriet on her cell after the attacks, concerned about how she was and whether she had been hurt. They decided to meet in Paris and Ari thought Harriet was hoping that perhaps they could reconcile. There was an article showing the couple at a holiday party. Although they were smiling, neither Gabby nor Ari thought Harriet's was anything but forced.

They had tried. Harriet wanted her marriage to mean something more than her parents' sham of a marriage. She couldn't believe she had not been able to see through the thin veneer of Prince Paolo. Even though there had been royalty in his family tree, Harriet thought "prince" was a stretch. His family cared as much about their station in life as her family, and she kicked herself for having bought into it. In the end, Paolo was more interested in the new, young and beautiful jet setters than he was in forming a deep relationship with someone, starting a family, or preserving any marital commitments.

Harriet steeled herself and began to revert to her old ways of isolation. Insecurity began to creep back in. Paolo made it clear to Harriet that he had no intention of giving up his lifestyle or any of the perks that went with it. Harriet understood, this meant other women. She couldn't understand why he had wanted to marry her in the first place.

The answer to that question became evident before Paolo left Paris to return to Italy. His attorney informed Harriet, "Paolo is willing to walk away without any further embarrassment to you if you sign over to him the Paris apartment and pay him a hefty lump sum settlement, ensuring a clean, uncontested divorce. Furthermore, Paolo will agree not to seek any alimony or drag you through the courts -- which in Italy can be a very long, certainly messy as well as largely reported debacle. And, oh yes, the terms I just outlined must be kept confidential." The *or else* was implicit and Harriet was just beginning to understand how vicious Paolo could be.

Harriet couldn't believe her ears. Paolo's family had a huge estate in Italy and lots of money, as well as a high social standing. Although Paolo's attorney never directly answered Harriet's questions, she began to understand that while they probably weren't broke, they perhaps weren't as well off as they led others to believe. Paolo also knew about her trust fund. She thought that he must have counted on that too. Understanding it all now led her to see that the settlement had been Paolo's goal all along, and would allow him to live in style outside of his parents' home and give him some money to play with.

After the initial shock of Paolo's proposition, Harriet began to think about what she would do. She certainly didn't want to admit her failure to the world. But that was nothing compared to the embarrassment she would feel in New York and her hometown of Thompsonville, should he choose to make this public. She understood that he could be nasty and say anything he wanted, whether true or not, and it would be reported for everyone to see. She was scared to death that if she tried to fight this settlement, she would be seen as an idiot to have been fooled by this "prince."

Harriet loved Paris, *although more so*, she thought, *before she met Paolo.* However, she also knew it would be much different for her now after Paolo. The friends she thought were hers, were really Paolo's. She was sure they knew the whole story, and Harriet didn't think she would ever be comfortable with them again. *Where to go?* Harriet wanted to hide, but she didn't know where. She couldn't count on her friends in Paris, anywhere she went she faced the paparazzi, and there was no way she wanted to discuss this with her parents. In a corner, Harriet ultimately decided she would sign over the apartment, and write Paolo a check in order to get out from underneath this whole mess -- but not until the divorce was final.

Harriet moved back to her apartment in New York while the divorce was in progress. She seldom went out and, when she did, she avoided the press. It was obvious to the European paparazzi that something was amiss. It didn't take long before a reporter discovered the filed divorce documents.

Harriet was at a low. She sequestered herself in her apartment with her dog, Winston, pulling the drapes, so that virtually no light would intrude on her. Sleep came often. Slowly, as the weeks passed, Harriet began to realize she couldn't continue like that. She thought about her life in New York, with all the social obligations, and knew that, while she wanted to come back to it at some point, she wasn't yet ready to face it.

As she thought about the house she'd purchased in Thompsonville just before her marriage fell apart, Harriet began to think about returning there until she could get her life back on track. She could throw herself into decorating the house and working in the garden. She would have relative privacy and her family there, such as they were, as well as Ari and Gabby.

Thinking then about her friends, she was buoyed by the fact that both Ari and Gabby had called to check in on her when they heard about the divorce -- Ari several times. Harriet began to realize how similar her story was to Gabby's first marriage. She found a certain sense of comfort in that fact, and thanked her lucky stars that she didn't have a child to deal with, as Gabby had. That really would have tied her down. This way, she could just do what she needed to do and go where she wanted until the time she would be ready to get back into the social whirl of parties and pretty people.

Frank hung in through the first week of January, although he hardly knew where he was during his last few days. Hospice aides took over in the end, and Linda was grateful for their help. The holidays, while subdued, were unbelievably sweet. Frank was so happy to see the family gathered together. It was almost as if he waited to pass until he could share the holidays with them one last time. Although they were mostly Linda's relatives, they had truly formed a strong family bond with one another. Frank's passing was silent. Everything he and Linda wanted to say to one another had been said, and Linda knew that Frank went peacefully, comforted by the fact that nothing was left undone.

It was quiet now. Suddenly, Linda and Ari were left with a silence that was almost unnerving. They worked to put the house back in order. They returned the hospital bed and other medical equipment to Hospice, and put the furniture back in place. But it just didn't look like it belonged anymore.

As they filled the first few days after the funeral with busy work, Linda was surprised to get a call from Stanford Lee asking if he could come by to see her. Linda couldn't think of why the President of The First National Bank of Thompsonville would want to see her, but she made an appointment for the following day. Linda was concerned that Frank may have borrowed money for either the business or even a personal loan, without her knowledge. Linda asked Ari whether she had come across any loan documents down at Bolan's, but Ari told her she hadn't seen any. They talked about the meeting scheduled for the next day, and the only thing Ari could come up with was that if Frank had taken out any loans, he may have kept the documents in a safety deposit box at the bank. Linda spent a very sleepless night worrying about what was going to be said the following morning.

Stanford Lee quietly offered his condolences to Linda as he made himself comfortable in the living room. Linda poured coffee and they both sat back as Linda braced herself for what was to come. "I'm not quite certain where to begin." Seeing the look of fear on Linda's face, he quickly said, "This is not bad news, Linda."

Somewhat relieved, but still with some degree of trepidation, Linda asked, "Then what *is* this about, Stanford?"

"Several years ago, actually quite a few years ago, Frank started putting money into certificates of deposit for you and Ari, rolling them over and adding more money as time went on. As these CD's were held jointly, you and Ari now have access to the money without having to go through probate."

Linda said with a sigh of relief, "Oh, good. Well that *is* very nice news. I had no idea Frank was doing that, of course, but that was just the kind of man he was."

Stanford Lee nodded and pulled out a pile of papers. He handed the stack to Linda and she was shocked to see that each piece related to a different CD. She looked at the top few papers and looked questioningly at the banker. He nodded his head and said, "Yes, it is a large amount of money when you total it all up. Frank wanted you and Ari to have financial security for the rest of your lives and, if invested wisely, this will take care of generations to come."

Linda was at a loss for words. As she sat there assimilating the news, Stanford Lee finished his coffee and asked Linda what she would like to do with the CD's? Linda hadn't realized how long she had been sitting there without saying anything. "I'm sorry Stan. This is so unexpected. I haven't really had time to understand all this, much less think about what should be done with it. Of course, I'll need to tell Ari about it, and then the two of us can make a decision. In the meantime, well, what would you recommend?"

"I am not a financial advisor, Linda, but these CD's have different due dates and there is a penalty if you cash them in prior to those dates. I think you and Ari should look these over, evaluate your individual needs and then make determinations based upon those needs. This is a great deal of money and I think it would be wise to retain a financial advisor to help you invest it. Frank bought these so that their maturity dates are staggered throughout the year, so you have time to get comfortable with an advisor before the bulk of these reach their individual dates of maturity. Take your time. In the meantime, these are only copies I had made for your review. The investments are safe in the bank, and will be until you tell me otherwise. If there's anything else I can answer for you, I'll be pleased to do so, now or later."

"Thank you, Stan. I can't think of anything now, but perhaps later. I appreciate your advice and the assurance that I don't need to make any rash decisions."

After he left, Linda stared at the stack of papers, still not comprehending how Frank had managed to do that for such a long time, particularly without her knowing.

When Ari walked in later that day, Linda asked if they could sit down for a few minutes. Ari was concerned and feared what was coming. She asked if this was something about the bank president's visit this morning and Linda said it was with a big smile on her face. After Linda told Ari about the CD's, she pointed to the stack of papers sitting on the dining room table, which was visible from the kitchen table. Ari's reaction was disbelief. They talked about the ramifications of the money and Linda told Ari what Stanford Lee had advised earlier in the day. They both decided that his advice was sound and besides they didn't need the money now anyway.

After the first few weeks of helping her mother at home and making sure they had a handle on the CDs, Ari began to go back down to the plant. At first, Ari was concerned about leaving her mother alone so much, but then she saw that Linda was dealing with the loss much better than she had expected – probably due to the fact they had known what was coming.

Linda was coping well. She missed Frank terribly but she was unbelievably grateful for the life they had shared. Theirs had been a wonderful marriage and no woman could ask for a better husband or father for her child. Linda's friends had tried to keep her spirits up during Frank's illness but, as the end neared, they knew she wanted to focus solely on Frank. Now, they were rallying around her, and she was finding her way back due to the support networks women form which are so essential to their well-being. Ari watched in awe. She knew how important it was to her mother that she be there during her father's illness. Ari was now watching an entirely different phenomenon. She saw her mother's friends surround her as if forming a cocoon which would protect her until she was ready to reemerge.

Ari kept up the plant, but knew her mother was ultimately going to have to make the decision about what was to happen to it. Frank had discussed his wishes with Linda and Ari, but Ari knew it was up to her mother, now that he was gone. Ari thought that the few employees who were left might want to buy the plant, but realized they wouldn't be able to run it by themselves; none of them had ever worked the business side of the company.

When Linda and Ari finally sat down to discuss it, Linda was at a loss as to what they should do. Business had been down over the past several years, manufacturing was down in the area and there were very few jobs out there, unless one worked at a big box store. Ari couldn't imagine George, or frankly any of them, finding a rewarding job at this point in their lives. Two of the five remaining employees were due to retire next year. George wasn't far behind, leaving the last two not due to retire until 2006. There was a pension plan in place and they were all fully vested. *Perhaps they would be interested in retiring early?* Linda and Ari decided that asking them what they wanted to do, might make their decision easier. Linda wanted Ari to take the meeting without her, thinking the employees would talk more freely to Ari, having worked with her for the past ten months.

On Monday, Ari scheduled the meeting for Friday afternoon, telling the employees they would be talking about the future of the company, and she wanted their input. She did this with the hope that some of these longtime employees would have a chance to think about their futures and offer some options neither she nor her mother had considered.

By the Friday meeting, the men were nervous which, in turn, made them quiet. Ari started by telling them this meeting was really intended to be a sharing of ideas. "As you all know, over the past several years, manufacturing has dropped off across the entire country, but even more so for us. The need for our products has decreased as jobs have been shipped overseas. Right now, Bolan's is maintaining it's own, but we've flat-lined. We cover salaries and utilities, but little else. My family owns the building, so fortunately we don't have to worry about paying rent. If we want to continue with health insurance or pensions, not to mention covering the insurance and taxes on the building, we'll have to increase our business. But where that increase will come from, I frankly don't know. At some point in the not too distant future, we probably won't be able to cover pensions and utilities. Then, we have the problem that my father ran the business end of the company and, while I stepped in to help him, this was only a temporary fix. I would really like to have your ideas here. Retirement is close for most of you and I need to know your thinking, including whether or not we keep the company open for business.

During his last months my father talked of you all often, and worried about his not being here to see you through to your retirements. Each one of you was special to him and he wanted to be able to keep the business going for all of you until then. Please tell me what you're thinking."

They began to open up.

Ray asked, "If we close, will that happen today?"

"No. We're not closing today or even within the next month."

They seemed to relax a bit. They exchanged "what ifs" and asked Ari whether she was willing to stay for the time being?

"I have no intention of leaving you until you've all had a chance to determine what's in your best interests."

There were questions about their pensions and also their salaries.

Ari tried to answer all their concerns. She finally said, "I think what we need to do is take the weekend to think it over, talk to your families and then meet again. I believe that it boils down to whether or not you want to retire early and we close the plant, or whether you want to keep going, knowing we can't stay open until the last of you retires. Besides, the plant needs at least three employees to function. Then you need to decide who will run the business end of it.

I want to assure you again that nothing is going to happen without your input and it certainly has not been determined that we are closing or when. Take the weekend. As a matter of fact, why don't you all plan to meet here Monday morning to discuss your thoughts and plans. I'll come in around noon."

George stood and took over. "I think that's a good plan. We all need to go home now and meet back here first thing Monday morning."

After they left, Ari turned to George. "I'm sure I didn't handle that as well as I could have."

"You did fine. It's not easy and they're scared. Not so much for losing their jobs, even though that's a big deal, but more so that they don't think they're ready to be put out to pasture; that their ability to make a difference has come to an end."

"Oh, George, I didn't mean for it to sound that way. I'm so sorry."

"Ari, it didn't sound that way, except to them. Take your own advice and go home for the weekend. I'll see you on Monday."

CHAPTER EIGHTEEN

It was spring and getting close to a year since Ari had gotten that awful call from her parents telling her of her father's cancer. It seemed as if it was an eternity ago, and she couldn't believe how much her life had changed in what was in truth a very short time.

George, Ray and the rest of Bolan's employees held their meeting on Monday, after spending the entire weekend thinking and talking with their families about what to do. When Ari arrived at the plant around noon, George told her that the employees were ready to meet with her again.

During the second meeting, it became clear that the men wanted to continue working until their retirements, but also acknowledged that it might not be possible. They admitted that they weren't trained to run the business end, and the fact that some of the overhead which Frank had been picking up, was beyond their means. Again, they asked Ari when she was planning on closing down the plant?

"We haven't made that decision yet. Right now we're still working on equipment for several old customers and we've also accepted work which will take us through at least October. We can't close our doors until that work is completed. The question is whether we try to keep going after that."

There was a lot of head nodding at this, but it was Ray who asked the group, "How can we run the business that long without Ari? And there still are expenses. We'd have to take pay cuts if we continue. I don't mean to sound ungrateful, Ari, but . . . "

"I know this isn't what you'd hoped to hear. It is a sad commentary that small manufacturing businesses such as ours are falling by the wayside, while many American businesses end up shipping jobs overseas. But the writing is on the wall about Bolan's. We can't continue with the small amount of business we have, and there is less and less every year. It hurts me for all of us that this is what's left, but you are all in my heart from almost as early as I can remember, and you will be with me forever. I know my father considered you family as you consider one another, and I believe we were all blessed to have spent such a large portion of our lives together."

Suddenly, Ari spoke up knowing how she could put a few of those CDs her father left her to good use. "Wait. I have a 'what if' solution. What if I continue through until we close the doors in October or so. My mother and I will cover the expenses which are not covered by our current income, and we'll pay you at your regular salaries through the end of the year.

Think about it. Let me know by the end of the week so that I know whether or not to accept any new work or we tell those who ask, we're closing down. Until then, let's get back to work."

They slowly rose from their seats and filed out the door back onto the factory floor. It was a solemn group but, to a man, they looked at Ari and nodded with respect as they left the room.

Gabby was pregnant again and this time it was under the best of circumstances. Jerry was thrilled. He adored Gabby from the moment he had seen her all those years ago and now that she was his wife, she was his love and best friend. They talked about everything. They laughed and they made a safe, loving home for Nicole. Gabby thought, *This is the way love is supposed to be,* before Jason had disabused her of that notion. Now with a new baby on the way, Nicole growing up so beautifully, and a wonderful husband by her side, Gabby was certain life didn't get much better than this.

Regency continued to grow, but not locally. Business was still off in Thompsonville with the loss of so many jobs and the young people moving away after college.

Gabby still loved to dabble in renovations and even conversions of apartment buildings in Thompsonville, but, ultimately, those jobs didn't keep enough of their employees busy and there was minimal cash-flow to keep Regency purring along. Gabby knew the only way to keep Regency healthy, was to build in larger, economically healthy cities.

Gabby was considering Pittsburgh and the suburbs of Columbus and Canton, but because of their distance from Thompsonville, she was thinking long and hard about it. It would require a commitment to add jobs, which was a risk in light of the current economy. But not to do so, might mean Regency would become a shadow of its former self.

Finally, deciding it was a chance Regency had to take, Gabby began building a large development in the Pittsburgh suburbs with the new open-design concept. The sales were unlike any Regency had previously experienced. Several months later, Gabby and Regency were featured in the business section of *The Pittsburgh Post-Gazette*. They couldn't build the houses fast enough.

While they were making inroads in Pittsburgh though, Gabby was concerned about spreading Regency too thin by expanding into Ohio in addition to Pittsburgh. There was a whole new set of difficulties facing a company where they didn't have a workforce and an eyes-on capability on a daily basis. As it was, TJ was already spending all his time with Regency's regular crew at their new development in Washington County, south of Pittsburgh.

She thought, *Sometimes, too much of a good thing is just too much.*

Harriet came home. At first, back to her parents' house, but found the constant questions and lack of privacy intrusive. She found herself screaming inside, while actually trying to catch her breath. After a couple of weeks of that, Harriet became convinced that even though her own house needed a little interior painting and was still mostly unfurnished, her sanity was worth more than some inconveniences, regardless of how major they were to her.

Her first move was to hire Amanda as a housekeeper. Amanda was Miranda's daughter. Miranda had worked for her mother for the past ten years or so. This made Harriet very comfortable offering a live-in position to someone whose family she knew. Now, with Amanda in place, Harriet was free to hire painters to work in the house while she was out shopping for furnishings and, of course, Amanda would be there to accept the deliveries.

The summer was approaching and so, too, unbelievably, was the ten-year reunion for the 1992 class of Thompsonville Hill School. Gabby and Ari were shocked by the knowledge that ten years had passed since the summer when their lives took separate paths, without truly separating them. Almost all of their high school friends were planning to attend and Gabby, Ari, and even Harriet were looking forward to the event. Jennifer Lee was coming in from New York where she was working at Chase after earning her graduate degree from Wharton as planned. Karen Dunwitty was coming in from Villanova, PA, where she settled after marrying a young Villanova Law School student she met while attending Bryn Mawr. Doug and Sean, Ari's and Gabby's prom dates, were on their way, as was Larry, who had gone to Peru and other foreign points over several summers in between school years with Josh. Josh wasn't able to get away. It seemed that all that time trying to help the underprivileged had reinforced his thinking that he wanted to become a doctor, traveling the world to continue his work.

The reunion weekend was almost a blur. From the welcome cocktail reception to the ceremonies at the high school, the tours to show off the upgrades that had been made at the school -- particularly the computer labs, which were largely funded by Jerry and his company – the big dance, of course, and then the closing breakfast on Sunday morning. Everyone had a great time. Everyone except, perhaps, HRH who hadn't had that many friends back then to relish this time together now.

Harriet's divorce became final over the summer and, as promised, she signed over her apartment in Paris and wrote out the settlement check, mailing it to Paolo's attorney along with the deed.

It wasn't more than about two weeks after her check to Paolo had cleared when HRH received a registered letter from the law firm which administered her trust. Harriet hadn't paid much attention to the statements she received quarterly from them, but this letter shook her up. She immediately got on the phone and made an appointment for the following day with the lawyer who oversaw her trust. Harriet never thought much about it, she just bought what she wanted and the bills were sent to, and paid by, the trustee.

Her meeting was even worse than she feared after receiving the letter. She was told that she had tipped the scales with the lump sum payment to Paolo and that it had perceptibly diminished the corpus of her trust. While she could do that under the terms of the trust, it had now depleted the principal enough to considerably reduce her monthly income and limit her ability to make big ticket purchases. Gone were the days of couturier wardrobe shopping, get away weekends, and certainly any short-term plans to buy another apartment in Paris -- at least until the trust could reinvest most of the interest income and replenish the principal.

Harriet had a choice. She could either sell her apartment in New York or rent it for a couple of years in order to supplement the trust. Either way, she would have to cut her spending appreciably. She thought she might even have to let Amanda go. But, on second thought, she knew there was no way she could cook or clean her own house. No, no way. She just couldn't do without Amanda *and that was that!*

Ari spent a long weekend visiting Emily in Chicago and generally checking out the job market there. Now that her father was gone and Bolan's was closing, she needed to think about what she would do with the rest of her life. *It's strange,* she thought. *Here I am back in the apartment I shared with Emily, and I feel as if I'm intruding.* It no longer was home to her, even though, through Emily's insistence, she had left many of her things there until she was ready to come home. It was somehow familiar, but it just wasn't a good fit anymore. She and Emily had a great time together, though. Ari was able to see some of her friends and visit some of the old neighborhood haunts, but there, too, many of the faces had changed.

Once back in Thompsonville, it seemed to Ari that everyone was limping along in some sort of holding pattern waiting for the economy to improve.

Brent was making ends meet – barely. His practice was slow and steady, the operative word being slow. Carolyn was sending some work his way, mostly the small cases that didn't require staffing one of her firm's attorneys in Thompsonville.

Gabby took her time thinking over any expansion into Columbus or Canton. She thought she would take the winter months to evaluate the upcoming economic forecasts and also the viability of being able to manage such a spread out operation.

Even Jerry's business was down -- not out, but definitely down. Few people were doing start-ups in the current business atmosphere and Ari was seeing several of the small local businesses close after years of service to the community.

Unbelievably, through all this, Bolan's was getting calls from several of their long time customers and even some new ones. It seemed that the smaller companies were in no position to move their businesses overseas. And now, with the current slow down, they were unwilling to invest in new machinery. This meant that their old machinery would need replacement parts and overhauling. Ari turned down business left and right, when she said to herself, *Wait a minute, maybe I can keep Bolan's going.*

Ari didn't say anything to anyone at first. She needed to think about it and her part in it. If Bolan's stayed open for the time being, she would have to make a commitment to the employees and she wasn't sure she wanted to do that. If not, maybe there would be enough new business to pay someone to run the business side, but she didn't think so. Then, what would George and the others think? She thought they would be energized and excited about the proposition, but maybe not.

Ari talked to her mom. Linda was all for it. "Ari, if you're up to it, we may as well give it a try. The building is of little value as an empty industrial shop in today's market. It's paid for, the taxes aren't much, and we can handle the insurance for the time being. This is your decision. But you'll need to discuss it with George and the others. With the increased business, their salaries would be covered, but the contributions to their pensions would be affected. They are fully vested though, so that might be all right for them since they won't be drawing down on them right away."

"Mom, this could work."

"Think about it Ari. You need to make certain you're willing to give Bolan's your time without any remuneration. After all, there won't be enough income to cover a salary for you. Are you willing to work for nothing?"

"Mom, it's not for nothing. Dad would have wanted it. And . . . I have those CDs. Besides, my other option is to go back to Chicago and go mad waiting for that perfect new job to come along. And, somehow, I'm just not sure I belong there any longer. I'd much rather try to get our Bolan's business family members through to their individual retirements, if at all possible. I'm going to talk with them next week, as long as you're sure you're on board with this."

Linda squeezed Ari's hand. "I'm certain your father would be very proud that you're being so unselfish to do this for these men. I'm also just as certain that he would not have been surprised."

It was September, the week after Labor Day when Ari walked into the plant and asked the men if they could take a break and spend some time with her in the office. Their fear was palpable as they nodded their collective assent. Ari tried to assure them this was not bad news, and they needed to smile. They thought they knew better. As they quietly found places to sit, Ari sat behind her father's desk and began.

"This really is *not* bad news. Lately we have been getting calls for more business than we anticipated." As Ari began to explain their clients' current needs, there seemed to be a noticeable release of tension in the postures of these fine, loyal men who had been with her father for such a long time.

Ari explained her plan, laying out the bad with the good. She told them that she would stick with them as long as business could cover their salaries and, if lucky, through their individual retirements. Everyone smiled and looked at one another with a nod, noting their agreement.

This time there was no need for them to go home and talk to their families or think about any of it. This offer was making them whole again. They hadn't failed the company, their families or each other, and there was no better feeling in the entire world.

George asked Ari, "Will you be covered under this new plan of yours?"

Ari understood he was asking about a salary for her, but she told him and the others that it was taken care of. Not one of the men believed it, but knew they would never get Ari to admit it. This was her way, and they loved her all the more for it. Ari suggested closing early for the day, but they wouldn't hear of it. They were back in business and they meant to work!

Adam Jerome O'Neil was born on November 21, 2002, the day before Thanksgiving. There was much to be thankful for at the O'Neil household, although their Thanksgiving dinner was moved back to Friday that year, in order to have everyone home for the occasion. And, everyone made it. Besides Gabby, Jerry, Nicole and now Adam, Gabby's mom and Brent were there, as was Ari.

Ari spent the actual Thanksgiving Day holiday with her parents' family at her Aunt Rose's house, but couldn't help participating in two celebrations, considering the event.

Jerry's mother and sister came by later, and there was a Norman Rockwell scene at the O'Neil's that day.

CHAPTER NINETEEN

Ari called Emily to tell her what had happened at Bolan's and that she thought this was the right thing for her to do. Emily said, "I know you felt somewhat unconnected over our weekend together in Chicago, but I have a proposal. I've been thinking about buying a condo, now that I've made partner. We can start anew in some new digs; we'd have so much more room and then you can feel as if you're moving forward instead of backward."

Ari loved Emily so much. Even so, she couldn't believe she would make such an offer. It went way above friendship and she would never forget it, even though she couldn't accept. After thanking Emily profusely, Ari explained. "Em, I can't exactly explain it. I feel a responsibility to my father and more importantly to the men who worked by his side for so many years. But, it isn't just a duty, it's a challenge, and one where I can make a difference. Besides, it's something that I *want* to do. Em, go get that condo, you deserve it. It'll give me something to look forward to next time I visit you in Chicago."

Emily was disappointed, but when Ari asked her to spend the holidays with her in Thompsonville, Emily perked up. "I'll do it." In fact, Emily had often wanted to visit Ari but, with her father's illness, it had just never worked out. "Ari, this will be great! Not only will I get to relax in the country for the holidays but I'm finally going to meet Gabby and Brent and Jerry and the children and oh, yes, Carolyn and Mrs. McCutcheon, just to name some of the people you've spoken about for so many years. And, geez, I almost forgot, HRH -- maybe I'll get to meet her too."

Along with the holiday cards this year, Brent was surprised to find a heavy formal buff-colored envelope in his mail. Noticing the Washington, D.C. postmark, Brent anxiously opened it wondering who would still remember him to place his name on their Christmas mailing list.

Opening it, Brent found an exquisitely embossed announcement stating that Stacy had married a fellow whose name sounded familiar as one of the partners of her law firm. It was the last thing he expected, and it knocked him off his feet. While they had not been an item in a very long time, and only spoken a couple of times since he left D.C., Brent had believed Stacy when she told him she had no interest in marriage.

Obviously, he simply wasn't Mr. Right. It wasn't so much that she married someone else, it was more that her marriage deepened his own sense of incompleteness, inasmuch as he hadn't found anyone with whom he could share his thoughts, discuss his ideas, or hold hands as they walked down the street.

All his plans and dreams were predicated on the notion that he wanted a family life and a career which complemented one another, rather than fought each other, each partner bringing to their union a dedication to each other, their family and their community. Was this a never-to-be-fulfilled dream?

Brent struggled to figure out why he was so alone. Had he left D.C. too early – a place where there were, many times over, more bright, sexy women than men? He could have probably had his pick. But then, would they have been the right partner to want to give up their careers to raise a family? Most of the women there were focused on careers. Oh, they had relationships, but marriage . . . ?

Was he too insulated from the social scene, such as it was, in Thompsonville? He had a wide circle of friends, most of whom were business associates, and a couple of girlfriends, but there hadn't been anyone special. Maybe he was reaching for the moon and not seeing the stars. He loved being home and a part of his sister and brother-in-law's family. There was true joy in watching Nicole grow and learn, and the love she showed him was unequaled. And, now, there was Adam to watch and teach and love, as well. But, as much as he loved being a part of that family, he longed for the day when he, too, could have a family of his own.

Brent thought perhaps it was time for a holiday – maybe he only needed to get away. He hadn't taken a vacation since returning to Thompsonville and he was now beginning to think he'd not only earned one, but he deserved one. Brent made a promise to himself that after the holidays he would look into a late January/early February getaway; *now where did he want to go?*

Harriet was finally getting out and about. Of course, she saw Ari and Gabby, and spent a lot of time with her mother, but she had sheltered herself from the rest of Thompsonville's society while she tried to come to terms with what had happened in the last year of her life. HRH spent the summer on her hands and knees in her new garden. She thought of it as therapeutic, rather than a self-imposed restriction from shopping and traveling in Europe.

Paolo was often in the society pages again. "Ridiculous," she said out loud, as she cursed to herself that male jet setters never lost their star power, as opposed to the women who, once they hit their mid-twenties or so, were pariahs, seldom invited by anyone and almost never seen again in the social section of any paper or magazine.

The American magazines were the exception, and Harriet was anxious to get back to New York and the social whirl of which she had once been a part. Sadly, that would not happen this year. But, if she really continued to curb her spending . . . maybe next holiday season. Until then, HRH was going to venture out to the big holiday gala at the country club. Of course her parents were going, but Harriet had decided to join Gabby and Jerry at their table which would include Brent, Ari and her friend from Chicago, as well as Karen Dunwitty and her husband, who were spending their holidays in Thompsonville with Karen's family.

The club was elegantly decorated as it always was for this affair. As soon as Harriet entered the main dining room, she found herself smack in front of her father's table, as she knew she would. Taking a moment to say hello to her parents and some of the movers and shakers of Thompsonville – her parents really didn't have any personal friends, just the current movers and shakers -- Harriet took a moment to slyly get the lay of the land.

There seemed to be fewer people there than in the past, certainly fewer than the affair she had hosted. But the room was lovely, the music upbeat, and from what she could tell everyone was enjoying themselves immensely.

Just as Harriet began to excuse herself, Ari and Emily appeared at the doorway. As Harriet greeted Ari and was introduced to Emily, Harriet turned and introduced them to the diners at her father's table. After the appropriate small talk, the three girls headed off to find their own table.

They found Brent, Gabby and Jerry standing by a table not too far away talking with a small group of people whose faces seemed familiar to Ari and Harriet. After introductions all around, waiters in tuxedos passed among the guests, balancing trays of champagne or wine, as others presented hor d'oeuvres for the ebullient partygoers.

The evening was a smash. Old friendships were rekindled, and new friends were welcomed and embraced. No one was passed over and they were all pleased with the evening's success.

One day, Ari and Emily ran into Brent at The Blue Frog, where they stopped after spending the morning Christmas shopping. While the restaurant wasn't near the shops where they'd been, Emily had heard so much about The Blue Frog over the years, it was a "must do" on her list for the trip. Brent joined them and they talked for what seemed like only minutes when, in fact, they had been chatting for almost two hours.

Brent was aghast he hadn't noticed the time, as he had a meeting back at his office. Making his regrets, he decided he would really enjoy continuing this get together – perhaps a little party in his apartment. He loved living upstairs in his newly renovated and stylishly-decorated apartment, but he had yet to invite anyone to dinner or a party. *This*, he thought, *could be a perfect time.*

As it turned out, Emily really did get to meet everyone. Brent's small cocktail party was intimate and warm. No one wanted to leave, so they ordered Chinese and stayed way too late.

Gabby invited Ari and Emily to her house for dinner one night and Emily was enraptured by Nicole and baby Adam. She couldn't believe that Gabby was a successful businesswoman, as well as clearly being a wonderful mother. Emily thought there was only a handful of women out there who could be that successful at both jobs simultaneously, and then remembered the story of her father's death and that, because of having to jump in and run the business, Gabby hadn't even gone to college.

To Emily's eyes, Gabby was truly remarkable. She found that Jerry was a terrific husband which, for some reason, seemed very reassuring to her, even though she had only known Gabby for a short time.

Gabby took Ari, Emily, Nicole and Adam over to Mrs. McCutcheon's house for an afternoon Christmas tea party. Mrs. McCutcheon's house was decorated with beautiful old family treasures, as it had always been when Mr. McCutcheon was alive. The children loved looking at all the Santas, elves and bears, some of which moved, that along with an old-time electric train, made the scene magical.

Mrs. McCutcheon hadn't been able to do the decorating herself this year. She admitted to being more tired, and Gabby noticed she did, in fact, look more frail. She made a mental note to herself to check on her more often.

On Christmas morning, Ari and Emily prepared a special breakfast for Linda, and the three girls spent the following few hours chatting, laughing and enjoying each other's company.

Ari and Emily finished up in the kitchen and decided to take a last spin around Thompsonville before Emily headed back to Chicago the next morning. They ended up at Logan Park, and decided to walk for a while. As they walked down the paths toward the tennis club, large, soft snowflakes began to fall. Emily thought, *Even the snow in Thompsonville is more beautiful.* In Chicago, it seemed to either be a nuisance when it was new, or else it was old and dirty. Here, there was a calm to the snow and Emily drank it in, reinvigorating herself as she looked forward to returning to her beloved fast-paced life in the big city. She had met some of the most wonderful people and enjoyed every minute of her visit, but she could never envision this life on a full-time basis for herself. She wondered how long Ari would really stay there.

CHAPTER TWENTY

The holidays were a particularly difficult time for Harriet. Even though she enjoyed the Christmas gala at the country club, she missed being part of the crowds in New York and Paris. She received several invitations that year – none from Paolo's crowd, not that she expected any. But, she thought that some of the women had been her friends, too. Apparently not. Most of the invitations came from her New York crowd, those who had been friends before Paolo. But, even those were mostly fund raising events. A couple invited her to their dinner parties, and she had all she could do to stumble through her regrets, making up other commitments, so she wouldn't have to tell them that she had sublet her condo and admit her dire financial straits.

Looking forward to spring, Harriet was eager to get back into her garden. She had rejoined, well, actually she had never really resigned from, the garden club. Her mother was still very active in the club, and it was something which had always been a bright part of Harriet's life from a very early age. This year, HRH, made it known that she was back and wanted to be very active in the club's activities. Some of the members were skittish, given Harriet's flitting in and out of town, but they needed someone to head up their activities' schedule and arrange for guest speakers. So, there she was, back in the thick of it. Having developed the Rose Hill Rose, Harriet was regarded by the younger members as somewhat of a celebrity. It wasn't New York or the Continent, but she was someone special again – if only on a small scale.

Most of 2003 was quiet for everyone and the country seemed to be plugging along, the horror of the 9/11 terrorists' attacks beginning to recede with the absence of any new attacks on United States soil.

Ari was hard at work at Bolan's and, while the work was steady, there were quite a few times during the year when they were idle, biding time until the next job. She worked tirelessly to find more work, and minimize their down-time. And, she was succeeding. Now, if she could just keep enough work coming in through 2006, the last of the employees would reach retirement age, and they could close the doors with dignity and a sense of accomplishment for everyone.

The curious thing was that some of the older employees were now working past their retirements in order to keep the company going for the three younger men. It was a strange and wonderful family, and they had truly adopted Ari as their chief, if not perhaps their parent.

When Frank was first stricken with cancer and Ari was helping him at Bolan's, not one of the men could have conceived of the impact her presence would have on their lives. As the cancer eroded his strength and Frank could no longer make it to the office, and, subsequently, ended his life, Ari took control and provided stability. They knew that without her guidance and tenacity, they would never have made it on their own. The little girl they had known for so many years, had earned their trust and their respect.

Gabby decided to expand into Columbus. She convinced Uncle Tony to come out of retirement temporarily so he could find the right construction boss and crew to work on-site. As it was, TJ was the construction boss in Pittsburgh and Mike Franconi was heading up the rehabs and conversions in Thompsonville. Gabby hoped Uncle Tony could find someone as good as Mike for Ohio. Mike had, after all, been plucked away from Detroit by Uncle Tony with the help of Mike's uncle, and Gabby relied on him as if he'd been with Regency forever.

The Columbus expansion was a large investment for Regency, both dollar-wise and risk-wise. Ari was anxious and confident, stressed and determined; these would indeed be interesting times. The real estate people were on the lookout for the right property for a large scale development in the suburbs of Columbus, while two small parcels had already been identified to mimic Pheasant Run closer to the city. In the meantime, TJ was busy with their major development south of Pittsburgh. Gabby found the challenges exhilarating. The real estate industry was solid and projected to stay that way for the next year or two.

Brent's work was interesting. Some cases far more so than others, but that was always to be. His greatest gratification came from interacting directly with his clients, not the book work he so enjoyed in law school. He never did criminal work. He worked with regular people with regular problems. Sometimes those problems were difficult and traumatic for his clients, but he seemed to be able to ease his clients' distress. He didn't win in every instance, but when he didn't win outright, he most often seemed to be able to minimize the downside for his client. He garnered a great deal of respect in the community and found himself sought out by other lawyers for his advice and counsel.

On the personal side, Brent never did find time to take that vacation. He started dating a young assistant District Attorney from Pittsburgh he'd met through Carolyn Maxwell. He dated Thursday – yes, that was her first name – for several months. In addition to it being somewhat of a long distance relationship, Brent realized he was perhaps a bit too traditional, as he found it exceedingly difficult to date anyone he had to call "Thursday." He wondered about parents that named their children such uncommon names. He guessed they never thought about the consequences to the children.

After his relationship, such as it was, with Thursday ended, Brent knew that trying to find the proverbial needle in a haystack was, perhaps, a lesson in futility and he began to re-evaluate his life. Brent had always known that he wanted children to be a part of his life. Since he didn't yet have any of his own, Brent decided that with the high unemployment rate in and around Thompsonville, there were probably many children who needed a friend.

Brent found out about the Big Brothers/Big Sisters program and promptly became involved, both on the organizational level locally, and by becoming a big brother to Tyler Mitchell, an eight-year-old, whose father had left to find a job elsewhere, and was never heard from again. Brent took Tyler out almost every weekend. They bowled, hit golf balls when the weather permitted, watched sports on TV, ice skated, went to the movies and spent lots of time just "shooting the breeze."

Brent was surprised to discover how much Tyler calmed Brent's own anxiety. Somehow, in the process of helping Tyler, Brent was more secure about his own life. The effort he put into mentoring the youngster diminished that unscratchable itch of not being married with his own children.

The year 2004 was equally uneventful, at least in Thompsonville. Nationally, we were in the midst of another presidential campaign. A good portion of the country questioned our government's claim of Iraqi stockpiles of weapons of mass destruction, and many believed we had been sold a bill of goods. Controversial at best, the country was in the middle of two foreign wars and antiwar demonstrations at home. Suicide bombers in Iraq were killing our troops daily, and support from abroad was shrinking. Nevertheless, in the end, a majority of the American people bought into Bush's promises and he accepted another four-year reign as Commander-in-Chief.

While Gabby was having success with Regency's ventures in Columbus and Pittsburgh, everyone else in Thompsonville was basically just managing to hold their own. There had been a downturn in the real estate market, particularly in the Northeast, but so far Regency had not been not affected.

The country as a whole seemed to be on a steady course, neither good nor bad. Plants were still closing, and many U.S. companies were still moving their customer service jobs overseas, although it hadn't seemed to negatively impact the stock markets or the employment figures.

Ari spent most of her time drumming up work for Bolan's. It was not getting easier. During the year, Ari had taken some time for herself and visited Emily in Chicago. The city was the same, and yet it was very different. Ari loved Emily's new condo and they were never at a loss for where to go or with whom. When they had quiet time just for themselves, they were as close as they had always been. Ari found it difficult to leave. There was such a contrast between life in Chicago and life in Thompsonville, and she felt the pulse of the city that had drawn her to it twelve years earlier.

Brent's practice grew along with his reputation. He became very active in the local Chamber of Commerce, which took up a good deal of his time, but also gave him a great deal of pleasure. He toyed with hiring an associate in order to take on more work and to free him up for more Chamber activities. He vacillated back and forth concerned that he might end up working even more hours. That meant time away from Tyler. But, in the end, he realized that he was already up to his eyeballs and, if he wanted more time with Tyler, he'd need that extra help. So, his search began.

Harriet became more visible at social functions. Her garden club activities allowed her to widen her circle of friends, join a local book club, and become a fixture at the ladies' weekly luncheons. Of course, when asked, she *had* to accept a position as part of the fund-raising board for the local hospital. It was, after all, a position for which she was suitably equipped and she felt as if she was on her way back up the ladder.

She hadn't yet allowed herself a trip back to New York, fearing she would be recognized. *How can I explain why I'm not staying at my own apartment?* Maybe next year – her trust fund was re-capitalizing. Curbing her previous spending habits was paying off, literally, and she thought in another year or two she'd be just fine, thank you.

Mary, Gabby's mother, remarried. It was time, Gabby and Brent thought. Mary and Brian Armstrong seemed as well suited to each other as they were when they first met several years earlier.

Sadly, Grandpa Bolan passed that summer. Linda and Ari felt very fortunate to have had him with them until the ripe old age of ninety-three. He was fun, feisty, and to him, life was an adventure to be relished daily. He would be sadly missed.

While 2005 started out almost status quo for everyone in Thompsonville, business again slowed at Bolan's. It seemed that even though their competitors were closing their doors due to lack of business which had given Bolan's a spurt over the last few years, now more and more of the

U.S. manufacturing facilities were also shuttering. The trickle, which had begun quite a few years earlier, grew to a steady stream of lost American business. Almost daily, or so Ari thought, there was an article about this company or that company relocating their manufacturing jobs to countries where workers were paid only cents on the U.S. dollar. The smaller mom and pop companies that were left in the States couldn't afford the massive retooling required to compete. And, as always, there was the high cost of labor, even when they could get the work.

The writing was on the wall and Ari knew it. So did the others at Bolan's. When it became apparent there wouldn't be enough work left to keep the plant going for another year, Ari met with the last five employees, just had she had in the spring of 2003.

Ray and Spike were the only two employees who had not yet reached retirement age. They both knew they had been given a gift by Ari keeping the plant open as long as she had. George, Joe and Tom, who were there to help with the work until Ray and Spike could retire, were thanked by Ari as well as by Ray and Spike. The decision was made that Bolan's would close its doors at the end of June and a final company picnic for all of Bolan's employees, past and present, would be held with their families on July 4th at Logan Park.

Ari was devastated that she hadn't found a way to keep the doors open past June.

When she sat down and told her mother about the need to close the doors earlier than their target date, Linda looked deep into Ari's eyes and told her without blinking. "No one, not even your father, could have done a better job holding the seams together for those men. You gave them two extra years they wouldn't have otherwise had. Ari, you've given so much. Now I'm going to give Ray and Spike their salaries through the end of the year, as if they were still working at Bolan's. There will be nice bonuses for George, Joe and Tom, too. They never had to do what they did for Ray and Spike and they deserve some recognition."

"Mom, that's wonderful. I know they'll appreciate it. It really was a group effort – a family effort."

"Honey, your good deeds will not go unnoticed either. While you didn't do this for recognition, someday your efforts will be repaid. I don't know how or when, but trust my words, God sees all."

Soon, Gabby was pregnant again. *What a great life*, she thought. She and Jerry were very happy. They both had successful careers, two wonderful children with a third on the way, and a marriage that was almost unique in today's world. She couldn't have asked for more. Now, if she could just slow down a bit work-wise and take some time to enjoy all that was good in her life.

Gabby had not stopped by Mrs. McCutcheon's for what seemed like a very long time. When the weather turned warm in early June, Gabby was out walking with Nicole and Adam when she took a chance and knocked on Mrs. McCutcheon's front door.

There was no answer and Gabby was about to turn and leave when Nicole said, "Mommy, Mrs. McCutcheon's on the floor, look."

In a panic, Gabby ran to the window and peeked in seeing exactly what Nicole had told her. Gabby immediately reached for her cell phone, dialing 911, while trying to break down the front door.

Nicole, sensing the emergency, ran around to the side porch and found the doors to the porch and, through it, the living room, unlocked. She immediately ran to the front door, opening it for her mother to get in and see what was wrong with Mrs. McCutcheon.

Just as she was beginning to stir, Gabby heard the sirens from the ambulance coming up the drive. Gabby told Mrs. McCutcheon to stay still until the paramedics had a chance to check her out. While Mrs. McCutcheon tried to dismiss the need for any attention by the emergency workers, Gabby would have none of it. She told her she'd sit on her if she didn't listen. Adam was about to do just that, when Gabby caught him. That made the old lady laugh and nod her head, indicating she'd stay as she was until she was told otherwise.

Mrs. McCutcheon said she felt faint as she came in from sitting out on the porch. She thought maybe she just needed some lunch; it had been awhile since she'd eaten breakfast. The paramedics, however, were not about to take her word for it. They insisted, and Gabby concurred, that she go to the hospital where she could be checked out properly. Begrudgingly, she agreed.

Gabby told her she was taking the children back to Ethel and that she would be right behind her, so that when the doctors released her, Gabby could bring her home. Gabby didn't really believe it would be that easy, nor did Mrs. McCutcheon, but she went off in the ambulance, smiling.

The good news was that it really was almost that easy. After the doctors determined it wasn't a heart attack or any other life-threatening emergency, Mrs. McCutcheon was admitted for observation. Then the battery of tests began and the doctors, specializing in all the various disciplines of medicine, came and went.

In the end, it was determined that Mrs. McCutcheon was in good health for someone her age. She was placed on some medications to thin her blood, lower her cholesterol, and generally keep her in good condition advising, however, that she should start looking into some retirement communities.

Brent put the word out that he was looking for an associate. He knew there would probably be only a few takers inasmuch as he was talking about Thompsonville, not one of the major cities. Most law students graduating in the top percentile of their class want to practice in big cities for prestigious law firms with big-name clients. In addition, those firms generally offered a slew of financial enticements, not to mention a really nice starting salary.

Slowly, Brent began to receive responses to his inquiries. After initial telephone conversations with the to-be grads, Brent had honed his choices down to two promising law students. In the end, while both were excellent candidates, the better fit seemed to be a young man graduating from Columbia Law who said he had enough of the big city and wanted to practice in a small town.

Brent wasn't sure that Scott had a town as small as Thompsonville in mind, but he liked him a great deal, and Scott convinced Brent that his aspirations were not as lofty as most of his classmates. Furthermore, Scott was from a small town in Michigan, and Thompsonville was close enough to be home for the holidays, yet far enough away not to be under his parents' thumbs.

And, so, Scott Silverman, became Brent's new associate and Thompsonville's newest resident. The more they worked together, the more Brent was convinced Scott was the perfect match for him. They were both people-persons and Scott had the same desire to help their clients on a level most big city attorneys couldn't fathom.

Gabby had not been feeling well. She was working on new developments for the Columbus and Pittsburgh suburbs. Now, she was worried about Mrs. McCutcheon. While she hadn't had any recurrences of her fainting spell, Gabby was concerned about her being alone so much. She visited more often and spent a great deal of time trying to find a retirement community Mrs. McCutcheon would like. She, however, was not having any of it.

One day in the early fall Gabby was feeling exceptionally tired and left work early to go home and lie down. She had been resting for barely an hour when the sharp pains doubled her into a ball. Struggling to reach her phone, Gabby was able to get Jerry just as he was stepping into a meeting. He ran home, but it was too late. Gabby had lost the baby in just that short a time. She sobbed uncontrollably as Jerry rushed her to the hospital. The doctors assured her and Jerry that it was nothing she had done and there was nothing that she could have done to stop it from happening. Gabby wasn't so sure. Maybe all this expansion into other states for Regency was taking its toll. The doctors and Jerry, however, convinced her that, right now, what she needed, was rest. Everything else would fall into place in time. This pregnancy simply wasn't meant to be, but there was always tomorrow.

Harriet figured out how she could go to New York for the holidays this year. She would merely tell anyone who asked that her apartment was being redone. "Damn the workmen," she would say. "They assured me the work would be done by Thanksgiving, but alas, I'll have to stay at the Waldorf. So, if you can't reach me at my New York number, please call me on my cell phone."

It all worked wonderfully in her mind. It would make a dent in this year's savings, but she'd earned it. She chose the first week of December for her Christmas holiday, which worked in quite well with the New York social scene. The timing also allowed her to get back to Thompsonville for the annual holiday gala at the country club, not to mention the hospital fund raiser/dinner dance. *Ah, life was returning to near normal!*

CHAPTER TWENTY-ONE

Ari took a long dreamed of vacation to China, Japan and Hong Kong after Bolan's closed its doors at the end of June and held it's last Bolan's summer outing on the 4th of July as planned. It was a wonderful trip and did wonders to help Ari realize her mother had been right. There was nothing more she could have done. It was incredibly hurtful though that, after losing her job at the brokerage house in Chicago, she had been unable to keep the doors open at Bolan's until everyone could walk into their own homes, knowing that they worked for a salary that kept their families alive and well until their retirement. In her head there was a nagging, an inner anguish, that if *only* she had tried this or that. Then, there was that spate of lost self-confidence from years earlier, which she successfully fought to re-bury -- whenever it reared its ugly head.

Now, in the early months of 2006, almost nine months since Bolan's had closed, the papers were filled with stories about new plant closings and American jobs being siphoned off overseas. The government was still forecasting a healthy economy for the country even though parts of it, particularly small towns like Thompsonville, had seen the effects, up close and personal, when their local factories shut down.

Gabby spent the winter thinking about her lost baby. It was a devastating experience, one which could never be understood by another, no matter how they tried to put themselves in the same situation. Jerry tried. He worked less, and found it hard to focus on his business when he did work. Gabby tried to keep up a good front for Nicole and Adam, but it was tough going. She thought about all the time she'd spent working. *Maybe that played a part in losing the baby, even though that's not what the doctors said.*

As she attempted to get her head around it, Gabby was reading the business reports. While Regency was doing well, she still didn't like how thinly they were spread over three cities. Uncle Tony had pretty much taken over in Columbus. He hadn't planned to, but the construction chief he hired ended up moving to Atlanta where he had a better offer. With no one to take his place, Uncle Tony jumped in and worked the two jobs that were still unfinished. Gabby was beginning to think that if she cut back on Regency's activities, she might not be on overload, and Uncle Tony could get back to his retirement.

Accordingly, Gabby made a plan to cut their business in Columbus and focus on Pittsburgh for further expansion, continuing in Thompsonville with their rehabs and condo conversions. It just made sense to her. Aside from the benefit of not having their business interests so spread out, it cut her overhead, her insurance and taxes. This could be a good thing, and the end result would mean more time with her family.

Mrs. McCutcheon was being stubborn. There was "just no way," she said, that she was going to live in some "old folks home."

Gabby and Carolyn had taken her around to visit some of the retirement homes in the area. There weren't many, unless you went close to the big cities. There were two which were considerably nicer than the others, but they had incredibly long waiting lists and, even at that, Mrs. McCutcheon was determined not to live in either one.

Eventually, Carolyn, her brother, and even Gabby got involved in finding a companion for Mrs. McCutcheon who would live in and take care of her on a regular basis. Gabby thought that it was the best solution and felt comfortable knowing that Mrs. McCutcheon's husband had left her well able to afford it. Otherwise, there didn't seem to be many options left to someone her age. Gabby was delighted that the residual benefit was that she would still be able to bring the children to visit the lovely old lady who had been so gracious to all of them since they first met.

Brent and Scott were busy. Brent thought that it would take a good deal of time for Scott to settle in; nothing could have been further from the truth. Scott was quick to pick up the cases, and his manner set Brent's clients immediately at ease. In fact, some of the business Brent had needed to turn down earlier because it was too much for one lawyer to handle, was now coming back through the door after hearing of Brent's new associate. Even with the additional work and Scott trying to cram for the bar when time allowed, Brent did find more time for the Chamber work he so loved and, of course, Tyler.

Harriet believed she was on her way to a banner year. After the previous winter's successful reintroduction to the New York social whirl, Harriet felt certain she would be embraced by New York society as she again spent part of the holiday season there. This year she also planned on taking a month in Paris. It was time that she tried that old shoe on again.

Admittedly, she hadn't heard from a good number of her old "friends" from Europe, but there were always new people to meet and she still had an entré to all the places where one went to be seen, photographed and written about.

The tenants in her New York City condo asked to extend their lease. Initially, Harriet was opposed to this plan but, after thinking about it, she realized that she would be in Paris and perhaps elsewhere on the Continent, and she still had social commitments in Thompsonville. So, building up that trust fund for another year didn't seem like such a bad idea.

By summer, Ari had grown restless. Not having Bolan's as part of her everyday life was like missing a limb. She had been so invested in the lives of her father's employees, that no longer having them around on a day-to-day basis was like shutting herself away in solitary confinement. She knew she needed to change her environment. Whether it was a new job, or going back to Chicago to see what might be there for her or even elsewhere, she just knew she needed a change.

Linda encouraged Ari to visit Emily in Chicago and see what it felt like now that her circumstances were different. Linda knew Ari needed to feel safe for awhile and Emily could offer that, and Chicago was a familiar city for her. Ari wasn't so sure but, after another month of seclusion without any new ideas, Ari decided to call Emily and see if there was any room at the inn for her.

Emily was beside herself. The thought of Ari's coming back to Chicago was the best news she'd heard in a long time. Emily had lots of friends, but none that were as special as Ari; it was difficult to explain the relationship between college roommates. Her male friends were okay, but the last longtime boyfriend was too possessive, and Emily couldn't handle that. *What is it with these guys?* she wondered.

Anyway, Emily couldn't wait until Ari arrived. It was August, so they could still go to the beach and enjoy Navy Pier and all the other outdoor activities Chicago had to offer, and there were plenty. And, if they could get Ari's resume up-to-date quickly, that could get her a head start on the fall hiring many companies did. She'd start asking some of her clients if they knew of anything. Networking was a great way to go. *Wouldn't it be great if Ari could find something in Chicago again?*

Ari and Emily set right to work on Ari's resume and Ari called her former headhunter to re-enlist his help in finding something new for her. She had kept in touch with him until she took over her father's business, but now she had a whole new slew of business accomplishments to add to her resume. With him in tow, Emily reaching out to her clients, and Ari responding to jobs posted on the internet from cities other than Chicago, Ari was busy.

She enjoyed the days when she was caught up with her job hunting duties and could just wander around Michigan Avenue, stop by the Cheesecake Factory, or take a walk in the park. It felt good to be among so many people, most of them in a hurry to go somewhere. Somehow, even though she was alone, she seldom felt that way.

She and Emily cooked and invited some of Emily's new friends, as well as some of their old crowd to dinner. On off nights, they ate at a few of the outdoor bistros near Carl Sandburg Village when the weather allowed and, as the cool fall weather moved in from Canada, they moved inside to some of the old-time pubs for which Chicago was famous.

By mid-November, however, Ari was getting anxious. She had gone on some interviews but thought that some of the positions which were available wouldn't use her skills to the full advantage. She had essentially been President of a company for three years, albeit a very small company which ultimately went out of business. But that was a function of the economy, not her business abilities. And, even though it was a small company, one had to know small companies face the same kinds of problems as large ones, just on a different scale.

She missed her mother, Gabby, Brent, and, well, everyone. She even missed being able to walk into shops where she knew the people who owned them and almost always running into people she knew at restaurants, or on the street while shopping.

Did she really want to go to work in a job that was not a challenge just because it was available, that required abilities less than she brought to the table? And, through all this, throw herself into her work, never knowing, whether, when the chips fell in the boardroom, she would be summarily dismissed by some higher up who knew little, if anything, about her.

Ari knew she was vacillating between home and the big city. She finally asked herself the big question. *If I land some sort of a management job in some mid-size company tomorrow, will I be happy?* Frankly, she didn't think so. She had now run the whole show, and she didn't think she would feel any sense of accomplishment in doing some run-of-the-mill job. *Now, what do I do?* She asked herself. "Go home," she said aloud.

Emily was so disappointed by Ari's decision. She begged Ari to stay a little longer to make certain that going home was what she really wanted. They talked and talked, and it soon became clear to Emily that Ari needed to do something to help bolster her self-confidence, and soon.

"Ari, have you ever thought about starting your own business?"

"Not really. Basically because I don't know what that business would be. My business skills are transferable to many types of businesses, but I have no real passion for anything in particular."

Emily felt so awful for her friend. "I wish I had an answer for you."

"Don't worry, Em. I'm keeping my name out there and my headhunter is still looking for the right fit. Maybe he'll come up with something." She told her, and believed it herself, "If I just had a job I could throw myself into, everything would be okay."

When Ari got back to Thompsonville just in time for Thanksgiving, she had terrific news waiting for her.

During Gabby and Jerry's dinner party Thanksgiving weekend, Gabby announced that she was pregnant again, and this time they were going to make it.

Gabby seemed like her old self. It was almost as if this was some sort of acquittal from above of a judgment imposed upon her for her demanding work schedule. Gabby, of course, knew better than that. But, she had nevertheless blamed herself, and, therefore, thought that God was blaming her, too. Ari and Gabby made plans to go shopping for the new baby and catch up on what was going on with each other. They included Nicole in some of their outings; she was at that age – twelve – where she was no longer a child. She needed some exposure to a more grown up world.

Gabby promised herself that she would cut back on her work hours and was unbelievably happy that she had decided to close down the Columbus operation, allowing her to do so. And, she was glad for another reason. Being in construction, Gabby had to keep her eye on the real estate market. Something just wasn't quite right. She couldn't put her finger on it, but something made her uneasy. Resale homes were starting to sit on the market a bit longer – really nothing that noticeable to those not in the business. Sales in the Northeast and the upper Midwest had been down for the last few years.

On the other hand, California, Arizona, Nevada and Florida were flourishing and it seemed that there was no end in sight for the increase in the value of real estate in those states. It was getting crazy. People were buying anything and everything, outbidding one another and taking out mortgages with nothing down, expecting the prices to continue soaring, thereby lining their pockets with money.

All in all though, Gabby was nervous. She wasn't certain she knew what she could do about it, if anything, or frankly whether she should even try. After all, her business was still good. Regency was about to begin the final two sections of the Pittsburgh development. They had a new large development due to break ground next summer, and had made an offer on a small Pheasant Run-type development.

She thought that, after finishing the two larger developments in Pittsburgh, Regency should take a timeout and get a measure of where the market was going. The small, planned Pheasant Run-type development, if their offer was even accepted, didn't have a start date and they could hold the property without any real expense, since it was still an undeveloped piece of land.

Gabby and Ari talked about this during their get-togethers when Nicole wasn't with them. Gabby was concerned for Regency and it's employees, Ari about her own job prospects, and those of the people who had lost their jobs in the massive layoffs during the past few years. Then, there were all the people in Thompsonville who lost their jobs over the years as business moved elsewhere. Both began to question whether the economy was really as healthy as the government continued to make out.

Brian, Mary's new husband, had been trying to sell his house ever since they'd decided to live in Mary's house. At first they held onto it knowing they would have to make some upgrades before putting it on the market. That plan was delayed while they took an extended honeymoon and then began to consolidate their furnishings. By the time that was done, Gabby and her mom began drawing up the plans, and getting the necessary permits.

When Mike and his crew finally began work, they were well into the fall of 2006. Then the holidays, and the slow winter sales season into Spring of 2007. By now, the market had really slowed down.

CHAPTER TWENTY-TWO

Most people in Thompsonville didn't move often. They bought a starter house, a larger one when they could afford it and had a family and then, perhaps, downsized when the children moved away. With the low turnover in local residential real estate, the almost no-growth population of the area, and the lack of jobs, that, even when spring came along, there wasn't much activity in the Thompsonville market. The cutbacks Regency made from large new developments to rehabs and condo conversions several years ago, while not making a large profit, kept the company in the black. Had Regency continued to build locally, they would have had a great deal of difficulty selling the homes, and it could have put Regency in deep financial difficulty.

By the summer of 2007, it was almost as if someone had pulled a plug, and all the real estate buyers were whisked down the drain. Mortgage companies, which had been handing out interest-only and zero-down-payment loans, were feeling the pinch. And, increasingly, homes were sitting on the market for longer and longer periods of time.

Gabby was not oblivious to all that was happening, even though she was a proud new mother to little Jacob. She had taken two months off with his birth, but was still keeping a close eye on Regency through conference calls with Uncle Tony, who was helping Mike out in Thompsonville, and TJ in Pittsburgh. By the time she returned to work, it was clear that the national real estate market was in quite a slump.

Gabby felt fortunate that they had their financing in place and that sales in their Pittsburgh developments, while lower than they had forecast, were still doing okay. Gabby questioned, though, whether Regency should continue building that last large development. She needed to make a decision quickly, as time was of the essence in terms of potential weather obstacles which could slow them down in the upcoming months.

Ari became increasingly frustrated. It was almost Thanksgiving, again, and there was nothing of interest coming out of Chicago. On a national basis, she had some nibbles, and a couple of interviews, one in Los Angeles and one in Phoenix. Los Angeles was just not for her. This, she knew immediately. The weather was nice but the city was just too big, and frankly, the job not that interesting. Phoenix was nicer, she thought, but she was not offered the position. And then the nibbles started drying up. By June she was just getting angry.

Calling Gabby to vent, Ari could barely contain herself. Gabby, sensing the frustration and anger, told Ari "Get over here so we can talk about this." Gabby was putting Jacob down for his nap when Ari arrived. Ethel had taken Adam to the park and Nicole was over at a girlfriend's house. Gabby told Ari, "Brent's coming by in about an hour. I need to talk to him as counsel to Regency about our legal commitments and potential financial exposure, should we decide not to finish the last two phases of Serenity Hills in Pittsburgh. I'm fairly certain that we're not going to go ahead with our next large subdivision in Pittsburgh either, at least not at this time."

Hearing that Regency was being squeezed too, to the extent that it may be in difficulty, was the last straw. Pacing back and forth in Gabby's living room, Ari could barely control herself and began spewing out all her pent up anger and frustration. "Look at what's happening here. And when I say 'here,' I don't just mean Thompsonville because, truth be told, what's happening everywhere in this country has been happening in Thompsonville for years if not decades.

The unemployment rate in Thompsonville is higher than it is nationally, with no end in sight. Our factories have all but closed down. The few that are left are dying. Look at what happened to Bolan's. We were a small family-owned company which had been around since my grand-father started it in 1934. That was more than seventy years in business. But, we couldn't hold on.

Why? Because we, and now I'm including the entire United States, no longer produce anything. So, plants that made parts for machines that no longer produce anything, can't survive. Almost everything that used to be Made in America is now being made elsewhere. And those few companies that still manufacture here have such high costs for labor, taxes, insurance, health care and who knows what else, they are finding it almost impossible to compete. Foreign countries subsidize their exports. Oh, maybe not directly or so blatantly that our government sees it or can prove it, but those subsidies undercut the prices American companies must charge to even cover their costs. And, this *isn't* news. This has been going on for quite some time.

Even our service industries or the service departments of our American companies are now based overseas. Hell, excuse me, you can't even understand most of their agents, and that's when and if you finally get through to them after spending what seems like forever going through the automatic prompts or the perpetual hold systems, while you wait for the 'next available agent.' And then, after all that, you promptly get cut off and have to go through the whole damn system again.

I'm just so tired of it all, that now I'm just angry."

Just as Ari was about to go on, Brent walked in, was about to kiss Gabby and Ari hello, when he noticed that kisses might not be the right thing at that point. So, Brent sat down on the sofa as Ari continued on.

"You know, it's not like this is all news to our government. They turn a blind eye. I understand our trade agreements – or at least the theory of them. But, these are moving parts and we're getting slammed.

U.S. companies have been moving jobs overseas for years now. We should have seen it coming when companies started moving their operations to states where the costs were much lower than the states where they had been located. And we're not just talking about labor. There were subsidies from those communities and states, which made it almost fiscally irresponsible for them to continue doing business in their previous locations. But no one saw it or else they just didn't think the next move would be outside the country.

We have all these incredibly highly paid senior executives in major American companies and yet it doesn't seem that they can put a plan together that will help ensure American business and certainly not America's interests in the long term. I'm not even sure what an American company is any longer. So many of them are now owned by foreign interests.

And now, Regency may be in trouble or maybe not in trouble but heading toward it. What is going on with real estate?"

Gabby jumped in bringing Brent up-to-speed on what Ari had been telling her before he'd walked in. Brent looked at Gabby and when she nodded, giving Regency's counsel permission to speak, he then looked up at Ari, who was now standing in place after all her pacing.

"Ari, you're absolutely right. Thompsonville has been getting hit for several years, even decades, now. Regency is not hurting, not yet. But there is concern about where it's going. That's a decision Gabby will have to make.

But, let's talk about what you've brought up and obviously something that has impacted you or is impacting you now. As a member of the Chamber, I am deeply involved in trying to assist local businesses, most of which are just trying to stay afloat. Whereas in many of the large cities in this country, the various Chambers are involved in trying to increase their area's business. We *wish* that was our problem. We're trying to *save* ours.

You're right, unemployment has increased significantly, not just in Thompsonville and the multi-countywide area, but the entire country. Here, we have factories which stand empty, many of them having been closed for years, in various stages of disrepair. The old fashionable area of downtown has become almost a ghost town. In fact, if it weren't that Thompsonville is the county seat, I'm not certain there would be anything left."

"Why can't we get other businesses to move their operations here," Ari asked?

"I'm almost certain Hiz Honor tried that several years ago, to no avail." Brent replied. "But, even if he tried to attract new business interests to our area, Thompsonville wasn't and isn't in a position to offer enough of those incentives you're so opposed to, Ari, for any company to take more than a cursory look."

Gabby jumped in. "What would it take for Hiz Honor to be able to make Thompsonville attractive to prospective businesses?"

Ari was becoming interested in where this conversation was going.

Brent said, "There's probably nothing we can really offer at this time. As Ari pointed out, most smaller companies are either being squeezed out, have been squeezed out, or the plants for larger companies have moved their operations elsewhere.

Besides, we no longer have the workforce necessary to work in any potential new plant. It's been several years, and in many cases many years, since our plants have closed down. Our workforce is older now, some of the younger workers have moved away, and, while we have a rather large unemployment number, it's not skilled labor. And that's just part of the equation.

How do we offer lower taxes and incentives to companies while finding it necessary to increase our electrical, water and sewer capacities? It would undoubtedly require considerable revamping of our streets and bridges, just to deal with the increased traffic and how do we pay for that?

Thompsonville is fundamentally broke. We look to the state and the state looks to the Federal government to help fund our needs. We simply don't generate enough here for our own services."

"Aren't we looking at this the wrong way?" Gabby asked. "Rather than looking at why we *can't* do something, let's look at what we *might* be able to do and then figure out how."

Okay, Ari was energized, now. "Wait a minute," she said. "It seems to me that we have several problems here, but maybe if we take them one-by-one it won't seem so onerous. Let's start with Thompsonville's lack of funds. What can we do to generate money coming into the coffers of the city/county?"

Brent just shook his head. "That's the million-dollar question. If we could have, the Chamber would have come up with an idea long ago."

Gabby, too, wasn't sure. "I'd love it if we could find some way to rebuild Thompsonville. Not only would it be good for the town, but it would be great for Regency and all our employees. But, I don't have any suggestions."

"Maybe we're being too traditional here," said Ari. "What brings money into a town, other than new business, is tourists. So, what could we offer in Thompsonville to attract tourists?"

Gabby looked up at Ari. "I think the idea of a theme park featuring cartoon characters is already taken. But, seriously, what if . . . What if we were to offer some sort of stopping place for the arts? Look at how successful Branson, Missouri is. Let's say we were to use some of our empty space downtown as rehearsal halls for promising playwrights. We could even have their companies perform in the old theater once they were ready to open and, if we have enough plays during the year, we could have a steady stream of income for the area. It would bring people who don't go or can't afford to go to New York City and pay those exorbitant ticket prices, not to mention airfare, hotels, and food."

"I like it. *A lot!*" said Ari. "What if we offered art galleries, too. Lots of art galleries with lots of artists who're just starting out or haven't yet been 'discovered.' The reason this comes to mind is that Doug's younger brother, Christopher, is an artist who had to move back to Thompsonville after many years of knocking on doors of galleries trying to market his artwork. I had lunch with Doug a couple of weeks ago and he told me of Christopher's heartache of having to give up.

There must be tons of artists out there struggling who would jump at an opportunity to show their work. I really think there are lots of people who would love to come and look at artwork and go to the theater in a nice, small, unrushed atmosphere as we have here. I'm really getting excited about this."

"Not to be the one to spoil all the fun, but how do we find the money to run these places, assuming we can afford to rent them?" queried Brent. "And, then, how do we attract the artists and playwrights?"

"Right. On to problem number two," Gabby said. "That is, assuming that we all like our idea as a potential solution to problem number one." No one disagreed.

Ari paced even more rapidly. As she thought about the ideas they were talking about, her mind starting clicking even faster. "Brent, do you know if all those empty buildings downtown are available? Are any of them just deserted properties that the city could own through some manner?"

"I'd have to look at the city charter, but almost every city has the right to take property by eminent domain. That basically means that if the city needs it, it can take it from the titled owner, with or without his consent, for what is determined to be 'fair market value.' The problem is that the city doesn't have the money to pay anyone 'fair market value.' We might be able to get some of the owners to lease their buildings to the city for some very low rent, let's say, ridiculously, a dollar a year or a month, that kind of thing. We'd have to raise some money from outside sources, of course, in order to pay all the other expenses such as taxes, utilities, insurance."

"We'll have to think about that one," said Ari.

Gabby said, "As far as finding the artists and playwrights, that's somewhere Jerry can help. With all the stuff on the internet these days, I'm certain he can put together some sort of an 'invitation to artists/playwrights' that, once sent to any group or organization, will be passed like wildfire among any who might find this the answer they'd been looking for or, at the very least, the idea interesting."

"We could end up being inundated. We would probably have to set up some sort of committee for each area to review and judge the artists -- there's some kind of name for that. We'd have to be selective, not only for our sake, but also for the benefit of the artists. But, we can do this," said Ari.

"Wait a minute," said Brent. "This all sounds well and good, but I think you're missing one of the biggest stumbling blocks to this whole concept." Both Ari and Gabby looked at Brent with daggers in their eyes, as if he had just squashed them to pieces. "Whoa, I think we're onto something," said Brent, "but I'm not so sure that we're going to get Hiz Honor or any of his merry little band of councilmen to go along with any of it."

As a group, they sat back deflated.

"Then," Gabby spoke up, "we'll just have to get rid of him."

Ari sat forward. "Can we do that? After all, he's an institution around here."

"Well, of course we can, we just need to recall him or something," Gabby answered.

"It may not be as difficult as all that," Brent said. "Look, next year is an election year, we'd just have to make certain he's not re-elected."

"Absolutely," said Ari. "All we need is a good strong candidate and he's out and, as a matter of fact, I know just the person."

Gabby looked at Ari and instantly she knew. They both said, "You, Brent."

Ari went on. "You'd be perfect. Look, you're held in very high esteem here. You know the law, plus you're a longtime member of the Chamber which has been trying to rebuild local business for several years. Now we have a plan, or at least the beginnings of one. Gabby, I think this calls for wine."

"We may have a plan, but I'm not sure we have a candidate for your little coup. I have to admit I'm intrigued with the idea, but I'm not certain I'm the right person for the job. You do, however, have my support in replacing Hiz Honor with someone reputable who has the best interests of Thompsonville at heart."

By the time Jerry walked in from his round of golf, the threesome was quite relaxed and extremely pleased with themselves. They poured Jerry a glass of wine and sat him down as they began to reveal their plan. Actually, Jerry thought it had a good deal of merit and began to think of how he could help. They broke up their little meeting when Ari decided it was time to head home. She promised to talk to Doug and his brother, Christopher. They all promised to think more about the different aspects of the plan and meet again in a few days.

CHAPTER TWENTY-THREE

And think about it they did. Ari called Doug and asked if she could have Christopher's number – she might have an idea for him and his work. Doug was delighted and didn't ask any questions about what Ari had in mind, thinking it was portrait work or something.

Brent was now seriously considering his part in this and whether he thought he could be the Mayor that Thompsonville needed at this point in time. This would be no ordinary mayor's job where one oversaw the budget, projects of the city and helped make laws which would benefit the entire community. This was *reshaping* Thompsonville, and would be no easy task. It required a vision. Did he really have it or was this Ari and his sister's vision? Maybe if he could enlist their help. *Ha*, he thought. *I'm being ridiculous.* In fact, he was certain there was no way to keep them out of it. *Good Lord, he really was thinking about doing this!*

Gabby was excited too. She thought that if they could turn Thompsonville around, that would be her gift. Gabby often felt somewhat inadequate in that she never went to college, other than a few night school courses. Somehow in her own mind, her own accomplishments, insofar as Regency was concerned, were just tasks that needed doing, and she was the one who had to do them. She thought about reviving downtown, how she and Regency could be a part of it, and what it would mean to all the people who had hung in there, waiting for some sort of turnaround in the economy. If this worked -- *No*, she thought, *When this worked* -- hotels and restaurants would thrive and there would be jobs for those who wanted them.

They met, again at Gabby's, on Thursday night when Jerry would be home and available to join them.

Ari told them about her meeting with Christopher and that he was ecstatic about being able to help them with the artists. "He told me about the difficulty artists face trying to find a gallery where they could hang their work. 'Seldom,' he said, 'are galleries willing to look at an artist's work. Even when the artist is standing in front of the gallery owner or manager, they just don't bother.' He said 'he understood that galleries represent many artists and often aren't in a position to take on another one.' Incredulously, he blurted out, 'But not to look? Perhaps the artist standing before them is the new Picasso or Andy Warhol or Peter Max.'

His frustration was evident. He'd been there. And there was no stopping him from letting it all out. He lamented, 'It's devastating to the artist and it costs them time away from their work, not to mention the dollars involved, traveling to galleries, packing their artwork, repairing damaged works, shipping, all the things we never think about. Just the time involved in looking up all the galleries on the internet and then looking at each individual gallery to see if his or her work was the type of art the gallery represented, took hours and hours. And, all this, just so that *if* they're successful, they can *pay the gallery owner* a percentage of the sales price and, most times, printing costs for receptions and handouts.' I *felt* his frustration," said Ari. "He then went on to predict that there would be similar interest on the part of playwrights. Apparently the cost of renting rehearsal halls is out of sight, the players' salaries of course had to be paid, and all this before they even knew if they had a viable product."

Jerry had done some initial investigation into artists' groups and associations, checking out various websites and told Ari, Gabby and Brent, "I'm sure it won't be difficult to get the word out, once the groups know that it's something which could be of great interest to their members."

"I can offer part of my crew at cost, once we've finished our development in Pittsburgh," Gabby jumped in. "I've also put the new development on hold. Of course, timing is imperative. I know I can't do it forever, and some of the workers might find other jobs at different companies. On the other hand, if this takes a long time to get off the ground, Regency may need them again. Again, timing. I don't believe our plan is going to take place right away, because it's unlikely anything can proceed without the backing of the Mayor and the City Council." This, she knew, was highly improbable under the current administration.

At this point, all eyes turned to Brent. He'd been quiet while the others had given their updates. Now, it was time for him to either commit himself as a candidate, offer up someone else as a potential candidate, or tell them he'd thought it over, and they were all nuts. Up until that very moment, even Brent didn't know what he was going to say.

Slowly, he took a deep breath and, looking at each one of them in turn, said, "This is crazy . . . but count me in."

What had ultimately turned him, he thought later, *was not only the look on their faces, but their intense dedication to the plan.* The fact that so many of his clients were in the same positions that Ari and Gabby had described the first time they talked about this, turned his arms-length support into unwavering commitment.

The people in Thompsonville were hurting. He represented some who had contract disputes with employers who had closed their plants, business and personal bankruptcies, real estate difficulties due to back taxes they couldn't pay, and so on. He had come back home from Washington to help the people and he knew that their plan might provide the best long-term solution for their problems.

"Before we actually throw my hat into the proverbial ring, I'd like to suggest that we invite some of the local business owners to listen to this and make any suggestions they might have. We may be *too close* to it, and we could be missing something that might be really important to them. How about we meet next Monday morning for an early breakfast at The Blue Frog? I have actually put together a list of people I think might be interested in this and, if we split the list in three, each taking a third to call, plus, of course, any others you think I may have forgotten, I think we might get a fair-sized turnout and a really good feel for whether or not we're on the right track.

I've already talked to Claudia about whether we could do this and disrupt her regular morning breakfast business, but, she assured me, it would be all right. By the way, she's planning on being there as an attendee – she said she'd put on extra help to cover her not working -- and is sworn to secrecy."

The enthusiasm was evident. There was little question in any of their minds that this was a splendid idea. Brent was still concerned that he might not be the best candidate, but he was certain he would be committed to defeating the mayor, *if* Hiz Honor didn't go along with their plan. With promises to make their calls, each went home that evening with a sense of direction and hope for Thompsonville, its people and their future.

The Blue Frog opened at 7:00 a.m. every day, so Claudia and the rest of her staff were there by 6:30. The meeting was scheduled for 7:30, but folks started showing up much earlier.

Claudia put some of the tables in a small circle in the back. As the local business owners began to gather and talk with one another, there was an air of mystery about what this meeting was all about. Of course, they had been told it involved future business opportunities and job growth in the city, but no specifics had been let out of the bag.

At 7:20 Ari and Gabby walked in. Not much more than a minute later, Brent followed. As they greeted everyone, and began to take their seats, all but one of the invitees had already arrived. They were looking over their menus and placing orders as Susan Cranston arrived, direct from the Petal Pushers Nursery outside of town, which her daughter ran while Susan manned the shop. There was a sense of excitement in the group and, after Susan finished ordering, all eyes turned to Ari, Gabby and Brent.

Ari started by thanking everyone for coming. "This is our first meeting after Gabby, Brent and I came up with the idea we're now proposing." If it wasn't already as quiet as The Blue Frog had ever been, it became even more so.

Ari took a deep breath and began again. "You're all familiar with the state of our local economy. As you know, over the last few decades, plants have closed, consolidated or moved their operations elsewhere and very little new business has taken over those facilities. Additionally all of us have watched what was a very vibrant downtown retail area crumble before our very eyes. What little business is left downtown is here to accommodate the business of the county offices. Local unemployment numbers are climbing and the best and the brightest of our young people can't find a reason to stay in Thompsonville.

You all know Gabby O'Neil and you know that she heads up Regency Construction, one of Thompsonville's largest employers. Even Regency in the past couple of years has had to reduce their operations in Thompsonville and concentrate their efforts in Columbus and Pittsburgh, where job growth and the need for new housing was still on the rise. This, too, is changing. Regency has already ceased their operations in Columbus. Real estate everywhere has slowed in the last year and Regency has found itself in a position where it put its plans for a new major development in Pittsburgh on hold. This means that after completion of its last section in their current project, Regency will have to try to absorb some of those employees here in Thompsonville. This comes as no surprise to most of you as Regency informed its employees of this several weeks ago. As I stated earlier, there's little work here with zero population growth. Obviously, many of those employees will be in jeopardy of losing their jobs.

Brent, Gabby's brother, you all know personally from his law practice and also through his affiliation with the Chamber, or at least you know of him. Brent has seen his practice here grow from his representation of various clients who have been on the short end of some of our area's lost business. Over the past couple of years, Brent has been working with the Chamber, and many of you business owners, trying to find a way to help bolster local business, without a great deal of success.

Last year, I had to close my father's business, Bolan's Machine Works, which had been operating here in Thompsonville since my grandfather started it in 1934. Before that, I was employed by a major stock brokerage/ investment banking firm in Chicago, which had to lay off thousands of its employees in 2001, of which I was one. Since closing Bolan's I've been looking for a position in Chicago and other major U.S. cities, but find that there are very few good jobs out there.

Contrary to what the national jobs' numbers show, most of the jobs that are available are in the service industries where minimum wage is the going rate. Many, many people laid off due to the dot com bust of 2000 are still out there, unemployed, and aren't even represented in the current unemployment figures. We know this not only from the available data, but also by what we know personally.

Last week, Gabby, Brent and I were talking about our individual situations and, frankly, became very angry. We talked about the fact that the situations we're facing here are just a slice of what's happening out there to the entire country. Then we talked about Thompsonville. We talked about the deterioration of downtown, the empty plants dotting our beautiful countryside, the lack of jobs, and the loss of our young people to more attractive jobs elsewhere. How do we stop this hemorrhaging? How do we rebuild our town? How do we pay for it without an increasing tax base? These are all questions we're certain you've asked yourselves.

A large part of this problem is that Thompsonville, with it's declining population, can't get enough funds from the state to get out of this quagmire. The state also has a declining population which means it can't get as much money from the Federal government. So, we lose out to other states which, in turn, build up their cities to which we lose more of our population, particularly the young, talented people. It's a vicious cycle.

Then we realized that we, and I mean all of us, have been relying on Washington to come up with some brilliant solution which will work for the entire country and then provide the tools which will put that solution into effect, saving us all.

Let's face it, we don't even have a local government that can do that and it's supposed to have our particular interests as its focus. And, Washington, well Washington doesn't recognize or has turned a blind eye to the fact that we're all in a world of trouble out here. If we wait for Washington to figure this out, Thompsonville will be a ghost town. We need an innovative idea which will bring business and jobs to Thompsonville, not just a band-aid philosophy of getting by until things turn around. We have to *make* things turn around. This brought us to our idea.

In order to rebuild Thompsonville into a thriving community, we need money coming into the area on a regular basis. To us, that meant tourists. Well, of course, we know we don't currently have anything here which would attract tourists. But, what if we did?

Our plan involves making Thompsonville into a center for the arts – at least the live theater kind and artists, painters, sculptors, photographers, etcetera."

As Ari explained the plan in detail, she, Gabby and Brent could see the look of concentration on each of the invitees' faces. By the time she had finished, everyone was talking all at once. Even the eavesdroppers from tables of other breakfast patrons were talking with the invitees with enthusiasm, at least most of them.

Breakfast was served. Somehow, Claudia had been able to hold off until just the right time, allowing Ari to get through her presentation. Actually, a good deal of everyone's breakfast ended up getting cold as they were too busy talking with each other to eat.

Vinny Patel, the owner of a local convenience store, said "Excuse me." Having not been heard over the din, he said, "Excuse me" again. Brent heard him the second time and asked everyone to be quiet for a moment.

"This idea sounds like a pipe dream to me. Tourism is a very good way to go and while your idea is interesting, in order to attract tourists, we'd have to find a ton, and I mean a ton, of money. We'd have to fix up Thompsonville, particularly downtown and its buildings in order to do this. We shopkeepers would have to invest money, money we don't necessarily have or would have to borrow on a whim, setting up our own new stores downtown.

And, what makes you think those artists and playwrights can afford the rent, utilities, etcetera, for this new downtown attraction? Are you suggesting we subsidize all the necessary costs for the artists and actors? This assumes we can even get any properties in the downtown area where the owners would go along with this dollar a year plan. My word, there's an awful lot of work to do and I'm not sure it's affordable, much less doable."

"Wait a minute," said Susan Cranston. "We can't just summarily dismiss this idea because it's difficult. We have to take it upon ourselves to *do something*. No one else is, and *I* think this idea has some merit."

Gabby spoke up. "We think we can get the buildings. I've offered my crew at cost, assuming they aren't tied up with other work for Regency or some other construction company. But, as Ari explained to you, Regency doesn't foresee needing its full crew after we complete our work in Pittsburgh. That means most of my men will be free beginning sometime this summer.

My husband, Jerry, has already started putting together a website that we will use to attract, hopefully, artists, playwrights, actors, etcetera. Other than utilities, our participation with the playwrights will involve only their rehearsal halls and the Thompsonville Theatre from time to time as they perform for the public. In the meantime, they'll need hotel rooms, restaurants, shops, groceries, laundries, all the everyday needs, which will be their own financial responsibility."

Ari took over. "The artists will need gallery space, again utilities, supplies, maybe models as well as their everyday living needs. The best part about the artists is that we'd have them create in public. Whether that means outdoors in the summer or in the window of some gallery or other, it doesn't matter, just so there's something for tourists to see and do while enjoying beautiful, newly-renovated, downtown Thompsonville."

"Okay, hold it," said Bernardo Pucci, owner of Augustino's Restaurant down on 7th and Columbia. "I have to tell you I have many concerns, not the least of which is the cost, as Vinny brought up. Personally, I'd love to see downtown revitalized. But, just as a marketing matter, I don't think the vacationing public would consider a vacation to a place called Thompsonville, no matter how great they'd heard it was. If we decide to do this, I think we're going to have to change the name to something more interesting and attractive."

"Well," said Brent, "Thompsonville was named after Ari's mother's family. I'm not so sure . . . "

"Wait a second, Brent. I don't think that'll be a problem. I've talked this whole idea over with my mother and, while we didn't even think about renaming the town, I know she thinks that we have to do something to save it. Let's face it, if we don't do something, the town will die, along with its name."

"What does Mayor Hill think about all this?" asked Arnie Schaub. Arnie's was the store where Hiz Honor bought most of his clothes, not to mention that the two were great golfing buddies. "I notice he's not here."

Gabby said, "We haven't even tried to talk to him about it yet. Frankly, we wanted to know if we had your backing before we proposed the idea to him. If we don't have your support, then there's really no need to present the plan to the Mayor."

"But what if he doesn't like the idea?" continued Arnie. "Do we just drop it then?"

"No, to answer your question. This is too important to just drop. If we have your support and the Mayor doesn't go along, well, in a few weeks we'll be into an election year and I, for one, know someone who would make an excellent mayor." Gabby paused and then continued. "My brother, with some arm twisting, has agreed that should Mayor Hill not see the value of our proposal or some other practicable plan, he will run for the office of Mayor."

The crowd murmured; some heads nodding slowly, others shaking their heads in disbelief.

Ari said, "It's getting late and most of you need to get to your businesses. We didn't and don't expect everyone to jump on the bandwagon. What we wanted to accomplish today was to present our idea, let you think about it, and then reconvene so that we can discuss any suggestions you have. You've made some good points. Think about solutions to some of the issues raised here today. We're looking to move forward, and we need your help. We'd like to meet in about a week. If anyone has an idea as to where we could meet without being rushed first thing in the morning, we'd love to hear it. Also, we want to thank Claudia for making The Blue Frog available to us this morning and disrupting her normal breakfast business."

Bernardo Pucci jumped up and said, "Augustino's is closed on Mondays, so if we want to meet there after work or after dinner, we can do that."

"That's perfect, Bernardo. Thanks," said Ari. "What about it, next Monday night at Augustino's, say, 7:00 p.m.? We can grab dinner beforehand." Everyone agreed and the next meeting was set.

All in all, the three friends thought that it had gone very well.

CHAPTER TWENTY-FOUR

After the meeting earlier that day at The Blue Frog, Brent received a telephone call from Bert Palmer, owner of one of the local hardware stores. He overheard the meeting that morning while enjoying his breakfast and reading the morning *Sentinel*. "Brent, I'm very interested in the idea being kicked around by the group and wonder if I can be included in your next meeting Monday night?" Brent apologized for not thinking of him in the first place. Bert said, "Not to worry. I understand that a hardware store isn't the kind of business that would jump out as the type you're considering for the new downtown. However, if the plan is successful, not only will tourists be heading to town, but there will be new jobs and therefore potential new customers for all sorts of retail businesses.

There were quite a few calls. Word gets around a small town very fast. According to Gordon Reed, one of Brent's fellow Thompsonville attorneys, Mayor Hill had heard about the meeting as well. Brent knew it had to happen, but he hadn't expected it quite that quickly. *It's not as if it's a secret,* he thought. *Otherwise, we certainly wouldn't have held the meeting at The Blue Frog where anyone and everyone could overhear.*

It was inevitable then that when the phone rang that afternoon, Brent found Hiz Honor on the other end of the line.

"Brent, what's this I hear about a major reconstruction project for downtown with you at the helm as the new mayor? That rather smacks of mutiny, my boy. Or, did you just think that if you could get everyone to go along, I'd have no choice other than to support it?"

"Mr. Mayor, it was never our plan to go around you. We were just testing the waters to find out if there would be broad enough support from the local businesspeople for us to present the plan to you. We're meeting next Monday night at Augustino's and we'd be extremely pleased if you would come and listen first-hand to what we've been discussing. It is not, nor has it ever been, our goal to remove or replace you. We would be delighted to have you run with whatever plan is agreed upon, assuming there *is* a consensus, and that *it will have* your wholehearted support."

"Well, that's more like it, my boy. I won't be able to make your little meeting next Monday night, but if and when you get a plan together, why don't you call me and arrange an appointment. I'll be glad to see you and hear what you have to say at that time. Good luck, young man. Goodbye." Even though Hiz Honor was fuming, he was bound and determined not to let Brent know it. He thought, *There's no one out there who can tumble my applecart.*

Brent was surprised by the Mayor's lack of interest in participating in the meeting the following Monday night, and further that he made no indication of wanting to be involved during any part of the planning stage. *Well,* Brent thought, *that isn't going to stop us.* Maybe it was just the Mayor's way of letting everyone else figure out the answer and then he would claim it as his own solution to the problem.

By the time Monday night rolled around, the excitement was palpable. It took little time to get everyone's attention as they all seemed so caught up in the potential for Thompsonville and, thus, the local business community. Issues were again raised concerning the attendant costs of such a monumental undertaking, but others were convinced that something had to be done for all their sakes.

Brent suggested they enlist his friend and commercial real estate agent, Jack Caldwell, to look into which buildings downtown were currently unoccupied, their location and ownership status. Jack was already preparing a list of the older buildings down by the river that had deteriorated to the point where they couldn't be saved – the cost of renovation would be prohibitive. They still needed to be identified, however. And, what was the cost of razing them, assuming they could get title? Then, could they raise enough money to renovate those that were still structurally sound? Maybe they should avoid the river area altogether?

Ari volunteered to work with Jack contacting building owners in an attempt to get promises from them to rent out their buildings for a very low annual rate. This, they would assure the owners, assumes that the plan would take effect and the buildings could be brought to code within the yet-to-be-established budget.

Gabby promised that when buildings were identified as potential sites for the redevelopment, she and her staff would inspect the buildings to determine the costs for rehabing them for their purposes.

Susan Cranston jumped in saying she thought that Bernardo was right about the name of the town. "I'd like to suggest that we have a contest, open to everyone in Thompsonville, to rename the town. I think that'll create public interest in the plan and, hopefully, some support."

"That's a terrific idea, Susan. We could even offer a prize for the winning suggestion." Bernardo exclaimed.

"In order to rename Thompsonville, we'll need to place a referendum on November's ballot for the voters to decide. It requires a petition, signatures, filing, and so on. Scott and I will put it together," Brent offered.

Susan then said that while the entire group should choose the top five or so entries, Ari, Gabby and Brent should then make the final decision since this was all their idea in the first place.

Jerry, at Gabby's insistence, stood and told everyone he was working on a site for Facebook announcing their plan to the artists and playwrights they were hoping to attract. "My laptop is on the back table and everyone is welcome to look at it and make suggestions. I'm also planning a website for Thompsonville – after it's renamed, of course. We'll use that in an effort to attract tourists. I'm still toying with the concept and layout, but as we move forward and have more information about the artists and playwrights, that site will also be available to you for comments before it's finalized."

"This is all moving way too fast and a website is entirely too premature." snapped Arnie Schaub. "While I'm for some sort of plan to increase business in town, I don't like the idea that this is being done without Mayor Hill's input." He again raised the issue of costs and how he didn't see that this plan was viable because, if it were, the Mayor would've already done it.

"Calm down, Arnie." Bert Palmer soothed. "Jerry said the website is only in the early creative process. In fact, the entire plan is still in its infancy."

Ari then asked, "Is there general approval that we continue to research the plan as we've discussed it tonight?" The vote was almost unanimous. Arnie was the lone standout, probably afraid that the Mayor would hear he voted for it. "Good. Gabby, Brent and I, along with those of you who've volunteered, will meet in an attempt to put this together on paper. We'll investigate the costs as best we can at this point, talk with others who might have information important to the plan and then schedule another meeting with everyone, probably in about a month, after we've enjoyed our holidays." With that, the meeting broke up as many went back to look at Jerry's beginnings of a page on Facebook.

Brent was in court several days later when, upon leaving the building, he unexpectedly ran into Hiz Honor. The Mayor offered his hand and, as they greeted each other, Hiz Honor pulled Brent aside. "I heard about Monday night's meeting and I wonder if you can spare me a few moments of your time?"

"Anytime, Mr. Mayor."

"Well, good then, young man. Now is as good a time for me as any other. Come along."

As they entered the inner sanctum of Hiz Honor's office, the Mayor pointed to a seat across from his desk and then sat without another word, and without offering Brent any refreshment.

Uh Oh, Brent thought. And it began . . .

"Young man . . . Brent, I am deeply disturbed by what you and your little group of businesspeople seem to be trying to do in *my* town. I've heard about the grand illusions you all have of rebuilding Thompsonville, and *even* going so far as to *rename the whole town for your own purposes.*

First of all, and let me say this so you get it -- *this town has no money.* Not just no *extra* money, but *no* money. We don't have a broad enough tax base to raise additional funds and even if we could raise taxes, many of the residents in this town are lower income folks, retired and living on fixed incomes, or don't have jobs period – so they'd end up losing their homes because they couldn't pay their taxes.

And, just who do you think is going to come to Thompsonville to look at some no-talent artists' work or watch some below-high-school-grade production of Peter Pan or whatever? I'm not sure what you all have been smoking, but this is about as practical as all of us selling our homes and lumping the proceeds together to buy lottery tickets, thinking we'll win."

"Your Honor, . . ."

"Don't interrupt me, young man. You're all dreaming and I'm not about to be dragged into it. So, go back and tell your friends that the plan is dead and to get back to trying to increase their businesses by conventional means. I have my hands full here trying to get more dollars from the state for things we need, not pie-in-the-sky ideas like this one.

And, if you think that this little scheme is going to get you my job, you've another think coming. The residents of this town are smarter than I guess you business folks are and they'll laugh at your plan and tick my name off on the next election's ballot. I don't wish you ill personally, my boy, but this plan and your aspirations for my job need to end."

With that, Hiz Honor stood up and walked over to his door, opened it and waited until Brent left, closing it after him.

The minute Brent got back to his office, he called Gabby and Ari to arrange a meeting with them for that evening without saying a word about what it involved. As they sat down, Brent said "I've called this little meeting to announce to you the formation of our committee to elect me the next Mayor of Thompsonville – or its successor name should we get that far."

Gabby's head snapped up. She looked over to see if Ari was as surprised as she about what Brent had just announced. Indeed, Ari knew that Brent was willing to run, but hadn't thought it was something to which he actually aspired. Gabby asked the question. "Okay, what happened?"

"Hiz Honor called me on the carpet this afternoon. It was a lecture in every sense of the word – his attitude was supercilious, and his manner demeaning, as if, *How dare I plan to run against him.* Hiz Honor didn't even ask about the plan, whether we'd determined any of the costs involved, the plan's eventual viability . . . nothing," Brent said. "Absolutely nothing.

If he thought he was scaring me away, he was way off the mark. If anything, the more he talked, the more certain I became that he needed to be replaced, and that Thompsonville needed new thinking if it was ever to move forward. I am more determined than ever, and I hope you still are convinced that we need to do something along the lines of our plan . . . that you still believe I should be the one to run against him."

Ari immediately said, "Absolutely, without question. And what if we make Bolan's your headquarters. That way, we won't be in your way at your office or disrupt your tenants' business. I was going to offer it as the renovation office anyway. What do you think?"

"I think it's perfect," said Gabby as she got up to give Brent a congratulatory kiss.

Meanwhile, Cornelia Huff raced past Dottie, the Mayor's secretary, and charged into his private office. "What the hell is going on in this town, Steve? I've just had a call from Abigail Spencer over at The *Sentinel* asking if I wanted to go on the record about the new revitalization plan."

"Calm down, Cornelia." Before closing his office door, the Mayor stuck his head out. "Dottie, will you bring Councilwoman Huff a Perrier with lime, please."

"What revitalization plan? Do you know about this?" she sputtered. "Does Harvey? Because *I* don't, and I have to tell you. . . ." Cornelia paused as Dottie entered and set a glass down in front of her, giving Hiz Honor a chance to collect himself.

"Let's take a moment here, Cornelia. Some kids got together and came up with an idea to rebuild Thompsonville. They're in the process of trying to sell it to the local businesspeople. It's pie-in-the-sky, and, as a matter of fact, just this afternoon I had a chat with Brent Romano, one of the forces behind the plan, and told him, *in no uncertain terms*, that the city can't afford it. According to Arnie Schaub, part of their plan is to replace me as mayor. You and I, ah, know that's not going to happen. Hell, I've been the Mayor here for almost thirty years. No young upstart is, ah, going to walk in with a crazy scheme and the town's going to buy it, hook, line and sinker."

"What does Harvey say?"

"Cornelia, you know our esteemed City Manager is off skiing and not due back until next week. We'll tell him then. In the meantime, I, ah, don't think there's anything to worry about."

"I hope you're right. Tell me about this scheme."

Mayor Hill explained the plan to make Thompsonville into an arts' center and that it was going to involve rehabing a large section of downtown. He admitted that he didn't know all the details, but that certainly it was going to cost a great deal of money. "Cornelia, they're still in the planning stages, but it's all very abstract. We'll keep an eye on it, I promise you."

"You're damn right we will. I'm not going to take this lying down. That, I promise you."

The holidays were obscured by the work they were all doing. As the early weeks of 2008 sped by, Ari found herself down at Bolan's daily.

When she wasn't putting together placards for Brent's campaign, Ari spent most of her time talking with The *Sentinel* reporter, Abigail Spencer, and other local papers about Brent, his past involvement with the Chamber, his work with the homeless through the Church, his legal career in Washington and Thompsonville, and his ideas to make Thompsonville a thriving business community again.

Ari took it upon herself to call some of the local businesspeople who were not part of the original group regarding the proposed redevelopment plan. Some stated they had heard something about the plan and others, like the local head of the electric company, hadn't heard a word.

She was able to get a commitment from that electric company that if the plan went through, the utility would provide electricity to the designated buildings at cost for a period of two years.

While the gas company didn't offer quite that, they did promise that they would give most-favored-nation-type status to those buildings, charging the lowest price available, whether or not through a promotional offer, for the first two years.

Harvey Dunlap returned from his skiing trip and found numerous messages on his desk from Councilwoman Huff indicating that it was imperative that he return her call before speaking to anyone else. Dialing her number, the City Manager said to himself, "Hell, here we go. What happened to get Cornelia all stirred up?"

"Cornelia, Harvey Dunlap here. I've . . .

"Thank God, Harvey. I thought you'd never get back."

"What's going on?"

"Well, I take it you haven't heard from anyone else yet. Good. Are you in your office? I need to tell you this face-to-face."

"Cornelia, I *am* in my office. But there's so much work piled up on my desk with my being gone . . ."

"Doesn't matter. I'm on my way up."

Councilwoman Huff sat in the City Manager's office detailing everything that she had discovered from anyone and everyone who would talk to her. She told him about the plan to raze some of the older buildings, rebuild them and Thompsonville, thereby creating a haven for artists, playwrights, actors and all those sorts of people. She then told him about renaming Thompsonville and that if the Mayor didn't support their plan, Brent Romano would be elected the new mayor and we'd be out. "You, as the Mayor's appointee, certainly, if Steve doesn't get re-elected. I'm on the ballot this year, too, so if I don't support them, I guess I'm out along with you. What are we to do?"

"Well, that certainly is an ambitious plan. I don't see how they can succeed, though. Coming up with an idea is relatively easy, but being able to get everyone behind it, fund it and then successfully market it – well, it's almost impossible. Thompsonville's residents don't have the money to accomplish this, no matter what this group thinks. Who *is* behind this?"

"As I said, Brent Romano, his sister Gabby O'Neil, and Ari Bolan – they're the main forces behind this. But, they've managed to get a group of the town's businesspeople together who appear to be supporting them in a big way. *It's terrible.*"

"Cornelia, I don't understand what the problem is. As I said, I don't think it's going to work – there's too much involved and it'll cost too much money."

"Harvey, *don't you see?* It doesn't *have* to work. They only *need* to convince the voters that it will, and, then, they'll be elected. *We'll be out!*"

"We can certainly put together our own set of numbers showing the voters how incredibly high the costs will be for them. We can also show them how we've been able to maintain our city services, even though we've had a declining budget to work with. There are ways to fight this. I think you're overreacting, Cornelia."

"Harvey, we need to fight this with everything we have. I *can't* lose my position on the Council – *it's my whole life*. You probably don't know that I was a big city girl with a very nice career which I gave up to marry Oliver and move here. We never had any children. Oliver had his practice, and I had nothing career-wise to do. Twenty-one years later, Oliver decides that his dental assistant is *his* one true love, and *I'm* left to fend for myself. *Twenty-one years, Harvey*. I gave up my career and my future *for what?* Fortunately, during those years I kept up with the local political scene, and my volunteer positions earned me a seat at the table. What do I do if we lose? The humiliation . . . and *then what?* I'm in my fifties – there's not much out there for my age group. *Hell, there's not much out there in Thompsonville, period.*"

"Then, let's not lose. Worst case scenario, though, you can run for the State Congress two years from now in the next election."

"Hmm, I hadn't thought about that."

Barely thirty minutes later, Hiz Honor knocked on Harvey Dunlap's office door. "Harvey, I heard you were back. How was the skiing?"

"Great, Steve. We enjoyed ourselves tremendously – lot's to do there. I heard that there's been a lot going on here, too. You just missed Cornelia. She sure has her panties all tied up in a knot over . . . "

"I know, I know. I, ah, don't think this, ah, plan has a chance in hell. But it sounds good, so we'll, ah, have to fight it."

"I'll put some numbers together, Steve. I told Cornelia I'd look into it too. We'll figure something out."

In March, Jack Caldwell submitted his preliminary report on the buildings downtown. Ari, Gabby and Brent were struck by the number of buildings down by the river that were in such a state of disrepair that they would, in all likelihood, need to be torn down. This, they thought could be their downfall. While they somehow, and they still didn't know how, believed they would be able to raise enough money to rent some of the downtown buildings at little cost, they couldn't figure out how they could buy some of the decrepit old buildings and then afford to rebuild them. Brent reminded them about the laws of eminent domain, but said they would need to have the backing of the City Council before that could even be considered.

And, where was the money coming from to renovate these downtown buildings? Of course, Gabby had offered her crews at cost, but there was still a cost, not to mention the cost of the materials necessary in order to do the renovations.

Ari dug in deeper. She called Gabby and asked her to contact some of Regency's suppliers to find the best deals available, explaining the plan to them and trying to determine if there were discounts on particular items, bulk pricing or upcoming sales.

Ari talked to Susan Cranston about trees. Ari hoped they could find enough money to at least line Main Street with beautiful trees at a relatively low cost. Susan thought her nursery could help, and she'd talk to her daughter about checking with some of the growers about pricing.

The estimates were coming in and, while they were all discounted in some way, the costs were overwhelming. Ari called Gabby and Brent and they decided to meet. They had spent more than two months in the trenches gathering data. It was now early June, the election only five months away, and the plans for Thompsonville's renovation seemed to have hit a major snag.

Ari seemed to think that Brent was doing well enough in the polls, such as they were in their small town. She was certain that if they could just find the solution to fund the renovation, Brent would be a shoe-in, and Thompsonville would be on its way to prosperity – or at least not economic ruin.

As the three discussed the estimated costs of their plan, they became quiet, each sensing the others' fear that they had hit the proverbial brick wall.

Ari said, "I knew it was going to cost a lot, but I never thought it would be this much. I just don't know how we can raise or borrow this kind of money."

Gabby snapped up. "Wait a minute. We don't know the first thing about how to raise lots of money. But the operative word here is 'raise.' While *we* may not know how, we sure know someone who has made it an art form."

Brent asked, "Who?"

Ari said, "You mean Harriet, don't you?"

"Of course," replied Gabby. "Well, I mean, after all, she raises money from all her rich friends for all those well-known charities, why couldn't she do the same for her hometown?"

Ari shook her head and said, "Well, think about it, you just made the point. She raises money for well-known charities from wealthy people who live in New York and other major cities. What makes you think she could get anyone to contribute to our plan here, in a town they've never heard of, much less visited? Besides, and maybe even more important, if we're successful, Brent will end up being the Mayor which means she'd be working against her own father's re-election."

Gabby said, "What if we made her an offer she couldn't refuse?"

Ari laughed. "Maybe everything does come down to The Godfather."

Undaunted, Gabby continued. "What I mean is, let's make Harriet *want* to be a part of this."

"And, just how do we do that?" asked Brent.

Gabby was on a roll now. "Okay, look. Harriet's big passion, at least here in Thompsonville, is the garden club. Let's say we end up taking the whole waterfront from 1st to 3rd, and Ashland to Dorrance, give or take, and make it a park. She could design it from beginning to end. I think that would cinch it."

"*That* could also solve another problem," chimed in Ari. " If we do end up taking those abandoned buildings by eminent domain, or seize them for failure to pay taxes, almost every one of them is going to have to be razed. So, let's raze them and *not* rebuild, saving the project tons of money and, yet, giving the town a park where artists can work and display their art during the summer months. Maybe an ice-skating rink during the winter."

"*Thereby* making this a big *plus* instead of a huge *minus*," Gabby picked up. "What do you say? I know this could work. If you agree, I'll call Harriet tomorrow. Whoever thought this whole thing could come down to HRH? Certainly never in *my* wildest imagination."

And, again, they came away with an idea they thought could work.

CHAPTER TWENTY-FIVE

First thing the following morning, Gabby picked up the telephone to call HRH. Half way through dialing, she hesitated, and put the phone down again. Gabby wasn't afraid of Harriet, but she thought they might have only one shot at getting Harriet to agree to help them. Knowing Ari was closer to Harriet than she, Gabby thought that maybe two were better than one in this situation. So, instead, Gabby picked up the phone and dialed Ari at headquarters.

Ari still didn't believe Harriet was the right person to help them, but agreed to help Gabby talk to her. Ari suggested that they plan a lunch or dinner meeting. *So much better,* she thought, *than over the phone.* At least a meal would keep Harriet a captive audience until she heard them out – and then turned them down flatly.

Now, armed with reinforcements, Gabby again picked up the phone, this time completing the call. As the phone rang, Gabby's heart picked up a beat. Amanda answered and asked Gabby to hold while she took the phone out to Harriet, who was working in her greenhouse.

Gabby and Harriet chatted for a few minutes but Harriet was somewhat reserved. She, of course, knew what was going on in town -- the plan and then the possible running of Gabby's brother against her father for mayor. Gabby, sensing Harriet's coolness, got to the point and asked HRH if she would join Ari and her for lunch the following week at The

Inn at Logan Park. Harriet, skeptical, but unwilling to accuse Gabby of ulterior motives, said she would love to join them and set the date.

While walking up the front steps to the lovely old inn, Harriet had the strange sense she was walking into an ambush.

Ari and Gabby greeted her warmly and were promptly seated by the maitre d'. The three women talked about everything -- everything, that is, except what was on each of their minds. Harriet was trying to avoid it all together.

While Harriet was not particularly shy about asking friends to donate money for any one of her charities, she was extremely insecure about her personal relationships, especially the ones with Ari and Gabby since they were friends from a time in her youth when she had no others.

Finally, Gabby broached the subject, gently. "Harriet, I know you've heard about the plans to revitalize Thompsonville and our part in it. This lunch is and isn't a subterfuge to have you help us. And, whether or not you decide to try, it will in no way affect our friendship."

Ari jumped in. "Harriet, we don't know what you've heard exactly. There are many rumors going around town, but we just want you to hear us out and, if there's any reason that you can't or don't want to help, we will understand and respect your decision."

As Ari and Gabby explained the plan for Thompsonville and how it was going to benefit the entire town and hopefully the surrounding area, Harriet began to see that the plan was nowhere near as self-aggrandizing as her father had made it out to be. In fact, Harriet thought it rather selfless, and wondered how her two oldest friends had managed to come up with such a concept.

As they talked, Harriet became more intrigued. What she couldn't do was understand how she could help, or how she could rationalize her participation in the scheme with her father's position as mayor in the balance.

Their desire for her expertise became clear as they laid out the plan for the park. Harriet was enraptured by the idea. While she had been asked many times to help raise money for charity, she had never been asked to help build something lasting with the money she helped raise. It was so tempting and clearly the hook they hoped would compel her to join them.

She admonished herself for thinking so cynically that this was merely a political ploy, but the doubt crept into her mind.

The women became quiet. Harriet's mind jumped from what she thought was one spectacular idea to another, and then envisioned the finished product. But, she was conflicted, too. She would have to sacrifice her time in New York and abroad, her shopping trips, and actually have to work. Oh, she worked raising money for those other charities, but those were easy -- established charities. But this, well, this was a major undertaking that would take months, if not longer.

Also, in the background, although less of an issue, Harriet knew that if she took this on it would impact her family and, perhaps, they'd never survive the rift. Well, if she decided to do it, she'd figure out a way to handle it later.

Finally Harriet spoke. "I'm thrilled you've asked me to do this and that you have the confidence that I can handle it. I understand why you felt you had to take me to lunch to propose this, but I wish it hadn't been so. I hope you're asking me because you truly think I'm the best person to design a park and help raise the money for it, as opposed to any political reason – my father being the current mayor. That's my old insecurity talking. But, whatever the reason, it is an exciting offer. I'll need to think it over.

As excited as I am about the chance to design an entire park, I can't forget my father's opposition to this plan and the inevitable loss of his position if the people of Thompsonville believe it will succeed."

Ari said, "Then help us convince him that this is the right thing for Thompsonville. Brent doesn't want to take your father's job, but we can't see how we can succeed without the mayor's backing. So, Brent is willing to run for mayor – and he'd be a great one – just in order to accomplish these goals."

Gabby added, "If you can just get your father to see the possibilities and be willing to undertake the plan, Brent would step aside, I'm sure of it."

Harriet nodded. "I'm really going to need to think about this long and deep. In the meantime, you have lots of work to do before it even gets to the stage where you'll need me. I'll try to talk to my father and see what I can do. Let's take some time. I'll call you in two weeks or you call me when you have some news.

Again, I can't tell you how excited I am you thought of me and have asked me to be a part of this. Oh, and thanks for lunch. It really was splendid."

Harriet went straight home and headed for her greenhouse, knowing that working with her plants was a way to get lost in her dreams.

Now, as she thought about the park and it's potential as the jewel in the wonderland Thompsonville could become, her mind raced. How could she get her father to see the possibilities? Of course, she hadn't seen them either. At least not until Ari and Gabby sat her down and explained the plan. Would he listen to *them?* To *her?* Harriet decided that her best line of attack would be through her mother.

Janet Dorrance Hill and her daughter decided to dine in at Hiz Honor's home the next evening. Hiz Honor was out of town at a mayor's conference, leaving them to talk freely.

Harriet excitedly told her mother all about her luncheon the previous day with Gabby and Ari. She spoke of the plans for Thompsonville, and her potential participation in them. Janet listened carefully. When Harriet finished telling all she had to tell, she sat back and asked, "What do you think, Mother?"

Janet spoke softly, yet pointedly. "Your father will never go for it, and he'll do whatever he can to make certain you never lift a finger to help them."

"But, Mother, why not? This plan is incredible, and it may be the only way we can help Thompsonville survive."

"Because, dear, your father doesn't like change. He also doesn't like to work. This plan will require a great deal of work. He is very happy just to sit back and chat with his old friends, play a few rounds of golf, meet and greet his constituency at the country club, and generally be everyone's good buddy. I'm not certain he would even know how to get this revitalization done. And, rather than be made a fool by showing his lack of ability, he'd just as soon not see it happen. Needless to say then, your participation would be a slap in his face, and his ego couldn't stand it.

Now, all that being said, I think you should go for it."

"What," Harriet exclaimed as she snapped her back against her chair? She looked at her mother questioningly, her mouth open.

280

"Close your mouth, Harriet, it's not ladylike. Look, Harriet, you've been out of school since 1992, you never went to college, and you have a failed marriage where you got suckered by a no-good prince who took you for your apartment in Paris and a great deal of your trust money. For the past sixteen years you have done little other than attend parties, be seen in the society pages and been a member of the local garden club. Oh, yes, you did develop a new strain of rose, but that was long ago, even before you left high school.

You have many good qualities, dear, but up until now, you've just not made the best choices. It's time you made a name for yourself and found something to do in an area where you really excel. This is perfect for you and this should be your time now, not your Father's."

"Mother, do you really think so? Won't Father be upset? I'm not sure I could stand it; he may never even speak to me again."

"Oh, he may not speak to you for a while, but he'll get over it. Besides, it'll give him more time to play golf."

Harriet left her parent's home that evening in a daze. Had her mother really given her the go-ahead? Would her father disown her? *Well,* she thought, *I'm putting the cart before the horse here. First, I'm going to try to convince him he should be doing this and then, if he persists in his position, I'll decide what to* do. With that resolved, Harriet continued to dream about her park.

Gabby watched the real estate market continue to dry up. The crash in resales pervaded the entire country now -- even the high-flying areas in California, Nevada, and Arizona.

Regency's home sales were also slowing, but, because they continued to have dedicated financing available to buyers' of their homes, they were still able to sell their product. However, because many of their buyers couldn't qualify under the new stricter requirements, or some couldn't sell their old homes, they weren't in a position to purchase a new home. Regency worked with their banks trying to arrange bridge loans, but it made many of the potential buyers too nervous, and they ultimately ended up staying where they were.

Several days after Ari and Gabby's lunch with Harriet, Ari got a call from Emily. Now, there was nothing unusual about that, but it came during working hours at Brent's election headquarters.

Ari was delighted to hear her friend's voice and, then, suddenly became wary. "What's wrong?"

Emily laughed. "I think I have a really good one for you."

Relaxed, now that she knew nothing was wrong, Ari sat back in her father's old wooden swivel desk chair and asked, "What's up?"

"Well, guess who I saw having dinner last night in the Cape Cod Restaurant at the Drake Hotel?"

"I don't know, your old boyfriend, Matt, or maybe one of my old boyfriends. Wait a minute. I don't really have any old boyfriends. I give up. Who?"

"What is it Brent calls him, Hiz Honor? Well, whatever, that's who I saw."

"And just how do you know it was Mayor Hill?"

"If you'll remember, when I spent the holidays in Thompsonville, we went to that gala at the country club and, you might recall, Harriet introduced us."

"OK, and this is important or funny because . . . ?"

"Because, dear friend, he wasn't alone, and it wasn't a business dinner – at least not like any one I've ever attended. They were quite chummy, if you know what I mean, and, oh, by the way, I took a couple of pictures with my cell phone – handy little devils," Emily giggled.

"You've got to be kidding! I've been hearing about his little, *um*, indiscretions for years but, you know, you never quite believe that stuff, particularly when it's one of your friend's parents."

"By the way, he/they were/are staying at the hotel. I saw him charge the meal to his room. So, what do you want me to do about it and/or the pictures? Assuming they're still at the hotel, I could have someone get more pictures if you need them for. . . .whatever."

Ari knew exactly what Emily meant. "Em, I don't think we should sink to that. It would be very hurtful to Harriet and her mother, and I just don't think that's the kind of thing we want to use in this campaign. I'm certain Brent believes we either win this campaign on its merits or he'll go back to his practice. I really appreciate your telling me this, just knowing about it could be helpful at some point. But I'm sure we won't want to use it. Thanks just the same."

"I understand and agree, but I thought I should let you know. I'll call you later."

"Thanks again, Em. Love you lots. Bye."

Ari had just about forgotten Emily's call when she noticed a new e-mail message from her. Ari knew that the pictures would be attached. She stared at the computer while she argued with herself as to whether or not to download them. Eventually, she decided that, although they may not choose to use the pictures, it would be foolhardy not to save them . . . *just in case.*

Brent was doing his best to get publicity for the revitalization plan which helped keep his name in the paper, hopefully benefitting his campaign.

He had been following the presidential race quite closely and noticed that the polls seemed to favor the candidate who chose not to slander his opponent. The more he watched the national political battle, the more convinced he became that running his campaign on the merits was the only way to go.

He spent hours crafting letters to the voters to publish in The *Sentinel* and other local epistles, hoping they could get a glimpse of him and to better inform them of the plan he envisioned for Thompsonville.

He invited Hiz Honor to a public debate. The Mayor apparently decided that he was well enough known and respected after all his years in office, that any debate would not help him and ultimately may end up benefitting Brent.

Harriet tried to talk to her father. *Damn,* she thought, *he's a stubborn man.* She didn't know him well enough to understand that he was, in fact, as afraid of being shown up as her mother had predicted. They almost came to blows.

She told her father of Gabby and Ari's proposal. He told her they were just using her and not to get too excited; they'd never let her actually do anything. That they had only approached her because of the way it would look if she supported the opposition. Besides, what did she have to offer?

This, of course, played right into her insecurities, which always made her retreat into her inner self. Harriet was in tears when she left him that evening.

Did he really believe that? she wondered. *Even if he believed everything he's just said, how could he have said it to my face?* Her heart and spirit broken, Harriet cried all the way home.

The phone was ringing when she walked in, but she was determined not to answer. Her caller I.D. identified her parents' home number, and she certainly didn't want to hear any more from her father.

A few minutes later, her phone rang again, but this time the number displayed was that of her mother's cell phone. Hesitantly, Harriet answered. She heard her mother try to calm her down. Apparently, her father had marched in and told her mother about Harriet's audacity at trying to go behind his back, even though he said he wouldn't allow it. He was convinced that Harriet was committed to the plan, and her part in it.

According to her mother, her father had calmed down some after she pointed out that Harriet was openly discussing the idea with him, not going behind his back. Her mother assured her that, with time, he would get over it.

Harriet wasn't quite so sure, but she was certain now that she wanted to take it on. It truly wasn't until she thought she couldn't participate, that she knew how much she wanted to be a part of it. Her father had convinced her all right, but not in the direction he'd intended. She would talk with Ari and Gabby tomorrow.

CHAPTER TWENTY-SIX

Regardless of Harriet's conviction of the previous evening, she was hesitant to make the call to Ari and Gabby. There was still that nagging sense of betrayal of her father, and she was struggling to weigh the positive impact of the revitalization of Thompsonville against his personal interests.

As Harriet stared at her phone trying to get up the courage to openly defy him, the phone rang, again identifying her mother's cell phone number. This time, however, it was her father's voice on the other end of the line. "Harriet, please let me apologize for the way I spoke to you last evening. I was totally out of line. And, forgive my subterfuge in using your mother's cell phone in order to be certain you'd pick up."

"That's pretty sad, isn't it, Father? In any event, I don't want to continue last night's conversation. So, if you'll . . . "

"Harriet, I understand your passion for this project and, certainly, I would like to see Thompsonville become a successful and vibrant town again. It's not that I'm against what you are trying to accomplish. It's just that I think the plan is a pipedream, a fool's errand. What you're asking me to do as Mayor is commit the city's money, which is so desperately needed elsewhere for other projects, to fund something I don't believe is possible. As the Mayor, therefore, I simply can't support the plan. As your father, I could never wish for anything except your success. A challenge this large, and the work required to see it come to fruition, can be monumental. I only hope you don't suffer any lasting sense of inadequacy, should it fail. Once you have considered that side of the equation, along with the exhilaration, and potential, but uncertain, chance for accomplishment, then, and only then, do I believe you should make your decision."

"Father, I have considered both sides and I will take a little more time before I commit, but I want you to understand that I believe that this is too important to the city to turn down any chance of making it happen. If it's a 'fool's errand,' as you put it, well, I won't be in it alone. Thank you for calling this morning, though. It couldn't have been easy for you."

"Harriet, you will always have my love, even if you don't see things as I do. Good luck with your decision. I'll talk to you later." And, with that, he hung up.

Harriet was surprised by her father's telephone call. Frankly, she hadn't really thought that her father cared that much about her. She had worried that he would be incensed by what she was planning to do -- not out of his love for her, but the damage that would be done to his lofty standing in the community. Oh, he was around a lot when she was growing up, but he always seemed to be busy; running the city, his next campaign, playing golf or just being at the club. Her mother was there, of course, and they had a closer, albeit superficial, relationship. But her father, well that was an entirely different story. She always hoped he loved her, but she couldn't, for the life of her, remember him ever telling her that before. *Well*, she thought, *maybe he was just saying that*. She wanted to believe him. But then she knew he was a true politician at heart, and generally politicians' words weren't worth their weight in dangling chads.

Harriet spent little time thinking about the negative aspects her father had raised. She was too enamored of the plan and her part in it. She called Ari and Gabby, accepted their offer, and asked where her office would be? Ari told her there wasn't much room, but that she was welcome to work out of Bolan's along with her and the few volunteers who helped with the campaign. With Harriet now on board, the team took on a new perspective.

Later that evening when the entire team met for the first time, Harriet told them she was somewhat concerned about the small number of

Thompsonville residents who might be in a position to donate money, but that she would do her best.

Gabby said, "Wait a minute, let's take a lesson from the Obama play book. He's raised millions by accepting small amounts from lots of people, as opposed to focusing on large donations from a small select group."

"But, how do we do that? Ask people to come in and give us their few extra dollars, assuming they have any?" asked Brent.

"Well, yes, as a matter of fact, that's exactly what we do." Needless to say, they all stared at Gabby as if she had gone off the deep end. "Look," Gabby continued, "this has to be a community effort. As Harriet points out, there just aren't enough wealthy people in town to collectively donate the dollars necessary to make this work."

"So," Ari picked up on Gabby's train of thought, "we write an open letter to the people and place it in The *Sentinel*, asking for small donations for the revitalization of Thompsonville and give them easy ways to make their contributions. Of, course, we'd have to have some very specific answers to some of our questions, because so far we've only broadly outlined our plan."

Brent jumped in. "We probably should have some sort of architect's drawing showing how we envision Thompsonville after all the work is done. Then, I think we need to have a town meeting. We can put the time and date in the open letter in The *Sentinel* – inviting everyone to attend."

"Okay, this is good," said Ari.

Harriet agreed. "But we still will have to have some major benefactors in order to carry this off."

"Oh, Harriet, I didn't mean this would be the only way. We certainly still need your expertise when it comes to raising big money." Gabby soothed the newest member of the team.

"So, tomorrow morning," Ari said, "let's start putting together the letter for the paper. Brent, Gabby, do you want to do the first draft? Harriet, since you've only recently joined us, you probably don't know all the behind-the-scene stuff yet, particularly not the numbers or who's doing what, etcetera. We'll want your input, though." Everyone agreed Ari should start the process and then they would all chime in with any other suggestions they might have.

Gabby said. "I'll follow up with Jack Caldwell while Brent's in trial next week. Also, I'll talk with some of the local architects we use for Regency's work to see if we can get some help with that drawing Brent mentioned."

Harriet said, "You know, it just occurred to me, what if we were to call Stanford Lee and the other local bank presidents asking if we could put donation boxes in their banks' branches? And, since we have the backing of so many retail businessmen, what about asking if they would be willing to let us put boxes in their stores, too? That way, anytime anyone went to the store or the bank -- maybe some restaurants -- it would be easy for them to make a donation. Charities do it, why can't we?"

"Great idea, Harriet," said Gabby.

Ari said, "It really is a good idea, Harriet. But before we do that, we need to get the open letter out and have our town meeting. We can't just ask people to donate money without first telling them exactly how we plan to use it. Otherwise, we could end up shooting ourselves in the foot."

"When do we think we can get the letter written, the costs closer to a realistic estimated budget, the architect's drawing, and the town meeting held?" queried Brent. "This is July, we'll be voting in four months and all this needs to happen very soon. Just because we have a town meeting, doesn't mean that we'll get the townspeople to agree. There will probably be concerns and plans may have to change to take those into account, which will surely involve additional town meetings. I think its crunch time. Our idea, our plan, such as it is, is basically good, but we must allow for variances and that means time.

Ari, we almost *need* the letter ready to go to The *Sentinel* next week. If we can get an architect to put together the drawing while we're working on the letter and the budget, even without final numbers, we may have a good enough estimate based on Jack's findings. Jack's numbers, remember, are strictly for the purchase of those buildings. Gabby, you'll need to take TJ over to the buildings Jack identifies in order to get a better handle on the renovations involved. Those renovation costs will have a significant impact on our budget."

"I'll schedule a meeting with Jack tomorrow, if possible, and then get Uncle Tony and Mike to go with me as their time allows. TJ is busier than either of them and besides he's in Pittsburgh most of the time now."

Gabby was busy writing down her assignments in her PDA as she finished telling the group her plan.

Ari chimed in. "I think that pretty much sums up our priorities for the next couple of weeks. If anyone has a problem getting anything done, don't sit on it. Call one of the others, except Brent, since he'll be at trial."

The meeting broke up and all of them went off to their own homes to figure out how they were going to accomplish all this in the next few weeks.

Bert Palmer called Ari the next morning all excited. "If Bernardo, or anyone else for that matter, hasn't come up with a prize for the contest renaming Thompsonville, I've talked with Bill over at the audio/visual store and he's willing to donate a 54-inch high definition TV for the cause."

Ari was excited too. She thought it was a grand prize and thanked Bert profusely. Bert said, "I'll call Bernardo. I know how busy you are with the revitalization plan and the campaign.

"Bert, let's keep it quiet though until we announce the contest, and please ask Bernardo to do the same." Ari then dug back into working on the draft of the open letter to The *Sentinel*.

Gabby scheduled a meeting with Jack Caldwell at her office, where Jack would have room to spread out his findings and discuss the properties in absolute privacy. Gabby found him as easy to work with as Brent had told her he would be. Jack had brought a map of downtown so that she could actually see the locations they were discussing and their proximity to one another.

A couple of the buildings were south of Main Street where the team really hadn't focused their attention. Gabby pointed that out to Jack, but he particularly wanted to point out two buildings. One was Bolan's, which Jack was fairly certain could be on the table, while the other was the huge cannery he had shown to Brent several years earlier and was still vacant. Jack said that the cannery was owned by a fairly well-to-do elderly gentleman whose estate, when he died, would end up paying tons of inheritance taxes on it. Given those circumstances, Jack thought that the owner might be willing to donate the property for such a venture. Apparently the gentleman had come to Thompsonville a pauper, well practically, and felt that he owed the town something. Based on Jack's tone, Gabby felt, with some degree of certainty, that Jack had already approached the owner on the subject. She remembered the building as having lots of wide-open space which might be ideal as a rehearsal hall for the playwrights and their players. She promised to consider it and bring it up to the others.

The other buildings on the north side of Main Street were, for the most part, in various states of disrepair. As Jack talked about each building and pointed to its exact spot on the map, Gabby was dismayed to see how many more buildings were now on the market than when Brent was looking for space.

Gabby made an executive decision and eliminated a portion of the downtown area because it was just too amorphous for their needs and their budget. She asked Jack to focus specifically on those facing Main Street, particularly those west of 6th down to the planned park at 3rd, and then any others north of Main up to Columbia, where he thought they might be donated, or leased for their much tossed around dream of one dollar a year.

When all was said and done, Gabby still had more than twenty buildings to look at and evaluate.

Jack also talked to Gabby about the properties on 1st and 2nd Streets. While the plan was to raze these buildings, Jack thought that, before the word got out, they may be able to get a few of the buildings donated so that the city wouldn't need to pay for them. That meant the city would only need to pay for those taken by eminent domain. Now, Jack reassured Gabby that fair market value was probably not a great deal of money in the scheme of things, but if they could get them donated beforehand, that was just so much less money that would be required to accomplish their plan. Jack also pointed out that some of the owners of these buildings may actually end up better off with a donation on their tax returns rather than the fairly low amount they may be worth through the eminent domain process.

Gabby liked the way Jack was thinking and knew she would be using him for any future projects Regency might have. Because business was slow, Jack indicated he was available for the next couple of days to show the properties to Gabby, her Uncle Tony and Mike too, if he was available. Gabby made plans to tour the buildings over the next two days and went away with her head swimming over all the possibilities.

Gabby was not having much success on the architectural side with regard to the drawings. Regency's architects were pleasant enough, but didn't seem to want to donate their time to the cause and Gabby was fit to be tied. She thought after all the work Regency had given the firm over the past thirty years, they certainly could have helped her out with this. She was further infuriated because it was unlikely that they were tied up with other work given the current state of the economy. This was ultimately very bad news for that firm because Gabby resolved that any future needs would most assuredly be performed by others.

Gabby opened the telephone book in search of other local architectural firms. *Certainly,* she thought, *there must be one who will be interested in working with the group, recognizing the importance their work might have with regard to future assignments.* As she was jotting down names planning to look them up on the web, Gabby noticed John Traymore's name.

She remembered John fondly from her early Introduction to Architecture class way back when she decided that she wanted to work with her father. She wondered whether John would remember her and whether he would be willing to help her out, or at least point her in the right direction. Gabby dialed John's number and was pleased to find that he certainly did remember her.

Gabby told John about the plan and what she needed in order to present it to Thompsonville's residents. John had heard about it and told Gabby that, while he wasn't certain he was the right man for the job, he would be more than happy to look at the map of downtown and listen to the plans as they now stood.

Not wanting to put anything off until tomorrow, Gabby jumped at the opportunity to get the ball rolling, and arranged a meeting with John for that same afternoon.

That afternoon in Regency's conference room, John listened to the plan, looked at the map, and rubbed his chin for a few minutes. "Gabby, this doesn't really look like that big a project to me and, while it's not my usual type of architectural drawing, it certainly is something I think I can put together for you in a fairly short period of time. I am fascinated by this idea of yours and I think anyone would be honored to help you out. So, if you're willing to let me go with it, I'm more than happy to offer my services to you as my donation to the project."

"Oh, John, I can't thank you enough. This means so much to the people of Thompsonville and I just know that, with your help, we'll pull this off."

CHAPTER TWENTY-SEVEN

Gabby, Uncle Tony, Mike and Jack met first thing the following day in order to tour as many buildings as possible. It was a full day and Gabby was very glad she had both Uncle Tony and Mike with her. By lunchtime, the group had only been able to inspect three buildings. It was slow going as each building had to be evaluated on so many different levels.

As they were sitting down at The Blue Frog for lunch, Gabby's cell phone rang. Gabby excused herself and answered the call. Norma apologized for interrupting. "The senior partner of our architectural firm has been calling all morning, insisting that he speak to you immediately. It must be urgent for him to call so often."

"Trust me, Norma, he's only calling to mend fences." Gabby wrote down his number. "I'll call him back later. If he calls again, simply tell him that you've reached me, and I'll get back to him when I'm free." Even though Gabby was still unhappy with his firm, she thought it important to keep the lines of communication open. *One can never tell . . .*

They ate quickly and spent only a few minutes chatting with Claudia as they explained to her they were out looking at potential sites for the plan. Gabby realized as she was saying the "plan" or the "revitalization," or whatever term any one of them used, they were all struggling to identify their goal. She added the point to her list of things to do, recognizing that if they were all having difficulty with what to call the plan, it would be difficult for them to get broad support for it. They needed a name which would easily identify what they were attempting to do, clarify it in the minds of the voters, and hopefully garner a great deal of interest and support.

The four finished up the day having toured only seven of the twenty-something buildings on their list. This was taking far longer than Gabby had anticipated, but she knew that Uncle Tony and Mike were being very thorough and that required a good deal of time if the job was to be done properly. Set to start early again the next day, the group broke up and went their separate ways.

Gabby headed over to Bolan's to catch up with Ari. The draft of the open letter was in its umpteenth rewrite, according to Ari, and she was glad that Gabby was there to take a look at it. Gabby thought it was a very good letter, but reminded Ari, "Writing isn't exactly my strong suit."

Ari said, "Ah, but you're *so good* in the idea department."

"Speaking of which," said Gabby, "it occurred to me today, as I was again struggling to think of what to call our plan, that we need a *real* name for it." After explaining her reasoning to Ari, Ari kicked herself for failing to recognize that they were all having the same problem. Gabby was right. In order to raise support for their plan and have a better chance for success, a more descriptive name for the project was necessary. The two immediately started coming up with ideas and began listing the really good ones to bring up at their next meeting.

Ari then asked Gabby about her day. "It's taking far more time than I anticipated, but we're getting a good feel for what's available," Gabby replied. "Jack drove us past the buildings on 1st and 2nd. Even though we didn't go through any of them, there really doesn't appear to be more than just one or two that might, and I stress *might*, be worth saving."

Ari said, "The more I think about the park idea, the more I think it'll be a terrific draw for the tourists, and while it is part of the plan by default, it may end up being one of our major attractions."

Ari put her head in her hands and softly said, "Damn. We've talked about the park, but we've totally overlooked it."

"What are you talking about?" asked Gabby.

"We've made a huge mistake here by not having Harriet start to work on the park. Not that she can actually do anything, but we need to have a better figure in our budget than the one we threw in there before we brought Harriet on. She can start pulling those numbers together now so that they can be included in the total budget as we present it to the people. We need to get her on the phone now."

"Uh oh, I think I sense the need for another architectural drawing coming as well," said Gabby.

"Okay, I'll get Harriet on the phone and we can both talk to her."

As Gabby and Ari explained the situation to Harriet, Harriet smiled. *Fortunately,* Harriet thought, *I've been so caught up in the idea of the park, I've been unable to think of anything else.* In her mind's eye she envisioned the beauty it would offer, as well as provide a setting for the artists who would become such an integral part of the new Thompsonville. She was exhilarated by the challenge and now it seemed she would be even more a part of the inner circle.

Gabby apologized for not focusing on that aspect of the plan earlier. "Harriet, I forgot to mention that Susan Cranston offered to help with the park. Maybe now would be a good time for you two to get together and come up with some ideas of costs for plants and labor, even if you choose not to use Petal Pushers' Nursery for the actual work."

"I'll be happy to work with Susan. We've done some work together in the past for the Junior League and I found her to be very knowledgeable and helpful."

"Great! Also, we're trying to come up with a formal name for the plan. Think about it. We'll need to come up with something at our next meeting."

With that, the girls hung up with Harriet, hoping they now were covering all the areas that needed to be considered.

"You know," said Gabby, "I'm not sure what the costs will be for the website and Facebook projects Jerry's working on. He told me they would be negligible – maybe a few hundred dollars – but they need to be included. Damn, I'll ask him about them tonight."

Ari said, "You know, things are starting to happen so quickly now, I think we need to schedule our next meeting for next week."

Gabby reminded Ari that Brent was in trial and might not be available next week.

Ari thought about it a moment and said, "Look, today is Thursday, tomorrow you'll be looking at more buildings and you may even need to finish up early next week. Since next week may be a problem for Brent, and because it's almost the weekend anyway, let's schedule our next full meeting for a week from Saturday. That way, we'll have your input, Harriet may have had enough time to start getting her numbers together, our open letter should be ready to send to The *Sentinel*, and I can check around and see if we can find a place large enough for our town meeting that'll be available within the next few weeks."

Cornelia was placing campaign posters all over town and was busy making the rounds of the various business associations making her pitch. She was making a lot of noise about the plan and her opposition to it. A formidable woman, Cornelia would bear some watching as the election drew near.

For the next eight days, everyone worked furiously to complete their assignments in time for the Saturday meeting. Brent's trial was over and he and Harriet had already given their input to Ari on the open letter. Ari assured him that she would have the final version ready for Saturday's meeting.

Brent reflected on the entire plan as it had evolved so far. He never forgot that this was the doing of Ari and Gabby. Aside from the fact that this had originally been their concept, it was on their wings that it took flight, thinking of and working on every aspect of the plan.

He also knew that he needed to devote more of his time and energy to the project now. To date, while he had given some speeches and written a few letters, his participation had been limited due to the responsibilities of his law practice. With his major trial commitment behind him, and Scott Silverman up-to-speed with all of their clients, Brent felt he could step back a little and allow Scott to carry most of the load. Brent also knew that if he won this election, Scott was going to need someone to keep the firm going, as Brent would have to step down from the practice.

Ari called the meeting to order -- not that they followed any "rules of order" as defined by anyone, but someone had to do it.

The first order of business was the determination of a proper name for the plan. Ari began, "While some of you may think this is a minor matter, it certainly isn't. Even the open letter can't be sent to The *Sentinel* because we must have a name in order to catch the readers' attention. Otherwise, this could end up being an exercise in futility – no readers, no residents willing to show up for our town meeting and, ultimately, no supporters and/or voters."

After discussion of the various names proffered, ultimately "Downtown Redevelopment Project" or "DRP" was chosen as the official name for the plan. They were particularly enamored by the "DRP" acronym, because they thought they could use it in Brent's campaign. Something like "Vote for Brent Romano and DRoP Hill." Clearly, they were getting ahead of themselves, but a little bit of levity is always a good thing.

Ari then presented her final version of the open letter, which was unanimously approved. Ari promised that she would get it out to The *Sentinel* for publication on the following Sunday.

They determined that Sunday was probably the best day because most people tended to read the entire Sunday paper, front to back.

"The town meeting is scheduled for Tuesday, August 12th at 7:00 p.m. in the gym at Thompsonville High School," announced Ari. "I hope this is okay with everyone. That will give us a few weeks to finalize our proposal, but still leave us almost three months before the election. Hopefully, a sufficient amount of time to make any last minute changes based upon the outcome of the town meeting/meetings. I've talked with a couple of the motel managers around the area, but their meeting rooms have limited capacities and we are hoping for a large turnout. If not, this could end up being very embarrassing. We may need to put up signs, and perhaps run the open letter in the paper a second time, just to make sure everyone knows what's happening and why."

Ari asked Gabby if she was ready with her recommendations?

Gabby handed a packet of papers to each of them and then went over to the easel where a huge map of downtown, adhered to some masonite, rested.

She ran down the list of buildings that she, Uncle Tony and Mike had visited, each one of which was outlined in the packets she had distributed. The buildings she thought might work the best, required the least amount of money to renovate and repair, and might be picked up at relatively low cost or rent, were marked in red on the map. There was also a small map, identical to the large one, in the packets and it, too, had been marked in red.

On the page following the map in each person's packet, was a schedule of estimated costs. It listed each building, its address, the number of square feet, the projected cost to buy/rent and the projected costs of repair. Gabby had also included some remarks under the address of each building indicating what she thought would be the best usage of each of the properties.

"Jack told me that there are several other buildings close by, but not within the area designated by the group, which could probably be acquired at a very low cost. One is the cannery on Preston, south of Main, that you looked at, Brent, when you were searching for your space. I know it's huge, but Jack pointed out that it would be excellent as a rehearsal hall and, even though it's out of the way, we don't need the rehearsal hall on Main Street, or even on the north side of town. It's not a venue we plan to open to the public, and it offers tons of space without having to tear down walls or provide retail amenities that the galleries will. All in all, I think we have about a dozen buildings here which have potential.

Now, I have something really exciting to tell you and I wish Jack could be here to tell you himself. Jack has called every owner of every building on 1st and 2nd from Main to Dorrance. While he has yet to reach everyone, Jack has obtained written, and I stress *written*, commitments from more than seventy percent of those owners to *donate* their buildings to the city if Brent is elected, and that the use of the land will be for the park as identified by our plan. Excuse me, the DRP."

Ari, Brent and Harriet sat there, stunned.

"No way," said Brent.

"Way," replied Gabby. "Now, remember there are contingencies attached to these commitments and we don't have deeds transferring any of these properties, but, *wow*, can you believe it? Jack just told me late yesterday, so I'm still absorbing the enormity of his accomplishments."

Harriet was truly dumbfounded. "Well, I guess there's no way we can allow Brent to lose this election now." This, having come from Harriet, silenced them all again.

Ari was the first to regain her speech. "While I was hesitant to tell you all this before I've had a chance to confirm it with each individual, it falls within the lines of what Gabby has just told us. I've gotten a call from

Claudia, who has been busy contacting some of the owners of businesses which have moved out to the strip malls over the past decade or two. Apparently, she has verbal commitments from several of them to reopen a small shop downtown when and if our DRP comes to fruition. Folks, I think this is really going to happen."

Harriet, not to be outdone, said she'd like to add what she had found out on her particular assignment. "I've met with Susan, and while it's impossible to know what the park will ultimately cost because we're still working on a final design, Susan gave me some estimates. These numbers are based on her research of similar sized parks that have been built in other cities over the past few of years."

Harriet proceeded to hand out her packet of information, a good portion of which contained the costs involved with the construction of those other parks. Harriet had added in the potential cost of having the skating rink they had discussed, benches, gazebos, and some sculptures she hoped would be provided free of charge by a few of the artists they planned to entice. Across the last page which listed the individual itemized costs as well as the total estimated costs, there was another column indicating a credit balance of one hundred thousand dollars.

"What's this all about?" asked Ari. "We don't have any money yet that I know about."

"Well, actually, we do," replied Harriet. This was Harriet's time to shine and she took a moment before saying, "I am now the first contributor to the DRP and, now that we have a name for our little plan, I have my check here already filled out, just waiting for the payee's name to be inserted."

"But, one hundred thousand dollars," said Ari, "that's a lot of money. Are you sure, Harriet? I mean you had a rough experience a few years ago."

"I'm absolutely sure, Ari, but thanks for asking. Actually, because I've spent so much time here in Thompsonville and because I've undertaken this challenge, I've managed to lease my condo in New York for far longer than I'd originally intended. I just thought that since I'm here for that extra year, I'd donate the rent for this year to our plan."

Gabby said, "Holy Cow, Harriet. That's terrific . . . "

"Harriet, that's extremely generous of you. What my sister and Ari are both trying to say is that we thank you very much. It was not expected and certainly not required."

Gabby said "Wow! Oh, I almost forgot. John Traymore is working on the drawing for downtown. I think I'd like to include some of those strip mall businesses which have indicated an interest in having a presence in our new downtown as part of the drawing. Can I get the names from you Ari?"

"I'm not sure they're willing to be identified at this point, but let me check it out. I don't see any reason why we can't use generic business names on some of the buildings, such as, 'The Main Street Hotel' or 'The Steak House' or some such other name which actually doesn't disclose any of the potential businesses. They may want their businesses identified, but, then again, they may be afraid in case the unthinkable happens and Brent here is back to being a full-time lawyer."

"Okay, that could work. As an aside, Regency's architectural firm's senior partner found out that some of his junior partners turned down helping us with our drawing. He fell all over himself trying to apologize for their shortsightedness and offered to help us with whatever we need. While I'm really happy with what John's doing for us on the Main Street drawing, if he finds that he can't give us any more time, we may need to use our old firm for a park drawing. What do you think, Harriet? Are we in a position to even have a preliminary idea about what this park will look like? And, can you work with these guys if we need them to get a drawing done by the August 12th meeting?"

"Well, I'm not certain. I can probably come up with something, but I'm not sure it will bear any resemblance to the finished product. What if I were to just find some pictures of other parks and use them as an idea of what the park could look like, making sure they understand that these are not actual plans for the park."

"That *might* do the trick, but it's iffy," said Ari. "I'm certain it's much more difficult to try and create something from scratch. And, while our Main Street drawing will not be exact, at least we have a starting point with existing buildings. But, I do think we should present a drawing at the town meeting as opposed to pictures of other parks. I just have to believe it shows we're really taking this seriously and have done some follow through work."

"That works for me," said Harriet. "I can find some pictures easily enough and then if you'll just let me know whether it's John Traymore or Regency's firm, I'll take it from there."

"Oh, one last thing from me," stated Gabby. "Jerry said the cost of putting the Facebook page together was only his time as was the creation of the website for the city, whatever its new name. He said there is a minimal charge for leasing the domain address we use to identify our site. These can be reserved for several years at a time and the costs, while a higher initial outlay, are lower per year the longer period of time we reserve the name. We'll need a name that's not currently in use. So, what Jerry's saying is that as soon as we have this contest and choose our new city's name, we need to immediately register it.

Finally, we'll need a service provider to host our site on the internet. Again, there's a charge, but there's no way to get around it. This is something which is absolutely necessary if we are to attract any tourists. Even established tourist spots such as Branson, Santa Fe, Taos, Vail, maintain sites. It proves the point that we'll need to have a website for years to come."

Brent finished the meeting by commending the group for the efforts they had put in and then recognized each of them individually on their specific accomplishments. "I know I left the burden on your shoulders while I cleaned up some existing legal work, but now I'm in a position to rededicate myself both to the DRP and the election efforts.

If there is anything specific any of you need me to do, please let me know. In the meantime, I'm going to be working with Ari trying to set up some dates to go out and speak to various business clubs and other groups in the community in an effort to let them get to know me, our DRP and why they need to get out and support both. Thank you all."

CHAPTER TWENTY-EIGHT

It was the morning of August 12th. The drawings were finally finished to everyone's satisfaction and there was a great deal of anticipation, not to mention apprehension as the hour of the town meeting drew near. Had they dotted every "i," crossed every "t?" They thought they had, but one never knew until it was pointed out that something had been overlooked. What could be missing from their presentation? The day dragged as they waited. And yet, before they realized it, it was time to drive over to the high school gym and set up their props.

They decided to use multiple easels to show the map of downtown that Jack had had blown up, still marked in red, and the two architects' drawings which, in their minds, had turned out beautifully. The format was to be similar to that of their last meeting. Each presenter would stand and talk about their specific part of the DRP and then Brent would stand and give an overview of why this was so important to the future of Thompsonville. At the very end of the presentation, they decided they would announce the contest to rename the town, the reasoning behind it, and the prize for the winning entry. Their goal was to let everyone leave thinking about the contest and what name they could enter, hopefully drawing them into wanting to participate in and contribute to the future of their town.

They all piled into Gabby's SUV and headed over to the gym. Jerry, in his own SUV, brought the easels, his laptop, drawings and the blown up map, along with another laptop, in case Gabby decided to show any of the digital pictures she had taken of the buildings they had identified as part of the DRP.

As Gabby's car turned into the circular drive outside the gym, Ari asked, "What's that truck doing there?"

Gabby said, "I don't know. Maybe they had to clear something out of the gym or put something in before their next game. Who knows? As long as it's gone before the crowd – we hope it's a crowd – arrives."

Just then, John Traymore walked out through the glass doors at the front of the gym. As he saw the SUV, he only smiled a huge smile and waved at everyone.

"Gabby, is John part of your presentation?" asked Ari.

"No, but maybe he had another drawing or something he wanted to get to us before the meeting."

"In a truck?" questioned Brent.

"Okay, let's not speculate. We can ask him as soon as we park the car," replied Gabby. She was somewhat miffed that John might be doing something that could jeopardize her presentation. Nervous, Gabby was grateful there was still more than an hour before the meeting was scheduled to begin.

John was pulling the truck away when the foursome neared the front door of the gym. John again just smiled and waved. Gabby was having none of that. She stepped onto the driveway in front of the truck as it slowly made its way out. John had to stop, because Gabby made it clear she had no intention of moving. He hopped down from the cab of the truck and greeted Gabby, and then turned to wave to the others.

"What's going on here, John? Did we forget something?"

Trapped, John knew he was busted before he could make a clean getaway. "Okay, Gabby, come on," he said. Following John, Gabby and he caught up with Brent, Ari and Harriet as they stood watching the whole scene, while trying not to pay attention.

John opened the heavy glass door to the gym's atrium entry hall and waited while all four walked ahead of him. Before them were the closed wooden doors which enclosed the gym itself and again opened the door, waiting for the four to go through.

When they entered, they were so concerned about what John was up to, they didn't carefully focus on the inside of the gym. John walked up to the group, stopped, smiled, and then looked in the direction of a collapsible table, on top of which was some sort of large object. Their eyes followed John's and suddenly it occurred to them that they were looking at a model of downtown Thompsonville. Not as it was, but what they envisioned it would look like once they had completed the DRP.

Slowly, very slowly, they walked up to the model, afraid that if they walked too quickly the model would disappear, like a mirage.

"Oh, John," said Gabby as she grabbed his arm. "This is spectacular. When did you have time? This is more than any of us could have ever dreamed. If anyone shows up, they can't help but want to be a part of this. Thank you so much from all of us, from the city."

All four of them circled and re-circled the model, pointing out the buildings, the trees lining Main Street, their park, and the county courthouse overlooking the entire new downtown.

They thanked John and asked him if he was going to pick it up after the meeting. John said, "I'm staying for the meeting, of course. After that, I'll move the model to wherever you want it. It belongs to the DRP and I think you should use it in any way you see fit to further your objective. Now, you all need to get your stuff set up before the crowd gets here. I'll just move my truck and join you in a little bit, when the rest of the townspeople arrive."

And the crowd did come. At first only a few people trickled in, but when Brent opened the wooden doors to the atrium entrance, he could see maybe a hundred people standing just outside the glass doors waiting for the exact hour of 7:00 p.m. Brent went over to the glass doors, opened one of them and invited everyone inside.

As the people entered the gym, almost every one of them was drawn directly to the model which John had placed so prominently under one of the overhead lights. The more people that came in, the more people ended up standing around the model, sometimes several people deep.

Brent leaned over to Gabby and said, "We may not even need the presentations, what with John's model there."

"Oh, yes, we will, and I'm very glad that we made hundreds of those packets for people to take away with them. It'll be helpful for them to have a visual reminder of how the town might look if this goes through."

Ari nodded in the direction of the model saying, "If I'm not mistaken, that's Abigail Spencer from The *Sentinel* over there. I'll bet a picture of that model ends up in tomorrow's paper and I think we'll have John to thank for that, too. Oh, I invited her, but I think the model is going to get us the front page."

The presentations were made. The map and the drawings viewed afterward by a large group of interested citizens. There had been lots of questions, not the least of which involved the kind of money that would be required for such an undertaking. Brent addressed most of the issues and told the crowd about the handout packets which detailed the estimates they had for the project on an itemized basis.

Brent turned the meeting over to Harriet to talk about the fund raising. She spoke about the plan for smaller contributions á la Obama's fund raising method, and the plans for donation boxes in retail shops, banks and restaurants around town. She talked about individual donors who might be in a position to contribute larger sums.

Someone suggested selling some of the bricks that were part of the plan for their park and also the benches. The contributors could have their name, or someone else's whom they wanted to honor, etched on the bricks. Everyone seemed to like that idea and Ari said that ideas such as that were welcome and could be called in or mailed to the office.

As the meeting broke up, way beyond its proposed one-and-a-half-hour time frame, many of the people lingered to look at the model, the map and the drawings. Some stopped Ari, Brent, Gabby, or Harriet, a few looking for further clarity about a particular issue, but most to offer a new idea or congratulate them on taking control of a bad situation and trying to turn the town around for the benefit of everyone.

Abigail Spencer stayed to take more pictures and ask a few follow-up questions for her piece in the paper the next day. Abigail finished up with Brent as the crowd finally began to disperse.

As they helped Jerry gather their props and John wheel the model into his truck, they finally allowed themselves some pleasure at what they thought was a job well done. When they finally piled into Gabby's SUV for the trip home, all totally exhausted, Gabby looked at the clock on her console. "Holy cow, do you all realize that it's 10:45? Some of those people stayed more than three hours."

Ari said she thought there had to have been more than two hundred people there. And everyone chimed in they thought that the project had been pretty well received, but that they would know better in a few weeks when they started hearing the talk on the street. With that, they all became quiet, lost in thought.

The *Sentinel* prominently displayed a very large picture of the model on the following day's front page. Under the picture was the beginning of the story Abigail Spencer had written. She split the article, after the main heading under the picture, to reflect the pros and cons of the DRP as she saw them. While there were considerably fewer cons, the big one, as always, was the cost of such an undertaking. Ari just filed it away as she made plans for the model to be housed in the plant section of Bolan's.

Now it was up to the people.

Cornelia was beside herself. She called a meeting in her office of all her fellow Council members and, by the time they all arrived, she could barely control her anger. "Have you all seen the front page of today's *Sentinel?* The picture of that model of the new downtown alone is going to lose us votes this November. Now, I know you're not all up for re-election, but if those of us who are end up losing, the Council, as we now know it, will no longer exist. This is out of control. We have to do something. I feel like *I'm* the only one out there trying to combat this thing."

As a group, the council members murmured to one another as they shifted uncomfortably in their seats.

"*What's the matter with you people?*"

Trisha Coleman stumbled as she tried to defy Cornelia. "Cornelia, I'm, er, not against this Plan. It, well, it looks wonderful to me and, well, I, for one, sort of think it, er, will benefit many of our residents."

"Have you *lost your mind, Trish?*"

"I agree with Trisha, Cornelia," Pete Peters said. "We've had to fund some of our priorities by short-shrifting others. At some point, there's not going to be enough to re-allocate any funds – and that point isn't too far off."

"Well, can't we come up with some sort of plan of our own? Wait. That's it! We'll come up with our own plan. We'll meet . . ."

Pete interrupted Cornelia's wailing. "We can't come up with a plan that will be more attractive than theirs, simply because we can't afford it."

"Then, *that's* how we'll fight it. We'll run ads, like that letter they ran in The *Sentinel*, and tell the people how they'll just be throwing their money away – this Plan is going to cost way too much and it'll never be completed. That's the answer." Cornelia was happy with her plan. "I think we can hit them hard, too, with the fact that none of them has ever held an elected position and Brent doesn't know the first thing about running a city. Yes, that's exactly what we'll do."

Brent and Ari made dates for Brent to speak and Ari and Gabby worked on placards to be displayed around town in the stores, on bulletin boards, and any other public places where such postings could be made.

When not out talking to the people, Brent was often found at food banks and churches, helping distribute goods for those in need. He worked with Father Frank in finding shelter for the homeless – the numbers staggering.

Ari tried to schedule a town hall meeting for Brent with Hiz Honor, but so far Hiz Honor had yet to accept. In the meantime, Ari reserved the auditorium of the high school for an open meeting with Brent, vowing to keep calling the Mayor's office in an attempt to have him participate.

There was a great deal of interest in the contest to rename Thompsonville – hundreds of entries piled up at the DRP office.

In the meantime, Harriet had been able to get many retail shops, bank branches and restaurants to place DRP boxes in their establishments. The boxes seldom contained more than $500 in any given week. But, once in a while, there were some really substantial dollars contributed. Donations by mail also started to come in, and the DRP bank account began to grow.

Harriet continued to get her ideas together for their park. As she and Susan played around with ideas, the plan slowly emerged. Harriet liked the suggestion made at the town meeting about raising money based on the sale of the bricks and benches in their park. She wondered whether there might be other locations in town where selling bricks might be a good idea.

The deadline for the contest drew near. The final date for entries to be postmarked was September 13th, but because so many entries had been dropped off, the group allowed hand-delivered entries as late as 5:00 p.m., Monday, September 15th. The plan was to let the working group, which now consisted of more than sixty business owners, vote on the top ten entries at a dinner meeting at Augustino's on Thursday, September 18th, with the winning entry announced in the following Sunday's edition of The *Sentinel*.

Ari, Gabby, Harriet and Brent worked on sorting all the entries on the Tuesday and Wednesday following the close of the contest. Some were duplicates, some were just silly or from someone who clearly wasn't supporting the Plan. They arranged the hundreds of entries in alphabetical order on the computer and printed the list for the working group's meeting on Thursday.

When all was said and done, they had more than seventy-five viable names to be reviewed and voted on.

When the foursome arrived at Augustino's Thursday evening, the entry was blocked by a large group of people huddled around the front door. Making their way through the crowd, they opened the door to the restaurant, finding standing room only on the inside, as well.

Ari chided herself. Believing they would have a nice, calm dinner with their working group was ridiculous in hindsight. *Hell, there are more than sixty business owners alone. Whatever made me think this was going to work?* Ari ended up taking control and announced to everyone that, obviously, based upon the huge crowd, the contest had been far better received than they had ever anticipated, and thanked them all for their interest.

Fortunately, Bernardo came to her rescue. He stood up and announced to the crowd that there were restrictions on the number of people who could be in his restaurant at any given time, and they had exceeded that limit. He asked those who were diners to request that they be seated, the rest could wait outside if they wished to dine at the restaurant that evening.

Although there was a great deal of disappointment that there wasn't enough room for the entire group of people to watch and cheer on their favorite entries, the disappointment was directed at Bernardo rather than at the DRP, for which Ari was extremely grateful. She knew that if there was any way this group was going to be able to come up with a short list that evening, it was going to require their uninterrupted attention.

The list was honed down rather quickly to twenty-two names. That was the easier part of the evening. Getting the list down from twenty-two to ten possible names was quite a challenge. The foursome found themselves glad they weren't part of that process. The twenty-two names still on the list were actually pretty good names. It ended up taking hours getting the list down to ten names, but it was finally done and Bernardo for one was glad. His staff hadn't stayed that late in the evening for years. With the final ten names agreed upon, the dinner broke up with a general sense of accomplishment.

On Saturday morning, again at Bolan's, the foursome met over croissants and coffee as they began to review and consider the name that would be artsy, catchy, strong, intriguing and a good marketing name for their town in its second life.

In the end, the one name that struck them as fitting all those requirements and the one they kept coming back to, was "Granite Falls." They didn't know about any granite in the area – there were some cascading creeks, but you really couldn't call them falls. Nevertheless, it just sounded like a good fit.

Gabby called Jerry, who immediately checked the availability of the name on Network Solutions, found it available, reserved it, and paid for its use for the next twenty years via his credit card.

And, so it was.

Ari called Abigail Spencer to announce the proposed name for Thompsonville and the name of the contest winner to be printed in Sunday's paper.

The campaign had grown very ugly.

Cornelia started her media blitz. She hyped everything that Hiz Honor and the City Council had done over the years to ensure that the residents' priorities were met. She slammed the DRP, throwing out astronomical numbers that would be required in order to revitalize Thompsonville as the DRP planned. She questioned where that money would come from? She questioned the DRP's ability to get it done. And then she personally attacked the foursome. Ari – she was fired from her job in Chicago and lived there with another woman. Gabby – she never even went to college and had to take a job in her family's business. Harriet – she never went to college either, and all she knew was jet-setting and parties. And, finally, Brent. Who was he but a lawyer who couldn't make it in Washington, D.C., a city that was filled with lawyers. Wasn't he living in sin with a woman in D.C.? And, what experience did he have running anything? This was who they wanted to run their town? Cornelia was relentless. She had gone off the deep end using smear tactics which were recognized as such by most people.

It seemed that Hiz Honor sensed what was happening in Thompson-ville. He knew that his popularity was declining as this crazy new idea of Granite Falls and its possibilities grew in strength. He threw everything he could at Brent and the DRP, but, if anything, it only seemed to make matters worse.

If Brent was following Obama's campaign plan, well, then, Hiz Honor would follow McCain's. Experience, and business as usual. The only problem was that he seemed to be having the same results as McCain. He only hoped he could turn it around. Mayor Hill assumed that McCain hoped the same thing.

CHAPTER TWENTY-NINE

By Sunday afternoon, September 28th, Mayor Hill was at a low point. He went to the club to play golf on what he thought may be the last really nice weekend before the cooler wet weather of fall began. He played poorly and decided to quit after only twelve holes; his heart wasn't in it. He went directly to the bar and ordered himself some consolation. Some of his fellow members were finishing up their rounds and also made their way to the bar. A couple of his buddies sat with him, but it was clear that a good number of men whom he had considered friends were steering clear.

He mentioned that fact to his two pals at his table and asked, "What am I to do? I thought I was doing a good job, crime is down, we have police on the streets. We have well-equipped firehouses, our schools are good, everything is running as it should. Yes, we have empty storefronts and our downtown has lost its appeal. But, this is no different from what's happening elsewhere in this country. Strip malls have taken over many downtowns. Oh, some of the cities are rebuilding, but they are, for the most part, major cities which also have strong business bases."

Bruce Kingman said, "Well, Steve, I think you have to let the people know that. You've only made a few appearances. You need to get in front of the people."

"I've tried, but, truth be told, I'm not getting many people showing up for my speeches. How do I get them to come and listen to me when they only seem to want to hear my opponent?"

"Steve, I know you don't want to hear this, but this DRP is quite compelling," Arnie Schaub spoke up.

"You, too, Brutus?"

"Look. The problem is that there are so many people out there who are in trouble and they see these young people and their beautiful plans for their town, they can't help but hope. Don't get me wrong, I'm solidly behind you and when you say we can't afford it, I believe you. But, you need to make this clear to the voters and explain why. And, if they're not going to your speeches, maybe you need to do something, like debate your opponent. That way those who come to listen to him will also have to hear what you have to say, if only by default," offered Arnie.

The Mayor was quiet for a moment as he thought. Then he said, "You know, his office has actually been trying to get me to do a joint town hall meeting on October 16th, and I've been ducking it. That might prove to be even better than a debate, because I can address the people with my own opening remarks and answer their questions without having to only speak to a moderator's questions, as would be required in a debate. Yes, that could be just the ticket. I know I *need* to do something, so I think I'll call them tomorrow and accept. Thanks, guys. Jack, put the next couple of rounds for these guys on my tab. I'll see you both later. I need to get home and start working on my remarks."

With that he stood, pushed his chair in, and walked off, waving at the other tables full of his "friends," thinking, *they'll see.*

Ari was shocked when she heard from Hiz Honor's office that he had accepted their offer to appear at the High School Auditorium on October 16th with Brent. Ari immediately called Brent, whose shock was as complete as Ari's.

Brent said, "He must be getting nervous. Otherwise, why would he accept?"

"I don't know, Brent, but I'll bet it has something to do with the fact that he's not getting much attention, either in the press or, so I hear, at his speaking engagements. Let's get something in The *Sentinel* right away announcing his participation. I think interest in the meeting will rise, as will the attendance. This may give us access to others who may have chosen to stay away from you and the DRP due to loyalty to Hiz Honor. I'll start work on a release as soon as we hang up. Talk to you later. I've got work to do."

The time flew by. While the pressure of the DRP was nowhere near what it had been before the town meeting, there was still plenty of activity.

Jack had made inroads with his hunt for properties which kept Gabby, Uncle Tony and Mike busy. He had also been successful in identifying some of the current owners of buildings which had been abandoned many years before. Some of the owners were individuals who had since died, and their heirs knew nothing of the building's existence. Others were companies that had gone out of business, or were acquired by new companies, many of which had also been acquired or gone out of business. Some were just abandoned with no trace of any person or entity responsible for the long overdue tax bills compiling interest as they rotted on the city's books of uncollectible debts.

Harriet had all but finished laying out her plan for the park. She worked with several of her friends from the garden club, some local landscape artists she managed to coerce into providing their services for free, and Susan Cranston. The park, which, when completed, would encompass an eight-block area plus that little frontage that existed overlooking the river, was, to her mind, a gathering place, yet offered many areas where one could sit, reflectively, without being on a main pathway or run over by children playing. She had defined several areas which would allow the park to draw different types of activities, and yet flow together through the beauty of the flowers, trees, ponds and gazebos, in different sizes and designs, scattered throughout the entire park. She approached several restauranteurs about renting the restaurant she planned to have constructed near the proposed ice-skating rink. While she had not heard from any of them yet, she was not deterred, and the plans included the site she had chosen. She took the plans over to the DRP and left them for comments.

By the time the foursome turned around, it was the day of the town hall meeting with Brent and Hiz Honor facing off, as it were.

Cornelia cornered Harvey Dunlap in his City Manager's office. "Harvey, are you going to the town hall meeting tonight?"

"I hadn't planned on it, Cornelia. Are you?"

"You're damn right I am, and I'm not going to keep quiet, either."

"Do what you want, Cornelia. But let me just warn you, you'll be cutting off your nose to spite your face."

"What are you talking about?"

"You've already made your position well known. Let it be, Cornelia. If you make a spectacle of yourself this evening, you'll never get elected to anything from this area again. Think about it. Are you willing to do that? Up to you."

Hiz Honor spent a great deal of time on his opening remarks and was as nervous as an about-to-be-groom as the hour approached. Hiz Honor won the coin toss to determine who would present his opening remarks first. He was relieved, as he was concerned that if Brent went first, there might be so much excitement on the audience's part that they wouldn't hear a word he said. So, gathering up all his courage, Hiz Honor stepped forward to the podium, and stared into a sea of faces.

"Ladies and Gentlemen, thank you very much for attending this evening's town hall meeting. I'd like to thank my opponent Brent Romano for sharing the stage with me on this important occasion.

As you know, I have been the Mayor of Thompsonville for over thirty years now, clearly earning your trust during that time as reflected by my long tenure. Your trust has not been misplaced. Over the years, we have maintained or lowered the crime rate by arming our police with the equipment necessary to conform to standards exceeding those of many other communities. In addition, our fire department has not lacked for the tools required to allow them to excel in their jobs, whether that be putting out fires, rescuing residents in need of help through the EMT services they oversee, or assisting other communities when they are in need. Additionally, we have maintained a high matriculation rate of Thompsonville High School students continuing on to college due to our superior schools and the excellent teachers who work so diligently on behalf of our children.

I will acknowledge that our downtown has fallen on hard times. This is not an uncommon phenomenon today. If one has been following the news over the past several decades, he knows that small towns all over this country have experienced the same desertion of their downtown areas, as strip malls have become the standard, growing along with the suburban areas. This is a function of a large percentage of the population moving out of the city to more family-oriented neighborhoods. While many large cities with broad job bases and strong city governments have begun to turn the tide on this outward movement, this is not the case for towns like Thompsonville.

Add to this the current national economic conditions, and you can probably understand how a town like Thompsonville with its negligible population growth rate is unable to invest in a beautification program. We have put our money, your tax dollars, where they are needed most -- educating our children and providing safety to our citizens.

After my opponent has had a chance to address you, I will be pleased to answer any questions you may have. Thank you for your attention, my friends."

As the Mayor stepped back from the podium, he received a hearty round of applause from the audience, and felt as if he had finally said what needed to be said about his performance as Mayor.

Brent watched from behind the side stage curtain, allowing the Mayor his moment. As the applause waned, Brent, with his erect bearing, strode purposefully on the stage, heading directly to the podium. The audience recognized him immediately, and the applause reached a level of enthusiasm not quite achieved by the Mayor. As he raised the microphone to accommodate his height advantage over that of his opponent's, he looked around making eye contact with members of the audience, nodding here and there as he acknowledged many friends, colleagues, and clients. The applause fading, Brent looked directly at the audience and began.

"I, too, would like to welcome you and thank you for attending this evening's meeting. What we have to talk about tonight is important.

Mayor Hill is correct when he tells you about the crime rate in Thompsonville, the important services available to all of us provided by our police, fire department, and EMT's. We are proud of them and we thank them for their service. Many of us are here today due to their efforts.

Our schools do have a high matriculation rate, but, aside from the computer lab at the high school, they lack state-of-the-art equipment as tools to help our children learn. Our teachers are dedicated and, to a great extent, only through their individual efforts could many of our children graduate, much less further their educations.

I see Mr. Findley out there. He teaches social studies, and Miss Cassiopeia, she teaches, I believe, 4th grade at the middle school and oh, way in the back there, is Miss Helen Thompson. In case someone here didn't go to grammar school in Thompsonville, you probably are not aware that Miss Helen, as she chooses to be called, taught here until she retired at age 75. That was more than ten years ago. But, Miss Helen didn't really retire. She continues going to the grammar school every day, where she spends her time in the school library reading stories to the children or helping them learn to read.

So, yes, Mr. Mayor, we have terrific teachers who do the best they can with what they have. But, what could our children achieve if they had state-of-the-art equipment? This is only one of the many questions I have for you tonight.

Mayor Hill has managed Thompsonville with a goal of maintaining the status quo. We, as Americans, must set goals, but ones which, on their face, appear unattainable. This is the American way, and the American ethic is not to settle. There are moral imperatives in this world, the first of which is to 'do no harm.' It is a sad commentary when one's plan for the future is merely to maintain the status quo. To aspire only to 'do no harm,' requires no vision, no inventiveness, and no commitment to making our world a better place. This complacency, of settling for the status quo, of not questioning our leaders, teaches our children to settle for things as they are, and ends up leaving them behind. One's greatest achievement can't be mediocrity. The entire world would kick sand in our face. If we reach only for the moon, we'll never reach the stars.

As things now stand, our children are leaving us behind -- literally. We educate them as best we can here in Thompsonville and they head off to colleges which prepare them for careers and lives which Thompsonville can't possibly offer. They outgrow us as teenagers and seldom come back to the nest, unless forced by outside circumstances.

We can't invest in Thompsonville because we don't have a growing population that can support our businesses. Over the last few decades, business upon business has closed in our area. We were a major manufacturing area, but I don't need to tell you the plants have closed, and the jobs have left. So, Thompsonville stumbles along. And yet, contrary to what I just said, now is *exactly* the time to invest in Thompsonville.

As you all must be aware by now, I am running for mayor in order to change the direction of our town. I'm not in any way impugning Mayor Hill's work; he has done as well as, or better than, his counterparts in other small towns across America.

But, it is time for a change and we need a vision, a fantastic vision, a dream. We need to set goals that envision a better future. We can rebuild Thompsonville, or Granite Falls as we would like to rename it. That too, will be up to you on November 4th. We would invest in making our town a destination point for weekenders, family vacations or anyone who just needs to get away.

I believe we can do this together, not just for the tourists and not just for ourselves, but for our families and our children. Let's rebuild our town to be all that it can be. Our future, their future, is in your hands. It is incumbent on us to strive for the greater good. Can you settle for mediocrity, the status quo? I won't, and I'm betting you won't either.

Vote for me and help us at the DRP rebuild your hometown and secure your children's future. Thank you."

The applause was enormous. Hiz Honor seemed to shrink in stature as he stood behind the stage curtain watching his opponent make his way backstage. He was beginning to think that the election was superfluous. It seemed evident to him that the future of Thompsonville was standing before him, and there was little he could do about it.

Brent took a few minutes backstage to take a deep breath and get some water before he and Hiz Honor would jointly retake the stage and be called upon to answer any questions posed by the attendees.

He had barely caught his breath when Ari walked to the podium and announced that the two candidates were ready to come back on stage and answer any questions put before them. Ari took a microphone in hand to traverse the stage in order to better see any raised hands. "Ladies and Gentlemen, let me again present to you His Honor, Mayor Hill of Thompsonville and his opponent, Brent Romano. Gentlemen, if you will.

Okay, let's begin. We are now open to questions from the audience."

A thirty-something woman raised her hand. "My name is Ann Murphy. My question is for Brent Romano.

Ari said, "Please go ahead, Ms. Murphy."

"Well, sir, I've been listening to you and reading some of the stuff in the paper about your plans. What I don't get is how we are going to pay for all of this? And, if we have the money just sitting around, why hasn't or can't Mayor Hill do it?"

"Ms. Murphy, I wish we did have the money just sitting around as I'm sure our Mayor does. However, that is not the case. Yes, this is going to cost a great deal of money, but we need to look at it as if it's our lifeline to the future, because it most assuredly is. Some of the donations have already started coming in.

What you may not know is that we have commitments from many owners of those downtown buildings to either donate their buildings or let us lease them at very attractive rents for the first several years. Likewise, we have commitments with regard to the utilities necessary to run the buildings. Regency, my sister's construction company with which many of you are familiar, has offered construction crews at cost. And the list goes on.

Furthermore, we have received cash donations, totaling more than $300,000 to date, a great deal of which was raised by small donations from our neighbors who put cash or checks in boxes located in businesses all over town. Clearly, there already is a good deal of support for the DRP. Mayor Hill is not one of our supporters. Therefore, in order to accomplish this Plan, I need your support.

The age-old question isn't whether we can afford to do it, but whether we can afford *not* to do it. I'll leave it to all of you to make that determination."

The next question came from a middle-aged gentleman. "Miss Bolan, I'm Jim. This question is for the Mayor. Mr. Mayor, what do you think about this Plan, this DRP?"

"Thank you for your question, Jim. I think the Plan, based upon the pictures I've seen is lovely, a beautiful dream. But I think that while most of us have dreams, they mostly remain just that. As children we have lots of dreams, but as we grow older we realize that dreams are fantasies -- unachievable, impossible, flights of fancy.

I would love to see Thompsonville prosperous again, but I am a realist. This realism comes from *years of experience, experience my young opponent here doesn't have,* at least not as an executive needing to balance budgets against the needs of a town with a dwindling population and tax base. He *doesn't have the experience* to make this dream come true. *I have fought and will continue to fight* for state and Federal funding to help us rebuild, and attract new business to Thompsonville. And, while this DRP has apparently raised some money, trust me, it is just a drop in the bucket of what would be needed to create this fantasy land of theirs.

"Ari, Miss Bolan, may I speak to that response?" asked Brent.

Receiving a nod, Brent started. "The government, whether local or at either the state or Federal levels, cannot be and never has been the entire solution to our economic problems. Look at what's happening at the national level as we speak. We have to stop expecting government to throw us a safety line. It is time to dig ourselves out of this hole and stop blaming everyone else for our current state of affairs. The Mayor's plan to continue business as usual also will not solve our problem. It's a Band-Aid, and, frankly, the Band-Aid approach won't work because we've already contracted gangrene."

Ari, sensing that Brent had finished, turned toward the audience, and pointed to Miss Cassiopeia, the 4th grade teacher Brent had recognized earlier. "My question is for Brent. Mr. Romano, you told us earlier that we are losing our young, talented people to major cities, with few ever to return. Yet you are here, Ari and Harriet returned to Thompsonville and Gabby never left. You are all leaders of our community; doesn't that seem to disprove your statement?"

"Miss Cassiopeia, Hi, it's been a while. Well, I'm certain we'd all like to thank you for the compliment, but let me give you some numbers. Out of my high school graduation class, I am one of only fifty-six seniors who are now living in Thompsonville. The rest of the class, which totaled more than 650 students, now live elsewhere. For the graduation class of '92 of which Ari, Gabby and Harriet were all a part, only seventy-eight students currently live in the area. Their class had approximately 685 students. These two years' statistics are not anomalies, nor is this a record of which we can be proud. It is our responsibility to provide opportunities for growth. The consequences of not doing so, will only seal our fate."

The next question was posed by an elderly woman in the back who identified herself as "Georgette."

"Mayor Hill, what do you think about the fact that your daughter is working for the opponent and the DRP?"

"Well, Georgette, my daughter is a grown woman and has her own mind. As I stated earlier, I think the plan to renovate downtown is lovely, I just don't believe it can work. My daughter has for many years had a passion for gardening. It only makes sense that her particular area of responsibility for the DRP is beautifying our downtown with a park. I am very proud of her and her efforts in that regard."

Ari said, "Next question, please." Over on the far side of the auditorium, Ari saw a raised hand. As she walked closer to that end of the stage, she recognized him immediately. George Swerling, Ari's friend and longtime employee of Bolan's, nodded to Ari, identified himself to the audience and cleared his throat. "Mr. Romano, your Plan, the DRP, rests entirely on the new Thompsonville, or Granite Falls, to be able to attract tourists here whose interest is art and/or theatre. Why do you think they will come to Granite Falls when they can go to huge theme parks or Disney World? But let's say they do come here. What happens after they've been here, seen what there is to see, and turn their interests to other towns which'll try to duplicate our efforts if we have any degree of success? What I'm really asking is, aren't we overlooking the fact that we need a strong business base in addition to the arts as you have outlined them?"

"Mr. Swerling, you have an excellent point. If I am elected Mayor, I promise to look into what businesses could be brought to Granite Falls in order to broaden our base. But just to answer your question about why not Disney World or other theme parks? Well, it costs a lot of money to go to these places, hundreds of dollars a day for a family not to mention the costs of travel and accommodations. Most people don't live near Orlando, Florida. We won't have an admission fee and we're only a few hours' car ride from almost the entire Midwest and several points in the East. The cost of gasoline, even at its current four dollars or so a gallon is a lot cheaper for a family of four than airplane tickets from anywhere. And, with the current state of the economy, people won't be able to afford those overseas trips, but they'll still want to get away."

"Excuse me," said a young man sitting near the front. "I'd like to follow up on that question, if that's okay with you all?"

"Certainly, please identify yourself and ask your question, young man," responded Ari.

"My name is Dean Franconi. You know my dad."

"You're Mike's son? I'm sorry Dean, I haven't seen you in years and I truly wouldn't have recognized you if you hadn't identified yourself. Please go on."

"Well, we need to do more in the area of all those green things the presidential nominees are talking about. I been reading and listening to all this stuff and I don't know why we can't do what they've gone and done up in Ohio. I can't remember the name of the town, but they took all those laid off auto workers and other unemployed folks and retrained them. Now they're makin' some kind of solar panels – so lots of those folks have jobs. And, my cousin, Jimmy, and me are workin' on a new kind of battery for cars so we don't have to use all that gasoline. But even the current batteries used in some of those concept cars that run on electricity, well those lithium ion batteries aren't even bein' made anywhere in the United States. Geez, Mr. Romano, I know this is a long question, but why can't we do some of that stuff along with all the other stuff?"

"Dean, this is exactly what I'm looking for, what the DRP is all about. It's about having all of us work together to come up with a plan to make Granite Falls a vibrant, healthy community not only to visit, but to want to call home.

Off the top of my head I'm going to say let's put your ideas in motion. Let's work on attracting some of those young and maybe not so young people out there with these new ideas. We have empty plants on the outskirts of town that we may be able to rent or acquire for use by the inventors. We could set up a Facebook page for green inventors offering some of the same incentives we have for our current plan."

A hand waved wildly in the back. This time Ari recognized it as another one of the Bolan employees, Ray. Ari saw that Ray was sitting with Joe and Spike, and smiled at them as she called on Ray.

"What if, excuse me, my name is Ray. What if we formed a group of retired workers who could work with some of these inventors, helping them do some of the labor and maybe even some of the brainstorming needed to help them build their prototypes. I'm speaking here for our little group of former Bolan's employees, but I know some other guys who have retired or been laid off from some of the plants that have closed. I'm sure we could get them to help, too."

Brent stood back almost unable to speak. Finally, he said, "Again, this is exactly what the DRP is all about. I need you, the town needs you, your neighbors, all of you. If we sit back and wait for our elected officials to act, we'd get nowhere. I can't do it without your help. Let's do it together.

I'm looking for your support, not to run the town but to help provide opportunities. My commitment to you is to work side-by-side with anyone and everyone who has a vision for the future. It is an investment not only of our time and money, but our ideas and hard work to ensure a better tomorrow for all of us. This Plan can only be as good as the sum of its parts. So, come, join us – be a part of the solution."

Ari scanned the audience for the next questioner. No hand was raised and no one seemed to be making a move to raise one. "If there are no further questions, I'd like to end the evening by thanking Mayor Hill and Mr. Romano for their participation here, as well as all of you in the audience for your attention. We all hope that you have found the meeting informative and look forward to seeing you at the polls on November 4th. Thank you all. Goodnight."

Councilwoman Cornelia Huff sat alone in the back of the darkened auditorium. The Mayor had taken a shellacking, and it was clear to her that she needed to consider her options.

As the auditorium cleared, the Mayor, Brent, and Ari shook hands as they walked off the stage. As they passed the stage curtain, the Mayor turned and walked alone toward the exit. Gabby and Harriet ran backstage from the audience in order to join Ari and Brent and offer their congratulations. Harriet caught a glimpse of her father walking slowly in a somewhat defeated slump. He opened the back stage exit door and disappeared alone into the night. She tried to catch up with him, but by the time she spotted him in the parking lot, he was already pulling out onto the driveway. They hadn't spoken in months and Harriet's heart went out to him. By then, the rest of the group caught up with her. Their enthusiasm was infectious and they decided that champagne was in order. They headed to Gabby's house, where Gabby knew Jerry was waiting with the proper libation.

CHAPTER THIRTY

The town hall meeting was very well covered by The *Sentinel* the next day. Abigail Spencer had outdone herself with her article. Abigail reported that the number of attendees had exceeded five hundred and that, based upon the questions asked of the candidates, there had been a great deal more interest in Brent than in the Mayor. In an apparent attempt at unbiased reporting, she speculated that this was probably due to the fact that the DRP was still an unknown quantity to many of the townspeople, whereas the Mayor, having served all these many years, was, well, known.

Cornelia determined that she couldn't stop the speeding bullet of the DRP. Her only course of action, as she saw it, was to continue addressing the public, emphasizing all the good she had done for Thompsonville, and promise to always keep the residents' best interests as her number one priority. The Mayor was on his own.

That Friday the phones at the DRP rang off the hook. People teemed into the offices, making donations and looking at the model for Granite Falls. Even George, Ray and Spike showed up at their old digs. Snagging Ari only long enough to tell her that they were going through with their volunteer support group they had talked about last night, George asked about getting that Facebook page done for green inventors, like the one Jerry was putting together for artists and playwrights. Ari said she'd check on it with Gabby and Jerry and get back to them. And so the day went.

By the next week, money was being stuffed into the boxes at the local businesses. So much so that the owners were calling to ask that the boxes be emptied in order to accommodate the increased number of donations. People dropped by Brent's campaign headquarters asking if they could put up signs or call voters, whatever was needed. Even Tyler, Brent's little brother from the Big Brothers Program, showed up with all his friends so they could get some handouts in order to distribute door-to-door in the neighborhoods where the voter turnout had been consistently low.

It was now just two weeks until the election.

There was fierce competition out there. Thompsonville, as well as the entire state, was polling largely in favor of McCain. While the foursome wasn't particularly invested in one presidential candidate over the other, their concern was that many voters would just stick to that side of the ticket, and that was where Hiz Honor firmly sat.

And, so, for the next two weeks, the group just held their collective breaths.

Finally, it was Tuesday, November 4th, the day of reckoning. Volunteers still manned the phones at the DRP, while others drove seniors to polling places.

There were long lines at voting centers everywhere. CNN showed the lines in some of the most unlikely spots, including cities and states where the weather was so ugly it would stop all but some of the most fervent constituents. Yet, it wasn't stopping them.

Gabby called early to tell Ari that she couldn't believe it. Although there were predictions for a large turnout for the presidential election, no one believed there would be any lines in Thompsonville. In earlier years, scarcely anyone showed up to vote. Was this going to swing with the national polls that showed Mr. Obama in the lead, or would Thompsonville's residents stick with their party of choice? They could do nothing now except wait for the returns.

Gabby and Jerry arranged for Ethel to spend the night with the children, except Nicole, of course. At fourteen, she was very much caught up in her Uncle Brent's campaign and the DRP where she was helping her mother and Aunt Ari whenever she could. So, Gabby, Jerry and Nicole, along with the rest of their adult family members, Mary and Brian, Jerry's family, Ari and her mom, Harriet, Scott, Brent's associate, and even Tyler and his mom, decided to wait for the returns at Brent's loft. There was plenty of food, and lots of beer and wine – sodas for the young people. Brent had begged off any spirits, wanting to wait until they had some hard numbers. The girls decided they were entitled to a glass of wine as they nervously awaited the results. The champagne was in the fridge.

CNN declared McCain the winner in the state, but the local votes were still being counted.

At 10:25 p.m. the phone rang and Brent found Hiz Honor on the other end of the line congratulating him on a war well fought. "My boy, I only hope you can follow through with half the promises you made. Good Luck."

Brent turned to his family and friends. "That was Mayor Hill. He called to concede the race and tell us that the referendum renaming Thompsonville to Granite Falls passed." A large whoop went up and everyone high-fived and hugged. Gabby ran to get the champagne.

As the glasses were filled and passed to everyone, Gabby quieted the group. "Hold on a minute, Brent has something to say."

"Ladies and Gentlemen, my dear family and great friends, this has been an incredible journey. One which could not have been made without each of you. In particular, I would like to thank Ari, Harriet, and my sister, Gabby, for their indefatigable perseverance against so many odds, and to let them know that they're not finished. I would like to announce two things.

One, it is my intention to appoint Ari as our new City Manager once I take office. Ari I'm sorry to ask you this way but I didn't want to jinx anything by making the offer earlier. I sincerely hope you accept."

Brent raised his glass to Ari, who bowed her head as she mouthed "Thank you" to him.

"The second, and no less important matter, is that, to no one's surprise, except, probably, hers, I'm planning to name the new park downtown 'The Harriet Rose Hill Park.' Now, Harriet, don't get all teary-eyed. Part of the reasoning behind this is now we're assured you'll get the job done, because your name will be on it. Seriously, you have done a phenomenal job designing the park and we all believe you when you say you'll get it done. Congratulations to you, too." He raised his glass to her. Harriet raised hers to him in return.

He turned to the rest of the group. "There truly are too many people who contributed so much to try and acknowledge them all here now. You all know who they are, many right here in this room. Now, let's enjoy tonight because tomorrow it's back to work, but this time with the approval of the town. So, thank you all, again."

"To Brent," they said in unison and they all drank.

Brent was now the Mayor-elect.

His duties as mayor would not begin until his swearing in on January 2nd, 2009. Until that time, Brent would be spending his time with Scott, attempting to find another lawyer who could help Scott with the practice.

Then there was the matter of trying to win over some of the old, as well as the new, city council members. Brent knew, as the new President-elect knew, one can't do it alone. City Council support was going to be imperative if Brent was going to achieve the objectives of the DRP. The City Manager's job was an appointed position, so, from the start, Brent knew Ari would be at his side, while also covering his back.

Cornelia was out by her own doing. There were two new members, one replacing Cornelia. Pete Peters managed to hold onto his seat, barely. He promised himself that he would work with Brent on the DRP to help safeguard him in the next election.

One of Brent's first tasks as Mayor, and one which he was greatly looking forward to, was accepting the properties committed by the building owners, which Jack had secured during the planning stages of the DRP.

Harriet began in earnest setting up functions and calling on individuals and business owners in an effort to raise the necessary dollars. Her work was cut out for her, and she was loving it. Harriet had been successful in finding the owner of a successful restaurant in Pittsburgh who loved the DRP and thought that his restaurant would lend itself to the park-like surroundings in particular, and the ambience of the new Granite Falls in its entirety.

Gabby was busy with the plans for the individual buildings they had chosen to be a part of the initial stage of the DRP. Jack brought others to the table, and they were busy doing the final evaluations.

Gabby also found herself involved in the artists' and playwrights' search. The Facebook pages were up and running and they were being overwhelmed by interested potential participants in their grand scheme of the DRP. Gabby ended up looking for help from current gallery owners and a few artists and playwrights Emily had recruited from Chicago to help out. Gabby, Ari, Brent, and Harriet decided that this had to be juried as if it were a real art show. The same kind of review would have to be done on the playwrights' side. They had discussed the potential need for such a panel early on, but had put it aside until the DRP was approved through Brent's election. It would be impossible to offer space to everyone who wanted to join them. If they were to attract tourists, it was going to be necessary to offer quality artwork and plays.

Jerry designed a Facebook page for green inventors. With the help of the newly-assembled volunteer group of retired executives, machine shop artisans, and assembly line workers, Jerry put together the internet page and the responses were being evaluated by retired engineers.

Jack Caldwell got involved in the real estate for that side of the equation as well. He identified two plants which would fall under the financial parameters they had used to determine which buildings would work for the downtown revitalization. The theory on the business end was that the more inventors/entrepreneurs who were housed together, the more they could bounce their ideas around, giving them all a better opportunity to come up with the best inventions possible.

Ari was on top of everything. She was in her element. She loved what she was doing and felt that being a part of the new town was the job she had been looking for all along. Her experience running Bolan's had served her well, and her administrative abilities made her the perfect person to become Granite Falls' new City Manager. She was very glad they had thought ahead and put the referendum on the November ballot requesting the authorization to rename Thompsonville, and that it had passed with the necessary majority.

Unbeknownst to any of them, Abigail Spencer had submitted a story to the *AP* about the previous year in Thompsonville; the DRP, Brent's campaign, and his eventual success at the polls. Ari received inquiries from reporters in small towns all over the country. Ari apologized to them for her lack of time as she referred them to Abigail's stories in The *Sentinel*. She told them that once Brent assumed office, and things settled down, she would be happy to talk with them. When the leading business newspaper in the country called however, Ari was astonished. She referred the call to Brent, saying that it was more appropriate that he be the one interviewed. And so it was.

On January 2nd, Brent Gregorio Romano was sworn into office as Mayor of Thompsonville. The swearing in ceremony itself was quite short and rather perfunctory.

The day would not have been all that memorable except that Brent was now the Mayor. That was until about 2:30 that afternoon when he received a call from someone identifying himself as the President-elect. Brent was about to hang up on the prankster when Ari came running in, giving him the thumb's up gesture, and switched the call to speaker phone. Apparently, it was not only the President-elect – fortunately Ari was there to recognize that – but he was calling to congratulate Brent on his election and the forward thinking of the DRP task force. He commended them on the realization that they needed to work together and dig their own way out of their predicament – that their future was in their own hands, the government only being able to do so much. He continued that if the rest of the country could duplicate Brent and his group's ingenuity and determination, perhaps his first few years in office trying to avert the current national economic quagmire would render itself an easier task.

"Mr. President-elect," said Brent, "you have a monumental task before you and I don't envy you that undertaking. It would be arrogant for me to offer you any advice. But, suffice it to say, the largest surprise to me in our little Plan here was the unexpected and unfettered willingness of the people to help with suggestions, time and money. Since the election, many more have stepped forward to roll up their sleeves and volunteer in ways we hadn't even imagined. On behalf of all the people here in Thompsonville, soon to be Granite Falls, we thank you for taking the time to recognize our efforts, and wish you nothing but the greatest success in your presidency. Thank you so much for calling."

"Goodbye Mr. Mayor and continued success to you as well."

With that Brent hit the off button on his speaker phone. He and Ari just sat back not believing what had just occurred.

The DRP was in full swing.

The town was officially renamed "Granite Falls" on the 5th of January, the first working day of Brent's mayorship. The buildings that had been donated were transferred to the city, and Gabby and her crew began working on the necessary repairs and renovations. Work went on with Harriet, Jerry, Jack and a whole host of others. The signs of the revitalization were in evidence everywhere.

The next matter of business was the City Council vote on reclaiming, through eminent domain, the old, deteriorated buildings down on 1st and 2nd which had not already been donated to the city. While this was a difficult sell to the Council, there was so much public support for the idea, they had put the heat on the individual members and they eventually capitulated.

By March the work to raze the buildings began. The few building owners whose properties were taken by the city, really hadn't opposed their taking. They were just looking for some compensation, which they received. So, they signed off on the properties, agreeing not to appeal. Another hurdle ticked off on their to do list.

CHAPTER THIRTY-ONE

Christopher Hale, Doug's younger brother and artist, provided invaluable assistance to Gabby and her crews regarding the layouts for the buildings which were to be renovated to accommodate the artists who would be en studio.

Ari and her mother offered the Bolan plant to the city for one dollar per year rent, to be used by sculptors who worked primarily in iron and other metals. Bolan's main work area was perfectly suited for it with the plant's very large open space, and was already wired for heavy electrical usage. While Bolan's was on the south side of Main Street, it was only a block and a half south of Main, between Westfield and Raymond, on 3rd Street. Because the buildings on the north side on 1st and 2nd were to be part of the new Harriet Rose Hill Park, the sculpture studio would only be a short walk for visitors to Granite Falls.

Harriet was very busy. Through fund-raisers she held throughout Granite Falls and the surrounding area, she had raised a fair amount of money, but it was the boxes in the local businesses that continued to over-flow with donations from the townspeople. Harriet also asked her society friends from New York and Paris to make contributions to her project, knowing full well they had to help out. Otherwise, they couldn't expect Harriet to reciprocate when their fund-raisers took place.

The young innovators were an entirely different challenge. While the volunteer group of retirees was well versed in the areas where they had worked, most of the ideas for this new green technology were way beyond their comprehension. They formed a research group with some of their members searching the internet, following up on new companies which had been reported on in the media, and talking with reporters who were experts in their field. The group found that most of these innovators, unlike artists, came in groups. They tended to be kids who came up with plans worked out on their computers. Many, people who had studied together in high school or college, had taken jobs after graduation, but continued to kick stuff around after work and on weekends. Or, just a group of like-minded mechanics who thought they had a better idea and ended up working out of their own or their parents' garages.

There had been inquiries from individuals who read about what was going on in Granite Falls. One gentleman who was working on developing a new type of building material contacted the group. He said his product would be green, low maintenance and, hopefully, by the time he was finished, relatively inexpensive. He was anxious to know if there would be a facility that he could use under the DRP. The volunteer group pounced on the possibility.

There were many others with ideas that were clearly out of the realm of the DRP. Another man wanted to find a way to make a new type of gasoline out of weeds. A young woman claimed she was close to coming up with a *clean* cigarette, whatever that meant, and a host of others, too numerous and too ridiculous to consider.

Ari was inundated by the national press on a daily basis, making it extremely difficult to keep the DRP moving ahead while attending to the ordinary matters that required her attention as City Manager.

One night, when she and Brent had been working late on forms of tourist transportation for downtown, Ari mentioned to Brent, "I've been thinking about recruiting Emily to help me with the press, leaving me relatively free to deal with the day-to-day matters of the DRP and city matters. The added bonus is that we'd get lots of publicity which will help promote Granite Falls as a destination point. What do you think?"

Brent thought about it a minute. "I think it's a grand idea, as long as we can afford it."

"I think I'll invite her here for a visit, show her all the progress we've made, and see what we can work out, if that's okay with you?"   B r e n t nodded. "I think it's an excellent idea, Ari. Go for it."

Emily was excited to be invited back to Granite Falls, visit with her old friend, and get a tour of the progress being made through the DRP. Memorial Day weekend was coming up and they both thought it would be a perfect time for their get-together.

In the meantime, Harriet was contacted by two of the many foundations to which she had applied for grants. One was contributing the full amount she had requested, while the other told her that, while they had already committed the bulk of their funds for the year, the members of the Board had decided to donate the remainder to the DRP, amounting to approximately one-third of the requested amount. Harriet had yet to hear about the Federal grant. But even without that, the two private grants were going to go a long way in completing the park.

While the renovations continued on the buildings chosen by the DRP, Gabby was busy working with the owners of the other buildings which were not a part of the DRP but would benefit from the Plan if only by their location. She worked with John Traymore to come up with interesting, yet different, facades for the buildings which would still reflect the flavor of the new Granite Falls. Most agreed with the concept, recognizing that if the Plan were successful, their old buildings downtown would enjoy a new life.

And, so, as Memorial Day neared, the facades for most of Main Street had been completed, several of the buildings that were part of the DRP were well under construction, and even some of the other buildings had been rented by business owners willing to take a chance on the success of the DRP.

The DRP buildings were designated as galleries or working studios. One large older department store had been converted to a small hotel. A donated building on Ashland near 5th, was in a state of such ill repair, it ended up being razed, but then transformed into a brick courtyard with wrought iron tables and chairs, sheltered by a few well-placed trees. The building next to it, which was not a part of the DRP, benefitted from the courtyard when it leased its downstairs retail space to a gourmet coffee house.

The Theatre was renovated from a movie house to a live production facility. The facade had not been altered, but had been restored to its former glory, and was ready for any production.

The old cannery, which Jack was so intent upon acquiring for the DRP, turned out, in fact, to be absolutely perfect for its intended use as a rehearsal facility. Granite Falls was visited by many young, up-and-coming playwrights who ended up being sold on the town. This was due largely in part to the rehearsal hall's size and facilities and their ability to test their productions on a small scale before moving onto other cities.

Several of the DRP buildings, which were several stories high and had been designated as galleries, ended up having the top couple of stories converted into studio apartments. This gave the artists a low cost of living, while Granite Falls was establishing itself and had the added benefit of making the downtown a thriving neighborhood with a certain elan not necessarily found in small towns.

Artists were invited to visit Granite Falls from the myriad of applications made via the internet. Just as their work had been studied and evaluated by the gallery owners and artists recruited by Emily, the working group of the DRP wanted a chance to meet them. They felt a certain sense of responsibility for getting a feel for their personalities and how they would blend with the idea of working in the public's eye, whether in the park on in a working studio open to the public.

More than forty artists were offered gallery or working studio space, as well as a low rent studio apartment on a trial basis. Each artist signed a commitment letter with the city to participate in city shows as well as working artists' weekends once a month in the park during the summer months. The plan was coming together.

Ari asked Christopher if he would design a flag representing the new downtown that they planned to place on the new lampposts along Main Street. Ari said the design would also become the first of the annual posters the city proposed to sell to tourists as an additional source of income.

Gabby had her hands full. Although, to the public's eye everything seemed to be going well, they were well behind schedule.

Originally, Gabby planned to have Granite Falls' official grand opening on Memorial Day. She had abandoned that hope in April. Building permits were a problem. Many couldn't be issued until ownership passed. That meant title searches, new forms of transference acceptable to the city needed to be completed, and the buildings taken by eminent domain also required that particular city documents be executed.

Storms created havoc during the first few months of 2009, putting some of their construction projects behind schedule even before they began. The razing of the buildings along 1st and 2nd Streets took far longer than expected, again due to the weather. Tornadoes, floods, electric storms – they all came, one after the other. Gabby could never have forgiven herself if something were to happen to any of the workers in order to meet some magic opening date she had set.

Memorial Day arrived and so did Emily. She and Ari spent the first night catching up, although a good deal of the conversation eventually turned to the DRP. Ari's enthusiasm was evident as she went on about the buildings, the artists, the park, well, just about everything.

On Saturday morning, Ari took Emily to The Blue Frog for breakfast where Brent joined them. The threesome enjoyed their breakfasts, though they were frequently interrupted by townspeople stopping to ask how everything was going. Emily could see that Ari's spark was duplicated by the interest of the residents.

Ari, Brent and Emily then toured the downtown area. Emily was astounded by the difference in the air of the street as they walked along. Main Street had been transformed, trees had been planted in parts of the sidewalk which had been cut out to make way for them. The lampposts were of classic design with solid bases. The buildings themselves spoke to a sturdy, prosperous town well-kept with interesting retail offerings.

They began at the new hotel, Maison on Main, which was nearing completion. It was very well done, along the lines of some of the small exclusive hotels in Paris. There they met Gabby who would answer any questions regarding the renovations Emily was about to see.

After leaving the hotel, they continued down Main Street toward the park, the bridge and the river. They walked through the galleries, the working studios, and the studio apartments. Some of the buildings which were not part of the DRP were also undergoing renovations, most of which were already leased to incoming businesses.

Emily became as excited as Ari and Gabby. While she was certain that Brent was extremely proud of their achievements to date, he obviously was not the type to jump up and down, but exhibited more of an easygoing confidence of a job well done.

As they neared the park, they were delighted to see that work was continuing, even though it was a Saturday.

The restaurant had been built close to the railed edge of the park overlooking the river. Harriet told them about the plan to add a covered deck to the end of the restaurant. It would have a view of the river and be enclosed with glass during the winter months. The exterior of the building had been completed and the interior was not far behind.

The rest of the park was a beehive of activity. There were stakes in the ground everywhere. The winding path was under construction, as were the gazebos that were slated to be scattered throughout the park.

Emily asked about two large areas which seemed to be devoid of any markings. All three replied that they thought one was going to be the site for the winter ice-skating rink, and a football/soccer field/picnic area during the warmer months. They were uncertain about the other area, they admitted.

Once they had finished the tour, Gabby excused herself. "It is, after all, a Saturday, and it's time to go home and be a Mom." She promised to talk to them all soon, gave Emily a hug and ran off to her car.

Ari, Brent and Emily went to Brent's loft to talk about what they thought Emily might do for Granite Falls and her interest in the project. As they spent the rest of the afternoon throwing around ideas, it became apparent to Ari that something more than Granite Falls was going on here. Ari noticed a chemistry between her former roommate and her best friend's brother that could not be disguised. She didn't know quite what to do; should she try to make an excuse and disappear for a while? Of course, that would be awkward since Emily was her weekend guest; yet somehow she felt superfluous in the little get-together.

Saved by the bell, as it were, Brent's phone rang. Gabby invited the threesome over to her house for pot luck. The three eagerly headed off to Gabby and Jerry's for the evening.

Most of the conversation centered on Granite Falls. Gabby insisted that Jerry bring out his design for the website, which was nearing completion. "I'm waiting for a few pictures of the newly renovated downtown, a few interior shots of a couple of galleries, a restaurant, and the hotel. With those, and a date when we'll be ready for visitors, the site will be finished and we can post it to the internet."

Emily made a cursory review of the site and thought it was very well done. "You know, Jerry, an opening date isn't really necessary. The best way to tempt the public is to announce that it is nearing completion. But that begs the question: When do you expect to be ready, open to the public?"

Ari jumped in. "We were shooting for Memorial Day. Obviously, we missed that date. Our current plan is for the 4th of July, with all the accompanying fireworks, but now I'm afraid even that's way too premature."

Gabby joined in. "We have at least two months' worth of construction, cleaning, decorating and getting everyone settled into their galleries, rehearsal halls and housing. Some of the buildings will be ready in the next couple of weeks and several of the artists are planning to move in then. They thought it would help them getting in early to set up their working space and become comfortable with their new environs. I agree. Settling in early will enable them to get to know one another, form their friendships and working relationships, not to mention adding any creative interior design elements to the galleries."

"Em, you probably noticed that the new gourmet coffee shop is already open and serving the local residents who are streaming into town to get a look at their creation." Ari added.

By the time the evening was over, entirely too much wine had been consumed, but a working bond had been formed with yet another new member. Though she had not officially accepted being their public relations person, Emily was certain this was an undertaking unlike any other she had worked on. She knew she wanted to be a part of it.

Ari and Emily spent Sunday out and about. They played tennis in Logan Park and then went downtown for a more leisurely walk around the renovations. That day there wasn't any work being done and, in fact, most of the work materials that had cluttered the sidewalk the day before, had been removed. Seeing Emily's questioning look, Ari told her they had made way for the Memorial Day Parade that would take place on Main Street the next day. Ari said that for the last twenty or so years the audience for the parade had dwindled, along with the downtown business population, but they were almost certain that they would have a fairly good turnout.

Ari and Emily took their time as they wandered slowly from one building to another, glancing in windows at the work in progress. Of course, there were a few businesses that remained untouched; perhaps their owners only waiting to see how successful the town would end up.

That night, Ari and Emily invited Harriet to join them for dinner at Augustino's. Harriet hadn't realized that Bernardo had redone the entire interior in anticipation of the business that was to come. It was beautiful. While the girls had always enjoyed the restaurant as it was, they were entranced by the renovation. Bernardo was tremendously pleased to point out the latticed screens, now making the tables more intimate, the pillars of plants, new indirect lighting, and soft candlelight glowing on each table. While the beautiful mural on the wall remained, gone were the checkered tablecloths, replaced by white lines and fine china

The friends talked animatedly about their work and their love lives. Harriet admitted, "I've pretty much begged off men since Paolo. But, I'm beginning to think it's time for me to get back in the market – right after we're finished with the DRP, and, more specifically, Harriet Rose Hill Park."

"I was dating the owner of one of my firm's business clients for a while, but that ended several months back. In the meantime," Emily said, "I've been going out here and there with a few different men, but no one special."

It was Ari's turn and she just blushed. Neither Emily nor Harriet was about to let her get away with that. They both stared at her and said, "Well?"

"Well, I don't know. I've been out with Gordon Reed a few times, but, er, well, there's nothing serious going on here, well, er, not yet, anyway."

Emily laughed uncontrollably. "Ar, I've never heard you put a sentence together quite like that last one. It can only mean one thing . . ."

"Yes," Harriet jumped in. "You're interested. How about that?"

Ari joined them in their laughter. They spent the rest of the evening sharing stories and having a delightful time.

On Monday morning, Ari and Emily got up early, put Emily's suitcase in the back of Ari's car and headed downtown for the parade, which was scheduled to begin at 10:00 a.m.

By 9:15, Ari and Emily reached the outskirts of town and ran smack into a traffic jam. Ari thought, *this can't all be due to the parade, can it?* as she tried to inch her way forward. After about ten minutes of very slow going, Ari turned the corner onto Chestnut behind the Courthouse and headed down to Normandy, right onto 3rd Street, then north to Bolan's parking lot.

They walked from Bolan's toward Main Street and the parade route. In front of them, they could see people on the sidewalk blocking their view. Turning the corner onto Main, Ari and Emily gasped at the hundreds of people, perhaps more, lining Main as far as they could see and on both sides of the street. Even the noise was staggering.

"This is incredible, Ari. You've a lot to be proud of."

"Yes *we* do. Not just me or our little group, it's everyone."

Ari and Emily brought cameras and began busily snapping pictures. Within a few minutes, the parade got underway. The lead car hosted Brent as it slowly made its way down the street. When he spotted Ari and Emily, he waved wildly, with a look on his face saying, "Can you believe this?"

They ended up seeing little of the parade itself, as they made their way to different spots along the parade route trying to get pictures from different angles. They ran into Abigail Spencer and Ari introduced her to Emily. As the three talked briefly, Emily told Abigail that she was the new pubic relations person for Granite Falls, and she looked forward to working with her. Ari gave Emily a big smile. After Emily and Abigail exchanged business cards, the two friends and former roommates made their way, arm-in-arm, back to Ari's car for the trip to the airport and Emily's flight back to Chicago.

CHAPTER THIRTY-TWO

As the summer slipped away, buildings were actually being completed and a good number of the artists, playwrights and actors had moved to Granite Falls.

The exterior construction work was all but finished and people now walked the streets without obstruction as they gazed into the newly renovated spaces, many of them open for business.

The biggest conquest, at least to Harriet's mind, was completing the park before the summer slid into winter. She had raised all the money necessary to create the park as she envisioned it, and was frantic to officially open it to the public – well, the Granite Falls' residents -- by Labor Day Weekend, when the restaurant in the park was also scheduled to open.

On the Tuesday before Labor Day weekend, a huge white tent appeared in the park on the spot that had been the focus of speculation by all who saw it. On Wednesday night, under cover of darkness, several moving trucks drove across the bridge into Granite Falls, and headed for the park. Harriet stood by nervously as she tried to keep the delivery people as quiet as possible. This was Harriet's personal gift to the people of Granite Falls and, she hoped, the crowning glory to the Harriet Rose Hill Park. Slowly, methodically, the pieces were brought into the tent to await the men who would covertly assemble it the next night.

By Thursday afternoon, people were wondering what was going on in the park. Several had tried to get close to the tent, but Harriet had anticipated those attempts and hired a security patrol to maintain the secrecy until the unveiling at the official opening. Even Abigail Spencer speculated in her latest article about what could possibly be concealed under the tent. Ari, Gabby and Brent claimed ignorance, or they just weren't talking.

On Friday night the crowd gathered to dedicate the park, and watched as the tarp was removed, revealing the main entrance with its bronze plaque, inscribed *Harriet Rose Hill Park*.

As the crowd applauded, they began to move farther into the park in the direction of the big white tent. Many marveled at the trees and flowers, but most couldn't keep their eyes off the tent.

Harriet raced ahead of the crowd as it moved toward the tent. Somewhat out of breath, she began. "I would like to thank all the residents of Granite Falls for your contributions, enthusiasm and endless offers to help create our new hometown. We were inspired by your confidence in us and in the vision of the DRP. I have been trying to find a way to show my appreciation to all of you for your efforts. So, without any further delay, I'd like to present my gift to all of you. Gentlemen, please."

With a nod from Harriet, the guards who had encircled the tent pulled back the sides to reveal a remarkable carousel with beautifully decorated horses, zebras, and all sorts of animals, as well as sleighs, poles, mirrors, and spectacular lighting, dramatically enhancing the entire attraction. At the same moment, the music began and the carousel started to turn proudly, displaying its grandeur. The exclamations were loud, as was the applause, as the new attraction captured flashes of almost everyone's favorite childhood memory.

The crowd lingered to watch or ride the carousel. Many wandered over to River House, the newly constructed restaurant Harriet had envisioned from early on in her planning stage. The restaurant had a clear view of the carousel, as well as the river.

Ari, Gabby, Brent and Jerry went over to thank, hug and congratulate Harriet. They reminded her that she had promised to join them for dinner, announcing that they had reserved a table at the River House in anticipation of its opening.

As the five of them made their way to their table on the patio, they found themselves sitting near a table where Harriet's parents, along with Arnie Schaub and his wife, were dining. Steven B. Hill, former Mayor of Thompsonville, and former critic of the DRP, got up and went over to congratulate Brent, Ari, Gabby, Jerry and most important, Harriet. It was the first time they had seen one another in months. They'd spoken, briefly, but she was certain that he was disappointed in her because of her activities on behalf of the DRP. Now, she happily jumped up and gave him a big hug, biting back the tears. It broke the ice. Hiz Honor proudly kept his arm around Harriet as everyone shook hands, and succeeded in taking the first step toward mending bridges irrationally constructed.

Back in Chicago, Emily was at full throttle. She managed to follow up with several papers that had reprinted Abigail Spencer's column. She then tackled the weekly news magazines, the financial papers and *USA Today*. She worked closely with Ari and Brent and took a couple of trips back to Granite Falls to watch the progress. She could barely contain herself when *The ABC World News* with Charles Gibson announced that Granite Falls would be highlighted on the show, as well as one of the lead stories on *CNN's* weekend spots.

One Monday morning, Emily's secretary announced that Brent was on the phone. She picked up the phone, wondering why he was calling her – it was she who usually needed to clarify something with him. As she heard his voice on the other end of the line, she focused her entire attention on his call.

"I'm planning to be in Chicago this weekend and wondered if you would like to have dinner with me?" Emily allowed herself a smile.

"Sure. What's the subject?

"No subject. Just dinner."

"Is this a business dinner, Brent?"

"Actually Emily, it's not really a business dinner, although we could discuss business if you like. Seriously, I'm sure business will come up since we're both working on the same project, but I'd like to make this something else. That is, if you're interested."

Emily smiled a wider smile. "I *am* interested and would very much like to have dinner with you this weekend."

Their dinner turned out to be the first of many dates over the next several months, and the beginning of a relationship which became very special to both of them. As the completion of Granite Falls' DRP drew near, Brent seriously considered asking Emily to marry him.

Although the official opening had yet to take place, business was already booming in Granite Falls. The owners of the Maison on Main hotel scrambled with last minute details before their December 18th scheduled opening. The media attraction and the internet certainly stirred interest in Granite Falls. The hotel was booked solid through the Christmas holidays, and almost every holiday weekend in 2010. As the media coverage continued, reservations neared capacity for weekdays too.

The galleries were selling their art, most of it from the new artist resident's of the town. The visitors were captivated by the artists in their working studios. People lingered, talked to the artists and ended up buying their work because they knew the artist personally.

The first theatrical performance was scheduled to open the week of December 20th, allowing the actors a few nights before the crowds were scheduled to arrive. They knew it was not only the opening of their show, but of a large part of the Granite Falls' concept, making them even more anxious.

Restaurants were busy and the horse-drawn carriages Ari had arranged to bring in for the festivities were a hit – their trek around the Park reminiscent of its Manhattan counterpart.

On Christmas Eve, Granite Falls officially opened to the public.

Brent, Emily, Ari, Harriet, Gabby and Jerry, along with Nicole, Adam and Jacob, and a whole host of others, were standing in one of the gazebo's in the park looking out at their creation. The children were especially delighted by the fairyland atmosphere. Nicole leaned over to whisper in Jerry's ear. "My mom and you did this didn't you, Dad? I know Uncle Brent became the Mayor, but mostly it was you, Mom and Aunt Ari, wasn't it?"

Laughing, Jerry squeezed Nicole. "Honey, your mommy, Aunt Ari and I did some of it. But, see all the people out there? They did this."

Ari had lights strung in the trees up and down Main Street, and intertwined in the truss of the bridge crossing the river. The lights in the park were mostly Christmas decorations and would come down at the end of the season. But tonight, this special night, it was a glorious sight. The crisp, cold air made the lights sparkle all the more brilliantly.

As the group savored the sights, they were enchanted by the glittering lights, the smell of fresh air, holiday music playing in one of the gazebos, and the carousel spinning with a magic all its own. Most of all, though, it was the crowd's laughter and enjoyment which was their crowning achievement. This was their hometown. The home of their future, and that of their children's – their Granite Falls.

LaVergne, TN USA
29 September 2009
158841LV00003BB/1/P